HOW REALLY PECU...
THAT'S ME.

I know that because it's like the pictures they've taken . . .

But I'm not really that person. I don't even know who that person is – she is made up, she is Mim's, her mother's . . .

I can see a long row of little hers that go back to Soho and Bertie and doing endless auditions, going to Miss Tina's, and Madame Blatsky's, doing her 'bit', dancing, singing, performing, in front of thousands of watching people . . .

Were any of them real? *Was* there a real one? Were they all an illusion of a someone, a mirage held together by a name, Liza Lee . . .?

# Command Performance

## NONA COXHEAD

'Who is it that can tell me who I am?'
SHAKESPEARE

SPHERE BOOKS

First published in Great Britain by
Severn House Ltd 1986
Copyright © 1986 by Nona Coxhead
First published in paperback by Sphere Books Ltd 1987
This edition first published by Sphere Books 1995

Printed in England by Clays Ltd, St Ives plc

Sphere Books
A Division of
Macdonald & Co. (Publishers)
Brettenham House
Lancaster Place
London WC2E 7EN

# CHAPTER ONE

'Oy, somebody . . . where's that little girl headed?'

Everybody in the front stalls of the theatre, all of the motley group of children on the vast, nakedly-lit stage turned to watch the small figure with the big red bows in her peroxide-blond curls trotting resolutely up the aisle towards the foyer doors.

'What's happened to the mum?' A bald-headed man in shirtsleeves stood up and looked about over the top of his glasses. The personnel involved with the pantomime auditions swivelled dutifully to join his search, their glances both irritable and amused.

From the shadow of a pillar, a thin muscular young woman with a top-heavy nest of brass-coloured hair shot into view, the cigarette clamped in her mouth, like a pointer in her lightning dash for the child.

'Aa – no you don't, me love. Not on your nellie. You do your bit, see.' The flat, tinny voice that cut through the silence had an under-bite of humour that did not lessen its authority. 'Thought you'd caught me nappin', did you. No waterworks, now. Watch the mascara.'

The child put up a futile struggle, cut short by the upward scoop of thin hirsute arms that bore her swiftly back to the stage, pushed her forcefully on towards the other children waiting their turn. 'Don't you dare to scarper again. Do your bit, and we'll go to Lyons for an ice.'

'Don't want to do my bit,' the child murmured, but under her breath, her over-sized blue eyes in the made-up

1

face blinking back insurrection as she became aware of not just her mother's attention, but of everyone's in that great big hushed, half-dark place . . .

Mim Hobbs gave the producer a V-sign, nodded, tugged her wide red mouth into a general smile of encouragement and returned to her position at the pillar, where she lit a fresh Woodbine and watched her child, her shrewd hazel eyes alert, eager, expectant.

The auditions resumed.

When little Elizabeth Hobbs came to the middle of the stage, there was new, if reluctant interest in her; several hard-bitten expressions twisted into faint smiles.

She wore a dress made entirely of frills, hand-crimped by Mim, showing equally frilly pink knickers, red silk socks, gleaming patent shoes. Her bleached-to-frizziness hair was tortured into so many ringlets that they shook like wires with her every move. Pink rouge had been added to her dimpled knees and elbows, and a black beauty-spot was placed to one side of her reddened mouth.

Mim frowned until the pianist struck up with 'Somewhere Over the Rainbow', then folded her arms about her muscled breasts, drew in a hard breath and gritted her teeth against the thrill in their nerves. 'Show 'em, me little darlin',' she said soundlessly. 'Hit 'em where they live!'

For just a moment, Lizzie, as she was called at home, couldn't make any words come out, or make her legs move. Her eyes had the glaze of a nocturnal animal startled in headlights. Then, suddenly, she began to remember all the rehearsing and practising, half-nodding to herself to bring them out into the open. Her voice, unexpectedly loud and clear, piped from her throat in the precise duplication of Judy Garland's record, broken only twice by an uncertain quaver.

She remembered not to look at all the faces out there, except to think of them all as being her friends, so she should make her bright smiles into nowhere, throw her kisses into the dimness – and, before there was time for anyone to talk or call out, to go into her little soft-shoe dance . . .

'All right, all right, little girl – that's enough . . .'

But she hadn't told them her joke yet, about what one cow said to the other in the . . . Or done her imitations of . . .

'Thank you. Next!'

'My God,' Fred Keeley said to his assistant, 'that mother should be shot. The kiddie's no more than five, let alone seven! Poor little tot, it's criminal.'

An austere woman taking notes in shorthand leaned towards him. 'Bears watching, though. If I were a Yank, I'd say, for her age, she was darn cute.'

'You're soft. She's a travesty. Still – keep her name. Give her a few years.'

The woman sat back, underlined Lizzie's name and put a special mark beside it. The child moved dazedly away, to be grabbed by her mother and borne off. The auditions continued.

'Want to talk to the big boy,' Lizzie said, as she was moved, faster than her legs could go without having to skip, and looking back at the tall thin boy with the big mouth and slicked-down brown hair who stood, hands on hips, waiting for his turn.

'What big boy?' Mim turned round, frowning.

'Him.' Lizzie pointed, tried to pull her mother back, to stop her.

Mim raised the thick dark brows, mercilessly plucked where they would have formed an unbroken line across the top of her long nose. She allowed herself to be halted for a moment, but only because the boy who had suddenly walked to the centre of the stage was doing an imitation that couldn't be mistaken. His chin raised, a slightly super-cilious smile on his mouth, his eyes barely open with wry

3

ennui, in a clipped, staccato voice he recited, 'Mad dogs and Englishmen go out in the midday sun . . .'

'Gor blimey,' murmured Mim. 'It's 'im to a tee . . .'

Lizzie giggled excitedly. 'Rob . . . That's Rob. He pwetended to pinch me bows. He's funny. I like 'im.'

Mim could not keep the grin from her mouth. Crikey, now he'd switched from Noel Coward to Stanley Holloway. She could do 'Sam, Sam, pick up thy musket' right along with him. The kid was a shout . . .

'We go back, Mum . . .' Lizzie tugged the hard hand.

'*Mim.* 'Ow many times I've told you? Mim.' The irritation turned her attention back to priorities. 'Don't be daft, love. He don't want to be bothered with a nipper like you – he's nine if he's a day.'

Lizzie's excitement faded. 'He likes me. He's me friend.'

Mim pulled her onward. 'You and your friends. You ain't got time, me gel. We've got big plans, we 'ave. Come on, we'll stop at Duffy's and get some sequins. Got to finish your costume tonight.'

'Lyons, Mum – Mim. You said Lyons Corner 'Ouse, 'ave an ice.' Lizzie tried to break from Mim's hand, which felt rough and lumpy from the work she did; but as they went through the carpeted foyer that opened to the street, Mim gripped the pudgy hand with the red-painted fingernails even harder.

'We'll have to forget that today, duck. More songs to get you – not to mention Bert's fags, and 'is Jack-the-Rippers.'

Lizzie's protest was diverted by the funny words for kippers. She wanted to laugh, as she always did at the rhymes Mim and Bert made, and to learn them for herself, but it didn't stop her from suddenly holding back at the doors, pressing her heels into the deep floral pile and looking up at Mim, her eyes luminous with daring. 'Take stuff off me face. Take bows off.'

'Don't be daft, you look a treat. 'Sides, I want Bert to see what I done . . .'

Lizzie's heels seemed to weld themselves to the carpet, making her small sturdy body a dead weight on Mim's hand. 'Wipe me face.' Her mouth was pinched, her nostrils flared in elderly grimness.

'Oh, all right, all right – don't get a cob on. 'Ere . . .' Mim took a large grubby handkerchief from her geometrically-patterned plastic handbag, jerked the child's face upward, applied spit and rubbed vigorously at the rouge, lipstick, blackened eyebrows, blue-shadowed eyelids. 'There you are, Miss Bernhardt, that's the best I can do. Now, take 'old me German band and stay put – no larkin' about with strangers today.'

Before allowing her hand to be recaptured, Lizzie felt at her face, braved her mother's impatient frown with the inconviction of experience. 'All smudged . . . More wipe.'

'Garn! I'll wipe it – with the back of me 'and!'

Lizzie blinked, her mascara-beaded lashes drooping to protect her from the sharp stare. In grudging truce she surrendered her hand, moved with the tide of Mim's renewed energy, skipped beside her in order to keep up along the crowded London street, a compact little figure of stoical cheer – undaunted expectancy.

Matinées were letting out as they made their way to Soho, and Mim was not displeased to note the attention Lizzie got. As they passed the Apollo where *For Amusement Only* was playing, people actually bumped into each other gawking. At the Lyric, where Noel Coward's *South Sea Bubble* caused a proper pile-up of nobs and taxis, there was such gaping you'd have thought they'd never seen the like of her, or herself. In 1956, in Shaftesbury Avenue, that weren't 'alf bad. Peering in the windows of a musical instrument shop, she looked at their reflections to see how it was they seemed to *them*, the public . . .

Yeah – the kid was an eye-popper, all right – ringlets bobbing perky as you please, the bouncy ruff of frills showing off a square little face so pink-and-white, eyes so big and blue as to make Shirley Temple seem a mouse. As for that chummy grin – well, the kid was a winner . . .

As for the woman with her – that'd be a teaser all right – foxy eyes, physog all nose, jawbone and red mouth, the upswept hair-do with roots like zebra stripes, the purple halter and drainpipes clamped to the muscle in her calves as she dragged the kid along, tottering in the high stiletto heels of once-white, too-big shoes bought cheap off a stall in the market . . .

Not the mother, they'd think, too young, no like-ness . . .

Well, I bleedin' am. Legitimate, an' all. Not so's it's any of your mind. You just keep your eyes on Lizzie, she told them with her po-faced stare – one day that little girl there will 'ave 'er name up in lights for you, and all the world to see. She'll be a great international star, the greatest ever – you just wait!

'Go talk to good big dog and blind man . . .'

Mim frowned as she almost lost the little hand, grabbed it deeper into hers. 'No time. Another day.' Crikey, if it wasn't a dog, a kitten, an old lady, another child, a baby in a pram, it was some grinning sot outa the pub or whore winkin' at her all cosy from a doorway; you couldn't let up a minute now she was goin' on five, it was like 'oldin' onto a goldfish . . .

'But 'e's a nice dog, Mum. Let me put my arms round 'im.'

The blithe skip had barely slowed, yet Mim did not feel the danger had passed and pressed the hot little hand tighter, pulled the bouncing shoulders closer as an arm-in-arm couple threatened to split them apart.

'Sulkin', are we?' Her downward smile was grim. 'Well, we'll have no more of that. Know why you didn't get into the panta? Wobblies on the high notes. We've got to get down to business, young lady.'

Lizzie looked up at her, the smile-wrinkles around her

6

lambent blue gaze lingering. For a moment her skip lost momentum and she dragged behind. But almost immediately, something had caught her attention, and before Mim had time to blink, the hand had gone – a glimpse of pink knickers and red socks, a flutter of peroxide ringlets and red bows, and the small, skipping figure, too, had gone . . .

Mim pushed through the crowd, jabbed with her elbows to make headway, her eyes narrowed in sharp search, the dark line of her brows drawn single, the cigarette clinging precariously to one lip. She saw the large blond dog sitting passively by the blind man, but no Lizzie. Scanning every shop doorway, the densely-moving traffic, up and down side streets, into the interior of cafés, she came to a halt. For a moment, she thought she was going to throw up, but spitting out the soggy Woodbine, she gulped some of the acrid air and forced herself to consider all the possibilities.

Where in bloody hell would the kid go? It must have been something that took her eye, sudden-like . . . Cripes, that could be almost anything! Everything interested Lizzie one way or the other. It was a ruddy nuisance at best – but round 'ere, comin' into evenin' it wasn't exactly a laugh . . .

She looked as far each way as her eyes would go, her heartbeat drumming against her ribs. Now, steady on, Mim, ol' gel, she said to herself in her mother's voice; no use to get your knickers in a twist – probably chasing after some filthy, scabby ol' moggy, or natterin' with one of the foreign restaurant owners or waiters she knew – or even an actor or rock star coming outa stage door . . .

The streets were beginning to congest with rush-hour frenzy, making it harder and harder to spot a small figure, even if it was somewhere within reach. If Mim knew how to cry, she'd have the full blubber right now. S'truth, if that little blighter showed herself at this moment she'd give her the hiding of her life . . .

'Miss . . .?'

7

There was a sudden tap on her shoulder.

'This little lady says you're her mother. Is this a fact?'

Two coppers stood there, Lizzie between them, each one holding one of her hands, while she stared wide-eyed as a doll, trying to smile.

'Christ!' Mim's tinny voice cracked like a flat bell. Her gaze was so fierce that Lizzie quickly lowered her head, pinched her lips into a tight pleat. 'Elizabeth Hobbs! What on earth you been up to! You 'ad me nearly in me grave!'

'Then you *are* the mother. Don't be hard on her, Miss.' The larger copper smiled wisely, benignly. 'She was trying to catch up to a boy she knew, but he didn't see her, and we found her about to cross Piccadilly on her own – not a good idea at this time of day.'

Patronizing bastard! Mim snatched Lizzie from his grip. 'Stupid little clot!' She shook her until Lizzie felt her teeth wiggle in their gums. 'You know better'n that. You coulda been run over, *kilt*!'

'Well – learnt a lesson, I'm sure.' The smaller copper bent at the knees to pat Lizzie on the cheek. 'Better stick to your mum in the future, eh?'

When Lizzie didn't answer or lift her head, he stood up. Expecting no thanks from Mim, the two coppers placed their hands behind their backs and moved on.

Mim stood with hands on hips, glowering at her child in a fury that sent waves of blood to her face. 'You must be off your rocker, round the twist!'

'Saw big boy. Rob . . .' Lizzie only managed a mutter, almost drowned by the traffic, but it was enough to make her mother grab her by the hair and squeeze.

'I don't care if it was Jesus hisself, do you hear? Never, never, do that again for nothin', for nobody!'

Lizzie was still. People rushed at them as they passed. 'You understand me, Miss Hobbs?'

Lizzie gave a slow nod which brought the ringlets into an agitated curtain about her face.

'Now don't start leakin' . . .'

Lizzie lifted her head. 'I *ain't*.' Anger glinted in her eyes now.

'All right, all right. S'pose I got a bit narked. Come on, then, let's get on with it.'

Lizzie gave up her hand, but did not skip. Her gaze went straight ahead, or lifted to meet the stares of passers-by in solemn desperation.

Mim shook her hand; gave it a squeeze. 'If you're a good girl and work extra hard with your new stuff, we'll go see Bert's new show sometime – not a matinée up in the gods, but at *night*, with house seats!'

Lizzie swallowed, faltered, but kept an eye on a girl of her own size.

'We'll go back and see Bert workin' the scenery, an' you can see the stars up close, and maybe peep out at the audience . . .'

Lizzie blinked in bewilderment as the little girl stuck out her tongue.

Mim stopped, pulled her round to face her, looked down at her a moment, then stooped and gave her smudgy-pink chin a pinch. 'Aw, come on, give Mim a penny-a-mile.'

Lizzie hung on, tightened her lips, screwed up her eyes – but it was no use. Her mouth twitched, then yielded.

'Ah, there. That's more like me little darlin'!' Mim hugged her up against her with wiry arms, put scarlet-grease kisses on her nose and cheeks. 'Now we're mates again. I won't even tell Bert.'

Lizzie's smile grew. When they continued back up Shaftesbury, she skipped along again beside her mother. At the costume shop she helped her choose sequins in reds and greens, and in the music shop she stood by while Mim went through sheets and sheets of songs, sometimes singing the words to her in a whisper, all hoarse and funny, making faces to go with them, with the cigarette going up and down at the side of her mouth. Then they went to shop for Bert's Players, *News of the World*, and Jack-the-Rippers.

'Nothin' much 'ere – boys comin' 'ome from Suez – no more third-class fares – Queen looks a picture with little Charlie and Anne . . .

Lizzie tugged up a red sock, gazing longingly towards Piccadilly.

'Dickie Valentine – done it again with 'Finger of Suspicion' . . . Crikey, wouldn't I like to be with them teenagers?' Mim re-folded the paper so as Bert wouldn't get cobby, and re-captured Lizzie's hand.

When they got to the little park at Wardour Street, Lizzie halted.

'Play hopscotch with kids, Mim.'

'You know better.' She jerked her chin towards the church spire, the sky.

Lizzie saw that the sky was a greenish colour, with bits of gauze like her fairy costume floating across it, and the spire and roofs were all cut-out black, and the birds were sitting in the trees singing a lot. She nodded wisely. 'Our Bert will be wakin' up wantin' 'is tea.' She skipped on.

'Well, 'ome, sweet 'ome. 'Ere – take the do-me-good outa me mouth.' Mim's arms were full as she backed open the side door of the small Italian café. 'Coo, it don't 'alf pong of sausage and garlic. As usual.'

Lizzie held the nasty wet cigarette between her finger and thumb as she followed Mim up the creaky stairs to their flat. 'And piss,' she said.

'Oy!' Mim looked back, grinned. 'We'll 'ave to get you to talk proper an' all, won't we?'

'So what's kept you, then?' Bert Hobbs' large, porous face undid its creases to make way for a relieved smile. He kissed Mim's cheek, took Lizzie up over his big pendulous stomach in an exuberant hug. 'How did you get on, Miss

Cuddles?' He seemed not to notice her streaked make-up. 'Did they love you?'

' 'Ey, watch them frills, Bertie, took me hours . . . You been at it already? Before your tea!' Mim gave a disgusted look at the bottles beside the sagging brown couch where Bert had volunteered to sleep ever since he took her in.

What a mess he made, crumpled bedclothes, fag butts, all over the lot. 'Yer eyes look like a boiled cod's, and you with a new job!'

Bert and Lizzie exchanged a downcast glance. 'Sorry, matey.' Bert's jowls quivered with remorse. He set Lizzie down gingerly. 'She's right, yer know. But go on, tell Bert the news.'

'They didn't like me, Bert – I did wobblies.' Lizzie hugged one of his sturdy, serge-trousered legs, gazing up at him in hope.

Mim plonked his Players and newspaper onto the oilcloth-covered table amongst the combined clutter of fabrics and patterns, pins, needles, scissors, tape-measures, beads, feathers, trimmings, her iron ukelele, sewing-machine, sheet music, Bert's wireless, betting slips, playing cards, playbill collection, socks and cardigans with holes, Lizzie's toys needing a mend, ringed teacups, the dishes from last night's meal of steak and kidney pud. 'It's the truth, so 'elp me. Just like this . . . If happy little bluebirds fly above the clouds, then why, oh, why can't I . . . I . . . I . . . I . . .?'

'I *didn't*, Mum,' Lizzie said. 'Not like that.' She ran first into the tiny bathroom, then the bedroom. The brass bed creaked.

'I told you she was too young – you shouldn't push her so hard, Mims, ol' girl. It just ain't fair.' Bert slumped heavily into the wooden armchair with the cracked black leather seat. 'I tell you, you'll be sorry. She's got to have a chance to be a kiddy, play, and make chums, and some day soon you'll have to let 'er go to school . . .'

'Yeah, yeah, yeah.' Mim moved briskly on to the narrow little kitchen. 'I read this script a thousand times, Bertie. If I listened to you she'd never amount to nothin' – just any little kid. That ain't what makes stars out of no-ones like us! You know that, ol' dear. There's only one way for the likes of us to climb over the fence to the somebodies – that's bein' so bloody good they can't turn their backs, they *got* to take notice. And the only way to do that is to work, Bertie – work an' work an' work!'

Bert nodded to himself, swigged some bitter, added the empty bottle to a small pile hidden beside the chair and opened another. 'You're right, lovey.' He pushed a hand through his thinning brown hair, stretched his eyes and face to clear the residues of a knees-up at the boozer last night. 'Watcher got to eat?'

'What d'ya think, ol' cock? I take orders, don't I?' She put her brassy head round the door and gave him a broad wink. ' 'Ungry?'

Bert grinned. 'I could eat *you*, darlin'.' At her coy chuckle, his grin widened. He picked up the paper. 'That Eden. What now . . .?'

Cigarette in mouth, Mim got on with it. Kippers sizzled, potatoes fried and cutlery and plates rattled with abandon. She hated cooking almost more than she hated washing dishes or taking a bath, but she liked to do her bit for her bloke. Who else would have stood by her when she found herself in the pudding club right in the middle of a show! What a good-hearted sod he was, giving up his batching and peace for a seventeen-year-old chorus girl, and then her squalling kid? Never a hard word when she carried on dreadful at her wretched luck, had the kid right in his poor old bed, hung the tiny bathroom with nappies, filled the whole place with the kid's dirty clothes and sour smells. How or why he kept on fancying her, she couldn't think. Even if he was fifteen years older, there was plenty of young birds in the theatre who took to him, particularly when he put on his best cardigan, cap and muffler, slicked his hair . . .

Wonder what Lizzie's doin'? Bloody-minded again. Piddled – hadn't flushed. Thrown herself onta the bed. Hugging Freddie for dear life. Talkin' and whisperin' to 'im – Gawd knows what she *said* to that bald one-eyed ol' bear. A right earful, no doubt. Like herself, Lizzie never cried – but she had other ways of doing it so's you'd never know the difference. Well – back to the guns . . .

Armed with plates, she ran an elbow over the keys of the battered upright. 'Liz-zie – grub! Bert, clear a space, pull up chairs. When you due at the theatre?'

' 'Alf six – better 'ave it on me knee – you an' Lizzie can eat proper after I go.' He looked up into Mim's bright, shrewd eyes. 'No, darlin', I'm not stoppin' off at the rub-a-dub. Got to be on me mettle – a lot o'shifts, three revolving stages an' the like.'

'Oh, yes, of course, 'and on the Bible. One of these days, Bert Edward Hobbs, you're going to make a right cock-up of them hemps and weights, whatever you call'em, an' kill a lot o' people, or get kilt.'

Mim cleared the table herself, set down his food, jerked her thumb in command. 'Eat, ol' darlin'. I'll sort out the prima donna.'

'Aw, don't call 'er that, Mims. She's a proud tyke. You 'urt 'er feelin's.'

'I'll give 'er feelin's. She's goin' to thank me some day for keepin' arter 'er. She's got a destiny, our Lizzie, Bert, a destiny.'

Bert thinned his lips, lumbered docilely to his feet, brought three rickety cane chairs to the table, sat down.

Mim patted the top of his bald spot, nodded, moved briskly, heels clattering on the wood floor where the carpet had worn thin, to the bedroom door. Shoving it open, she peered in, then closed it behind her.

Bert gazed after her, his brown eyes baffled and doleful.

13

It seemed that in the last ten years, ever since the War, he'd been going through a tunnel backwards. He hadn't wanted to go and fight and kill, but once over there he'd done his best and they'd given him a medal or two. Then, when he got home, it was as if it had never happened, except that he'd lost part of a kneecap, his mother's house had been bombed with her in it, and his sister, married, had no room for him . . .

He'd done a lot of odd jobs to keep going; nothing much came of them even though he worked hard and everyone seemed to like him. Then he'd helped a mate out who was a prop man at Drury Lane, and he'd got him in as a hand, and he'd gone on from there. None of it was what he'd dreamed as a kid from the Docks – a life of big adventures, maybe at sea, never to marry but have a lot of loving girls he made happy when in port . . .

Wouldn't you know he'd take a fancy to a bold-faced little East-Ender, not even pretty, though she could make you think she was when she danced and grinned at you with the lights making her eyes shine, making you forget she was skinny and hairy and built more like a little man?

But, of course, she hadn't really fancied him back. She played with him, teased, while she kept her sights on bigger fish, on getting ahead. Well, he hadn't suffered. There were dozens of far tastier birds with their eyes on him – and there were his mates to have a laugh with, the gee-gees, and a bit of cheer – as long as his liver held out . . .

Then, sudden as the drop of a curtain, there she was, hanging onto a rope behind him, green as scenery, losing her lunch right onto the floorboards, her mascara making great squiggles of black down her greasepaint. 'Use yer crust,' she had said when he asked her what was wrong.

Naturally, the penny dropped. 'You know someone to go to?' he'd asked her. 'You must be jokin,' she'd answered. 'Me Irish grandmother'd turn in 'er grave.'

So, there it was. She'd got bigger and bigger, and soon they'd have her out of the show. She didn't have a clue who the father was – a one-nighter – and the idea of having a basket changed her from a youngster jokin' and larkin' about, to a bitter, sharp-tongued little biddy with a face like granite.

It was more than he could bear. He'd asked her home, shown her his living quarters. 'Not your Buckingham Palace,' he'd said, 'but you could stay here, have the kid . . .'

'What – in *sin*!'

Funny, looking back, how he hadn't laughed.

'I'd marry you, of course, give the kid a name.'

He'd always remember the look she gave him. It made him randy, like bursting into song. She didn't look any prettier, uglier if anything, but there was some kind of gleam in her eyes he'd never seen.

The next thing he knew, they'd gone to a registry office, he'd moved out of the bedroom, and because one night it was all too late to get her to the hospital, she'd started screamin' and yellin' and he'd helped her bring out the kid right on his own Uncle Ned.

What a kerfuffle! She didn't want the kiddy, and he had to walk the floor with it at night. It was the end of his peace . . . Yet, he was still stuck on Mims. And he couldn't resist the gurgling little infant she later named after her beloved queen. It didn't matter that she wasn't 'is. He didn't want to know about the bloke who was the father, and it was never mentioned.

But now – ever since Mim had had her arse-about-face, laid her own dream on the poor trapped mite – he could feel himself moving further along the tunnel, the light at the end getting fainter and fainter . . .

Ah, well. Bert pushed at his thinned brown hair, reached to the wireless and switched it on, recovered a half-full bitter from the floor, finished it, then took up his knife and fork.

Ten minutes later, after a furtive trip to the lav and a quick wash, he got his cap off a hook on the door, settled it solidly above his large ears and, moving with quiet haste to the door, shut it softly behind him.

Cripes . . . Mim heard the latch click. Must have fallen asleep beside Lizzie. Well, they'd both been up half of the night gettin' her ready . . .

With a deep frown, she lifted Lizzie's thumb from her mouth (revoltin', nearly five!), removed the bear from under her arm. 'Come on, sleepy-mouse – wake up. It ain't bedtime yet for the likes of us.'

Lizzie did not stir. Her lips were open, her breathing short and even.

'Look at me frills – mashed. There's gratitude for ya.'

Mim propped herself on an elbow to gaze at the clownish little face, innocent as an angel. 'If only you knew,' she thought . . .

'Not eighteen, I was, Lizzie, when you nipped me life in the bud. Made it into *Kiss Me Kate*, I had. Never would've believed it, with no Bristols to me name and Scotch pegs like a pony's. But, you see, ol' darlin', I danced the lot to shame. Cartwheels, nip-ups, backbends, high kicks, jive, tap, tangos, Rogers, Astaire, Kelly – I did 'em. And then, with make-up trowelled on, they must a' thought I'd do in the back line.

'So, I got in. They never thought I would – Effie, your gran, Alf, your granpa. They always used to say it was one thing to entertain scared people in the air-raid shelter, everyone wantin' their minds kept off the bombs – another to get took into a West End show. *Cheek*, they said, weren't enough. But cheek with workin' yer arse to the bone, that's what they didn't think of, see.'

Mim lay back into her nest of hair, arched her arms above her head.

'Yeah . . . It's a funny thing, life, Lizzie. When I was your age, a big war broke out. Most of me li'le mates were

16

sent away to the country. There was big barrage balloons hangin' over the river, whoppin' great lights crossin' the sky, and Bale Street was all quiet – we was waitin' for bombs to come and blow us all up.

'But they didn't come. Kids came back, and we ran round in the streets and played because no-one went to school and a lot of mums got jobs in factories and stayed away all day . . .

'Effie went back to being a dresser . . . I don't remember the play, but she brought 'ome a signed picture of Gertie – Gertrude Lawrence – you wouldn't know 'er, darlin' – she was a big star. Died the same year you was born. So did the King, of course. That's when Princess Elizabeth became Queen . . .

'Anyway . . .'

Mim let her shoes slip off her feet, her thoughts drift farther into memory . . .

She could see the little house so clearly still, its dingy brick front, battered front door, damp-streamed windows – and, when you went in, walls, too, as if they were always crying. Effie's collection of signed pictures curled up under the wetness, and her mother would take an iron to them, dry the walls and put them up again. The lav was in a wooden shed out in the yard, and the old tin bathtub hung on a big rusty nail outside the kitchen. On Friday or Saturday nights they would bring it in, fill it with kettles of water heated on the coal stove, and take turns washing in it in the middle of the kitchen floor . . .

They didn't have two taps in the kitchen, like Bert. Nothing so grand. One tap, with water so cold in the winter you couldn't touch it, and it dripped all the time; all through the night you could hear it . . .

And the smell of the house . . . You could never get the fish and chips off Alf's clothes. He brought the whole of his shop home with him and fat that had had fish fried in it, over and over, went into everything. They all smelt of it. Effie put Ashes of Roses scent all over herself (she wasn't so stout then, and used to curl her red hair up with the tongs, and the stars sometimes gave her a smart dress they no longer wanted) before she went to the theatre . . .

Mim stirred, reached for a Woodbine from the little table next to the bed, lit it, and stretched back out. Let the little tyke kip on a bit, she thought, so's she could put in a good couple of hours on the stuff for Friday . . . All Lizzie had to do was get into Bettina's troupe and Bob's yer uncle, she'd be on the way!

Mmm . . . Effie was different then. Hadn't taken to drink. Several times, even after the bombs had come and done in a lot of the docks and made big fires by the Thames that went on all through the night, she had taken Mim with her, got them to let her sit out front or in the wings – and one night Ellen Patrick herself actually asked her into the dressing-room, talked to her while she made up, let her look over all the costumes . . .

'I understand you can do extraordinary things with your legs,' she had said, smiling so graciously. 'Do show me.'

'Go on,' Effie said, stopping her bustling about and giving her signs behind Miss Patrick's high black wig.

Not wasting time, Mim had lifted up her serge dress, got down on the floor and put her legs around her neck.

'Amazing,' Miss Patrick had said, clapping once.

'Go on,' Effie said. 'Roll, dearie.'

So she'd rolled around, tipped back and forth, and was just about to leap up and show her some splits, when there was a shout outside and Miss Patrick got to her feet in a great rush and left.

'Shame,' Effie said. 'Never mind. Maybe she'll remember you for something.'

Later, of course, the bombers kept coming back, and Effie didn't go to the theatre any more, and Alf's shop was hit, and so was Auntie Lil's, and most of the time, from

18

late afternoon on was spent down Tilbury Shelter under ground, with thousands of other people of every age, even ill people in bathchairs . . .

'You wouldn't 'ave believed it, me love. Hawkers came sellin' foods, wicked ladies sellin' you-know-what, everyone brought things to do an' make. There were fights, an' people got sick from being down there so long . . .

'All the time, up there, everythin' was bein' laid to ruins. You'd come out and find nothin' but masonry and wires and parts of rooms stickin' out on their own, an' all the insides of 'ouses in bits and pieces, an' furniture all over everywhere, an' you would be shown 'ow to 'elp, and then you would all go down under again . . .

'It wasn't a lot of fun, darlin' – but I used to practise me dancin' an' singin', just for the time when the Germans would all go away and I could get started becomin' a somebody . . .

'Because that's what I wanted. Not to be rich, Lizzie. Don't think that. Just never to be a nobody. To be looked at, noticed, recognized by the somebodies. And what other way could I, a nothin' from Bale Street, do it? None.'

She had danced to her own playing; Alf's uke – from the days he was a busker before he bought the fish shop – had come in useful. She had sung all the songs she knew: the Cockney ones she'd learnt from Alf and hanging round the pubs; the latest tunes played on the radio; the ones from shows that Effie played on their battered upright with the aspidistra on top. She did her acrobatic tricks, tap, and got everyone joining in with her in 'The Lambeth Walk'. How they laughed and cheered when she borrowed their clothes and did take-offs of Music Hall stars, of Hitler, of upper-class twits with monocles . . .

She could feel the tingle of it now . . .

Then, when the doodlebugs came, they frightened people even more than the bombs, and when they waited for them, in the silence, to explode, they had no more interest

19

in her, even if she was trying to cheer them up . . .

'An' that wasn't the end of it. Next, there was the V2 rockets, tall as 'ouses, Lizzie. They basted the 'ole of Petticoat Lane, and later on, a whole block of flats in Vallance Road, killin' 'undreds of people . . .'

No wonder no-one wanted to bother any more with an eleven-year-old 'performer'. The war finished and everyone celebrated and then got on with clearing up the mess. Bale Street was never the same. All the Jews gone, the shops wrecked, the market stalls moved, only a few houses left standing . . .

'Ours was never 'it directly, but it's got a big sag an' lots of cracks where moss grows, an' it won't be long before Effie an' Alf will be carted off to one of them big highrisers, which they won't like, I can tell you. Could kill Effie, in 'er state . . .

'Well, at least I got away. It wasn't easy, Lizzie. They wanted me in school, but I generally scarpered. Got into a gang o' girls, an' we'd go about playin' tricks on the newcomers movin' in, the Blackies an' Wogs. Mind you, I like 'em now, but in them days, you didn't know nothin' about 'em. Then – took to comin' up the 'Dilly . . .'

Mim nodded to herself as she remembered waiting in the long queues to get into musicals, getting money off older women by saying she was lost so that she could pay for cinemas. With a couple of girlfriends, she had gone to various dancehalls and practised on any willing victim, making sure she could still get attention. One afternoon, the three of them, Nellie, Mabel and herself, had gone to the stage door of *Piper of Dreams* and dared to ask to see Ellen Patrick . . .

Miss Patrick *did* remember! She gave her a note of introduction to the Dance Director. 'How's darling Effie?' she asked. 'I do miss her. Give her my love. And, best of luck, dear.' She had smiled at them all and waved as she got into a big gleaming car with a chauffeur.

The girls couldn't believe it. They giggled and chattered and made fun of her for her big ambitions. 'I'll get there,' she told them. 'Just you watch.'

But she didn't get far with Percy Snell. He seemed to find it hard to take her seriously – particularly when she *spoke*. 'I'll do my best,' he said, 'for Miss Patrick – such a poppet.'

He had passed her on to another dance director with another note, and she had made herself a dress of gold lamé with feather trim for the interview. He also seemed unable to look into her face. 'But you sure can dance,' he said. 'Maybe they could use you in the new musical they're about to cast . . .'

That had been *Kiss Me Kate*.

She had been making beds, emptying pos, trying to clean up the chaos and dank filth of the house as best she could, when there was a heavy knock on the front door. The postman had a letter, a real letter. She had dried her chilblained hands before taking it from him.

It was a call to audition for the chorus. She had thrown her arms round old Frankie, who'd known them all as friends, given him a kiss on his blotchy nose.

'Glad someone's got good news round 'ere,' he said . . .

Mim grunted, opened her eyes, looked at Lizzie.

Was she still asleep, or pretending to be?

Mim's eyebrows drew together. The kid did look like *him* – dead ringer. Same brownish-blond hair when it wasn't peroxided. Same light fair skin, short, pudgy nose, dimples . . .

'A charmer, 'e was. Never 'ad so much fun in me life. Took me all over the place, 'e did. Fancy bars, restaurants, nightclubs – what a time we 'ad! "Help me drown my sorrows, little one," he said. Grabbed me as I came out the stage door, you see. Swayin', blue eyes all bleary, smilin' like 'e loved the sight of me. "Come on, baby, you just *slay*

21

me with your funny way of talking. Let's paint the town. Whaddya say?" '

'He was dressed nice, Lizzie, a gent, even if he had a Yank accent. Said he'd come over to marry someone, and they'd changed their mind, and "Here I am in pain, sweetheart, in *pain*." '

He had put his arm right round her, she remembered, cuddled her so sweet and hiked her off to a long red sports car, the kind she never thought she'd ever ride in, and she'd just got in, never said a word, as if they were old friends.

And it was like that all night. The more they drank, the more in love they were. 'I don't even miss her,' he kept saying, as they danced . . . 'and, oh, that bloke could dance, Lizzie! Not clompin' all over yer feet like the rest, knowin' just what 'e was doin' without even thinkin' about it . . .'

And, then, stopping to kiss all the time, they went to his hotel.

'No. Lizzie, don't even know the name of the 'otel. Just *big*, and so posh I nearly fainted. Up to 'is room we went – 'e called it a suite, pronounced like sweet. Two rooms – expected *her* to be with 'im, 'is wife by then . . .'

Everything had been going round, the satins and velvets, the grand sparkling lights and gold mirrors – and the huge royal-looking bed . . .

They'd fallen into it, laughing and laughing, kissing and kissing, and then they seemed to be undressed and something good but faraway was happening to her, and to him . . .

And then there was silence, a long quiet time she could not remember, but in some part of it she felt a shaking and then heard sounds like crying . . .

In the shelter, she'd heard that sound, a man's crying . . .

'Oh, God,' he said, over and over. 'Oh, dear God . . .'

And suddenly he was standing beside her, asking her if she would mind leaving him. He was sorry, hoped he wasn't being unkind. He put a wad of money into her little gold handbag, kissed her so softly.

She could remember getting dressed, still not sure on her feet, her curls and make-up all messy. 'That's all right, mate,' she'd told him. 'We 'ad a wonderful time, didn't we?'

He had such a sad smile. He still looked handsome. She could have loved him if that had been on the cards. But it wasn't.

'The doorman will get you a taxi, baby,' he said, giving her a hug that seemed more like relief than affection.

'Right. Ta-ta. Thanks for everythin'. All the best, ol' darlin'.' She'd given him a bit of a salute.

Mim touched Lizzie's cheek. 'An' that's where you come in,' she whispered. 'An' no kid was ever less welcome, I assure you. Blasted me career. Knew I'd never make it back with a scarred bread-basket added to the rest, a kid in tow. Could've smothered yer, I could . . .

'Then one day, while you was suckin' I took another look at yer. Suddenly I saw what 'ad 'appened when I lit that candle, just in case like me grandma used to say . . . I had got me a little corker, a *gem*. What was I worried about? It didn't matter any more about *me*. The Saint 'ad given me you instead.' An', oh, me little pearl, what you could do that I never could, even if I worked me arse to the bone for the rest of me natural!

'Why, one day – you'd not only be a great star . . .'

'Upsey-daisy.' Mim tickled her still-rouged knees, and gave her a push.

'No more work . . .' Lizzie rolled away, recovered the bear. ' 'Ave me tea.'

' 'Course yer'll 'ave yer tea, nit. But then it's up an' at 'em.'

'What about me bath? Where's the boat Bert got me to float?'

23

Mim's next push was hard enough to send the rumpled figure off the edge of the bed. 'In good time, Miss E.'

Lizzie jumped up, pressed the bear to her chest, ran from the room towards the front door . . .

Mim had to laugh. 'An' where do you think you're goin', me love? Want to get in trouble with the coppers again?' She grabbed her, turned her smartly around, marched her to the table and pressed her onto a chair. 'Now, you sit there till I 'eat up your Jack-the-Rippers.'

Lizzie's eyes rolled upwards at her, reflecting the light from the overhead bulb, holding all the protest she knew how to express, yet not so much that she'd get a shaking.

'And 'ere – let's get rid of Freddie . . .'

Lizzie clasped the dilapidated bear with all her strength.

'Aw, not forever, silly. Just so's you can eat an' attend what you've got to do. See – I'll just throw 'im on the bed, real nice, so's he won't be 'urt.' She would, of course, she thought, have to get rid of him soon; 'e was a bloomin' pest.

Lizzie did not like kippers, but she ate them, and had lots of Marmite on toast and drank two cups of milky tea, and finished off with a rock cake. She slid off her chair, went to investigate the toys Bert was going to mend, saw that he hadn't, and sat down on the floor with the doll whose wig had come off, leaving it with a bare head streaked with glue. 'Poor dolly . . .'

'Oy – up with you.' Mim shoved the big table back, turned over the sticky, threadbare carpet, lit up a Woodbine and started going over the sheet music on the old piano Effie had let her bring here. She felt a moment of weariness, an ache in her back, soreness in her feet, and she had to rub her eyes to get the sting out of them. 'Pour us a cuppa, ducks, nice an' strong, an' bring yerself over.'

Lizzie did not answer immediately. She made a further attempt to make the black, coarse-haired wig stick on the bald head . . .

'Elizabeth Hobbs! You *mind*!'

Lizzie started; struggled to her feet. Lips pressed, she managed to pour from the big brown teapot, to put in the milk and sugar and carry it, the tea slopping over the sides, to the place at the side of the piano already thickly ringed. 'Ta . . .' Mim murmured. 'Right – now let's go over the words again, so's you won't forget 'em.'

Lizzie moved to her side; gave a prolonged yawn.

'Now pay attention . . .'

Mim played with sharp vigour. 'Oh, what a beeutiful mornin',' sang Lizzie, 'Oh, what a beeutiful day . . . I got a . . .

'Glorious feelin' . . .'

'Glorious feelin' . . .'

'Everythin's comin' my way . . .'

'Everythin's comin' me way . . .'

'Not me way, *my* way . . .'

Lizzie let out a sigh, started tracing the cracks in some of the yellowed keys.

Mim slapped her hand away. 'Stand up, remember to smile – sing out real high an' loud, like you wanted everyone in London to 'ear.'

Lizzie tried again. And again. Finally, she got the words in her head and put the actions with them, lifting her small fat arms outward at the finish and doing a quick bow.

Then it was into the middle of the floor to her new tap dance to 'That's Entertainment!', wearing her shoes with the cleats and a funny bowler hat that would go with the sequin costume Mim had to finish.

Mim kept getting up to show her the steps, to make her do them again and again. The ringlets began to collapse, and the bows hung undone, and the knickers kept falling down over her knees.

Mim peeled off her own clothes, put on her leotard, and made Lizzie get into hers. Then they did a few acrobatic steps to 'Night and Day', to show how well Lizzie could do slow backbends and splits . . .

'Ow!' Lizzie said, when Mim pushed her down farther, 'that 'urts between me legs!'

'Never mind, you'll get used to it. You get bendier, love, as you go on. Now, let's recite your poem, and we'll end up with "Maybe It's Because I'm a Londoner" – that'll leave 'em gaspin' for ya.'

Lizzie sat down on the floor. 'Tired, Mum.'

'Snap, snap. Up on your tootsies – we're near done.' Mim turned back to the music in front of her, scowled, nodded . . .

'May – be it's be – cause I'm a Lon – don – er . . . That I love Lon – don so . . . Come on, sing up, don't lisp like a baby!'

Though she did it over and over again, Lizzie could not do it the way Mim wanted it, and finally she went hoarse, and no more words would come out, and there was a look on her face very like crying.

Mim grunted, stopped. 'Right you are – that'll do for now. Needs a lot of work, though.' She got up, gave Lizzie a hug and a kiss on her sweaty little brow, went to run her a bath.

When the child was clean, her teeth brushed, her hair put up in fresh curling rags, she helped her settle in the big brass bed, which wasn't even a double one, and where they would end up fighting for space and covers. She let her snuggle up with the bear. 'Sweet dreams, me ol' darlin'.'

Lizzie kissed her back, settled her nobbly head into the soggy-white pillow, shut her eyes . . .

But when Mim closed the door and put her ear to it she could hear her nattering away in a husky whisper to the wretched bear.

She shook her head, went into the kitchen and made herself some strong fresh tea. Then she put the room to rights, put on her nightie, and got out her sewing equipment.

26

It wouldn't be long before Bert came in, back from the theatre. He'd bring sausage rolls, pickled onions, Guinness . . . He'd have a lot to tell her. It'd give her a chance to get the little costume finished.

# CHAPTER TWO

Miss Bettina's School and Agency was one flight up in a building in the heart of London's music business known as 'Tin Pan Alley', but it was as silent at this time of the morning as the inside of a church; Mim had got Lizzie ready, pushed her through streets filled only with tourists and office workers, and now stood with her outside the still-locked door, on which a printed card said AUDITIONS TODAY 10 a.m.

It was, by the wall clock Mim could just see by peering through the glass panel, not quite *nine*.

'Cor. We 'ave got a wait. If I weren't so skint I'd take us for a cuppa. Nowhere to sit, neither . . .'

'Go 'ome?' Lizzie suggested, with a brave upward glance.

Mim gave the child's shoulder an impatient shake. 'Go over your stuff, more like.'

Lizzie tightened her reddened lips. 'No more.' With determined suddenness, she slid down the wall beside the door, extended her short plump legs with the rouged knees, folded her plump arms with the rouged elbows across her chest, leaned back into the shelter of her red sateen cape and fixed her gaze on the shining ends of her blunt-toed tap shoes.

'And what do you think you're doin', young miss?' Mim gazed down through the smoke of her cigarette. 'Get yerself all over dirt, you will.' When Lizzie didn't answer, she nudged her with her knee. 'Got cloth ears, 'ave we?' Still there was no answer.

Grunting with recognition of the distant expression on the cleverly made-up little face (she looked eight if she looked a day this time!), Mim slid resignedly down the wall beside her, lit a fresh Woodbine, wrapped her arms about her knobbly, purple-trousered knees. 'I suppose yer 'avin' one of yer "thinks" – well, don't come up with none of yer trick questions, like why was we born, and 'oo is God, and why ain't we got no fur, an' such. I ain't in the mood. We got enough to think about keepin' ourselves alive. You just think about bein' a big star, 'ear?'

Lizzie drew her knees up to her chin, hugged them close, cast a wistful, furtive look towards the light at the top of the staircase . . .

'An' you're not goin' nowhere neither,' Mim said. 'Aw, come on, me li'le duck, this is goin' ter be your great day – let's 'ave a penny.'

When Lizzie tried but couldn't, Mim shrugged, flicked ash impatiently to the floor, jabbed a bobby pin more securely into one of Lizzie's ringlets, got a powder puff from her plastic bag to dab at the end of Lizzie's nose. 'Got ter get us some proper theatrical greasepaint,' she muttered, 'an' don't you eat off yer lipstick . . .'

Suddenly there were sounds of doors, rapid footsteps on the stairs. A woman appeared, grey-haired, with glasses and a hunch to her cardiganed shoulders. She put a key in the lock of the door. 'Been waiting, have you?' she said, nodding at Lizzie's drooping lids. 'Well, you may come and wait inside, at least. Miss Tina should be here soon.'

Mim shook Lizzie awake, propelled her into the square room which was furnished with assorted oak chairs, a low table holding theatrical magazines and papers, two questionably-living potted palms, a notice board on the wall covered with press clippings showing Miss Bettina as a beauty-contest winner, her various troupes, and photographs tacked up everywhere of her famous children

29

doing their routines in seaside hotels, on piers, in music halls, even in a London theatre or two.

'Sit down,' the woman said, then went on sensibly flat shoes to air out the office, riffle through the post, start a kettle to boil. Almost at once, the telephones began to ring, and she answered in a flat, disenchanted voice, as if being there and involved were beneath her.

'Everyone wants priority for their children,' she said.

Mim stared at her from under a single black brow. 'I 'ope you got Lizzie on that list,' she said curtly. 'Lizzie Hobbs.' Mim put the *h* on with care.

The woman stared back, cast a curious pitying glance at Lizzie, did not answer.

In a few moments, the door opened and another mother and child came in, took seats. Mim studied the heavy-set brunette mother and child with frank hostility. Miss Bettina surely wouldn't consider such a lump of dough! She nudged Lizzie not to smile at her.

Two more children came in, one boy with a mass of curly black hair and two front teeth missing, one tall plain girl with thick mousey plaits, wearing an outgrown velvet dress. The man with the boy kept smiling and nodding at everyone, and the woman with the girl did nothing but stare at Lizzie, looking as if she had just bitten into a lemon.

Jealous, thought Mim. Recognized a real professional kid. She looked down proudly at Lizzie, whose legs swung from the edge of the chair in happy excitement at the possibility of new friends. 'Not a dicky bird to anyone,' she told her. 'This is business.'

Mim sat up even more alertly as two children came in with a woman who seemed more like an older sister than a mother. The girls were both perky and bright-eyed, with shiny red curls and neat little bodies that moved knowingly, as if at any moment they would break into dance and song. Trained, of course. Mim knew old-timers when

30

she saw them. Yeah, the woman carried a case – there'd be costumes in it, an' make-up. Mim's mouth tightened on her cigarette.

Lizzie squirmed in every part of her body. 'Talk to sisters, Mum . . .'

Sisters, eh? That was it, of course. Lizzie didn't just have wool for brains. A clever little double-act – an' only two places open today . . . 'You go over yer words, young miss, 'ear? Think about yer steps. This ain't no social lark.'

Lizzie plucked at a curl, put its end in her mouth.

'An' don't do *that*. Yer supposed to be seven, not a baby.'

Lizzie took the curl from her mouth, sat up straighter.

Now, as the room filled up, the other children began to talk to each other, the mothers or sponsors to gossip. Mim kept her po-face and listened. Troupes, apparently, were on their way out. Miss Bettina was losing money. She was only looking for *special* talent . . .

Ah. That was where Lizzie would come in. There'd be no-one like her here! She tightened her hold on Lizzie's hand, gave it a hard squeeze, did not notice Lizzie's grimace of pain.

When Miss 'Tina', as everyone called her, pushed in through the door, every eye went to the portly figure with the huge amorphous bosom, the cascade of coarse yellow-blond hair, the ruggedly handsome face with its frank layers of make-up, the incongruously thin legs and ankles in totteringly high heels. As her huge, wrinkle-surrounded dark eyes swept around the room, it was as if a current of electricity had been sent through it, stunning the children to stillness, shocking the adults to ingratiating smiles of acknowledgement.

'Sorry to be a bit late,' she said loudly. 'Got caught up in Trooping of the Colour traffic; murder. You may all go into the studio and get yourselves ready. I'll be with you in a moment.'

Mim gave Lizzie a quick nudge to get ahead of the crowd, and walked briskly with her into the large adjoining room. It had mirror-lined walls and was bare except for benches against the walls, a big chair and desk, an upright piano. One large unshaded bulb suspended from the ceiling provided the only light, though its many reflections gave the impression of dazzling brightness. 'Quick.' Mim pushed Lizzie towards a bench near the desk, which was spread with papers, an ashtray, cups for tea. 'Let's 'ave a look at yer.'

As the children and their guardians surged in, looked for a place to change in privacy, Mim could not repress a smile. *Nits*. They should've known to come ready. She looked at Lizzie with sharp pride. The sequin costume fitted her small body neat as skin; the ruffle round her neck stood up like starch itself; there were sequin butterflies in her hair and on her bright green socks, and when the actual moment came, Mim would hand her the funny sequinned bowler hat that had kept her up past three to make. 'Lift up yer chin, that's me girl; smile saucy. Don't forget, everyone loves ya, everyone's yer friend, an' you're goin' ter knock 'em cold. You are Miss Tina's big discovery, 'er great new shinin' star.'

Lizzie kept her chin up, where it had been jerked, and looked into Mim's eyes. 'I got to piss, Mum . . .'

'No, you ain't. You bloody ain't. You 'old it. If you don't, I'll . . .'

Mim realized her voice was rising. 'That's a darlin',' she said. 'Good girl.'

Lizzie crossed her knees, pinched her mouth, while Mim watched, one corner of her mouth lifted. After a moment, the plump knees moved apart again. All was well.

There was a close smell now of sweating bodies and powder, and some awful scent they used these days under their arms. Hair was brushed, twisted, bobby-pinned up on top. No-one, but not one single one, had Lizzie's spiral-

ling light blond curls all standing out from her head ready
to go into action when she danced . . .

In fact, no-one was even in a costume, only in darned
and patched leotards or shorts and cotton vests. It seemed
almost a shame to have so little competition . . .

'All right, everyone.' Miss Tina took her place at the
desk, lit a cigarette, took a quick sip of tea, nodded to the
thin, pale man in shirtsleeves, pencil in mouth, who sat
waiting to play the piano. 'I'm going to ask you to come
out singly and dance to whatever Billy plays. Do whatever
you like. This will show me how inventive and resourceful
you are, as well as adjustable. You see, we never know
what conditions we may find in this business, lost music,
out-of-tune pianos, rotten floorboards. Be able to dance
to anything, anywhere, under any conditions. Clear,
kiddies?'

There was a high chorus of 'Yes, Miss Tina.' It did not
include Mim's voice. 'What about the rest – what we got
ready to show?' she asked, with a rasp of threat.

Miss Tina smiled charmingly. 'That, of course, will follow.' She raised a large square hand with red hooked fingernails. 'Now, line up. Look slippy. Billy . . .'

Billy nodded, struck up smartly with 'Hernando's Hide-
away', and the first child, a boy of about nine with a rise of
blond hair like a pincushion, and mouth and eyes equally
wide open, placed his hands aggressively on his hips and
began to twirl and dip in tango rhythm, ending up with a
bow and snarl-like smile.

'Not bad, not bad at all. Your name is Rudi – *à la*
Valentino, no doubt.'

Everyone except Mim and Lizzie laughed politely.

Miss Tina clapped. 'Next, please.'

Now came the two bright-haired little girls, and this
time Billy struck up with 'Singin' in the Rain', and they
immediately went into a smoothly rhythmic tap routine
taken straight from Gene Kelly. Gawd, thought Mim,

who wouldn't know how to do that? Lizzie'd been doin' it since she was three . . .

'Bravo, girls,' said Miss Tina. 'Next.'

The line of children moved along, each child straining with grim resolve to outdo the others with winsome, adorable or sophisticated appeal, putting so much energy and vigour into their interpretation of the assigned music that sweat mingled with their bright smiles like clownish tears; but when the plump brunette girl broke into hip-twisting gyrations to 'Shake, Rattle and Roll', her fat, developing little breasts wobbling up and down, side to side as she jerked her shoulders, grimaced, and even moved her pelvis forward in seductive bumps, Miss Tina threw up both hands and brought both down on the desk in a resounding thump.

'No, no, no! Stop! I'm sorry, dear, but this simply isn't my style. Where's your mother . . . Ah, Mrs. Wilder – really, my dear, you must see that your daughter needs to lose at least a *stone* – apart from anything else . . .'

'We've come all the way down from Blackpool, and you wrote . . .'

'You sent a very obsolete photo, as I see it. Sorry – time is too valuable for this. Next.'

Mim nudged Lizzie as the big child, her face crumpled with desperate weeping, was led away by her infuriated mother. 'Serves 'em right,' she whispered. 'Na then. Your turn comin' – give it all yer've got, Miss Cuddles, for me an' Bert.' Mim tweaked Lizzie's rouged chin. 'Love ya.'

'All right,' said Miss Tina, with a strange new expression on her rubbery, mobile face. 'The little girl – you, dear.'

As Billy struck up with 'Shall We Dance', Lizzie looked up at Mim with a sudden fearful stare.

'Ey! 'Old on . . .' Mim stepped forward in front of her. 'That ain't fair. You got to 'ave two people for that!'

Billy's hands hovered over the keys; he looked forlorn,

34

wilted, as if at any moment he might just get up and walk off. 'Brats and their mothers,' he muttered audibly.

'Take it or leave it, Mrs. – uh, Hobbs.'

Mim's outraged comment was drowned by Billy's opening thumps of the famous tune from *The King and I*. With sudden agility, she was out of the way, dipping into the plastic bag, producing the little sequinned bowler, setting it firmly on Lizzie's head, thrusting a small sequinned cane into her hand.

'Do it now,' she whispered, with a hard little push, 'the whole routine, like for "That's Entertainment".'

Lizzie, left alone, stood for a stunned moment without any movement at all; even her face seemed to have frozen into a grotesque little mask. Then, suddenly, one cleated shoe began to tap, and her head nodded to the beat, and she was off into her exhaustively-rehearsed bit, doing each step and making each gesture like a furiously wound-up mechanical toy.

When Billy came to the end of the tune, Lizzie simply went on, singing 'That's Entertainment' without accompaniment. Her bowler hat came off, and she picked it up and put it back on. Her cane fell to the floor and she retrieved it, still singing and dancing. But when in the middle of the high point of the lyric her red cape would not undo, she came to a halt, tugged, pulled at the cord clasp, her face turning bright pink as it only became more firmly knotted.

'Forget it,' came Mim's hoarse whisper. 'Just finish the song . . .'

Nodding, Lizzie resumed her singing, but now panic lifted her voice to heights beyond her reach. It thinned, cracked, went off-key, developed a definite babyish lisp with a coarse edge that finally ended, before the climaxing phrase of the song, in a small grunt like the first effort of a young frog.

There was a moment of complete silence in the room,

while Mim gathered Lizzie to her in a fierce hug of protection. 'Never you mind, me darlin',' she whispered. 'You did wonderful.'

Taking her by the hand, Mim prepared to move away in the full dignity of betrayal. She was just waiting, just waiting, for that smug old cow to say one word . . .

'Thank you, Lizzie,' Miss Tina called. 'That was very interesting.' She tapped her big teeth with a pencil. 'Please wait.'

Aha! Mim broke into a gleeful smile, almost laughed aloud. She ground her cigarette out on the waxed floor, drew Lizzie to a bench, sat her down, put an arm around her, put a quick kiss that left a bright stain on the plump cheek. 'You done it, me li'le gem, you done it. You're me pride an' joy.'

'Go 'ome now?' Lizzie asked.

' 'Ome? 'Ome? You make me laugh, you do. But you know what I'm goin' ter do when we get there?'

Lizzie shook her ringlets.

'I'm goin' ter knit that bear of yours a red jumper.'

Lizzie's blackened eyebrows rose. 'An' twousers to match? An' an 'at wiv 'oles for 'is ears?'

'Well . . .' Mim's mouth jerked the cigarette further to the side. 'Why not? In fer a penny, in fer a pound, eh?'

Lizzie drew her shoulders together, shivered. 'Oooh . . . 'E *will* be pleased!' Her grin devastated the impressions of age; reduced it to no more than four.

Pleased with her sacrifice and generosity, Mim kept her arm about Lizzie and did her best to withstand the other performers, tried not to let her contempt show. At last they were done. Billy stood up, stretched, closed the lid of the battered piano.

'Will Mrs. Watson, Mr. Frith and Mrs. Hobbs please wait and see me in the office,' Miss Tina said at last, with firm dismissal.

There was a long pause now, while the other parents

and children were interviewed in a tiny room concealed by a firmly closed door; even the secretary remained outside.

Eventually, after what seemed an hour, but was probably only twenty minutes, the other children and their parents left, and Miss Tina loomed in her doorway to beckon Mim.

'Sit down,' she said, and sat across from them, over a desk inches high in mounds of dusty papers, photos, clippings, framed photographs of herself at earlier stages of her life when she was a voluptuous young woman held round the waist by handsome beaming young men. 'Now, then – let's have a talk about this young lady.' She smiled and winked at Lizzie.

'I'm glad you want 'er,' Mim said, tilting her brassy crowned head graciously. 'You'll make no mistake. She's a one-orf, is Lizzie.'

Miss Tina sat back in her huge worn-leather chair. 'Look here, Mrs. Hobbs, I want to be very honest and frank with you. I don't want you to get your hopes up and then be let down.' She cast a soft-eyed glance at Lizzie, almost loving. 'She's a dear little thing, most beguiling. And I can see how hard she's worked to do what you want her to . . .'

'Yeah?'

'But, the point is, I'm afraid, that she just seems horribly precocious and bratty. The way you make her up, the way you make her present herself – well, she's merely a – curiosity. I'd have to completely re-train her . . .'

'Wait on . . . What're you sayin' – curiosity? What's that, then?'

Miss Tina did not flinch, though Mim's eyebrows made a ferocious line of black above blazing eyes. 'An oddity. That's what I mean – instead of a bright five-year-old with a lot of spirit and potential, who might – I say *might* – with care and patience, be directed to become a competent little entertainer, with who-knows-what bright future.'

Mim's face became a taut, angular frieze. 'Well, I've 'eard everythin'! Of all the cheek . . .'

Miss Tina made an abrupt upward move of her heavy body, reached for a leather handbag at her feet. 'I see we don't understand each other. So, if you don't mind, I've got an appointment to keep.'

Mim grasped Lizzie's hand. 'You're turning 'er down, ain't you, just like that!'

'I'm not turning her down, Mrs. Hobbs. All I'm saying is that I'm willing to take her on for training, if you're willing to accept my terms . . .'

'Terms? You didn't mention no terms . . .'

'I was going to, my dear. I was going to suggest that I take her on for a year, as a sort of experiment, see what I can do. You'd have to leave her entirely to me, and she'd have to come here several times a week. When she's had the chance to develop, there could be a possibility of fitting her in. I once had a student, younger than Lizzie, who did amazingly well, became one of my top performers . . .'

'So, you'd want 'er comin' 'ere just to learn, not to be doin' no performin', just to be learnin' what she already knows – for a *year*!'

'Mrs. Hobbs – please forget I even mentioned it. I must be on my way.'

'An' that's yer last word? That's all Lizzie means to yer, a li'le kid ter practise on, like a guinea-pig!'

Miss Tina stood to her full height. 'Good morning. Good luck with Lizzie.' She reached over and patted one of Lizzie's cheeks. 'Sorry we won't have a lot of fun together.'

Mim interrupted Lizzie's shy smile with an abrupt shake. 'Don't you get at 'er. She's my kind, an' what's more, she's goin' to be a great star. You don't know nothin' or you'd see that yerself.'

'Apparently, you're not going to let me.' Miss Bettina held out her hand, but Mim ignored it.

'An' if I did decide to let you 'ave a go with Lizzie,' she

said, pointing her nose towards Miss Tina's, 'when would she start? What would she 'ave ter bring? What time would she 'ave ter be brought and fetched?'

Miss Tina paused. 'We could work out those details. And she could start – well, Monday, if you like. I happen to have a rest period for the moment.'

'You do, eh?' Something like suspicion chilled the back of Mim's neck. 'Maybe yer think yer onto a good thing. Well, I wouldn't blame yer. Only remember, I'd be keepin' me eye on yer. I'd be watching' everythin' yer do. If you exploit my kid in any way . . . My Bert, 'e's a big bloke, a stage 'and at the Drury Lane!'

Miss Tina's sudden laugh was genuine. 'Oh, Mrs. Hobbs, really. You'd think I was trying to harm your little girl, instead of trying to help her – and you.' She moved towards the door, opened it. 'Now, please.'

'S'pose I said I'd give it a bash,' Mim said quickly, tugging Lizzie back from her quick spurt for the door. 'What then?'

Again, Miss Tina paused. 'Well, I don't know. You'd have to want your child to be here with me, cooperate *fully*. On top of that . . .'

Mim met Miss Tina's sudden sharp glance with a start. Somethin' was fishy . . .

'You'd have to be willing to pay three guineas a week.'

Mim's mouth dropped open. She forgot Lizzie's hand, forgot her cigarette. 'Three guineas a week – *me* pay *you*!'

'That's right. Everyone pays me, Mrs. Hobbs. How do you think I maintain a business? Not only are fees paid for training. I also deduct a percentage for all engagements. Now, if that isn't satisfactory, then this is a waste of time.'

Suddenly Mim was running after Lizzie, running after the large woman who stopped to speak to her secretary. Patches of red stood out over her arms and shoulders. Her armpits oozed sweat. Christ, what a turn. What would Bert say, with nothin' comin' in these past weeks between shows – lumbered they were, lumbered proper . . .

' 'Old on, wait . . . Look 'ere, Miss Tina . . .'

'Yes, yes . . .' The woman did not even glance at her.

'Uh . . . Seein' as 'ow you ain't been exactly draggin' yer 'eels all these years, I'm game to give it a Scapa Flow if you are.' Mim put out her sweaty, muscled hand and grasped Miss Tina's in a hard downward jerk.

Blinking at this onslaught, Miss Tina forced a last smile to her mouth. 'Right. I'm glad. I really admire your little girl and I think she'll have a lovely time with us. It's not all hard work. And . . . oh, yes; the fee will include some elocution lessons.'

'Ow, yes?' For a moment, Mim thought she might let go with a one-two to that big double chin. What made 'er think '*er* voice was so posh? She could tell it was only a bit up on 'er own, *made* like that . . .'

Still, Lizzie would have to be made some time. 'Right, then.' She took hold of Lizzie. 'Monday. What time?'

'Ten o'clock. Sharp! Fetch her at four. Bring leotards and a sandwich.'

Mim touched an imaginary forelock. Lower lip curled, shoulders braced, she drew Lizzie along with her, her heels making an aggressive clatter.

'Ah, Mrs. Hobbs.' The secreatry moved forward, peered over her glasses. 'That's payable in advance.'

'In advance! Of what? I ain't got it *on* me, if that's what you mean!' Mim's saliva thickened. The cords on her neck stood out.

'Never mind, Mrs. Carter,' Miss Tina said. 'It's all right, Mrs. Hobbs. Monday will do. Goodbye.'

Mim moved on, dragging Lizzie behind her like an after-thought, down the stairs, out onto the street. 'Pissin',' she said, as they moved out into the heavy downpour, the waves of raised umbrellas. 'That's *all* we need.'

'Twelve guineas a month, that is,' Bert said, as he and Mim

lay wrapped together on his couch-bed. He patted her hard little bottom comfortingly. 'Not to worry, ol' girl. I've got some good tips on the gee-gees, and I'll put me medals into Uncle's, and cut down on the booze an' fags.'

'Gawd love ya!' Mim prodded his unshaven jaw with the tip of her nose. She was glad she'd decided to muck about with him a bit without his even hinting. She wasn't nearly good enough to him, even if he was too elephant's most the time to notice . . .

' 'Ey – what time is it, Bertie?' She wrenched herself upward out of the grey twist of bedclothes. 'Christ! I'll be late!'

Bert's big bare arms reached out to her futilely. He pulled gently at her mass of brassy hair. 'Don't go yet. We miss you shoutin' at us, me an' Cuddles.'

She gave him a twitchy smile. 'Light us one, darlin'.'

Bert heaved himself over, knocking down several empty bottles at the side of the bed, and fumbled about until he had one of her Woodbines ready to slip into her mouth.

She took a deep drag, another, then suddenly was out of bed, padding off to the kitchen. 'I'll make us a cuppa . . .'

'No, I'll do it. You got enough on.'

She nodded to him, grateful. Once she got to the offices, there'd be no let-up till it was time to get over to the restaurant.

' 'Ow's yer back, ol' dear?' Bert asked, as he shuffled to the kitchen in his long vest that did not quite reach his crotch.

'Not so bad as me feet!'

They both laughed.

'It's the lav's the worst,' Mim called from the bathroom. 'You wouldn't believe them business tycoons could 'ave such ro'en aim. The stench, Bert. Worse than the ol' Bale Street days. Still – I ain't complainin'. Just so long as I don't get 'ousemaid's knee. They say it 'urts som'ink awful.'

'What about Frenchy's – they got any more 'elp yet?' Bert brought in two cups of tea, saucerless, slopping the dark brown liquid straight to the floor, and carried them to the bathroom.

'Ah, ta, ducks.' Mim had scooped her hair up under a scarf that she tied neatly on top. Without make-up, she looked like a gaunt waif and, as she gulped the hot tea, half-starving. But beyond the scarf and overalls, she conceded nothing more to the role of a char . . .

Bert leaned against the lintel, as she applied make-up with abandon, fascinated, forgetting he was tired, had had little sleep, that his head pounded dully from the booze. 'You do wonders with yerself, ol' darlin'. Bet they all flirt with you at Frenchy's, eh?'

She pinched his chin. 'No time, luv. Dishes clatterin', everyone shoutin', more tables than I can 'andle. They don't notice ya, only what they get to eat!'

Bert shook his head, looked sorrowfully into his cup. 'I don't like it. If only . . .'

'Bertie!' Mim snapped her fingers. 'None of that. We both want this for our li'le darlin', right?'

He nodded, sighed, rubbed at his big stomach dolefully.

'So – that's *it*, then. Get on with it. Just you see she gets there on time, that she don't take down 'er ringlets, that she's got 'er lunch-box. An' what's more, that you clean this place up a bit, an' keep outa the boozer.'

Mim winked at him, then went past him to the bedroom. It was still dark in there, even though light was beginning to lift the darkness outside the window. Lizzie lay with her arms flung over her head, a small mound under part of a blanket, Freddie close beside her. Mim stared down at her for a moment, struck by something like panic. Would that crafty ol' cow get her bands on the kid, take 'er over so's she was some'ink different, maybe never ever get to be a somebody? Maybe they should've listened to Harry Org from upstairs, when 'e said 'they all look alike once old Betts gets through with 'em.' An' 'e oughta know, bein' an ol' Music Hall man who'd played on the same bill over the years with what 'e called 'er 'brats' . . .

Suddenly, Lizzie was stirring. 'Mum? . . . You goin'?'

'Yeah – off to me work. You don't 'ave to wake up yet.'

'Why d'you 'ave to work?' Lizzie pushed at her rag-wrapped hair.

' 'Cause I gotta pay Miss Tina, that's why. An' don't knock them rags off.'

'She won't let me 'ave 'em, Mum . . . Mim. She bwushes 'em out.'

'I know she does.' Mim put her hands on her bony hips. 'So, I put 'em back in. We'll soon see who wins.'

Lizzie leaned up on one elbow. 'I don't like 'em. I want me 'air straight.'

'Oh, yer do, do ya? Want ter look like a plain li'le no-one, do ya? Well, I'm not lettin' ya, see? You tell 'er to put that in 'er pipe.'

Lizzie lay back. 'When are yer goin' ter make Freddie's sweater an 'at an' twousers? 'E's been askin' an' askin'.'

'Mmm.' Mim put some low-heeled shoes in a bag, slipped her feet into the white high heels, took out her waitress uniform and folded it in beside the shoes. 'What time I got, I ask yer? Soon, me darlin', soon. Now, give us a hit-or-miss, an' be good for Bert. I'll fetch yer as usual. Ta-ra.'

Lizzie watched her go, then drew Freddie up to her chest. 'Never mind,' she whispered in his threadbare ear, 'when we go on the picnic, I'll take yer with me. You'll see weal twees an' other animals, an' I'll tell yer stories, an' we'll go fer walks wiv Bert. I pwomise yer, Freddie, pwomise.'

'Well, me ol' boot, I'm off,' Mim said to Bert, closing the bedroom door, and giving him a quick peck in passing. 'I'll see yer when I get 'ere.'

He grinned. 'No doubt.'

She gave him a perky salute, closed the front door sharply behind her.

Bert got his old army dressing gown, wrapped it around

43

him and sank into the leather chair. There was just time for a kip before he swung into action with the little Miss.

'Escaped!' Mim's fingers drummed on her plastic bag. 'Whaddya mean?' She was done-in, aching in every bone, and now dragged out of Frenchy's before she'd got 'er tips, before she'd even had time to change out of her uniform; Bertie in a tizz; the ol' cow lookin' at 'er as if the world 'ad come to an end . . .

'What I mean, Mrs. Hobbs, is that Lizzie has been escaping from school, running off each day on her own, wandering about the streets, doing God-knows-what with the time she was supposed to be doing her work here . . .' Miss Tina looked over her desk at Lizzie.

'Goin' to the libwawy, readin' books, playing wiv the kids in the school yard, 'op scotch, an' ball, talkin' wiv me fwiends an' the big dog an' the kitty-cats . . .' Lizzie moved up and down on her toes with the terrible excitement of what lay in store, the ringlets, which she had taken down and flattened, hanging in forlorn tails about her bright pink cheeks.

Mim stared at her. 'You *got* to be jokin',' she muttered.

There was an intense silence in the room. Each tick of the wall clock sounded with ominous sharpness.

'What kind of a teacher are ya, I ask?' said Mim, returning her stare to Miss Tina. 'I could sue you. Bring the law on you. 'Ere'm I workin' me arse ter the bone; Bert sells 'is medals so's yer can give our Lizzie a proper trainin'; an' what do we get for it?' Mim's fists balled, lifted, so that Miss Tina's eyes went to them in apprehension. 'Bleedin' awful. Our kiddie runnin' aroun' the streets, where anythin' might 'ave 'appened to 'er, anythin'! You understand?' The fists lifted a bit higher.

'I know, Mrs. Hobbs. I kept on trying to get her involved and interested, kept on hoping I'd win her over and make headway – I tried every persuasion, I promise you. And the children all loved her . . .'

'An' what's that gotta do with it? You know what you done – you've wasted an 'ole year of our Lizzie's career! You should be run outa business. The 'ole world should know 'ow you get parents to give ya twelve guineas a month, then just let their kiddies run about loose . . .'

'That's not . . .'

Mim stood up. 'Yes, it bloody is. If you'd been doin' what yer should've, Lizzie would never've done what she's been doin' – right, Lizzie?'

Lizzie gave a start. Her body, not as chunky as it had been, shuddered to a more upright position – stood at attention.

'Mrs. Hobbs, you really do know how to twist things around. If I told you the truth, that Lizzie simply cannot follow the others, cannot work to set routines, is unable to do anything at all, except what you've taught her; that she was, poor mite, totally lost – you'd undoubtedly tell me it wasn't so, that it was all lies . . .'

'An' so it would be! Ro'en excuses for not knowin' 'ow ter deal with genius, with a real, genuine star, instead of li'le sheep what you can turn into nobodies no-one will ever 'ear of. Come on, Lizzie, me girl, you an' me is leaving. Where's all yer gear?'

'Everything's in her carrier, Mrs. Hobbs.' Miss Bettina's face was greenish-grey round the edges of her pancake tan. Her ringed, red-nailed hands shook, and she kept her eyes from Lizzie's.

'Put yer things on then, Miss, an' take yer last look. Yer'll not see this place again.'

Lizzie did not look anywhere, even at Miss Tina, even towards the back room where some of the kids were rehearsing and making a lot of wobblies on the high notes. She followed Mim, scuffling along as fast as she could in the cleated shoes, the big fake fur jacket Mim had bought off a barrow, the wool hat that dangled pom-poms into her eyes. 'Goin' ter give me an 'idin', Mum?' Her breath made little puffs of smoke in the frosty air.

Mim did not pause. Her bulky sweater and drainpipes didn't do the job in this weather! Her bum was freezing, her nose dripping. 'Come on, move yer plates!'

'Are yer, Mum?' Lizzie broke into a trot that caused backward looks in the neon-lighted gloom.

Mim came to an abrupt halt. 'Now, look 'ere, Miss Clever-Boots. When 'ave I ever? Eh? When 'ave I ever laid an 'and on ya?'

Lizzie stared upward, the puffs of smoke coming faster. 'I dunno.'

'O'course ya dunno. Neither me nor Bert has ever touched ya, that's why. But don't think yer're goin' ter get away with what yer've done. It may be the ol' cow's fault, but yer went be'in' our backs, didn't ya? Me an' Bert what was workin' our arses off for ya, an' yer just scarpered.'

The eyes meeting Mim's had a stricken, liquid look. 'I'm sorry, Mum . . .'

'Sorry, eh?' Mim stared back at her, her chattering teeth vibrating the forgotten cigarette. 'Is that all? Sorry! Well, we'll see about *that*.' She grabbed Lizzie's hand, pulled her on so that she stumbled, tripped along beside her. 'We'll just see about that, me little flower.'

'You goin' ter do Freddie in?'

Mim wheeled on her. 'Now, who said that?'

'Put 'im in the dustbin, in the muck?'

Mim wiped her nose with the back of her hand, then did Lizzie's nose as well. 'You give me a good idea, you 'ave. Yeah – an' next time you scarper, or don't work 'ard like what I tell ya, *Bert* ain't goin' to save 'im, neither, see? You got that?'

Lizzie stared into her eyes, gritted her teeth . . .

'Right, then. Give us yer 'and and a nice penny-a- . . .'

After a moment, Lizzie did both.


In the following two years, scarpering or wandering off

46

became the least of Mim's problems with Lizzie. Far worse was the interminable wait for her to age. No matter how much progress was made with her voice, Lizzie would give herself away with her hand-over-the-mouth giggle, or the funny lisp caused by the gaps where her baby teeth had been.

There was nothing to do but soldier on. Mim got Lizzie into a week-long version of *The Gingerbread Man* as a little biscuit that could do tumbles and splits, into a Cockney musical where she sang 'The Cokey Coke' with a chorus of children, and into a children's play where she spoke one line: 'My name's Alice. What's yours?'

When none of this made the slightest impression on anyone, Mim decided Lizzie needed her own little solo act, a clever turn that showed all her talents off and made them see what a real knockout she was. After that, they'd come clamouring.

She made Lizzie a quick-change screen of tinsel remnants which she stretched on a nailed-together wood frame, got a carton from downstairs and lined it with sateen to hold the six little costumes Lizzie would wear, then put together six different kinds of routines.

Bert did not approve of the idea, but had no say, while the flat filled up with even more clutter, and there was nowhere safe from pins, needles, beads and sequins, to hide from Mim's interminable croaking and banging at the piano, her pony-tail jerking, her bony face scowling and miming, or poor little Lizzie dancing and reciting, rolling her black-circled eyes and making curious grins. He found himself exiting more and more frequently into the friendly warmth of the boozer.

Here, expansive and reconnected to the world outside, away from Mim, Lizzie and the theatre, he was appreciated for his kindly wit, his views on politics and what was happening to post-war society. With mates surrounding him, he spoke of the Wolfenden Report, the whores-off-the streets campaign, tight jeans, X-films, the increase of porn shops, the 'rock 'n' roll' fad and Elvis Presley shoving his willie at the girls and getting them all started.

Kids were taking over the world, he said. What thanks for the ones who fought and died to save them! 'Dupes, we was, mateys,' he often observed, with the doleful grin that made him so popular at the elbow-polished bar. ' *'Ad*, good an' proper. A conned generation.'

Still, they did have a good royal family, he admitted. Sending young Prince Charles off to a school was a good step – would change the monarchy, bring it closer to the way things was.

Bert's reasoning was not always clear, and there were arguments, sometimes loud, and he would have to be sobered up with coffee and sent out into the night to get to his job. He would forget he hadn't had his supper. On the q.t., the doctor had told him to watch it; the lining of his stomach was in poor condition. In fact, he should never touch another drop of the stuff as long as he lived.

This would make him think of Mim's mum. Dear ol' Effie was in the same hole. Trapped up there, she was, in that great concrete high-riser, her entire life in the East End, the markets, the street life, the comrades of poverty and survival all gone as if they'd never been; and with no more connection with the theatre and stars she'd worked for, the ol' girl was drinking herself right down the drain. Alf, the poor blighter, was helpless as a babe to stop her . . .

Gawd, Bert would be reminded; he'd better take Miss Cuddles to see her before the kid's ol' gran croaked. They'd get away from Mim for a day, take Alf and Effie some of the stewed eels they still fancied. Afterwards, maybe, they could do one of the rambles through Whitechapel, Petticoat Lane, and other of their old haunts. She'd love that, little Lizzie . . .

Meanwhile, to the salt mines, the pulleys and flying systems, the double handling, and pray he kept 'is 'ead about 'im.

At last, Lizzie was word-perfect in the six routines: Mary Martin singing 'I'm Gonna Wash That Man Right Outa My Hair'; Mae West cracking jokes and saying 'Come up and see me sometime' (Lizzie wearing big padded Bristols); Eliza Doolittle, doing 'Wouldn't It Be Loverly!'; Vera Lynn singing 'We'll Meet Again'; Ella Fitzgerald singing 'I've Got a Crush on You' (Lizzie in a black curly wig) and, last, a street-walker by a lamp-post singing a song she (Mim) had made up for Lizzie: 'Stars over Soho' (which brought a lump to your throat).

Lugging the big box of costumes with her, she took Lizzie to one theatre after another, one agent after another, one audition after another (pushing her way in, even when refused), but the results were always the same. The kid was 'amazing', 'professional', but far too young for the sophistication of the material. 'Why not let her develop in her own time, Mrs. Hobbs?' one producer said in a down-the-nose voice. 'You do the wee thing a grave disservice.'

Mim had glowered; there was no way to answer short of a raspberry. As a row of big fur-hatted blokes burst into loud shouts and started kicking from the knees, she grabbed Lizzie's hand, the box of costumes, and moved grandly to the exit.

'Silly sod,' she muttered. 'Never you mind, pe'al. We're not done yet – not by a long chalk!'

Lizzie didn't say anything. She didn't say so much these days. And only occasionally did she skip.

# CHAPTER THREE

'You say your little girl is eight, Mrs. Hobbs?' The tall, thin young man with the prominent Adam's apple and big pale blue eyes looked over at Lizzie with a gentle smile. 'She doesn't look it. We'd have to see a birth certificate, in the case that Madame took her on.'

Mim lifted one side of her lip, which today had been left free of a fag in deference to the occasion. 'You sayin' I'm a liar?' she asked in her most polite tone.

'No, no, of course not. It's just that there are rules and laws – Madame takes no-one under eight, you see.'

'I know that. That's why I been waitin' for today. Midnight tonight, Lizzie'll be exactly eight years old. That near enough?'

The young man smiled again. 'That should do it. If other qualifications are met. Well, now,' he rose from his desk in the small office. 'I'll take you down to the theatre.'

Mim jumped up. She had worn her best dress, a fake leopard-skin velvet, fitted tightly from her chest to her knees, which she had copied from Marion Ryan, the singer. (That was one good thing about Harry Org getting a telly, she and Lizzie could now go up there and watch all the new pop singers and rock 'n 'roll groups, and Lizzie had learned how to do some of Petula Clark's numbers and Connie Francis's 'Stupid Cupid'.) Luckily, it being late August, she hadn't needed a coat, and her hair, hanging long, helped to make her neck and shoulders look less bony. A pair of second-hand gold sandals with extra high stiletto heels completed her well-off appearance; it would be obvious to the woman she was not coming here cap in hand.

For this reason also, Mim had dressed Lizzie in a pink satin evening top with a full matching skirt under which there were three mauve tulle petticoats, lifting it away so you could see real nylon stockings (a little suspender belt held them up!), and she wore small-size real grown-up high-heel shoes of silver. Mim had cut a fringe across Lizzie's forehead and lifted the curls on to the top of her head; with your eyes half-closed she could have passed for twelve.

Since Lizzie was not entirely steady on her feet, Mim took her firmly by the elbow as the young man led them down the same stairs they had come up, which, being bare and wooden, reminded Mim of the dreadful days she'd spent at school. It was an immense place, rambling and chaotic and not at all what Mim had imagined. Several buildings seemed to have been joined together with covered walks. There was an assortment of big bare rooms with desks, a room filled with easels, a big gymnasium, a jumble of different-sized rooms filled with supplies of all kinds, huge crates, costumes, props, glimpses of a vast kitchen, a dining room . . .

'You should see it in two weeks from now,' the young man said to Lizzie, as if Mim were not present. 'Filled with kids going this way and that . . .'

'I can go to weal school?' Lizzie looked directly into the pale eyes as if seeking harbour.

'You'd have to, love. The only difference here is that we concentrate on stage training, you see. All our children want to be in the theatre. Like you.'

Lizzie blinked. 'Yeah . . .'

'That's what she's goin' to be. In the theatre. A big star.'

The young man smiled vaguely. 'This way – here's the actual theatre, and Madame will be seeing you in due course.'

'You mean we'll 'ave to 'ang about – I've 'ad this appointment three months!' Mim stopped where she was, in the bare outer hall that bore a big sign over one door, saying QUIET.

'Mrs. Hobbs – Madame Irayna only holds these auditions twice a year. You naturally wouldn't be the only one. You do, however, happen to be first. Which isn't a bad thing . . .' His smile towards the sign was vaguely sorrowful. 'Madame does tend to tire these days. So many young people wanting to be in the theatre, so few with real talent.' He patted Lizzie's bare arm. 'I wish you the best of luck, love.'

Lizzie looked up; met the gentle smile. 'I like you,' she said.

He laughed. 'My name's Pete – maybe we'll get to know each other. I hope so.' He turned to Mim. 'I'll leave you now. If it works out, come up to my office. If not, all the best.'

Mim eyed him coldly. 'You say that to all of 'em, eh? We'll be seein' ya – count on it.'

Pete nodded, moved off, vanished.

'Well, I s'pose we park our arses 'ere.' She led Lizzie to some austere-looking chairs lined up against one wall. Lighting up a fag now, gasping for it, Mim contemplated the various posters that lined the hall. 'They say she gets her students into all the good shows, Lizzie. They nearly all become famous. No-one else like 'er. You'd better show off real good today, 'ear?'

Lizzie swallowed. She felt stiff all over. Her toes were pushed together in the shoes, the petticoats scratched, the nylons were like loose skin rubbing her legs, and she was sweating under her armpits. 'I'm getting patches, Mum,' she said.

Mim shook her head. 'No, you're bloody not. There's nothin' to sweat about, see. You know your songs, you know your bits and pieces, you know your dances . . .'

She stopped, grasping her by the shoulder. 'You do, don't ya? You bloody better.'

'I . . . thinks I do, Mum . . .'

'MIM.'

'Mim.'

'Whaddya mean, *thinks*? An' don't do baby-talk never again. 'Ow can you think you know – you either know or you don't know. Which bloody is it?'

The patches were definitely forming. Lizzie could feel the moisture creeping slowly between her armpits and the satin. 'I know 'em,' she said. 'I know 'em.'

'Well, I 'ope you perishin' do. If you let me down today . . .'

Prickles of fear made Lizzie's fine hairs stand up on her arms and under the nylons. As another child came in, considerably older, wearing a plaid cotton dress and small white gloves, the woman with her in a nob's sort of suit and hat, Lizzie shifted closer to Mim. Closing her eyes, she went over her words, over and over.

Gradually, as Pete ushered them in, young children and their parents or sponsors filled the chairs. There was no conversation here, only everyone eyeing everyone else, restrained curiosity, small tight smiles.

When Madame Irayna Blatsky came in and nodded with gracious detachment, all the smiles broadened – but only for a moment, because she moved with speed, head forward, cane ahead of her, limp imperiously ignored, even her eagle-like profile seeming to abet flight. Pete, behind her, lingered. 'This is Nikki,' he said, turning to a short, dark-haired young man beside him. 'He will be in charge and will call you in turn. There'll be a short wait now while the staff arrange lights, *et cetera*. Thank you.'

Nikki, carrying a large pad, a pencil pressed across the top of one ear, stood for a moment, his thick dark lashes lowered.

'I must tell you that Madame has had some indisposition.

We cannot promise that all of you will be heard today – but she will make it up. I propose to call you according to the alphabet . . .'

'Oy – I was 'ere first. Been 'ere ages – ask your friend . . .'

'Your name?' The lashes did not lift.

' 'Obbs.'

'The letter "o".'

'No! The letter haitch!'

'Oh, Hobbs. Well, let me see. You're third, in any case. Safe, I'd say.'

Mim grunted. 'That takes the cake.'

'My goodness,' said the lady in the suit, 'I can't imagine wanting to go *first*.' She looked around and got sympathetic nods.

'Don't want to be first, Mum,' Lizzie whispered quickly, 'I want to . . .'

Mim grasped her arm.

'No, you don't. You just 'ang on, 'ear? Tighten yer legs, 'old the muscles.'

Lizzie ground her teeth tight as well. After a moment, the feeling went away, but not altogether . . . She thought hard of Freddie, of Freddie being thrown out, gone forever, and at last, she could undo her knees and breathe.

An hour and a half later Nikki emerged, beckoned Mim.

Mim jumped up, grabbed Lizzie's elbow. 'All right, darlin', 'ere we go!'

Lizzie moved the best she could on the high heels. Despite her practice on them, they still wanted to go over sideways.

Nikki nodded, closed the door, sat down beside Madame Irayna.

While the two whispered together a moment, Mim had a chance to size up the great Madame Blatsky. Why, she was just an ordinary little woman, a bit like Effie, except for the beak, but with more hair, Effie's having thinned since the bombs, the red gone grey. Madame was very white and pasty, and her eyes when Mim looked them over, were dark and sharp as a bird's. Her lipstick seemed made of black stuff, and her teeth like a little set of false ones for practical jokes. Cripes, you wouldn't want to meet 'er in a dark alley at night . . . An' all that braid, like a bleedin' general – or one of them lion-tamer ladies at the circus about to crack a whip . . .

'All right, Lizzie,' Madame Irayna was saying suddenly, in a very thick accent, 'come and sit by me and tell me something about yourself.'

' 'Ey – I'd better do that, Madame – she ain't much of a one with the words . . .'

Madame looked at Mim, her eyelids drooping over her dark eyes like small hoods. 'Mrs. 'Obbs, yes?'

'That's right.'

'Mrs. 'Obbs. It is not our custom to talk with the mothers. If you please, unless you have something very important to say, to wait outside. It is better for the child.'

'Ah, no. Not for this one, it ain't. She don't do nothin' without me watchin', unless it's on the stage itself. She 'as to know I'm there, see.'

There was a silence. Madame whispered again with Nikki. 'Perhaps, then, she is not yet ready?'

'Of course she's ready. Never readier. You just start 'er off an' see.'

Madame Irayna looked down at the notes given to her by Pete. 'We can't possibly do all these things you say here . . . I shall need only a little, to hear her speak and sing and read a few lines.'

'That's no good – you gotta see it all. She's got it all learnèd!'

'All right, all right. Sit down, my friend. Let us remain calm.' She nodded to Lizzie. 'Come here, my dear. Let me have a look at you.'

Mim nodded sharply, and Lizzie went forward, allowed her hand to be held by the old woman with the black lips and eyes. Close to, she was not so frightening. Lizzie was sorry for all the cracks in her face, and the way the mascara caught in them around her eyes. She gave her a smile.

'Dear little thing.' Madame Irayna continued to stare. 'Nice eyes, charming freckles. Pity to cover them with make-up. What's the real colour of your hair, darling?'

Lizzie looked at Mim, sitting on the edge of a hard chair, her fag unlit. 'What's it matter?' Mim said sharply.

'It is quite terrible what you do with it. What colour is it without the peroxide?'

'Bwown,' said Lizzie. 'And stwaight.'

Madame Irayna and Nikki broke into delighted smiles. 'I love it,' said Madame. 'What a pity they have to grow up and speak so-called correctly. So, it's bwown. Well, that would be much better. I'd like to see it, and just combed down nice and stwaight with a fwinge.'

Lizzie looked from one face to the other, unable to tell whether they were laughing at her, or with her . . . 'Yeah . . .' she said.

'And you're *not* going to dance – or even sing – in those high heels, surely! Why, that's the first rule we have here – to be absolutely steady on your feet. Could you take them off . . . ?'

'Yeah,' said Lizzie. 'Take 'em off. Mum's got me tap shoes in 'er bag.'

Mim jumped up and produced the tap shoes, helped Lizzie put them on, took the high heels and quickly returned to her seat, where she lit a fresh fag and sat upright with a frown and stare threatening to erupt into protest.

Nikki told Lizzie to go up to the stage and walk to the middle. Someone else turned a spotlight on her. Her musical arrangements were handed to an accompanist.

Lizzie looked at Madame's face. It gleamed whitely at her. The mouth was a black gash, the black eyes like beads, the red hair like a fire bursting from her head. Lizzie felt sick, and the pee-feeling came back almost too strong to hold.

'Don't be frightened, darling,' the funny-sounding voice growled at her from a long way off. 'We're all your friends.'

Lizzie's eyes would not budge from the white face, and a trickle moved warmly into the centre of her under-knickers.

Christ! thought Mim. She's scared of the old Russian bear!

'Don't look at *no*-one, love,' she called out, her voice scratching like a rusty gramophone needle. 'Listen to the pianner.'

Lizzie did the little blink that meant she'd be okay now, and Mim let out her breath as she started into 'Loverley', sounding for all the world like Julie Andrews' Eliza Doolittle . . .

But – Madame was not smiling. Madame was holding up her hand. 'Enchanting – but the Cockney is too like herself. What else can she do?'

Crikey – there was a twist for ya. But no problem. 'Do the next one, young man . . .' she wagged a forefinger at the accompanist. 'Right in front of ya.'

He squinted over his glasses, nodded, began to play 'That's Entertainment', always one of Lizzie's best, and her little voice rang out with amazing force and clarity, favoured by the careful acoustics of the school theatre.

'Yes, yes – all too much show biz for us, Mrs. 'Obbs. Can she speak lines? It says here that she's been in plays . . .'

' 'Course she can speak lines!' Mim moved quickly to Lizzie's side. 'Do your bit from the *Fairy People* – yer remember.'

'Don't wemember.'

Mim's face was taut, her eyebrows in one ferocious line. 'Don't use w's, an' yer do remember, see?'

There was another warm spurt into her knickers. Lizzie's

lips pressed with the effort of holding on. She looked desperately towards the side door marked EXIT.

Mim grasped her elbow. 'I 'ave very special powers, if you are a good, kind boy, I can take you to your mother . . .'

Lizzie's eyes opened into hers. 'Oh, yeah.'

'You got 'em; you just do it – real clear, like it was. Good girl.' Mim patted her arm briskly, turned and went back to her chair.

Lizzie drew herself into tip-toe position, held out an arm. 'She is holding a wand!' Mim called out. 'She is a fairy.'

'Fairies,' muttered Madame. 'Is there nothing else these children learn to play?' Nikki drew down his eyelashes in response.

Lizzie's voice piped out, word-perfect now she remembered, her expressions fitting them with a kind of precision that could not be faulted.

'Nice, dear,' Madame called. 'Now – can you read?'

Lizzie's gaze shot to Mim. 'Can I, Mum – Mim?'

Mim stood up. ' 'Course she can read. But what kind of thing?'

'Well, a play, obviously. Lines from a play – something more general, like . . .'

Nikki bent to her ear.

'Yes – like *Peter Pan*. Let her read one of Wendy's speeches.' She raised her hands, clapped them, and a young woman at a desk in a far corner took a book off a pile and brought it quickly to her. Madame put on glasses, ran her finger down a selected page. 'Here we are, Lizzie. Start halfway down here.'

Mim felt an icy chill on her neck. Lizzie did read, all the time when she wasn't supposed to – but how much did she understand without having learned proper – and, even though she'd taught 'er Wendy's lines, would she be able to recognize them in the book!

' 'Old on,' she called. 'Let me show 'er.'

Madame closed her eyes in pained ennui. 'We cannot have this woman,' she muttered to Nikki. 'No, Madame,' he whispered. 'We *cannot*.'

Mim scanned the page as she bore the book to Lizzie. Ah, thank Gawd! All she'd 'ave to do was start 'er off – she'd remember this bit about children who never grew up . . .

'Start right 'ere, love,' she whispered, 'where me finger is. Pretend you're readin'. Say, "I shall always want to stay and look after you . . ." Just that bit until Peter speaks. Right?'

Lizzie's brow puckered under the fringe. She peered at the words in the book as if blind.

'I shall always want to stay and look after you . . .' Mim repeated.

Slowly, her lips gathered into soundless words. Lizzie began to nod. She took the book that was thrust into her hands, held it up to her face. Before Mim had got to her chair, she had started to 'read' the lines, each word half-sung, a high-pitched monotone.

'Good God,' said Madame. 'That will be enough,' she called.

Lizzie stopped at once, in the middle of a word, stood, waited for the next command.

'I would like to speak to this child alone. Mrs. 'Obbs, please wait outside.'

'What're yer goin' to talk to 'er about – she ain't got nothin' to tell ya. I'm the one to talk to. I trained 'er, didn't I?'

'Yes, indeed. And a *remarkable* job you've done, my friend. Truly astonishing. She is already more professional than most professionals, of *any* age.' Madame waved a heavily-ringed hand with black fingernails. Her tone grew weary. 'As for talent – well, there *is* a certain appeal in her singing voice – which, by the way, needs complete re-training. You've taught her to sing from deep in her throat, like this . . .'

Madame opened her mouth, made a guttural sound in

the region of her tonsils. 'Ruinous. She'd have no voice left by twenty. She must sing from here.' Madame closed her mouth tight, patted her nose, sang part of a scale without moving a muscle, sonorous, reverberating. 'She could sing a lifetime; never harm it.'

'Well, maybe. I done what I could . . .' (Nobody'd never said nothin' about 'er voice down in them air-raid shelters. She'd just opened 'er mouth, let it come out.)

'Of course you did. And that's what we have a singing teacher for. She would learn to place her voice, both for speaking and singing, learn to project it to the back of the largest theatres . . .'

'So, you'll take 'er on, then?'

Madame looked away from the blazing eyes, the cords in the neck, the jumping jaw muscles, the hands that wrung a brocade handbag to a rag. 'I am not at all sure. Her diction, it is so bad. But – more important – I must speak with the child alone, please.'

For a moment, Mim felt the same fury she had with Miss Tina, but this time there was too much at stake. This old bat wouldn't take much to turn into a right proper witch. It would be curtains for Lizzie, her best ever chance down the sink.

She turned to Lizzie, still standing on the platform, hands at her sides, waiting for her next order. 'You talk nice to the lady, now,' she called. 'Watch yer p's and q's, d'you 'ear?'

Lizzie didn't speak. Her eyes seemed to grow larger.

Mim walked briskly from the room, showing the dress off to best advantage with a straight back, slight undulation of hips. She allowed Nikki to hold open the door for her, nodded regally. Nikki closed the door and came over to sit beside Madame.

'We cannot be long, there are others,' Madame said. 'Come, child. Sit here.'

Lizzie came over quickly, sliding a little on the bare

boards, her stockings now in little bags around her ankles. Dutifully, she lifted herself onto the chair, felt with her toes for the floor, could not find it, settled for a slight dangling motion of her sturdy legs.

Madame smiled at her with secret humour. 'What a funny little girl,' she said. 'Very, very clever. A lot going on in that fuzzy yellow head eh?'

Lizzie looked at her blankly.

'So, you want to be on the stage, do you? You want to become a famous star.'

Lizzie's expression was concentrated, intent. She thought the lady was not so black-white-and-red now; that her face was like someone poorly, someone who needed a friend . . .

'You must answer me, darling. You are old enough to have some feeling of your own about all this, and I must know what it is. It is a very important decision. I take on only those who are sincere and dedicated. A great deal of work goes into making a star performer, for the teachers, for the pupils. You must think, and honestly tell me – is this what you want, to be making your whole life the theatre?'

Lizzie could not make herself think. 'Where's me mum?' she said. 'Me mum wants me to be in the theatre. She wants me to be a famous someone, not a nobody.'

'Yes, yes – that is more than clear to us. You can see by the way she dresses, and dresses you, that it is her greatest fear, that you might be *mistaken* for a nobody.'

'Uh?' Lizzie's brow gathered so that the fringe trembled.

Madame and Nikki exchanged a glance. 'Never mind that. Come, now, the question is quite clear, and it is you who must answer.'

'Me?' Lizzie's toes stopped wiggling. Her shoulders drooped and she adjusted herself to sit on her hands. 'Well . . .'

'Yes? Come on, child, I have others waiting.' Growing irritation thickened Madame's accent.

'Umm . . .' Lizzie's head lowered. 'Ask me mum.'

The silence was broken by discreet coughs in various parts of the theatre, voices from the street, distant traffic.

'Well, darling, if that's the best you can do, I can only assume it is not what you want, but what your mother wants that counts with you. That is not good enough here. We do not encourage stage mothers. We will not put up with pushy ones. We welcome their co-operation and support, of course – but you, the pupil, must have your own genuine ambition. We could not possibly train you otherwise. Do you understand at all?'

Lizzie knew they were all looking at her, all waiting. She still could not make her head come up. 'Yeah . . .'

'So we have to turn you down, Lizzie. Do you see? It is a pity. I wish for you the best, and a good life. Goodbye, my dear.'

Lizzie felt herself going all soft and pink inside. She almost looked up to see whether it showed. Freddie would have known about it, but he wouldn't have told. 'G'bye,' she said.

'You're not disappointed, I can see. I am glad.' Madame had her secret smile again. 'Nikki, you inform the mother.'

'Yes, Madame.'

Lizzie slid off the chair. 'Me shoes,' she said, running to where they lay beside the stage.

Madame smiled, looking like an evil granny. 'What a love . . .' she murmured.

Suddenly, Mim was back in the room, her face white, her shoulders strangely hunched. 'You've turned 'er down,' she said. 'You've bloody given 'er the gate. Lizzie – what you been an' gorn and said? What you been tellin' 'er, eh?'

'Oh, my dear. You mustn't blame the child. She said nothing, nothing at all. In fact, that is really the trouble – she has nothing to say. It is only you that have the ambition – the child has none.'

Mim stood suddenly still, frozen in misery beyond words. It was as if the whole world had gone dark around her, with a great hole in the middle into which she was sinking, drowning . . . It was worse than when Lil's 'ouse had been bombed, than when nothin' was left of their street . . .

'Come, my friend, brace up. You're not the first to be disappointed here. I do not like to be ruthless, but I must. Now, please, I will ask you to take little Lizzie and leave. Nikki – we will have the next one.'

Nikki nodded, went with turned-out feet towards the door – but as he reached it, it opened towards him and a tall boy came rushing in. 'Madame, madame!' he said, in a high false voice of urgency. 'A missive, a telegram! I have been deputed to deliver it with haste!'

Madame's frown cleared. A low chuckle preceded the impatient reach of her hand 'What now – a summons, another demand from the tax man, a death? Now, Rob, stop looking over my shoulder . . .'

'Is it a contract, Madame?' the boy called Rob said. 'Has one of your students got a star role in Hollywood?'

'Well, not exactly, but a good part.' Madame nodded contentedly, looked up at him, but he was no longer looking at the telegram or her.

Madame followed his gaze. 'The little girl with the red bows,' he murmured. 'Elizabeth. Elizabeth Hobbs.'

'You know her?' Madame's eagle-like nose pinched at the nostrils.

'Big boy!' Lizzie said to Mim. Her face was creased with smiling, the beginning of laughter. 'See – it's *im*, it's *im!*'

Rob walked over to Lizzie, clicked his heels, bowed. 'I believe we've met before,' he said.

Lizzie broke into giggles. ' 'Ello,' she said. ' 'Ow *are* yer?'

'Rather well. How are you?'

'Yeah – I'm well, too.' Lizzie giggled so hard she had to hold her hand over her mouth to hold it back.

63

'You've grown, of course. Not so round about the middle.'

'You're bigger.'

'Well, that's natural.' Suddenly, his voice altered. 'Whatcha doin' down 'ere, anyway – auditionin' fer the school?'

'Yeah – only she don't want us . . .'

'She don't?'

Rob raised his thin, angular face, curled an eyebrow. 'Hmm. I'll 'ave to 'ave a word with Madame.' Adjusting his grey jumper with the darned holes in it, hooking a thumb into a back pocket of his navy serge trousers, Rob strode back to Madame.

Mim held Lizzie firmly by the hand. 'What's goin' on?' Who the 'ell's '*e?*'

There was a vigorous whispered conference round Madame's chair and table, hands turned upward, shrugs, shaking heads. 'You're sure? You'll take responsibility? I promise nothing.'

Madame's voice rang out abruptly. 'Mrs. 'Obbs. My star pupil, Rob Grover, who is here on a council grant, has interceded on behalf of your little girl. If it is agreeable with you, I will give her a trial period of six months' training. If it does not work out, she will have to leave, with good grace on all sides. What do you say?'

Mim's lower jaw dropped. The misery was so instantly replaced by triumph, that she could hardly contain the flow of insults that had jumped to her mouth but, somehow, for Lizzie, she did.

'Yeah – that's agreeable with me, with us. That's smashin', innit, Lizzie?'

Lizzie's eyes were on Rob's face, her hand still over her mouth to keep herself serious. She nodded, up and down.

'You can see, she's over the moon! An' you won't regret it, Madame Blatsky. You got a winner 'ere. You'll thank me for bringin' 'er 'ere today.' Mim held up a thumb. 'Bombs away!'

'God preserve us,' Madame whispered to Nikki.

They all watched Lizzie run after Rob, put her hand in his, grin up at him, and at Mim pressing on behind, trying to regain Lizzie's hand, frowning with exasperation at the tall, long-nosed boy.

# CHAPTER FOUR

In a small studio at the top of the Blatsky School, a voice rang out with such belting force and clarity that it penetrated the soundproof walls and echoed into the silent corridor where Rob Grover stood waiting, making him shake his head and smile one-sidedly to himself. Folding his thin arms around his thin chest, he leaned against the opposite door, adopting an expression of wise detachment tinged with kindly forbearance, at the same time trying not to cast impatient glances at the big clock above the studio door.

Inside the studio, Cynthia Sterling lifted her hands from the piano and brought them together in a loud clap. 'Well done, Lizzie,' she said, 'At last you're getting it into the diaphragm!' She screwed up her sparkly hazel eyes so that her lashes made spikes against her lids. 'Oh, I do think Madame will be pleased. But, of course, there's still a lot to do with your pitch.'

'Yes, Mrs. Sterling.' Lizzie pressed her lips and nodded. She knew just what her pretty singing teacher would say next. She said it every day, twice a day.

'You must keep practising. At least half-an-hour tonight.' Cynthia Sterling pressed a bobby-pin into the extra tress that gave height to her upswept dark hair, gazed with affected sternness at the sturdy ten-year-old who remained so singularly unimpressed with her incredible voice. 'It's the only way to the top.'

'Yes, Mrs. Sterling.' Lizzie didn't tell her that Mim would never let her *not* practise, even though she could hardly drag herself to the piano after being on her feet all day at her two jobs, the restaurant through the day, the cashier's job through the dinner-hour; or, that Bert would be lying passed-out on the couch, where he was most of the time since he didn't have any work at the theatre; or even that she never got a chance to do her school home-work, which was what she wanted to do most. 'Well, then – I'll be on me way . . .'

Cynthia Sterling stood up, put a slim, ringed hand on Lizzie's head. 'On *my* way,' she said. 'You're doing so well, better go the whole way.'

Lizzie looked up at her, the wide fringe she wore these days with her straight brownish-blond bob, falling away from her self-deprecating blue gaze. 'I'll never – will I?'

'Why, of course you will, my dear. It's a matter of time. One day no-one will suspect you ever dropped an aitch.'

'Garn . . .'

Cynthia Sterling broke into a laugh that made her look more like a schoolgirl than a twice-married woman of forty-two. 'You're a sketch!' she said.

With an embarrassed grin, Lizzie picked up her music case and schoolbag, her big coat and wool hat for the blizzard, her scarf and wellies. 'G'night, Mrs. Sterling. See ya, then.'

'Good night, Lizzie.'

Lizzie opened the door, closed it behind her.

'Hi there, pardner . . .'

Lizzie put a hand over her mouth. At the sight of Rob, she felt so happy she wanted to jump up and down. 'Hi . . .' she whispered, 'watcha doin'?'

'Waitin' for Godot. What d'ya think I'm doin'! Wanna go up? We got half an hour till your mum comes . . .'

Lizzie's eyes were bright with intrigue. 'Yeah . . .' She looked furtively along the corridors of closed doors. 'Yeah – I *do* – let's.'

Rob gave a sober nod, hoisted himself from the wall,

sauntered towards the stairs that led up to the vast attic room where all the school's costumes and props were kept.

Lizzie followed, leaving her things at the foot of the stairs in a shadowed niche. Although Rob, with his quiff of brown hair that made him look much older than thirteen, his wide mouth that curled at the side like the bad man's in a film, his dark blue eyes that seemed to know everything in the world about everything, now started up the stairs like their leader, she knew that he was actually waiting for her to take his hand. She knew, too, that he didn't know this himself. It was funny, but when Robbie wasn't making people laugh with his take-offs, he wasn't at all brave. It was on account of having been an orphan, of course, and all them foster homes, and even though 'Mum' Grover had got him 'the Grant' (a lot of money they gave you free so's you could be taught), he hadn't ever had anyone of his own . . .

Even so, she didn't take his hand until they were safely out of sight. The whole school teased them because they were always together, because Robbie hung about outside whatever class she was in, carried her books, took 'charge' of her when they went from one building to the other, and, naturally, since he was supposed to help her with her training, was always hanging around in the theatre when she was learning a part. 'Robbie loves Lizzie,' they sang at them, and in the lavs they drew big arrows on the doors and walls going through two big hearts marked R and E. Robbie sneered, pretended he was much too grown-up for such 'infantile behaviour', but Lizzie saw the way his Adam's apple would bob and his face go red, and she tried to protect him by keeping separate when they could be seen.

Now that it was all right, she took his hand firmly. 'Watch you don't bump your shin on that . . .'

But it was too late. 'Gow!' he muttered, and swore like a

navvy as the piece of raw wood by the top step dug into his thin leg.

'Oh, dear – 'ave you 'urt yourself bad . . .?'

Rob made quite a fuss; let her look to see. 'It's nuffink,' he said.

Lizzie saw this was so; there was not even a scratch. What a baby he could be! She noticed how he spoke, too, like himself, as if he'd never learned better, never learned nothing about all those accents he could do, that upper-class talk like Noel Coward . . .

'Come on, then,' she said. 'We got to hurry – don't want Mum askin' where I am, do we?'

'No, indeed!' Rob lifted his eyebrows, rolled his eyes at her, and Lizzie laughed carefully into the sleeve of her navy-blue sailor blouse.

Hand in hand they moved quickly past the great ghostly room of hanging costumes that were like a lesson in history, the boxes piled high with wigs and masks and headgear that spilled over onto the bare floor, the mounds of carpets and dust-laden curtains, the shelves of props and stacks of scenery, until they came to the big heap of many-coloured and -sized cushions. Here, on two big hooks they had found, they hung the velvet curtain that they had folded away out of sight and quickly ducked behind it, carrying several large cushions. These, they arranged in squares, to indicate separate rooms.

Lizzie smoothed her navy skirt, pulled up her knee-high socks, tightened the laces of her brown Oxfords. 'I'm ready,' she said.

With a nod, Rob moved to the outside of the door. 'My key is unlocking the door,' he called.

Lizzie took off an imaginary apron and put on a sweet smile the way they did in films about families. 'Hello, husband dear. 'Ave you 'ad a good day?'

Rob took off a hat, drew a newspaper from under his arm. They kissed each other's cheeks. 'Not bad, but the traffic was terrible. How about you?'

'The children were very naughty. Really, dear, you must give them a talking-to.'

Rob nodded with authority. 'I will. How about the baby?'

'Oh, she's in good nick. 'Er new tooth is comin' through nicely, thank you. Oops – that's 'er now. I better change 'er nappy before you 'old 'er.'

'Shall I do it for ya?'

Lizzie's smile was indulgent. 'Not likely – you never get the pins right.'

'Ha, ha, ha,' said Rob.

They moved in mutual accord to another division between the cushions and looked down with fond smiles on a pierrot doll lying in a long shoe-box. 'Ain't she more and more like you, dear?' Lizzie said, sighing, blinking her eyes up at him with adoration.

'More like 'er mum, I'd say – a real beauty.' He put an arm around Lizzie's shoulders. 'We're such an 'appy family, ain't we.'

Lizzie nodded enthusiastically. 'An' with our nice big 'ouse an' garden, our dogs an' cats, all our nice friends comin' to visit, an' real lovely neighbours – ah, 'usband darlin', we are never goin' to part . . .'

'Never. We'll 'ave six more, won't we . . .?'

'At least. I once seen a family with so many children they could make a team for rounders!'

'You didn't!'

'I did! S'truth!'

'Well, dear, I can see that I will 'ave to work 'ard an' get a lot of promotions to support us all!'

Lizzie gave him a quick kiss on his chin. 'Thank you. Now, I'll just change the little one – there . . .' Lizzie did a few passes around the doll, then handed it to Rob, who held it in his arms and made faces and clucking noises. 'Now what?' he said.

' 'Ere. I'll give 'er 'er bottle and put 'er back to bed, then I'll see to our tea . . .'

'Dinner, dear,' said Rob. 'Tea is workin'-class. Nobs say dinner.'

'Of course – how silly of me.' Lizzie almost forgot for a moment, to tell him how Bert's sister still had the high-chair with the hole in the middle, where Bert had sat as a little baby so he could have his 'high tea' with the family and pee at the same time. It would give him a laugh, it would – but she had to be careful not to break into all the other things they told each other and shared . . .

'I got a nice piece of beef, dear,' she went on quickly, and I'll make Yorkshire pud the way you like. You sit and read your paper.'

'What about the children?'

'Oh, they're watchin' the Beatles on telly singin' "Love Me Do". Before they has their bath.'

'Ah, telly. I suppose it keeps 'em still, don't it.'

They nodded at each other. ' 'As its uses,' said Lizzie.

'As long as it don't 'urt their eyes.' Rob moved back to another division, sat on a large tapestry cushion with fringe tassels. 'Ain't very good news, I'm afraid,' he said, flicking open an invisible newspaper.

'Tell me – I can 'ear ya while I cook,' Lizzie called in a muted shout.

'The worst snowstorms in England since eighteen 'undred and somethin' . . .'

'Oh, yeah?' Lizzie took down pots and pans and opened and closed an oven door, stirred, poured, wondering if her husband or her children should set the dining table.

'They exploded this 'ere nuclear thing under the ground, British it was, in a place called Nevada . . .'

'Oh, yes?'

'They got a Russian space thing on its way to Mars . . .'

'Cooo . . . Anythin' about Princess Margaret's 'usband?'

'Yup. They makes 'im an Earl. Lord Snowdon 'e is.'

'Just fancy . . . Well, dear, dinner's on the table. Call the children.'

Lizzie, Rob and their children sat down to their dinner which, because time was rushing by, they ate delicately, wiping their mouths often on their serviettes . . . Lizzie washed the dishes, Rob dried them. The children and baby were swiftly put to bed. It got late, and because Rob had had such a long day, they decided to retire.

'Don't forget the lights, dear, and put the cats out . . . ooh, am I ever knackered . . .' Lizzie yawned with vigour, got into a nightgown.

'You look a treat in that,' Rob said. ' 'Ere, move over and let your 'usband cuddle up.'

They knelt, one each side of a cushion, cradled their heads in their folded hands. 'Ain't it lovely, to be in our very own bed together, wifie?'

'Loverly, 'usband . . .'

Lizzie was about to say 'sweet dreams' and give Robbie a kiss goodnight when suddenly there was the squeaky sound of floorboards, a burst of voices . . .

'Me Gawd!' said Rob. 'It's *'er*!'

They jumped quickly to their feet, stood shoulder to shoulder like mechanical dolls stopped in the middle of a movement.

The curtain was ripped aside. ' 'Ello, 'ello – an' what's this lark? What you two up to?' Mim's bony face, protruding from a soaking-wet wool hat, thrust itself at them with the keenness of a bird-dog. 'Why'r'ya 'idin' be'ind this?' Her scowling gaze focused significantly on Rob. 'What you been *doin'* to my Lizzie, young lad, eh? You been doin' what you shouldn't . . .'

'Mrs. Hobbs, really!' said Pete, who had been unable to restrain her since they'd found Cynthia Sterling's studio locked and the rest of the school closed early because of the weather. 'They often play up here – just some sort of game . . .'

'Game, eh? I bet it is. I 'eard that 'usband-wife, cuddle-up carry-on. I weren't born yesterday. I'm goin' to see Madame about this, I am. An' right now. Come on, me girl. You're goin' to tell 'er the truth about 'er darlin' genius!'

'Madame cannot be disturbed, Mrs. Hobbs. She is doing her schedule . . .'

'I don't care if she's makin' 'er will!' Mim grabbed Lizzie's hand as if she were still a toddler and dragged her away from Rob, back through the big, dim room, causing waves of musty air to rise and sending the costumes into a swaying dance.

Looking back over her shoulder, Lizzie tried to give Rob a warning glance not to follow. In spite of his lifted nose and contemptuous smile, she knew he was scared. Mim had it in for him proper, always had . . .

But Rob was following, doggedly, lifting his hand in their secret code of alliance, and all Lizzie could do was keep going, down, down through the silent halls, trying to get her hand back, feeling more and more scared herself . . .

'Come!' called Madame Irayna's sharp, accented voice as Pete gave a timid, reluctant knock on the blue-painted door with PRIVATE written across it in bold black.

Mim pushed past the tall young man, yanking Lizzie with her. 'Not 'im!' she commanded, as Rob followed closely behind, but Rob did not falter.

'What is this – Pete? You know I'm not to be disturbed!' Madame Irayna looked sternly at her Administrative Assistant.

'I'm sorry, very sorry . . .' He did not have to go further; as Madame looked over the top of her bifocals with the black dangling chain, and registered the full assault of Mim's expression, Lizzie's big eyes under the lowered fringe, Rob's tucked-in mouth and lifted chin. She sighed, put down her pen, straightened some papers on her desk, adjusted the side-tilt of her lamp. 'What *now*, Mrs. 'Obbs?' she said.

'What now, you might well ask!' Mim advanced, leaving Lizzie behind. 'This time, you'd better 'eed my words about this boy!' She ignored the drops of water sliding down from her hat, tightened the belt of her red rabbit-fur coat. 'I come to fetch Lizzie – not a sign of 'er. I twiddle me thumbs, an' then ask 'im . . .' she jerked a thumb at Pete, hovering uncertainly at the door, "Where is my daughter? She is not with 'er singin' teacher – where is she, then?" 'E says, "I don't eggsactly know." "Egg-sactly," I says. "Well, then, young man, we'd better 'ave a look, wouldn't you say?" '

Everyone in the small room, stuffy with gas-heat from an antiquated burner behind Madame's desk, stared at Mim as if hypnotized. Lizzie tried to close her mouth, but it was stiff. She wanted to reach to Rob, but her hand wouldn't move.

Mim fixed Madame Irayna's eyes with beady direct-ness. 'So, I goes to them steps I never gone up before . . .' She pointed a battered, red-nailed finger at Madame. ' "What's these?" says I. "Oh, that's the attic," he says, "where the costumes and such is kept. She wouldn't be up there . . ." '

Mim pushed the wool hat up from her furrowed brow so that the fierce gleam of her eyes seemed all there was of her face. "So, what's all this, then?" I ask 'im, seein' Lizzie's gear stacked there in an 'eap. "She disappeared into thin air, been murdered, or something"?'

'I didn't know, Madame,' Pete said. 'Sometimes, they do play up there . . .'

Madame did not stir. 'And . . .?' she said, her gaze riv-eted to Mim's.

Mim stood back a little, and Lizzie knew she would fold her arms around herself and make her eyes look small – like when she'd finally thrown Freddie away in Antonio's dustbin and wouldn't even say she was sorry . . .

' "Well, up we go then," I tells 'im. An', sure enough, we 'ear sounds – right down the end. We go on, an' there's voices! An' as we come up close – who d'ya think we find – be'ind a curtain, all 'idden-like and secret?' Mim stared harder at Madame, waiting like a trained actress to deliver her bombshell of revelation. 'My Lizzie – an' '*im!*'

'Yes?' Madame stared back over the top of the glasses. 'And? So?'

Mim drew in a breath. 'And so – *So* – What was they doin' there, then, eh?' Mim's lips had the suggestion of a leer.

'Playin' a game . . .' said Lizzie, grasping Rob's hand and drawing him closer. 'That's what. Just 'avin' a bit of fun till Mum come . . .' Rob nodded down at her, with calm dignity.

'Really, Lizzie . . .' Madame made a clucking sound. 'Aren't you forgetting your diction?'

Lizzie's toes turned inward, her shoulders rose. 'Sorry, Madame.'

'So you should be. You mustn't lapse into your old ways the moment you're upset. All right, dear. Go on. You and Rob were playing a game . . .'

'Ask 'er what *kind* of a game!' Mim put her hands on her hips with such fervour that her handbag, sliding up her arm, just missed hitting Rob.

'I hardly see what it matters, Mrs. 'Obbs – these two are always playing at something up there . . .'

'Ain't you crafty?' Mim drew up one eyebrow. 'Don't want to know, do ya – it don't ma'er to you that 'e's a big boy of near fourteen an' takin' Lizzie be'in' the curtains to play muvvers and favvers, 'usband and wifie, 'er all innocent, 'im a real slum brat who knows just what 'e's doin' – I ain't fooled by 'is take-offs. I don't care who 'e can imitate or 'ow much 'e pulls the wool over your eyes . . .'

'Mrs. 'Obbs!' Madame Irayna brought her fist down on

the desk, causing everything on it to vibrate and shift. 'That will be quite enough! You've gone too far, this time! You are quite the worst nuisance I have ever had to bear – but I've done it because of Lizzie. Not because I'm fond of her, which I am, or because she will ever be a great actress or dancer – which I am sorry to say I don't think she will – but, because she may one day be a very good singer, because she has a truly outstanding voice which, with careful training and relentless practice, over the course of time, could bring a great deal of pleasure to a great many people.'

'Aha! You've finally caught on, 'ave ya! What I've been sayin' all along. *Now* you don't want to lose 'er, eh? Well – I tell ya one thing, and I tell yer straight, Madame Blatsky . . .'

Mim swivelled to face Rob, raised her finger again, pointed. 'If 'e don't go, you don't get Lizzie. An' that's final.'

The silence in the room allowed the weather to creep in, the tap of sleet on the darkened window, the faint howl of wind. Lizzie thought she could hear her own heart, except it was really the tick of Madame's little clock with the gilt angels, the one that had been in her home in Russia. She looked up at Rob. If only she could help, take away his hurt . . .

'If that's the way you feel, dear lady,' Madame rose stiffly, moved to a coat stand made of deers' horns, lifted down a huge fur coat so worn that it was barely recognizable as mink, a big hat to match with a large ruby brooch lacking a stone or two pinned to its front. 'My heart will mourn to lose dear little Lizzie – but you must know that I could not possibly share your unpleasant suspicion of Rob. He is more than a clever, talented boy; he is a fine and good one, and I have the utmost trust in him.'

While Mim whistled through her teeth with shock and fury, Madame looked at the two youngsters facing her.

'Whatever the game is that you play, my dears,' she said, with her thin, dark-lipped smile, 'I'm sure it *is* fun – I've never seen you both so happy.'

To Lizzie, the dim, mysterious little room with its heavy, peeling gilt furniture and dark old paintings was suddenly less awesome. 'Oh, Madame!' She ran over to her, pressed her face into the prickly fur. 'I don't want to go. I love it here!'

'Don't worry, anyone,' said Rob suddenly. '*I'll* remove meself. Plenty of places to go. Got offers galore!' He spread his hands, adopted the expression and intonation of Hughie Green of the famous television show, 'For Rob Grover – *Opportunity Knocks!*'

It was so exactly like the man that Lizzie almost forgot what he was saying and laughed and clapped – then her face crumpled with horror. 'No, Robbie, no – you can't, you mustn't! I'll go. It don't matter about me. Oh, Madame, you wouldn't *let* him.'

'No, darling, I wouldn't.' Madame drew brocaded gauntlets from the pocket of her coat, reached for her cane. 'It will be very sad to lose you, but, if I cannot have you both, well . . .'

'See,' said Mim, reaching for Lizzie's arm and pulling her with her towards the door. 'She don't give an 'oot fer you – it's 'im, only 'im! It don't matter *what* he does!'

'But he ain't done nothing, Mum! What you *on* about? 'E's me best friend in the world . . . I ain't goin' with you!'

Lizzie pulled away with such sudden force that Mim almost fell. Pete, still hovering, righted her, retrieved her fallen handbag, looked anxiously at Madame for instruction.

But Madame was looking at Lizzie, at the way she had run over to Rob, put her arm tightly through his, her light-freckled face a bright pink, her mouth a formidable, down-turned arc – and the awkward way Rob stood, looking sideways down his nose, his long thin arms and body grown out of the maroon sweater and serge trousers futilely denying his mature detachment.

'Ah, me . . .' Madame sighed deeply within herself.

'Is that all you got to say?' Mim braced herself up, clenched her teeth, moved to Lizzie and yanked her arm in a vice. 'Right. You come with me. Get yer things. This is the last time you'll see 'er – or 'im!'

'No!' Lizzie tightened her grip on Rob, stood even closer to him.

Suddenly, Madame's voice rang out in sharp command. 'Lizzie – go with your mother. We shall have to have a talk about your schoolwork, of course, and other matters – but not now. I shall write to you.'

Lizzie's eyes widened in shock. 'Don't you want me no more, Madame? I can sleep on the floor. I won't be no trouble . . .'

'I'm sorry, my dear. I cannot come between a parent and child.' Madame gave Mim a long, hard stare. 'Particularly this one.' She raised an eyebrow at Pete. 'I am ready to go – you will take charge here. Lock up as usual.'

Mim relaxed her grip on Lizzie's arm. There was a sudden uncertainty in her sharp gaze at Madame. 'Well, I never . . .' she said. 'So much for this great talent of Lizzie's, eh. You don't give a cobbler's for 'er voice – she were just another 'undred quid a year in the coffers, weren't she. Wait till I talk to the papers about this!'

Madame lifted her shoulders, walked in slow, limping solemnity to the door. Pete opened it for her. She went out.

# CHAPTER FIVE

'Aw, come on, me love – give us a penny-a – talk to me proper,' Mim would say in the long weeks that followed. 'I only done it for you. Couldn't 'ave that kind o' thing, could we? *Couldn't* let 'im get away with it, could I?'

Lizzie didn't even try any more to tell her that Robbie hadn't done anything to get away with, and didn't even know what she was on about. But she still couldn't smile for her, and had nothing she wanted to talk to her about; nor did she want to learn new routines or songs, or do auditions for anything, shows, films *or* TV. At first, Mim commanded her, then coaxed, then brought her treats, or put on jokey faces to make her forget and laugh, and give in.

All Lizzie wanted to do was to lie on the bed and read her school books, especially *Romeo and Juliet*, over and over, and think about Robbie. When the knots in her tummy from missing him got too bad, she would go out and wander about Soho, chatting to her friends in the shops or cafés, sit in the square watching all the different people go by, steal into a back pew in the church and kind of listen for God in the candle-lit dimness. Did he know about her and Robbie? If he did, did he care? She never seemed to hear him answer . . .

'Lookit, me darlin' – if you miss bein' at school so much,' Mim had said, 'you can go 'ere, to the local. I'll 'ave a talk with 'em. Would ya like that?'

Lizzie had shrugged. It wasn't just any school she wanted. She could hardly bear to think about Blatsky's, the ink and pencil-lead smell of the classrooms and desks, the nice but strict teachers that made you work at your lessons – geography, history, maths, English, composition – so hard, but such *fun*. (Her best friends, Nancy Crooke and Jennifer Tate, who *only* wanted to be actresses and thought she was mad, would crib from her copybooks!)

But she would never think about Mrs. Sterling, or even old eagle-face Madame; next to Robbie they gave her the loneliest feeling of all. If only she'd worked harder for *them*, if only she hadn't always been doing it just for Robbie . . .

Was Robbie lonely, too? Missing her the same way? How would he get on with no-one to tell his secrets to, no-one to know what he was thinking behind his superior smile and clever take-offs, when he was hurt or afraid . . .?

If only she could see him! If only he could come and see her! But, of course, he wouldn't – because of Mim.

One day, when Mim was at work and Bertie was out cold and snoring on the couch, Lizzie got dressed, gave her hair a good brushing, took some money out of Bertie's jacket pocket, and set off for Paddington where Rob lived with Mum Grover. Because it was Easter hols, she knew he wouldn't be at the school.

All she wanted to do was see him, talk to him, find out if he was all right. It would be quite nice if she could meet the Grovers too, and all the other foster kids, and take a look at the house, and where Robbie slept. 'It's like Euston Station,' he'd told her, 'except everyone's a kid and the 'ole 'ouse pongs of nappies, sour milk and bangers. The telly is always on, and Mum is always washin', feedin', or carryin' a baby. Apart from that, it ain't that bad. It's 'ome.'

Lizzie hung onto her grown-up handbag and tried to look as if she knew just what she was doing, that her heartbeat under the yellow suit Mim had made her was normal, not jumping about like a trapped mouse . . .

The trouble was, she got lost. She wandered about until it was almost dark, never finding the street, and when she finally asked a copper for help, she didn't have the address right. The copper took her to a bus stop, saw that she got on the right bus to get home, and she was so frightened she just went, without ever having seen Robbie.

Mim had been home by then, and the worry on her face was enough to make Lizzie hide her head. She remembered that Mum did love her, that she did everything *because* she did.

Still, it didn't make her want to talk or smile at her any more than before, and Mim almost gave up trying to make her practise and do auditions. Sometimes Mim would just sit and smoke, her eyebrows so low over her eyes that it looked as if she was sleeping, or crying . . .

But it could have been Bert she was staring at – Bert, who was getting more poorly every day, turning a yellowish colour, twisting about in the soggy grey sheets, groaning and muttering, begging for his only 'comfort', his fine-and-dandy, which Mim had to keep refusing him because the doctor said it would polish him off.

And then, one night, Mim had had to run down to Antonio's and ring for an ambulance. Lizzie wouldn't let go of Bertie's hand, wouldn't let them take him away . . .

'Please, Bertie, don't leave us,' she begged him. 'We loves ya so much!'

'Sorry, Cuddles,' he wheezed. 'I ain't been much good to ya, but I love ya, darlin', Take care of 'er, won't ya? Do what she wants. Make 'er 'appy.'

'I will, oh, I *will*, Bertie!'

They'd carted his big body off on the stretcher, shoved him inside the white van with its revolving light, Mim following – and that was the last time she'd ever seen him. He'd 'gone' in the night.

Mim, who'd sat with him till the end, said it was 'sudden

as a light goin' off. One tick 'e were there, lookin' at me the way Bertie looked – the next tick his eyes didn't 'ave no look – they was just . . . eyes.'

Lizzie crumpled up inside. She hugged Mim, and Mim let herself go. Lizzie never knew so much water could come from eyes, or that there could be so many big hard sounds with it; she held her mother for a long time, until they both fell asleep on the bed they had always shared.

After that, Lizzie was almost more worried about Mim than about Robbie. She helped her with breakfast, helped her get ready for work, helped with the housework, did the shopping. At eleven, she was like a small woman, a substitute husband, everything she could be to help Mim keep going.

Then, just like that, without a word, Mim announced one night that she had '*news*'.

Lizzie was sure she would say it was a show, a chance to be in TV, a panto – whatever. It had had to come, and Lizzie had made up her mind she would do it, anything to make Mim smile again, to be her old self . . . Besides, that was her promise to Bertie.

'I've 'ad a letter from 'er 'ighness, darlin'.'

Lizzie had been about to eat a sausage roll. 'The Queen?'

'Don't be daft. Not 'er – *yet*. No, me love – your old friend, Blatsky. She's goin' to take you back. What do ya think of *that*?'

Lizzie shoved her fringe to the top of her head. 'What! *Why*, Mum? What's changed her?'

Mim raised a chilblained thumb. 'Me. I ate the 'umble, didn't I? I played me violin. I sent me apologies to the kid, I told 'er you was pinin' to a corpse, 'ow me good 'usband 'ad bit the dust, the lot. Nothin' left out.'

Mim had leaned forward and put her hands on Lizzie's cheeks, giving them a hard squeeze. 'It worked, sweet-'eart. It worked! You can start back there Monday!'

Lizzie couldn't take it in. When she did, she hugged Mim

and danced with her around the little flat – and, now that she was almost as tall and getting stronger – lifted skinny Mim right up in the air and swung her.

That night she drank a bitter with Mim, to celebrate. It made her pee more than usual, and go to sleep in a minute, muttering like Bertie used to, and mixing Freddie and Robbie up in her dreams.

It was funny, going back. It made her feel shy, as if she was a new girl. Some of the kids looked at her as if they had forgotten her, but others gathered round and acted as if they were pleased, and Jenny and Nancy kissed her. Mrs. Sterling hugged her, even had tears in her nice pretty eyes, and couldn't wait to start work, though she wasn't very happy with the 'rusty' sound of Lizzie's scales and high notes. Madame actually gave her a kiss on the forehead and said, 'I shall expect lots of attention and effort. We have several opportunities for you, one of which might bring you to the attention of a very important producer.'

Robbie, who seemed to have grown much taller and to look more like fifteen than fourteen, did not change his expression when he saw her, but suddenly took a leap to each side, the way they did in tap routines, and said 'Tarra . . . Re-enter Lizzie Hobbs, coloratura soprano with grin!'

Though it made her grin even more, it also made her feel strange, as if they weren't so much together. Perhaps it would never be the same. Perhaps he had grown up, didn't *need* her to be his friend any more . . .

If that was true, then there wasn't near so much fun being back in the school, only the lessons to look forward to, and maybe, a little, the singing.

But after a day or two, when he seemed to keep bumping into her by accident everywhere she went, she began to feel a bit happier. She saw that lots of girls looked at him now, 'gave him the eye', as Mim would have said, but that he didn't give back in the same way, except in a kind of take-off of 'Sexy-Rexy' Harrison, or Elvis, making them look a bit daft.

Soon, they were being teased again, and it was as if all the trees and flowers that had got their summer colours again were blooming inside her as well, and she could not wait for each day to dawn to get on the bus and tube and be back in school.

They never played up in the attic again, or even mentioned their family, their house, their children. It made her feel silly that she still wanted to. Robbie was more different than she was: his voice had gone downwards and sometimes split into a high, a low note at the same time, which she pretended not to notice, and he suddenly guffawed in a strange way at jokes in magazines with girls inside lying about in their birthday-suits.

It didn't make her feel too good, neither, to see how small her new tits were ('*bosom*, dear, please – or *breasts*,' said Mrs. Sterling). She wished there were some way to make them grow faster, or to pump them up so she could wear a bra. At least, they were as big as Mim's . . .

Poor Mim. She was getting thinner and thinner, working so hard, day and night, still making clothes for her, not costumes, but outfits to wear to school. She didn't make only her own ideas any more, but looked at fashions in shop windows and what they called 'boutiques' in the King's Road and Carnaby Street and copied them, and Lizzie didn't have the heart to tell her that they sometimes laughed at how she looked. 'Now you're twelve, me love,' she said, 'they won't expect you to look like a little school kid no more. We can make you smart, give you a bit of chick.' (She did not even like to tell her that *chic* was not pronounced chick – that was the trouble with lessons: they made her hear how Mim spoke, to want to correct her the way *she* was being corrected.)

'You look fine to me,' Robbie said, when she grumbled to him about it, and all of a sudden, kissed her. It was only a quick sort of kiss, just between the lobe of her ear and her jaw, but Lizzie felt herself go pink and faint.

After that, in class, in the playground, in the theatre between rehearsing and resting, going through the halls or walking to the bus, they held hands all the time. And though they talked and talked about everything on earth, Lizzie was always wondering when, at what moment, he would kiss her – and she was ready. She had used some of her allowance to buy a little bottle of Tweed, a scent that an older girl in the school wore. Rob didn't say anything, but the end of his long nose twitched, and he leaned a bit closer.

They were sitting under a tree in the school yard, studying the lines of a sketch in a revue Madame had put them in, when it happened . . .

*She* kissed *him*. Her lips landed on some needle-like growth on his chin, slid a little and only just missed a bared tooth. He looked startled, then gave her a kiss back, very quickly, and gazed into her eyes as if he had never seen them properly before. 'Gawd! what minces!' he said, in a voice that sounded like his own, yet different. 'It shouldn't be allowed!'

'Me eyes – mine?' She blinked them at him, all coy.

'No – your twin sister's.'

She laughed, feeling soft in the head, peculiar.

They leaned back against the tree, forgetting about the sketch, just looking at each other.

'Let's go to a picture some time, Lizzie. Would ya?'

Lizzie wanted to say, of course, in a grown-up way, but there were prickles under her skin. What would Mum say?

'Don't tell 'er,' Robbie said, reading her thoughts. 'She don't 'ave to know. We'll go in the afternoon, say the school's rehearsin' outdoors somewhere, like we do – you know . . .'

Lizzie tucked her thick, streaky-blond hair behind her ears. 'Cripes, I dunno . . .'

He ringed her wrist with his long narrow hand. 'Aw, come on, Lizzie.'

She noticed how he had light-grey specks in his navy-blue eyes, that his mouth hung in a big careless dip, sort of like Mick Jagger's (who he could take off to a tee) and she felt a vibration in her tummy and wanted to squeal the way girls did at the Rolling Stones. How could she ever have called him husband and played such silly mother-father games with him?

'Whaddya say, Liz-zie, eh?' he slid his fingers more confidently up and down her wrist.

What *could* she say, Mum or no Mum?

And so they began to sneak away, quite often, to see films in West End cinemas where, between big bags of popcorn and ices bought in the intervals, they sat, hardly watching the pictures, no matter what big stars were in them or what they were about, with Rob's arm round the back of the seat, her leaning her head against his shoulder, their knees pressed together and, every now and then, turning their faces to each other and gazing. When the gazing got too long, one or the other would turn away.

In between times, they would talk and talk and talk. There was now hardly anything they didn't know about each other, even the most private thoughts and feelings. They were like one, interchangeable person, and hated to be apart.

At night, she would sit with Mim in the stale-grease-smelling flat over a meal of beans-on-toast or chips with vinegar, listening to her daily grouses about the customers or management, the state of her arches and veins, and answer her sharp questions about what she was doing at the school and why *she* wasn't the star in everything – and, of course, about the 'boy-genius'.

Lizzie got her answers down pat, just like a vaudeville routine. After washing the dishes, she would get Mim to play for her practice, pretending not to notice how many wrong notes she struck and how out-of-tune the old piano had become, or the banging from Antonio's, who kept complaining that high notes had grown so loud and penetrating that they disturbed the customers.

When Mim went out again to her cashier's job at Romero's Nightclub, Lizzie sometimes went upstairs to Harry Org's and watched telly. Because Robbie would be watching it too, she tried to watch the same pop shows, like *Ready, Steady, Go!* and *Thank Your Lucky Stars*, so that they could talk about them the next day. But it was more and more boring to be away from him . . .

Going to bed in the little room that was getting shabbier by the year, Lizzie would sometimes stand and stare at herself in the damp-stained mirror on the wall as if she were someone else. Her legs were getting long, but her tummy was still too plump. She sucked it in to make it flat like the older girls at the school, but it bounced out again the moment she let her breath go. There was a new womanish look to her breasts, though, and there was a little triangle of brownish-blond hair between the tops of her thighs that made her wonder about all sorts of things . . .

What would it be like to be naked with Robbie? What would they *do*? She'd heard a lot of talk about it at school, read a lot of descriptions in novels and books that were meant for grown-ups, seen oodles of plays and movies that almost showed what went on – and on telly now the girls took off most of their clothes and writhed about in bed with men you could tell had nothing on under the sheet, first one on top and then the other in strange positions.

It made her face hot with embarrassment that they would do such private things in public like that, that girls would actually let their tits – breasts – right out, nipples and all, for millions of people to look at . . .

The very idea made her cover herself up, quickly put on her nightie. One thing for sure, she and Robbie would be married before anything like *that* went on!

The thought would make her shake her fringe and groan . . . Blimey, that wouldn't be for donkey's years – 'absolute ions,' as Jenny Tate would say.

Meanwhile, Robbie was even worse than Mim, always going on about her *Voice*, how she was going to be much greater than Julie Andrews or Petula Clark or even Shirley Bassey. He would listen to her every chance he could, his arms folded, his head cocked, his eyes narrowed, and whenever she came to the end of a song he would nod several times – or perhaps raise his long hands over his head in a silent clap. The way he didn't smile, and looked so sure and knowing, made her want to giggle, but she tried not to giggle so much these days, to be more like *his* age.

Every now and then, too, Robbie would give her a bit of a lecture: she should be more serious about her *Talent*; she shouldn't ever worry about hurting his feelings if she had to practise instead of being with him – 'First things first, Lizzie!'

'That's you, then,' she'd said, sharp and saucy. 'You're the one got the Grant. Madame says you're going to be a leading impressionist, and a fine actor besides . . .'

'That's good,' Robbie said back. 'You got her voice down to a tee. But it's codswallop, of course, I don't even like doing take-offs no more. And I don't fancy meself an actor.'

'What! But, Robbie . . .' She'd tried not to look as surprised as she was; he'd never mentioned this before. 'What *do* you fancy, then?'

Robbie had curled his eyebrows a moment, then shrugged. 'Buggered if I know. Sing like Mick, play a guitar . . .'

That had made them both laugh.

Ah, well . . . Tomorrow was another day, as Scarlett O'Hara said in *Gone with the Wind*. There were picnic lunches between exams, taking the wireless with them and listening to rock 'n 'roll, bossanovas, jazz, swing – or sometimes news and people talking, because that's where Robbie got a lot of his ideas for take-offs; there were walks along the river, rides on the tops of buses; and, of course, there was Madame's big event of the year to look forward to, when everyone connected with the school could bring their friends and relatives, and all the biggest-wig theatre, film and TV people were invited to a display of Blatsky's student talent (with a reception and nosh after).

Lizzie would lay out her things for the morning, her clothes, books, music, do her teeth till they gleamed, brush her hair till it rose from her head and sparked, then settle into her side of the bed. Every night, like a silly nit, she would reach under her pillow for Freddie before she remembered he had been gone for years. Another sadness came then – Bertie and his big hugs, the way he had called her Miss Cuddles . . .

She would squeeze her eyes shut, try to be asleep before Mim plonked down beside her, smelling of tobacco and sweat, grunting and swearing at her aches and pains, going on about her horrible job, how she missed Bertie, how hard it was to keep up with the rent and school and all the other expenses.

Most of all, what Lizzie didn't want to hear *again* was that it was 'all worth it', because it wouldn't be long before Lizzie hit the top; 'Just keep at it, me love,' she would say, like a record going round and round in a groove, 'in no time at all we'll be outa this rat's-nest for good. We'll 'ave us a nice big flat in Mayfair, or some place we got a view right over the park. We'll be livin' like nobs, eatin' chicken an' duck an' lobsters, drinkin' champagne, ownin' a car with real leather seats . . .'

Being asleep was even better than pretending. Pretending just made her feel mean and awful for not listening, for not reaching out to her poor tired mum . . .

She would shake her thick, jagged fringe from her face, fold her hands under her cheek, and wait . . .

Almost at once, in the small lighted stage behind her lids, there would be Robbie, doing one of her favourites: like James Cagney saying 'You dirty rat, take that and that and that'; of Humphrey Bogart saying, 'Play it again, Sam'; or, best of all, Harold Wilson puffing away on an imaginary pipe saying ridiculous things for a Prime Minister, in a North Country voice . . .

She would fall asleep, still grinning.

# CHAPTER SIX

'I don't know what to make of her. She's only *thirteen*, you say?' David Pendy leaned on his elbow towards Madame Irayna, kept his deep voice low.

'That's right, David. She has been with us since she was eight.' Madame felt a pleasure she knew less and less these days. In this, what they called the 'permissive' age, young people were slipping into a mode outside her understanding. The kind of contribution she could make to their careers threatened to become obsolete. Even dear Rob was changing course, wanting, to her deep disappointment, to become a pop singer. But, at least Lizzie, singing 'Climb Every Mountain', and 'Summertime', with the sweet, true pitch of Cynthia's brilliant training, was living up to her highest hopes. She smiled up to her on the stage, nodded.

David Pendy, a slender man in a blue pin-stripe suit, with the kind of long scruffy hair Madame despised, turned to another man, Tony Clayton, sitting on his other side in the long line of producers, agents and other potential bidders for exceptional performers. 'A range of at least four octaves,' he said. 'And did you ever hear such high notes from a kid?'

'From anyone,' said Tony Clayton, his seamy face almost gloomy confirmation. 'Who is she like?'

'A young Marianne Faithfull? Lulu? A mixture?'

Tony Clayton twisted his mouth. 'Yeah – a strange one. Time, maybe. Another couple of years?'

David Pendy nodded judiciously. 'Perhaps. But there's that spot on Doolican's show . . .'

'Mmm . . .'

'Irayna . . .' David Pendy turned back to her. 'What's the background here – do I detect a Cockney edge?'

'You shouldn't, dear David. But it's possible. It's very ingrained. That's her mother over there.' Madame tried to indicate Mim, sitting in the section given over to parents and friends, so that the attention wouldn't be spotted – but Mim's gimlet-eyed stare picked it up like radar. It was obvious, by her cocked head and lifted chin, that she had noted the men's reaction, had been unaffected by the roar of applause, was almost off the chair in readiness to take over.

'My God – what an extraordinary outfit.' David and Tony both restrained laughter. 'I've never seen so much black!'

'Is she in mourning, perhaps?' Tony whispered, leaning across to Madame.

'No . . . It's supposed to be sophisticated, I think.' Madame gave a subtle shake of her own black-dyed french-twist. 'Careful, or she'll pounce – and there's no escape.'

'That would be who we'd have to deal with, then?'

Madame made a wry face. 'Ultimately. I have never found an answer. She is like a fate.'

They all looked up at Lizzie, who was now walking back to the piano to an encore.

'She's got good legs, style, a kind of sparkle.'

'Professional as hell.'

'Too bad about the mother . . .'

Madame cleared her throat. She had done all she could, would continue to do so until such time as Lizzie was launched, but there was a foreboding in her mind that clouded the pleasure of Lizzie's beautiful performance. There were times when she had to cross herself at the ugly feelings *that* tiresome woman put in her thoughts. 'Yes,' she said. 'But I urge you not to let it discourage you.'

The two men were now doubly attentive, as Lizzie, in her short gold dress with long sleeves (copied by Mim from a Mary Quant style), gold stockings, long gold earrings, belted out with force and power 'You'll Never Walk Alone', ending with her arms thrown out, her head thrown back, her thick neck-length hair and fringe tossed behind her and an uplifted smile on her mouth.

'Great,' said David Pendy, joining Tony and the rest of the audience in ecstatic applause. 'We'll have a talk, Irayna,' he whispered to her.

Madame Irayna drew in a glad breath. While there were several students this year with exceptional promise, it was Lizzie she most believed in, Lizzie who, despite her youth, was the most outstanding; she had a saying, familiar to her students and staff – 'training without talent is a game of chance; talent *and* training together is a certain winner.' Not that there wasn't still a long way to go . . . she stole a glance at Cynthia Sterling. A great deal would depend on her. Would she be content to stick with Lizzie after that last outburst from the mother? Certainly, there was no animosity in sight tonight, as she sat radiantly smiling beside her new fiancé. The main thing was to keep the 'Obbs woman away from her – particularly during the reception. After that, there'd be the half-term break, time for harsh words to lose their sting.

'What have we got now?' David Pendy was saying, looking at the hand-painted programme. 'Readings from the works of William Shakespeare. Not my scene, but more yours, eh, Irayna?'

Madame smiled thinly. She could not remember the number of students she had placed in serious drama over the years, from those currently in the ranks of the Royal Shakespeare Theatre to repertory companies all over the country. Nevertheless, her reputation didn't stop there. 'Don't worry, David,' she whispered back. 'You will also note scenes from musicals, and some comedy . . .'

'Right. What about this boy I've heard about who does imitations? Should we be interested?'

Madame raised a black-nailed forefinger. 'Extremely. He is quite ready. There is almost no-one he can't do – brilliantly. You will see.'

'How old?'

'Sixteen.'

David Pendy nodded, relayed the information to Tony Clayton. The curtains lifted. On the dimly-lit stage, characters in sixteenth-century dress moved forward. In the hush, young voices spoke out, clear and strong, delivering lines from *As You Like It*. This, with a re-grouping of performers, was followed by *Hamlet*, and then *A Midsummer Night's Dream*, ending with *Romeo and Juliet*.

The applause was enthusiastic. With speed and dexterity, the scene was blacked out, reconstructed. Down came a backdrop of a pirate ship. Out came the younger students to do an excerpt from *Treasure Island*.

Well-received, this was followed by an original one-act play written by Isabel Ashton of the English Department (her students cheered loudly for this), and then came Rob Grover.

For his act, nothing was required but a spotlight, a chair, a small table holding hats and wigs. The contrast of this simplicity caused a stir in the audience.

'This is the kid,' David Pendy said to his colleague.

Along the same row two well-known and powerful agents shifted straighter in their seats.

Rob was extremely uncomfortable in the blue velvet jacket provided at the last moment, when his own choice of a long sweater and jeans had been vetoed. Also, as he waited in the wings, he saw that Mum Grover's seat was empty. He hadn't really thought she'd get there, with the new nipper in the house and Dad Grover down with Asian 'flu. With a hollow feeling in his gut, he scanned the crowded theatre for sight of Lizzie . . .

Ah, there she was, sitting with Mim and that old vaudevillian, Org. Why was she looking so stiff and po-faced? What was that bloody cow of a mother on about *now*? Couldn't she leave it out for one night? Poor kid, not allowed to enjoy the first big success she had ever had . . .

Well, there was Jimmie Bruce as the M.C. announcing him, Felix Wheeler rolling the drum. Rob walked briskly on, went to the middle of the stage, bowed. The velvet jacket constricted his arms and shoulders, and he was suddenly boneless with panic.

There was a silence that seemed to go on forever. Someone called out from the back of the theatre, 'Come on, Rob – Lost your tongue?'

There was a restrained titter.

Rob pushed at his quiff, which felt like lead on his forehead. His underarms were getting clammy. With absolute clarity he knew that he could not do Dick Emery's coy woman on wobbly high heels saying, as she pushed a man's chest, almost knocking him down. 'Ooh, you are awful – but I like you!'

Something was happening to him. He couldn't bear doing these take-offs. He wanted to be *himself*.

But – who *was* he?

Turning involuntarily to Lizzie, he saw that she was sitting forward, her eyes huge with encouragement and love, a kind of message that travelled to him like light . . .

In an instant, he was in charge. Rubbing his hands and clapping them, he started off with the chorus of 'All The Way' which he sang in the style of Tony Martin.

This got a burst of applause, and he was able to speak confidentially to the audience now, and go into a series of his, by now, standards: characters familiar to all, in well-chosen variety (thanks to Madame, et al.).

'This boy is fantastic,' David Pendy said to Madame, hardly holding down his voice. 'Is he another Cockney?'

'Not exactly – how could you tell?' Madame frowned.

How difficult it was to submerge roots . . .

'It couldn't matter less, Irayna. It's rather endearing.'

Madame was not sure this was advantageous, but her frown undid itself, and she leaned to him. 'You ought to take him in hand soon – he needs recognition. Do you know what I mean?'

David Pendy folded his pinkish lips. 'I think so . . .'

'Youngsters these days – so easily lost. Not a happy background.'

'You're very fond of him . . .'

'I don't want him to flounder. Several of our youngsters have taken to cannabis and other things.' Madame felt a nasty flutter around her heart. 'It's an age of protest and disruption, of confused morals. This boy was unwanted, an orphan, fostered . . .'

'Say no more, Irayna. We're not philanthropists, but we can support genuine talent.'

Madame Irayna closed her eyes, breathed inward. Whatever happened to her, dear Rob would not be a victim of his own death-wish.

Finally , the show ended, and the audience rose, excited approval prevailing. Eyes met eyes in bright interest, some of it frankly exploitative. For here, at Madame Blatsky's yearly talent-display, the mixture of old students now firmly established as stars, some very famous, the highly influential representatives of production, management and agency in open accessibility with hopeful parents, students and staff, was an exceptional, if not unique opportunity for all.

Madame herself, overwhelmed by the strain of preparation, wished only to retire, and longed for Nikki's arm as she rose and leaned heavily on her cane.

'Please,' said Nikki, appearing instantly, eyelashes fluttering, dark eyes wide with ingratiation, 'do not surround Madame. She will see you at the reception. Just follow the arrows . . .'

Madame was grateful for his arm. She could not help feeling that her life's work was approaching culmination, but that it had had, after all, some contributive purpose. Not least of which might be dear Lizzie . . .

'All right, me love, come with me,' said Mim. Her massive diamanté earrings (found in a theatrical costumier's going-out-of-business sale) swung like miniature chandeliers from her pendant lobes, scraped her bony jaw like claws. 'An' don't *you* say a word, you 'ear me!'

Lizzie swallowed what seemed small lumps of cement. 'You aren't going to make one of your stinks, are you, Mum? This is Madame's big night – can't you 'old off?'

Mim's answer was a sharp swing to her hips that made her black-sequin dress an accessory to her fury. 'What right, what bloomin' right, 'as this bleedin' gargoyle to leave yer outa all that actin' – an' the dancin'? You what 'as 'ad the best trainin' than the 'ole bloody lot put together – eh? Answer me that, Miss, answer me that!'

'I ain't no ruddy good at actin'!' Lizzie's veneer of speech reached a point of collapse. 'Or dancin' neither! I ain't got no inspiration. I'm an automaton . . .'

Mim wheeled on her. 'A *what*?'

'Never mind, it don't matter – everyone says I'm good at singin'. So I sings. Ain't you pleased they like me?'

Mim stared at her daughter as if she had sworn at her. 'Why, o' course you're good at singin'. 'Oo taught ya from the time ya could gurgle? But that ain't all you're good at; there's somethin' fishy goin' on 'ere. I don't work me arse off for bloody great fees to 'ave yer touted as just a pair o' tonsils, me girl.'

Mim turned and pushed on through the crowd milling towards a long table at the back of the theatre where the food and drink was being served by students in dresses and suits instead of their usual jeans and t-shirts. Her sharp elbows cleared the way with ease.

'I ain't comin' with ya, Mum!' Lizzie suddenly pulled

back. Her hair swivelled this way and that as she looked for Robbie, a terrible feeling in her tummy, almost like the curse.

Mim stopped so hard she knocked two people off-balance. More people were beginning to falter in their smiling acknowledgement of Lizzie to stare at the bizarre woman with her, whose heavily made-up face looked like a black-eyebrowed bird under bronze head-feathers, eyeing a prey. 'Yes, you bloody *are*, me darlin'!'

Lizzie was aware of all the eyes on them. It was all she could do not to turn and bolt – but that would be even worse for poor Madame. Cripes – this was the limit, this took the cake. If it weren't for Robbie, she'd just scarper, once and for all . . .

Oh, where was he? He was the only person in the world who would know what to do, who could stop Mum . . .

Suddenly, even as Mim's hand grabbed at her arm, Lizzie saw him – in the middle of a group of the big-wigs, Madame at his side, all of them talking, looking serious. Gawd, he wouldn't see her, even if she waved.

But just at that instant, Rob lifted his chin and swept the gathering with a keen, searching look . . .

Looking for her – she knew! Raising her arm high above her head, she waved it side-to-side in their code.

At first, he didn't seem to see . . .

And then, he did!

But, instead of understanding that she wanted him there, he raised his arm, not responding, but beckoning her to come there, drawing his hand towards the group in vigorous message.

'Oh, well,' she said, turning back to Mim. 'All right. Madame's over there.'

Mim's eyes narrowed. 'What you up to?'

Lizzie's gaze was blue innocence. 'Nothin', Mum. Lead on.'

The effect of this sudden capitulation was already

showing by the time they approached the group at the far end of the table. A puzzled caution had modified the ferocity of Mim's expression. As she and Lizzie were greeted, hands extended, introductions made, Mim resolved into the alert expectation of earlier, before she had realized that Lizzie's songs were not to be followed by any other accomplishments.

Lizzie and Rob exchanged meaningful, furtive glances; behind their backs, their hands met in a brief clasp.

'Lizzie,' Madame said, 'Mr. Pendy and Mr. Clayton were very impressed with your singing . . .'

'Were you, now?' said Mim. 'That's very nice to 'ear.' The ferocity was now replaced by a sidewise smile. 'Enough to 'ave 'er in one of yer specials, I 'ope.'

'Really, Mrs. 'Obbs . . .' Madame began, but David Pendy, in wry acknowledgement of her previous warning, only smiled.

'That's what we thought of discussing,' he said. He turned to Lizzie. 'We might want to hear some more, other kinds of songs . . .'

Lizzie flushed. 'I know all kinds . . .'

'I *said* these was too 'igh-brow,' Mim broke in. 'I *told* 'er teacher she oughta be doin' 'er ding-dongs an' pop, not just show stuff . . .'

'Then, that's fine. You'll come and sing for us one day at the studio?' Tony Clayton joined David Pendy in smiles at Lizzie.

'O' course she will – expenses paid, I 'ope.' Mim winked, cast a look of defiance at Madame.

Lizzie blinked, looked downward. In spite of Robbie's nudge of comfort, she could hardly go on standing there.

'I should like to suggest, gentlemen,' Madame said, 'that you write to me when you want to make an appointment with Lizzie. I will confirm it and see that she keeps it.' She turned her attention to a balding man with a long fleshy nose. 'I'm delighted, Ben, that you're interested in Rob. A good agent is just what he will need when he leaves us.'

'He should have a great future, Irayna.' Ben Wolfe nodded at Rob, patted his arm.

'Ta,' said Rob, with an expressionless nod.

'Well, now,' Madame smiled graciously all round, extended her elbow to Nikki for support, 'I have many to talk to – enjoy yourselves.' She moved off in slow, uncertain grandeur.

'Gawd! What cheek!' Mim looked at the group remaining in conspiratorial alliance. 'Didya ever 'ear the like! Tryin' to squeeze me out, *er own mother!* Well, mates, I got news fer ya. I ain't bein' squeezed out. If yer wants me little girl to sing for ya – I comes with 'er. 'Er career is my business – understand?'

The men looked at her with glazed eyes. They did not even seem aware of Lizzie's red cheeks, tightly-pressed lips.

'Considering her age,' David Pendy said at last, 'it doesn't seem unreasonable. Does it, Tony?'

Tony shrugged one shoulder.

'So, then, Mrs. Hobbs – Lizzie – until we meet.' He nodded, tapped Tony's elbow. 'We mustn't forget the Tate girl . . .'

'Right.' With more nods, a final smile for Lizzie, they moved off.

'Whaddya go on like that for, Mrs. 'Obbs?' Rob said. 'Now you've probably been gone and done in 'er first big chance!' He shoved at his quiff, squared his chin at her.

Mim stared at him as if she had never seen anyone more odious. 'What does a kid like you know? Nothin' – that's what. Them producers is vultures. They seen a good thing. They'll be eatin' 'er to the carcus if I don't watch 'em! So you just stay out of it. An' keep away from 'er, too. Know what I mean?'

'Mum – you stop that. I won't 'ave you talk to Robbie that way – never again, see!' Lizzie moved to Rob, put her arm through his and held him tightly against her, her eyes brilliant.

Mim looked at them both for a moment, then she smiled to herself, took a cigarette from her fringed handbag. 'One day, me love,' she said to Lizzie as she put the cigarette into the corner of her mouth and lit it, 'you'll look back on 'im an' know just what I was on about. Look at 'im – see – 'e knows hisself. Don't you, Robbo?'

Rob, to Lizzie's amazement, didn't spark back. A funny look she had never seen before came into his eyes – they seemed to shift away, to have a sad expression. Where was his boldness with Mum, the clever words that could put her down, even if it was only for a tick while she got something even spikier ready to say? Why did his arm seem to loosen its tight grip on hers?

'Aw, forget it,' Mim said, with her jokiest grin. 'Come on, we got somethin' to celebrate – let's tuck into the free grub an' booze!'

Lizzie and Rob both looked at Mim as she stuffed her mouth, gazed about with triumph in her eyes, raised her glass and called out jolly 'ellos to one and all.

Somewhere, far back in the shadows at one side of the theatre, Harry Org, completely forgotten as her escort, waited to be summoned.

# CHAPTER SEVEN

'Better take your Auntie Ella, darlin',' Mim said, as they prepared to go to the Studio. 'It's rainin' pigs.'

'Don't want it.' Lizzie walked slowly to the door of the flat, hating the stupid grown-up dress she was wearing because Mum had sat up two whole nights making it, and the stiff stuff she had sprayed on her hair to make it stay high on her head. She felt sick in her stomach at missing a whole school day, and she wouldn't see Robbie now until Monday, which was *ions* off . . .

'Lift up yer lips, me love – you look like you was goin' to a funeral.' Mim, in a white zebra-striped mac that showed her knobbly knees, smacked her jauntily on the bottom. 'This is the biggest day of your life. *Anyone* can go to school, only special somebodies get a chance to sing in a big television show!'

Lizzie didn't even shrug. She had learned not to argue with Mum about anything. It only wasted your breath. One day, she'd be old enough to marry Robbie and have the home they wanted – and that would be that. No matter how sad and disappointed Mim was, she'd just have to lump it.

' 'Old them shoulders back; you look like an old woman!'

Lizzie kept on going, down the stairs, along with her mother, but just slightly behind, as if to deny they were together. She still loved Mum, but sometimes she saw her in a different way, like other people might see her. Though if anyone said anything nasty about her, she would want to fight them, because there was no one in the world so good, who worked so hard or did so much for their kid. And all without Bertie, all alone, with not a bloomin' soul in the world to help her and nothing more to go by than plain guts. 'She's a livin' marvel, your Mum,' Robbie said. 'Sometimes I 'ates 'er, Gawd knows. But I wouldn't mind 'avin' 'er on me side.'

That was one thing you could say: Mum was on her side. Trouble was, she wasn't on no other. Everyone else was like enemies. Cripes, she didn't even like Jennifer, or Nancy, who were real mates, didn't ever want her to go to their houses, because, she said, they was upper-class twits who would give her ideas that weren't no bloody good to her, besides making her feel like a nobody. Which was just what they *didn't*. When she was with them, she really felt a somebody. They thought she was funny, told her their secrets, and – they envied her, they said, because of Robbie.

If only Mum could see things different, how *all* the girls in the school fancied him – even more since he'd been doing pop songs instead of take-offs. Madame hadn't half been narked when he took some of his Grant allowance to buy a guitar! (What a lark that had been, going round all the music shops she knew in Soho. She had helped him pick it out, a real beaut with two different shiny woods. And he'd got a pick – though now he was growing his thumbnail long . . . )

'For Gawd's sake watch out where you're goin', an' 'urry – that's our bus!'

Trying to look ordinary in the short dress and tights, the scarf that rode on her backcombed hair-do, Lizzie followed her mother, who somehow pushed a way through the passengers ahead in the queue and found them a seat, causing a busful of staring eyes. If only Robbie didn't want the same things for her – if only he weren't so excited about her singing, and getting this chance . . . If only it was still *just* being a family . . .

She gazed away from Mim's alert eyes, through the window at the changing scene of London en route to Shepherd's Bush – so many, many people in the world, so many kinds, all going about, hurrying about millions of things that weren't nothing to do with being a star, with singing and singing your head off, always practising and rehearsing and dressing up and talking special . . .

If she weren't a singer, if Mim didn't make her – what else could she be? There must be hundreds of things – like . . .

Well, like a secretary, or a salesperson in a shop, or a teacher (of small kids, 'cause she liked small kids a *lot*), or a book writer, or an artist who did pictures that showed how things looked, like now, with the rain going all sideways, and all the umbrellas bobbing along, and shop lights reflecting in the puddles . . .

'What you dreamin' about, then?' Mim's voice was flat with exasperation. 'Got yer 'anky, and yer Kotex safe?' She tapped Lizzie's little black patent handbag.

'You know I have – you put them in.'

'Well . . . I got your music . . .'

'You needn't. I know it.'

Mim gave a sharp nod. 'You better. Just remember everythin' I told ya . . .'

'Yes, Mum.'

'Mim. You'd think by now, near fourteen, you'd 'ave got that right!'

'I thought I *was* fourteen.' Lizzie's lips tugged.

'I saw that. You don't 'ave to get uppity just 'cause you got an important audition. I say what I 'as to say. I tells 'em what they want to 'ear. You'll thank me one day . . .'

Where have I heard that before? Lizzie thought, but said nothing; she wanted to continue her think, which was very interesting . . .

'Come on, then, wake up – 'ere's where we get off and run to the tube. Look nippy! We don't want to keep 'em waitin', do we?'

Lizzie didn't answer that, either. She wouldn't mind if they had forgotten the whole thing. As usual, as she and Mim half-ran towards the big complex of buildings at White City, she felt a pee coming on. 'Be sure to go before you leave,' Mim had warned, 'we don't know where there's a lav in a place like that. An' there's takin' down yer tights an' dealin' with the pad . . .'

'Suppose I bleed through it?' she'd said.

Mim's expression was what stage directions called a 'smirk'. 'You won't – you ain't really got goin' yet. You wait!'

Ugh, Lizzie thought, wrinkling her nose. But it didn't stop her from wanting to pee *now*.

'You just 'old it,' Mim said. 'It'll go away – it always does once you're on.'

Lizzie gritted her teeth.

'An' don't do *that!*' Mim said, nudging her as they went into the big reception hall, 'they'll think ya got the wind-up. Give us the old penny-a . . .'

'Can't.' Lizzie didn't dare unlock her teeth.

Mim gave her a harder nudge at the desk, where she asked for Mr. Pendy.

'Hey, watch it, Mum, Lizzie whispered. 'You made it come.'

'Oh, me gawd!'

'Please take a seat,' a busy-faced young woman said. 'We'll call you.'

'Where's the lav?' Mim asked her quickly.

'Ah – the nearest Ladies is around the staircase and down to the left.'

'Right. That's where Miss Lizzie 'Obbs will be.'

The receptionist exchanged glances with two others behind the big half-moon desk. Cheeky lot, thought Mim.

Lizzie, half-pushed by Mim along the waxed floor, could hardly stay upright in the thick-heeled, box-toed shoes that now replaced her stilettos. 'Mum, leave off, will ya – I'm about to fall on me arse!'

Mim's eyes opened with shock. 'You don't talk like that no more. You got elocution now!'

Lizzie looked away. It happened whenever she got excited. And when she was with Robbie, she didn't even try. Maybe she'd never speak *real* proper – but, at least, now, she knew the difference. And – so did Mim . . .

'Glad you noticed,' she said, with a saucy look.

'Get on with ya . . .' Mim's eyebrows almost separated as she winked.

Once she had re-sorted herself in the nice fancy 'ladies', Lizzie felt better. 'Okay, Mum,' she said, stepping out with her back to the reception hall. 'Let's get it over with.'

Mim's thin mouth made a downward arc. 'Is that all – ain't you even the *least* pleased?'

Lizzie couldn't bear that look. 'Aw, Mum – stop, I was only pullin' your leg.'

'You are pleased?'

Lizzie nudged her thin, hard arm, even more muscular these days with the bed-making she'd taken on at the hotel. 'Course!'

Mim's mouth returned to normal. 'It's me what's got the willies,' she said, reaching into her pocket for a crumpled pack of cigarettes. 'You'd think it was me goin' to do the audition.'

Lizzie restrained a nod, a retort.

The wait seemed forever. Lizzie watched the hands of the clock go very slowly around. She felt twitches beginning in her feet, then her shoulders . . .

'Ah,' said a male voice, 'there you are. So sorry to keep you waiting.'

David Pendy shook their hands. He looked quite different in very tightly-fitting denim jeans, a roll-neck white jumper, some kind of a thick medallion hanging from a chain around his neck, his hair even longer now and quite greasy; and Lizzie wondered how he could see anything in the big, mauve-tinted glasses. But his smile was very nice and friendly, and she smiled back.

'My word, you do look grown-up,' he said, as he led them quickly along several corridors of closed doors and all sorts of signs that Mim craned her neck to read, 'they'll think I'm having them on about your age.'

Mim looked at him in smug accord. Lizzie didn't know how to look, or what to say.

'I've only just got a studio for us, had to wait for a Victorian set to be dismantled – and, I'm afraid, we've only got it for about twenty minutes before they want it for something else.'

'Cripes!' said Mim. 'It ain't what you'd expect,' as she followed him into a big room with bare brick walls, on which were hung boxes of padding, cables, poles and odd bits of equipment. Ladders, more cables leading to cameras, microphones, loudspeakers, monitors, made a general clutter.

He laughed. 'If we get time, I'll show you something more impressive. Meanwhile . . . Oh, there's Tony, now, and some of our production team for the Doolican show. You've got Rod, over there, at the piano. I hope the piano's in tune.'

Lizzie felt a shiver go from her head to her toes. Looking at all the kindly, expectant faces, she had only one urge – to take to her heels, and keep going. She would get on a bus or train and just disappear – forever . . .

' 'Ere,' said Mim, 'take off the scarf – careful, don't muck up me hair-do. Give us yer coat. Let me put some powder on your I-suppose – crikey, what a shine! Lean down a bit. You been *eatin'* your lipstick?'

Lizzie stiffened in every part of her. 'Go away, Mum, *please*!'

Mim blinked upward into the staring blue eyes. 'Keep your wig on, I'm only doin' the necessary!'

'It ain't,' Lizzie whispered. 'Don't you *see*. They'll think we're daft!'

Mim pressed her mouth, cast a sharp resentful glance at the waiting faces. 'Right. Well, I'm finished, any'ow.'

'Do sit here,' David Pendy said to her, indicating a chair at the end of a row. 'Lizzie, you just tell Rod what you want of him.' He bent chivalrously to pick up the music case.

' 'Ere!' said Mim, grabbing it from him. 'I take care of that! I 'ope 'e knows 'is stuff. Come on, me love.'

David Pendy stared after them as they moved to the piano, in a mixture of irritation and bemusement.

'It's the mother . . .' someone whispered, loud enough for the seated spectators to hear.

'Good God,' someone said. 'Poor kid!'

Everyone in the room studied the bony-kneed little woman in the zebra-striped mac as her sharp jaw and bronze, black-rooted head bent over Rod like a bird of prey, as her peeling red nail scraped the music or tapped it in emphatic description. Rod kept nodding, frowning, and nodding. 'I know . . . I follow . . . That's okay, *thanks* . . .'

'Mum . . .' Lizzie whispered, 'pack it in – 'e knows!'

Lizzie could hardly look round. A great blush was coming up into her face.

'Mrs. Hobbs,' David Pendy called, 'time's moving on . . .'

Mim looked up. ' 'Alf a mo,' she said reasonably, 'it won't do no one no good if it ain't played right.'

'Rod's had a lot of experience,' David Pendy said, with irony meant for his colleagues.

'Go on, Mum – or I'm off.'

Mim stared at her daughter as if she had misheard. 'You're *what*!'

Lizzie didn't repeat it; it would only lead to something worse. All she wanted, now, was to get on with it, sing, scarper, forget the whole thing.

In sudden decision, Mim stood up, puckered her mouth, walked in dignified briskness to the chair that had been indicated. For a moment, the black-eyebrowed scowl on her stiff-jawed face drew more attention than Lizzie standing beside the piano.

As if coming to, David Pendy clapped his hands. 'Let's begin, dear. Tell us what you're going to sing. Don't forget, I'd like the others to hear a sample of the kind of songs you sang that night, as well as a couple of more recent ballads, *et cetera*.'

Lizzie nodded. It was at a time like this that she was glad of all the training she'd had, Mrs. Sterling's, even Madame's with her constant harping on 'the absolute poise of inner confidence, of knowing exactly what to do and doing it with complete assurance'. You didn't really have to think or feel – anything. You just did it. It didn't matter *who* was looking, or where, a little place, a large place, a few people, or hundreds.

'I'll start with "You'll Never Walk Alone", please.'

David Pendy nodded, sat back, folded his arms about his chest, smiled in restrained anticipation of her effect on the others.

The bright-eyed young man called Rod nodded, struck up.

Lizzie stood straight and tall. No light was on her hair, but it cast a pale-gold aura around her fresh-complexioned, lightly-freckled face, the fringe giving a half-elfin, half-mysterious piquancy to her great blue eyes. Her figure was both child and woman in the sleeveless black dress, hanging straight from neck to hem but just brushing the nipples of her small breasts. Beneath the dress, her legs descended in undeveloped slimness that seemed to elongate them, and her absurdly stylish shoes with the box toes accentuated the thinness of her ankles. Her arms, as she hung them in a low clasp of hands, were vulnerable with adolescence, yet promising of subtle maturity. She lifted a chin just barely indented with a lingering dimple of childhood, to show a flawless creamy throat, the beauty of which the tawdry necklace could not diminish, drew in a breath, opened her small reddened mouth . . .

The sound that emerged from her, if eyes were closed, could not have been distinguished from those of an eighteen- or twenty-year-old. Every word of the lyric, as it rose in emotional crescendo, came out crystal-clear, with exactly the right emphasis, the right expression. She not only sang with powerful force, but seemed to understand precisely the meaning, feeling, mood of the song's concept. Every shift of expression in her mobile little face was radiantly knowing, every gesture she made was beautifully fitted to the inflexion of her voice, the significance of what she was conveying. There was nothing naïve, no slightest falter to give away a gap between age and comprehension, not the faintest trace of self-conscious aping or appeal to her audience for tolerance of her youth.

When she came to the end of the song, she raised her slender arms in inspired reassurance and confirmation, offered with love to her audience – 'and you'll ne – ver walk a – lone!'

There was a spontaneous outburst of approval, tinged with surprise, a mumble of questions and comments.

Lizzie shifted her shoulders, licked her lips, prepared for another song, another mood. This time she put her hands on her hips, planted her feet apart, indicated a wry yet grim determination and launched into 'I'm Gonna Wash That Man Right Outa My Hair'. (It was not Mrs. Sterling's doing that she sang it with Mary Martin's gusto, *and* American accent, but Mim's. Mim's Cockney seemed to *become* American when she did American songs. ('It was all them films, weren' it? Spent 'alf me life watchin' Yanks in the cinema, on the stage . . .')

Lizzie didn't really know what impelled the girl to wash the man out of her hair, but the idea of it, the vigour dinned into her by Mim, created the impression that she was an experienced young woman at the end of her rope with a 'guy'.

More applause.

'Utterly amazing!' an elderly man with side-swept pieces of hair said to Tony and David, who nodded complacently.

'Now,' said Lizzie, feeling sticky under her arms, wondering if the pad was holding up, 'a song called "Yesterday" . . .'

There was a shift and stir in the row of watchers. This was in the charts, one of the Beatles' records. Mim lit a fresh cigarette with possessive vigour, raised a thumb at Lizzie.

Lizzie sang this one without much thought; neither Mrs. Sterling nor Mum had had to tell her what to do because after listening to Robbie and watching them on telly, it just came sort of easy . . .

'Good, Lizzie – very, very nice, indeed! That'll be all we have time for . . .'

Lizzie nodded, but Mim bent forward alertly. 'Don't you want to 'ear 'er Cockney song? We got it perfect.'

Everyone turned to Mim.

'I'm sorry, Mrs. Hobbs – I'm sure it's delightful, and I'd love to hear it, but we must move on now. Thank you for bringing Lizzie, it's been most interesting.' David Pendy gave her a beaming smile, shoved his hair behind his ears, and turned to his colleagues.

'Well! I like that!' Mim stood up, walked quickly to Lizzie. 'Come on, me girl. There's no sense 'angin' roun' this nu'-'ouse. Plenty o' places we're *wan'ed* . . .'

'Mum – shut up, will ya?' Lizzie drew in a breath, closed her eyes, prepared to get her music and make a quick exit.

'Lizzie,' called David Pendy. 'May we have a word with you, dear?'

Lizzie paused, turned, walked over to him. 'Yes?' she said. Because she did not feel like smiling, she didn't. Monday, she and Robbie would talk all this over when they went over to Hampstead Heath for a walk . . .

'Sit down a moment,' Tony Clayton said, indicating an empty chair on David's other side. 'Apart from your mother, darling, do you think you're going to be able to carry a prominent spot on the Doolican show? You see, we can't promise she will be at your side – it's quite a different world . . .'

Lizzie just looked at him. She was not at all sure what he meant. Her tummy hurt with the curse, and she longed to be out of here and lying on it in bed. He was such a nice man, and she wished she could think of something to say . . .

'We very much want you on the show,' David said.

The rest of the group were picking up notebooks and jackets and preparing to leave, but all were looking at her with approval.

'Don't be afraid to speak,' David said.

'I ain't,' said Lizzie, with a sudden surge of annoyance. 'What do ya want me Mum to do – disappear?'

'Now, now, dear – of course not. Naturally, she would be with you – up to a point. What I want to know is, do you need her to have confidence?'

Suddenly, Mim was standing between them. 'What you on about, Mr. Pendy, eh? You want Lizzie but not me, eh?'

'Mum . . .!'

Mim pushed her out of her way. 'Is that it?'

David Pendy bit at his top lip with a gold-edged tooth. 'Mrs. Hobbs . . .'

'All right. Lizzie – come on, duck – let's 'op it.'

Lizzie gave David Pendy one long look, her eyes moistly brilliant. 'Sorry . . .' She turned and began to follow Mim from the studio.

'Lizzie, Lizzie . . .' called David Pendy. 'Come back – please.'

Lizzie stopped. Mim pushed on, but when she saw that Lizzie was going back to the group, she shoved her hand on a hip and with her cigarette clamped like a finger of challenge, waited, one foot tapping.

'Lizzie, look . . .' Tony and David and two other men, as well as a smiling blonde woman, all looked at her.

'To put it plainly, dear,' said David, 'we want you on the show. Do you want to be on it?'

There was a short silence. In the soundproof studio only breathing and the rustle of clothing could be heard. 'Well, yeah – yeah, of course,' said Lizzie. She turned to look for Mim. 'Mum . . .' she called. 'You got it all wrong. They *want* me on the show . . .'

'Mmmm . . .' Mim walked back, taking her time. 'All right, me "good" friends,' she said, 'let's 'ear the deal.'

# CHAPTER EIGHT

It all started one day when he took off Elvis Presley for a bunch of the kids in their lunch break. A sudden March squall had kept them from their usual exodus for air and physical outlet, and they hung round the games machines and juke box an old student had donated, joking, shouting, over the top of the music, or dancing to it . . .

Rob had broken away from Lizzie to go over and put a coin in the box, choosing an early Presley he still liked. As 'Blue Suede Shoes' broke forth, almost everyone got up and began to rock'n'roll and Rob and Lizzie, with their familiar, much-practised steps, were easily the most vigorous and adept.

When the number ended, someone shouted, 'Encore! Let's have it again!'

Rob, sweating but not out of breath, lifted his left eyebrow at Lizzie. She nodded, grinned, and he dug into his pocket quickly for another coin. This time, he went and turned up the volume.

Again, the Presley voice filled the big barn-like room with its poster-covered walls and wooden benches, and couples, some girls dancing together, other boys or girls going it alone, sprang back into action, looked on by tolerant staff and help.

Rob felt a great surge of happiness as he lifted or swung Lizzie's light, slender body, met her eyes as they moved together in perfect rhythm. ('This Lizzie,' Mum Grover had teased, 'she must be a knockout. With all them pretty girls in the school, don't you *never* fancy *no-one* else?'

'Nope,' he'd said, 'no-one.' And it was true.) 'You my girl?' he asked now, as they bumped and retreated, swung back to back and over.

' 'Course.'

'D'ya love me?'

' 'Course,' she said, landing deftly on her feet, hair swinging out behind her.

'For ever and ever?'

'*And* a day. What about you?'

Rob slid her between his ankles and up over his shoulders. 'Silly question. When are ya goin' to marry me, then?'

'Tomorrow?'

He almost grinned himself to a stop. 'Hardly! You got to do your show – and, get older.'

For just a moment, Lizzie leaned against him and they barely moved, just looking into each other's eyes . . .

Suddenly Rob leaned back and raised his arms in the air, emitting a great cock-a-doodle-do! Then, as Lizzie burst into laughter, he rushed up to their table, picked up his guitar, tore over to the juke box and stood in front of it aping Elvis, wriggling hips and all.

The kids howled with approval, shouted for more, and once more a coin was inserted and out came Elvis's voice with the beat they couldn't resist. This time they only jogged mildly about while watching Rob, and finally everyone in the entire room was still, listening raptly, calling out when he rotated his hips in the exact way of Elvis . . .

Rob was somehow out of mind and time. He felt one with Elvis and the music, but more than that, as if it was the first moment of his life – as himself. Although he was imitating Elvis Presley, he was also playing and singing from *inside* some real, live feeling. He had told Madame he wanted to be a pop singer, but not until now did he know why.

When the music stopped and they were all clapping, he didn't walk away, but strummed for a few seconds on his guitar and began to sing on his own, singing several different songs that were in the charts, in the manner of various singers and current groups. But even as the kids clapped and asked for more, and Lizzie's joyous face rose from the others, beaming encouragement and support, he was moving about in his new feelings, groping for a way of his own, his own style . . .

When it didn't come clear, somehow it didn't matter; it was there, somewhere, and he'd find it. He drew in a rasping breath, put the guitar back with his and Lizzie's gear, went over to her. 'Oh, Robbie,' she said, 'Oh, Robbie – that was wonderful.'

They put their arms around each other's waists and strolled to the Coke machine, the blue-jeaned figures looking oddly similar in their closeness. 'You know what, Robbie?' Lizzie said, as they raised the bottles to their mouths. 'I'd much rather just look art'er you, take care of you, you know, than singin' meself.'

Rob shook her shoulders. 'Don't be soft. You got to sing, you got a great set of lungs. He nudged her cheek with his nose. 'There ain't nothin' wrong with us both bein' performers is there? Maybe Mim wouldn't be so 'ard on me. Maybe she'd think I was good enough for ya, eh?'

They grinned at each other in perfect understanding. Rob thought: I'll win the old ogre round yet, get her on *my* side, too! Meanwhile, he put this down in his memory as the happiest day of his life. He had found out where he was headed, and had got himself what the nobs called a 'fiancée'.

'Would ya like a ring, then?' he asked, as they moved back to the floor to dance to a slow, dreamy ballad. 'It'd have to be glass, of course.'

Lizzie sighed, nodded, leaned her head on his shoulder. It was the happiest day of her life, too. It would never have occurred to her then that the little fake opal ring he bought her at Woolworth's could cause the bull-an'-cow of all time.

Mim had been in the kitchen getting their supper when Lizzie got in from school, later than usual; now that she did the journey alone, she was generally the first home.

'An' what kept ya, me love?' Mim asked, as she peeled some spuds. 'Not larkin' about with '*im*, I 'ope.'

Lizzie threw her books onto the cluttered table which, though Bert's things were no longer part of the mess, was still loaded to the edges. 'Come on, Mum – don't start.'

Mim eyed her over the top of the granny glasses she was now forced to wear for close seeing. Her hair was bedraggled, the roots an inch wide, her face sallow with fatigue and even her tights, stretched from kneeling to wash floors at the hotel, sagged on her bone-thin legs. Lizzie felt a tug of worry, went to kiss her before she could add words to the suspicious look. 'I'll do that, Mum – go put your feet up and have a beer.'

'*You're* bein' extra charmin' – what's up? What you been doin', eh?'

'Nothing. Go on, Mum. Sit.'

' 'Ang on. You been somewhere – it's Friday, school's finished early. An' why're ya all pink an' sparky? Just what you been up to?' Mim stopped peeling, pointed the knife like a threat.

Lizzie grunted, took off her bulky blue sweater, threw it across the wall pegs that still held Bert's old caps, landing it with practised neatness. Then she took off her shoes and kicked them aside so that she could be in her favourite outfit: jeans, shirt and bare feet. Padding into the kitchen, she took the knife from Mim's hands. 'Off with you,' she said.

Suddenly Mim's eyes caught sight of something that caused her mouth to fall open, her eyes to bulge. 'What's *that*?' She jerked her thumb downward on the small opal

117

ring (so small, in fact, that she and Robbie had wondered if it served the purpose – but even that had cost all the money they could dig up between them. 'I'll buy you a real, ruddy great diamond someday, me sunbeam,' Robbie had said, looking so awkward and embarrassed that she'd simply had to hug and kiss him right in the shop in front of everyone!).

'That?' said Lizzie, drawing her hand away quickly. 'It's a ring.'

'None of your sauce – I can *see* that! But what's it for? Where d'ya ge' it?'

'Someone gave it to me,' Lizzie turned away. It was stupid, but she couldn't tell Mum lies even for peace. 'If you won't let me help, I'm goin' to rest me eyes a minute. We had lots of work today.'

'Work! What d'you know of work! I'm the one what works – so's you can play about with books – an' 'im!' Mim moved after her, throwing the spuds into the sink in passing, grabbing at her arm. 'Let me see that thing again. I bet *'e* gave it ya, eh. Come on, be'er tell me the truth, young lady!'

Lizzie turned back, faced the angry woman without a blink. 'If you mean Robbie – yes, he did give it to me. What's wrong with that?'

'What's wrong? What's wrong? Because, boys don't give girls rings, me darlin', less there's somethin' between 'em. You got somethin' between you?'

Lizzie wondered why the cords in Mim's neck didn't just burst. 'Mum – you get so narky,' she muttered. 'Honest, you should see yourself.'

Mim's hand rose so swiftly that Lizzie was sure it would land on her face, but she didn't duck.

'Narky – narky, eh? Well, why shouldn't I be? That kid is *seventeen*, a young man – what's 'e doin' givin' a girl your age a ring?'

Blimey – that awful scowl – how hard it was not to

back off and run to the bedroom, slam the door as she had done when she was small. 'Well – if you must know, Mum – he *loves* me. And I love him. And the ring says that some day we're going to get married, to each other.'

Mim stared speechless into the big eyes that kept wide open into hers. 'Now I've 'eard everythin',' she murmured after a while. 'Bloody everythin'! So – in the meantime, you're 'is, an' 'e owns ya, an' 'e can do as 'e likes . . .'

'What do you mean – he *doesn't* own me, and I don't *own* him. And he doesn't *do* anything.' Lizzie raised her chin. 'We're just engaged.'

'*Engaged*, eh?' Mim's thin mouth arched upward so that the forgotten cigarette pointed to the ceiling. It seemed for an instant that she was going to burst into laughter. Then, with increased force, her scowl returned. 'Well, *I* know what 'e's up to, me li'le innocent. No doubt you've already let 'im do you over. Tell me – still a virgin, are ya? Or 'as 'e 'ad yer maiden'ead as well?'

This time Lizzie knew better than to listen. 'You've got a nasty, dirty mind, Mum. You know that? You should be ashamed of yourself.' She moved off, too fast for Mim to grab her back. It was childish to make for the bedroom, but there was nowhere else to escape what was coming.

'No, you don't!' Mim came after her like a bolt of aproned lightning and backed herself against the bedroom door. 'You're a fourteen-year-old kid, Lizzie 'Obbs – *my* kid, see. *I'm* the one what 'ad ya, an' what's goin' ta look after yer till yer old enough to look arter yerself. Un'erstand? It won't 'elp you none givin' me the big blue-eyed 'urt look. Not this time. You're goin' ter tell me eggsactly what you an' 'e done together – an' then you're goin' ter throw that ring in the dustbin – an' arter that, you're goin' ter stop seein' 'is 'ighness Rob Grover ever again outside of class. I'm goin' to talk to 'im 'isself, to Madame 'erself, and to that woman 'e lives with, the foster woman. Now . . .' Mim folded her bare, muscled arms across her chest. 'Shoot.'

Lizzie's eyes narrowed and her lips pressed shut. Not a word would she get out of her. She wouldn't even explain that all they'd ever done, she and Rob, was to kiss a lot, and cuddle, and sometimes lie close in the grass and hug and hug and maybe talk a bit about when they would be old enough to make love in a real serious way. Darling, good Rob – how dare Mum speak of him like this!

'Right – we'll stand 'ere all night, if yer like. I ain't ge'in' yer grub, an' I ain't even goin' back ter work till yer've spilled.'

Lizzie stiffened her shoulders, did not speak.

'I can stay 'ere all night – or, you can be'ave an' we can 'ave a jolly supper of bangers an' mash and be good mates.'

If only she didn't look so wiped out, Lizzie thought. If only I could just hate her plain and simple. The poor, worn-out scarred and chilblained hands with the cracked nails moved through her anger, taking away its support. She could feel her lids flutter, her stare breaking . . .

'All right, me love – yer've arst fer it!'

With a lunge so sudden that Lizzie almost fell under it, Mim grabbed at the hand with the ring on it and began to pull it off. 'Might as well give it to me,' she half-shouted, ' 'cause I'm goin' ter 'ave it off yer!'

There was no choice. Lizzie had to defend herself, to fight the hands off with all her strength. Her mother's muscles were suddenly like steel to her hands as she pushed at her, thrust at her.

'Fi'in' yer own mother! I never thought to see the day . . . Come on, give it me, or I'll bust yer one . . .'

Rage rose like a jet of fire inside Lizzie's hand. 'I'll bust ya right back, Mum – you're round the bend!'

'I am, am I?' Mim's palm landed with such a loud smack on the side of Lizzie's head that she thought a gun had gone off. She struck back automatically, as if something outside herself drove her hand, but it went wide of Mim and came down through the air, and when she hit out again,

Mim already had her other hand in a vice and had the ring off before she could get back her balance.

'Right,' said Mim. 'That's that. Now get an 'old on yourself an' set the table.'

Lizzie stood where she was, every part of her shaking. I'll never speak to her again, she thought. On Monday, I'll tell Robbie. If he wants, I'll run away with him.

'Come on, gel,' Mim called from the kitchen. 'No 'ard feelin's – I got ter do what's best for ya. I'm all yer've got. 'Sides, Bertie would 'ave backed me up, done the same. *You* know that.'

Bertie never would. Bertie would have stopped the row even starting. Bertie would have understood . . .

For a moment, Lizzie thought tears were coming at the back of her lids, there was a warm feeling there; but they didn't. Blinking, she moved with as much dignity as possible towards the bedroom.

'I said, set the table, darlin',' Mim called. 'Did ya remember it's me birthday tomorra'? *Thirty-bloody-two!* Would ya believe it? You won't mind if 'Arry takes me to the pub for a couple, will ya? You can watch 'is telly.'

Lizzie opened the door, went into the dim room, closed the door behind her. Reaching for the key, she found it gone. Mim had threatened to do away with it if Lizzie persisted in hiding herself in there. She flung herself onto the creaking bed, lay on her back, gazed at the crack-etched ceiling. Till Monday, she thought, till Monday . . .

# CHAPTER NINE

'No, sunbeam – we can't do no flit. It'd be barmy – it wouldn't be right for you.' Robbie kept kissing her, holding her, and Lizzie could feel that he wasn't just being sensible, like thinking of her age and what they would do or where they would go; he had a different kind of look when he gazed into her eyes, sort of far away at the same time as it was full of love.

'What are you thinking, Robbie?' she asked, as they lay in the grass in the park under a sun just like summer, with two colours of tulip-beds all around them and the songs of birds almost louder than the traffic beyond.

Rob pushed back the thick fringe of her hair for a better view of her upturned face, her clear yet puzzled gaze. 'Lizzie, love – I 'as to say this, but it *was* a daft thing to do, gettin' that ring. You got to see it like she would – 'ere she 'as all these plans for ya – works 'erself like a black and what do you do but come 'ome with a ring, sayin' you're "engaged" – an' to *me* 'oo she wants to think is up to somethin' nasty.'

Lizzie sat up, put her hands on his face. 'But I know you're *not*. Isn't it what we know is true that counts?' It was her turn now to push back the fringe of *his* hair that was cut even more like Mick Jagger's these days, which made him almost too dishy to bear. 'We got the right to be in love, Robbie, ain't we?'

'Lizzie,' he said, 'don't you twig? She wants better for you than *me*. I'm like what *she* knew, where she come from, if you know what I mean. I'm like goin' back. If I take you away from 'er, that's the end of 'er dreams for ya. She's got to do me in, don't ya see, or *she's* done in.'

Lizzie kept searching the dark-blue eyes with the little grey flecks, a great ache starting in her chest. 'What about me, Robbie? Ain't I got a say? I love you.'

Robbie grabbed her to him and they sank back, kissing as they'd never kissed before. Lizzie suddenly knew that fourteen going on fifteen wasn't being a kid any more. 'I'll never give you up, Robbie,' she whispered into his ear, 'and don't you ever go on like that again – there ain't no one better, and never will be!'

Rob leaned away a moment. His big mouth tugged side-ways. 'Blimey – do I want to believe that! Life without you, sunbeam, wouldn't be – life! Hey, that wouldn't be a bad idea for a song, would it?'

'Write it, Robbie. Maybe it'll be your first big hit.'

'Yeah – and you can make it Liza Lee's theme song!'

Lizzie's grin drooped. 'That ruddy name – don't even sound like meself. Don't know why she let 'em give it me . . .'

' 'Cause it sounds more like a star than Lizzie 'Obbs, and *that* matters more than 'er 'urt feelin's. See? All you's got to do now is open up your north-an'south and wow 'em, as they say State-side!'

'You'll be there, at the show, you'll be near . . .'

'You mean, in spite of the dragon? Well, of course – even she couldn't keep me away!'

Lizzie sighed. In that case, she thought, nothing would be so bad . . .

But it was. When the night came, and she was surrounded on all sides by the production staff, the crew, the musicians and other members of the show, when the size and splendour of the 'dressed' set bore down on her, when Tolly Doolican, so big and grand in his white satin suit, hugged her, smiled on her with such teasing humour, when she was dogged not only by Mum but the make-up people and all sorts of other men and women with note-books and last-minute directions and she became aware of the big studio audience, the great array of cameras and lights and the keyed-up excitement under the grown-up calm, when nowhere in all of this was there any sign of Robbie, or any chance that there would be, her smile became so stiff that she was afraid she would not be able to open her mouth to sing, let alone to let it 'roll out . . .'

'Bloody 'ell . . .' whispered Mim, 'you're gettin' stains under the arms – the bloody deodorant ain't doin' its job. Just 'old yer arms out a bit, no-one'll notice.'

'It'd be better if you left now, Mum,' Lizzie said through the stiff lips. 'I'm all right, I'll see you after.'

'That's another thing,' said Mim. 'I'll be right in front – you'll see me wave, so there's nothin' to be afraid of – pretend you're singin' just for me, eh?'

Standing outside the set in a sudden silence where everyone seemed to be caught into a sort of conspiracy to halt and freeze, Lizzie gave her mother a glance like that of a stranger. Her hair – piled up almost double the height of her face and head . . . the little beads of mascara like stage actresses wore for the footlights . . . the red satin dress trimmed with feathers and barely longer than her bum . . . the jagged red mouth with the fag stuck into it . . . This was her mum, who loved, her, who lived for her, who was all the family she had!

'Go on, Mum, will ya . . .' she whispered, with a soft push. 'I'll look for ya, honest.'

Mim shot her a sharp look from under the eyebrows. 'O' course you will!' She gave her a pinch on the chin that was meant to be soft but scraped Lizzie's skin like sandpaper. 'This is it, me ducky-dear. We're in the door at last. Now, sing like you never sung before. Show 'em, right?'

Lizzie's muted make-up gave her face a translucent glow. Her blue gaze struck through it in sharp contrast.

Only her expression seemed at odds with her youthful radiance. 'Right,' she said; and breathed out as her mother, with a wink and a lift of her thumb, retreated out of sight.

The show commenced. Its idea was to present Tolly, so famous for his relaxed manner, pleasant open face and charming, nostalgic voice, in a variety of different moods and backgrounds, with three guest stars and an all-girl trio imported from America, the Wonder Sisters. Lizzie was to be one of the guests, a complete novelty and surprise.

Lizzie saw how they 'primed' the audience first to respond to Tolly's entrance, so that it seemed that he must be the most beloved performer in all television. The band in the background joined in, smiling at him as they played his theme song, 'There's No Business Like Show Business', which he sang with an American accent. He then told some funny stories that made him seem a berk, though he still looked as though he loved himself. Then he introduced Derek Emerson, who did take-offs (not nearly as good as Robbie's), then a little lot of dancers came out, with almost nothing on, and knocked themselves out doing strange movements with their hips and breasts and looking at the audience with half-asleep eyes. (Lizzie was amazed at the way the cameras moved around, and was so interested in the *way* television shows were made, that she thought she might like to work in telly – so that was *another* possibility.)

Then another man came out, Biff Barraclough, a famous comedian from the North who joked with Tolly at such speed that Lizzie couldn't really hear the points, even though she'd heard them before at rehearsal. A lovely tall woman with beautiful big breasts and long dark hair came out next and sang something from an opera in a grand voice that made Lizzie want to hear more operas and feel that her own kind of singing was silly . . .

But the Wonder Sisters got her back to liking swing

again, and they were each so pretty and had such nice dresses . . .

At least Mum had had to listen about *that*. Mr. Pendy would not even let her *talk* to the Wardrobe people, and the blue silk dress she had on was the nicest she'd ever had: without looking lah-di-da posh, or like a kid, its closed-up top and swinging skirt made her feel just right for the first time ever . . .

Not that it would help if she made an arse of herself when she got out there and opened her mouth.

Oh, if only Robbie were there!

Suddenly, there was no more time for thinking about it or caring. Tolly was saying, 'And now . . .' and talking about someone called 'Liza Lee', and she was listening to all the ridiculous things he said about her – and the music began . . .

Emerging from the top of a staircase, she walked down quickly, smiling as she had been taught, and walked forward to the mike, which Mim said she didn't need, but which they insisted she use.

The damp patches under her arms turned wet, dripped down the inside of her arms. Although she *always* thought she wouldn't be able to make a sound come out – *this* time, she was sure of it. The place at the back of her tongue that led down to her throat had stuck tight. Her knees weren't even there, and the ground seemed to be coming up at her in waves . . .

And then, she thought of what she'd been taught, of Mrs. Sterling, Mum, Madame, Robbie – and it just came. And, once it started, everything went together, the music, the words, the movements, expressions – *and* all the right feelings.

It was even fun, in a kind of way, hearing the sound of her own voice, using the breath control to make the songs go soft or loud, as she wanted; to squeeze down to almost a whisper, to climb out of her diaphragm and rise higher

126

and higher, then stay there as long as she liked . . .

It was nice, too, seeing the interested looks on the faces watching her, so many of them, more than she'd ever sung for – and it wasn't many compared to all she couldn't see, who were out there by the thousands, maybe millions, listening, seeing her standing there and singing. Coo . . . That wasn't a good thing to think about . . . Soft at the knees again . . .

But the applause was so loud and long, that the feeling came back in them, and she was able to look out and smile and bow. Mim had wanted her to blow kisses the way she had done before Blatsky's, but Lizzie couldn't have done that now. She just raised her arms outward to the audience as if in humble thanks, smiled again – and suddenly, it was all over, and the show was on to someone else.

'That was wonderful, love,' David Pendy said. 'You were a smash. Let's talk further in the canteen . . .'

She wasn't even panting now, and the patches were drying up like puddles in sunlight. 'Thanks, Mr. Pendy – thanks very much.' She smiled at him happily. (Golly, as Jennifer would say, that's a relief. Now she could go back to being herself, find Robbie. I won't even care what Mum says – he's coming with us to the canteen!)

Only the fact was that when Mim suddenly appeared, caught up with her as she went to change, she knew at once by her expression that Robbie wouldn't be anywhere to find . . .

'I saw your friend in the audience,' Mim said, walking briskly along with her. 'I told him we was goin' to a party and to take 'isself off.'

Lizzie paused to look at her, her eyes, still dilated from the excitement of performing, shocked to blankness. 'You wouldn't – you *couldn't* . . .'

Mim grinned with one side of her mouth. 'Well o' course I would, and I did. I already told ya – 'e don't belong in your life. Sooner 'e gets the message, the better – for the both of ya.'

'Come on, Liza,' someone called. 'We've got some bubbly for you!'

'Bubbly, for "Liza", eh?' Mim's eybrows rose. 'Seems you made it, sweet'art. The next time I doubles yer fee!' Mim laughed cosily, took Lizzie's arm. ' 'Ow about a skip, like ol' times?'

'Mum,' said Lizzie. '*You* go to the party – I'm going home.'

'What? Like 'ell you are! You're comin' with me, an' you're goin' to stop actin' barmy over this cocky larikin once an' fer all. 'Ear me? What you got ahead of you ain't got no room for the likes of 'im. You're goin' straight up the ladder to the top, me love – *you're* goin' to perform fer the Queen!'

Lizzie jerked her arm away, started off in anger that had no special aim except escape – but the corridors were full of chatting, hurrying people in every direction who called out to her or just blocked her way. On top of that, she couldn't run off in the dress and shoes that weren't hers – and she didn't have any money for fares – and if she went home, Mum would come there, anyway . . .

And, not even Robbie would want her to go to him.

She slowed down. Mim caught up. 'Aw, come on, me ol' darlin',' she said. 'Let's not 'ave any more barneys over 'im. 'E ain't worth it. Let's just enjoy ourselves. I loves ya, ya know that. I'm proud as a peacock of what you did tonight. It was like seein' all me dreams come true before me eyes.'

Lizzie felt her arm taken again. It seemed impossible to thrust it off.

# CHAPTER TEN

It seemed to Lizzie that nothing after that night was ever the same again. With just two songs that took no more than five minutes to sing, she had become a 'celebrity'. Agents wrote to her offering to take on her career. Antonio was always running upstairs with messages that she should get in touch with this or that producer. 'Why don't you get in your own phone,' he grumbled to Mim, and that was just what Mim did.

Mim gave up one of her jobs and cleared off a space on the table and bought a big exercise book, and, fag in mouth, granny glasses on the end of her long nose, entered in the names of everyone who enquired, their addresses, telephone numbers and other of her own comments, such as 'sounds like a twerp, but bees-'n-'oney good.'

When Harry brought her down his old portable type-writer, Mim learned to type with two fingers and within a week was writing and answering letters.

Although Lizzie continued at Blatsky's, it was under-stood that she would be absent whenever she had a job, which was more and more often. She sang on radio, at the London Palladium, at the Olympic, on another Doolican show and in a spectacular on ITV, where she sang with the star herself, Shauna Lang.

'See what it says 'ere,' Mim had said, pointing to a write-up in the *Evening Standard*, ' "A natural. Sings from 'er 'eart, but with a true professional's discipline. It also doesn't 'urt that she 'as a gamine-like charm, a bit of a Cockney accent along with that inimitable radiance of youth. Should go far." Well, sod the Cockney bit – but that ain't 'alf bad, eh?'

Lizzie had made a sort of Stan Laurel face, shrugged. It had nothing to do with her; they might just as well have been writing about somebody else.

Mim didn't notice. She was on to the next thing, like a one-man-band. At least, she finally listened and agreed to use some of the money for herself. Grumbling at the cost of things not off a barrow, she bought some decent underwear, new shoes, a proper winter coat, a couple of Mary Quant-style dresses, and started to get her roots done at a hairdresser's . . . At times, to Lizzie's faint surprise, she saw that her mother *could* look smart, even if in an odd sort of way – but she could never understand why they were so unalike. Only in faint glimmers could she see past Mim's gipsy-like colouring to some angle or expression that related to her. If anything, it was easier to see Bertie when she looked into the mirror. He had had lightish blue eyes, and his complexion had been clear and light before the booze had turned it red and purple. Not that she could explain – Robbie didn't have a clue what either of his parents had looked like. What a strange, awful feeling it must be – no wonder he was so excited about getting noticed in the pubs and clubs, not doing take-offs of all kinds of other people, but being part of a group where he felt natural and fitted in as himself . . .

The school was so lonely without him, though. If it hadn't been for old Madame and Mrs. Sterling (even Mrs. S. was leaving soon to start on her own), she wouldn't have kept going; it would have suited Mim if she didn't but Mim did admit that if she stayed until her sixteenth birthday, she could claim she'd gone through school according to law, that no-one could call her an uneducated brat from the slums, which one famous singer whom she'd replaced in a show had done, to her face.

Lizzie would never forget Rob's last day. Everyone was

sad, but they knew it was a good thing, too, so they made him a huge square cake (chocolate – his favourite) with a guitar drawn onto it, and his name in big white letters, and Madame got up on the stage dressed in a splendid purple gown and made a speech about how he had 'endeared' himself to all the school, and how they wished him well, 'one and all', with whatever he did in the future. There was a lot of applause and a lot of people called out nice wishes – and then they asked him to sing and play, and Madame, doing her best to tolerate the 'appalling sound of modern music', sat and kept time with her old ringed hand on the arm of her chair and tapped her brocade shoe and nodded.

There was a lot of hugging and kissing – and then it was all over. Everyone went home. The lights were put out and Pete shut the place up, and she and Robbie ran together for the bus, kissed goodbye and made plans to meet the following Saturday.

Crikey, how she'd looked forward to it, dreamed about it, planned how she would look and what she would ask him – and how it would be when they could hold each other and kiss again . . .

The only trouble had been getting away from Mum for the afternoon. She thought and thought of different stories, different events that might convince her she wasn't seeing Robbie . . .

And, finally, it had come to her that there was no other way but to tell her the truth – and then not to let her stop her!

With her mind made up, it no longer seemed so big a step. After all, she was now taller and bigger than Mum; she was nearly sixteen; she had the authority of her success.

It was only a matter of when and how to do it without a barney.

A wonderful bit of luck happened. The men came to

131

deliver the new couch and to take the old one down to the street. That was Saturday morning. During all the commotion, with Mum directing them and giving them each a cuppa and pieces of her mind about the weather, the government, Lizzie shut herself into the bedroom and got herself dressed for meeting Robbie later, wearing jeans and a bulky sweater, a band in her hair, and plimsolls.

When they were all busy taking directions from Mum and staggering about making the exchange, Lizzie called out in a loud cheerful voice, 'Ta-ra, Mum – I'm going to the pictures with Robbie. Back for tea. See ya!'

The men all paused to smile, and she smiled at them and waved, threw Mum a kiss, and simply turned, before Mum could recover and say a word, and tore down the stairs and out onto Wardour Street.

Not daring to look back, she moved off at a near-run, wondering how she would fill in the next two hours. Oh, how Robbie would laugh when she told him.

After a while, she looked back. There was no sign of Mum, so she slowed down and began to browse in the various shops she passed.

Although it was cold, the sun was shining on plate glass windows and red buses and London looked freshly new as well as ancient and Lizzie felt at one with the light breeze, free, separate, a someone on her own. It was great fun to sit in a Lyons and have a bun and a cup of tea and pay for it herself. But, all the time, there was this deep feeling that simmered underneath that soon, soon, she would be with Robbie. Her heartbeat was like a secret message of anticipation. She could feel his arms, that had grown so big and muscular, close around her, the bigness of his chest when they hugged, the feeling of his mouth on hers . . .

' 'Ell . . .' she muttered under her breath, 'I'm as soft as all the slosh in movies and novels.' But, still, it was true . . .

At long last, it was time to walk along Leicester Square to the Empire. He would be waiting outside with that casual expression that didn't show at all what he was feeling, made her have to *know* that he was just as excited and glad as she was. He'd only say, 'Watcher,' or 'Hi, Lizzie.' But when they were seated and the lights went down, he would reach first for her hand, slowly squeeze it, hold it against his chest, then he would let it go and slide his arm round the back of her shoulders and draw her close to him . . .

She tried not to actually run. How nice that it wasn't raining or snowing, just breezy; that she could stroll up to him, perhaps one hand in the back pocket of her jeans, her hair blowing away from her face, lifting the fringe from her forehead the way he liked . . .

As she came up to the theatre, though, there was no sign of him. That meant that *she* would be there first, waiting for *him*. Which would be the first time; Robbie was always sort of anxious, ahead of time, and she was always the one to be a bit late.

Now, she had to stand about. She struck different poses, tried different expressions, studied them in the glass doors and decided she was better off being still and having no expression at all.

Time went by. Soon, the picture itself would be starting. Not that she minded being late for it; she couldn't have cared less if they missed the whole thing – as long as he was there with her.

As two became half-past, and half-past became three, Lizzie could no longer fight off the worry, the misery. Over and over she went through the various reasons why he might be late, or might not come at all. Could Mum have something to do with it? Although it was sure that she would if she could, it didn't seem likely.

Lizzie bit her lip, rubbed her arms, began pacing in frank distress that made the usher, theatre manager, box-office lady, keep looking at her. At least four times, some man tried to pick her up, and even one woman tried.

133

At quarter to four, Lizzie drew in a deep quivering breath, gave up, walked slowly away.

Looking back on that afternoon – when she was seventeen – Lizzie thought of it as the turning-point of their lives. It wasn't just that Robbie hadn't shown up. There had been a perfectly logical explanation for that, once all the facts were known – he had had this sudden opportunity to play with a group in a club in Coventry; because she hadn't been there when he rang her, risking confrontation with the ogre, he'd been forced to leave a message with Mim. The upshot of that was obvious: Mim hadn't given it to her. 'Slipped me mind,' she said later, 'arter the men left, I 'ad to go see this agent down Denmark Street – that's when I got you the special, remember?'

It was useless, at that point, to fume. When she got together with Robbie again, a week had passed, and it wasn't any use for him to fume, either. They had talked it over in a coffee bar. 'I'll be doin' this 'ere 'oppin' about from now on, sunbeam.' He'd held her hand even more tightly than usual. 'If we get known, we could 'ave work all over the country, wherever there's a pub or club will 'ave us. We're goin' to call ourselves the Roots – d'ya like it?'

'Not much,' she'd said. 'Sounds vague, square.'

'What, then?' He'd looked at her in the way that had made the girls at school squeal like stuck pigs.

'I dunno – how about the Grover Five?'

'Mmmm . . . Not bad. That'd get me name known, too, eh?'

So that, from that time on, had become the name of the group, which made her feel like it was part of her and Robbie, no matter where he went!

Robbie had told her that day about the other thing that was to change. Mum Grover, he'd said, couldn't have him practising when the small kids were asleep. There really wasn't room for his gear, and his hours disturbed Dad, who had to be up at five for his job at the brewery. Mum G. had told him there was no hurry but that it might be better if he found a place to live. After all, he was twenty, and much as she would miss him about the place, maybe it was time to be on his own.

Well, he'd said, she was right, of course. You couldn't hang onto people for ever just because they'd given you a home. Most kids, when they got older, *wanted* to leave, didn't they?

'So where are you going, and what are you going to do, Robbie?' Her heart felt tight. She so wanted to take care of him, look after him.

'Would you believe me luck? Pete, he's the drummer, 'as this old 'ouse in Muswell 'Ill and there's a room another bloke's just moved out of. It's a real mess, but we all muck in together and it ain't so bad. All of us, 'cept one – he's an artist, queer as a bent wire – are musicians.'

Lizzie smiled. She was pleased for him, but uneasy, too.

As if he knew what was on her mind, he hugged her against him, ran his hand back through her thick straight-cut long hair. 'Don't worry, love. I'll keep on the narrow. Don't appeal to me, all that stuff. Let them as likes it use it to their 'earts' content – me, I just want to work, to get the group goin', break through, make records, write me own songs.'

There was a shift of focus in his gaze, as if he was seeing something beyond her, that might include her but was not *just* her.

Why did she feel such sadness?

'Aw, lookit, Lizzie – nothin's changed between us. Never will. Only, we both got things to do, ain't we? You're already up there with the stars – you got to keep goin' up, up, up!'

'Hold on, Robbie, Why? Why have I got to do this up, up, up bit? Who says?'

'Ey, don't bite me 'ead off.' Robbie had looked baffled. 'Not just 'er. If that's what you mean. Or me. You got the talent, sunbeam. You're born to be great, don't yer see?'

Lizzie had looked at him, her lips tight. It was as if a lot of doors had slammed shut and locked behind her. Her breathing felt funny, cut off.

It was then that she had known that it was the turning point in their love; that much as they wanted to keep it forever, they would move away from each other, like two boats gliding off on different streams.

'Lizzie, love,' Robbie said, hugging her closer and closer, 'what you on about – we'll 'ave great times. You'll come to me gigs, we'll 'ave parties an' weekends, an' maybe get away for 'olidays. When we get the bees, we can do a bit of travellin', eh? – foreign climes an' such! Just picture it, sunbeam, no more grubbin', no more doffin' the cap – 'avin' good gear, cars, all the world knowin' yer, wan'in' to know ya. An' I'll be the proudest bloke of all, with Liza Lee, the marvellous Liza Lee, as me very own girl!'

She had given him a look something like Mim's when she raised an eyebrow. 'Did you forget?'

'Eh? Forget what . . .?'

'About being engaged, about marrying me?'

'Forget! You've got to be jokin'! Of course we're goin' to get married – soon as we've got a bit of bread together, soon as we're ready to settle down. That goes without sayin' – unless you've gone and changed your mind?'

'I haven't, Robbie.'

'Well, then. If you want the truth, sunbeam, I'd never marry no-one but you, can't even *picture* it!'

They'd kissed, very gently. Lizzie couldn't understand then why tears, the first ever since she was a small baby, came into her eyes.

Robbie had been right about one thing: she did keep on

getting more jobs, more notice. Mum seemed to have forgotten those endless auditions when no-one wanted her, and now sometimes had to turn offers down. Lizzie didn't ask her how she decided between one thing and another, because Mum made such a study of the pros and cons, and it took so long to explain them that it seemed best to leave it all to her. 'You do the singin' and signin', me love,' she'd say, 'I'll do the dirty work. There ain't no agent nor manager goin' to poke 'is nose in for 'is tenner. An' ain't no management goin' to put one over on Mim 'Obbs.'

The result of this was that Lizzie lived in a separate world of non-stop practising, rehearsing, performing, a sort of twilight place where the only glimpses of other ways of living were on the way to and from theatres, halls, studios, some near home, some in outlying parts of London, some in the provinces. Without the constant work with Mrs. Sterling, her vocal chords might have become strained, but she kept on at her breathing and pitch until her voice continued to strengthen and develop.

She didn't mind going to Mrs. Sterling's studio in Earl's Court, because it was full of plants and books and beautiful cats that sat and watched, and 'Cynthia' was so pretty and loving and gave her tea and real home-made cake when they were finished. Her lessons were like little islands set apart from the constant push of presenting herself, winning and pleasing audiences – but most important of all, a time when she could speak of Robbie, mention his name aloud, be listened to and sympathized with . . .

'It's so often this way, darling, with first love. I had someone I felt like that about . . .' Cynthia had sighed, looked down at the new wedding ring. 'I'm not saying that you and Rob won't be different. Your love may survive everything.'

'He says it will. But I hardly see him any more . . .'

'Do you write to each other? That sometimes helps.'

Lizzie had looked into the sparkly hazel eyes wistfully. 'Mum knows his writing. I'd hate it if she read his letters.'

'Surely she wouldn't.'

'She would, I'm afraid.' Lizzie had been able to smile; at least Cynthia knew what Mum was like.

'Then why not get him to write to you here – I'll be your go-between.'

'You will! Oh, that would be great!' Lizzie had rushed over and kissed her, upsetting a half-asleep cat from her lap.

'A pleasure, Lizzie. I'm fond of you both. By the way, you sure you don't want one of Desdemona's kittens?'

Lizzie shook her head so that her hair swung across her eyes. 'You don't know how much I want a kitten. Mum gave a little black one I brought home with me to some shop and I never saw it again.'

'How sad. Oh, dear. Well – you are travelling about a lot now, too. It doesn't really make sense to take on an animal, does it?'

'No . . .'

'Don't be downhearted – you'll have them some day, I'm sure. Meanwhile, you've got a marvellous career going. I'm so proud of you.'

Cynthia's help made a difference. For a while she and Robbie wrote endlessly to one another. Robbie wasn't articulate, and Lizzie knew it wasn't easy for him to write down the things he would have said. There were times when it was almost more agony to hear from him than not, when he didn't say something she longed for him to say, or said something that could be read in different ways. If he didn't use the word 'love', she worried for days. If he told her about his gigs and mates and seemed happy and optimistic, she felt left out, losing him for sure, but if he didn't have gigs or was disappointed or worried, then she wanted to rush to him with comfort and support.

For Rob, it was the same. Wherever he was, he wrote,

she was the centre of his life, the centre of his thoughts. He could manage anything if she was there and still loved him. He was thrilled with her successes, but until he did better than he was doing at present – the Grover Five didn't seem to be going anywhere, and there was talk of breaking up – he wouldn't be much good to her. Perhaps Madame had been right and he should have stuck with take-offs. Trouble was, he hated doing them now. What he wanted now was a really good quartet with the kind of music the Kinks were doing, only his own songs.

Lizzie thought of the Kinks with mixed feelings. Rob could do it – but if and when he did, where would she fit? Even if she gave up her whole 'Career', as people kept calling what she did, which she would be more than willing to do, wouldn't she be like all those girls who hung round the edges of the famous groups, someone to be a convenience, mostly in the way?

Anyhow, what would happen to Mum? She would have to consider that; Mum simply didn't have any other life at all. She didn't scrub floors, wait on table, or do the 'loos' (a smarter word for lavs) of business execs any more, and she didn't sit up all night sewing – but still she never stopped. She put herself into Lizzie's climb to fame with all her heart, strength, energy and time. Even Harry Org complained of her 'one-track' dedication. Much as he admired it, he felt she ought to have at least a bit of diversion, some outside interests of her own. 'What are you goin' to do if Lizzie gets 'erself spliced?' he'd asked once. 'Lizzie ain't goin' to get 'erself spliced,' she'd come back at him. 'Not until she's way up there, a world-famous star – maybe arter she's done 'er command performance.'

Harry had laughed and shaken his head, but Lizzie knew Mum meant it. 'You're daft, Mum,' she'd said. 'You don't think I'm going to be a *spinster*, do you?'

'I didn't say that, me darlin',' Mum said. 'You'll have your *romances*, bound to. But nothin' so as to knock ya off-course. 'Usbands, they get in the way. An' when it don't work out, you got to make up all the time you lost.'

'How do'you know all this, Mum? Where do you get your facts?'

Mim had raised one nicotine-stained finger, lowered her brows. 'Whatcha think I read them magazines for, eh? Been readin' 'em since before you was born. There ain't mor'n an 'an'ful of 'appy marriages with the big'uns. You ask me to name 'em – I will.'

'No, *thanks*.'

Lizzie had shut up. It had been another of those moments when the doors closed and locked behind her, and there was nowhere to go but on . . .

And 'on', at the age of eighteen, had been Mim's demand, made to David Pendy, relayed to those on high and accepted, that she should have her own spot – the *Liza Lee Show*.

'There you are,' Mim said. It proves you got to 'ave ideas and keep arter 'em. Now they decided to do it, you'd think *they* thought of it. Don't even want me suggestions.'

'I don't suppose you'd consider not making any?' Lizzie had said, 'or even asking me if I *want* to have my own show?'

Lizzie would always remember the look in her mother's face. In the very middle of anger too strange to describe, she had stopped, gone over to her where she stood by the phone that had brought the news, and held her thin, hard little body to her.

# CHAPTER ELEVEN

'She's made it. She's a star.' Kit Cameron raised a hand from his control panel, snapped his fingers, nodded to himself. Straining forward to study Liza in multiple version on the monitors as she wound up her first show with vibrant ease, his normally hostile expression had an inspired speculation. 'Well, well,' he murmured. 'Hmmm.'

Henry Marsh turned his grey head to him, eyed him with distaste. He did not even like working with him, let alone sitting beside him. He had despised him from the moment he had been lumbered with 'fitting him in somewhere' at the request of Ed Vaughan, Head of Light Entertainment. Not only had he been a thickly-bearded, long-haired drop-out with body odour and bad breath, but also challengingly aggressive towards any sign of resistance from the establishment. His deep-set, knowing dark eyes were like scanners, alert for discrimination, ready to assert the right of rebellion, to attack the very implication of aversion.

'I'm sorry, Henry. I do apologize,' Ed had said, explaining the situation to him in confidence. The story was that Alister Cameron, Kit's father, had rescued Ed from poverty and despair at the end of the war, lent him money, housed him and helped him find work. The Camerons were wealthy landowners with a great Georgian house in Dorset, whose main interest was farming and horses. They were, according to Ed, fine people who brought up their four children with the best of values and examples, spared no expense on education, gave them everything

141

they wanted that was within reason. But, gradually, with the youth protest, instead of gratitude, their children began going 'astray'. One of the daughters went off to live in London with a boy they had never met, another got expelled from college for smoking cannabis, and Kit had started wearing filthy clothes, growing his hair to his shoulders, deriding everything his father said or the family stood for, condemning his father for fighting in the war, mocking the comfort in which the family lived, refusing to go back to university, constantly urging his youngest sister to defy their mother's conservative training and 'do her own thing'. One night, at a formal dinner party of County people, Kit had come to dinner in tight, raunchy jeans, farted and picked his teeth. No-one said anything then, but Alister had had to decide on a final confrontation. Before he could do so, Kit had packed up some of his clothes, taken some money from his mother's handbag, and driven off in one of the helps' Minis.

Despite their heartache, the Camerons had resigned themselves to Kit being gone, making it in his own way, or not. Christmas came and went with not a word from him. Then, suddenly, in the middle of the night, there he was at the door. No regret, no explanation, no apology; he had simply wanted some money, and a letter to someone at the BBC so he could get a job. That, he said, was what he had decided would 'suit' him. Dad could help him – with that chap he knew there, who was some sort of big-wig now.

'The rest, Henry,' Ed explained, 'is obvious. The lad came to me with a letter from Alister. What could I do? You must bear with me, do what you can. If it's utterly impossible, if he's of no use whatever, I'll simply sack him. At least I'll have given him a chance.'

The rub, of course, was the fact that Kit wasn't absolutely impossible. If he could rouse himself to be in on time, if he wasn't so involved with some new girl, or taken up with Anna Croft, Ed's secretary, to the extent that he turned up half drowned in sexual fatigue and could hardly remember his name, *if* he actually studied the technicalities of what was wanted with even a quarter of his brainpower without the haze of pot or alcohol, he had a moderately keen mind, some last-minute creativity that precluded putting in the final boot.

Now, by the thinnest skin of his teeth, Kit was an associate on the production staff – but everyone was watching, waiting, hoping, that his next lapse would be the last. The trouble was that Kit was well aware of this. In the rise of Liza who, like almost all females, for reasons Henry could never decipher, was becoming vulnerable to him, Kit was seeing his possible salvation.

People were getting up, moving about, discussing the success of the *Liza Lee Show*, the wonders of this eighteen-year-old girl who had the professionalism of an old vet, who could handle herself in every facet of hosting and starring in what was a substantial production, and emerge utterly delightful, appealing, and, yes, sexy, too, with her peek-a-boo fringe, big eyes and little mini skirts . . . 'A great find', 'Great future . . .' were some of the comments Henry overheard as he walked out of the control gallery.

'Mind if I don't hang round, Henry?' Kit said, moving alongside him. 'There's something I've got to do.'

Henry glanced at him before answering. The beard had been trimmed for this 'something', he thought, the black wavy hair actually washed, the usual un-ironed shirt replaced with a clean high-necked tunic covered with braid – but now, more than that, the speculative look in the dark eyes had a sharper gleam.

His own ruggedly-assembled features hardened. He could, of course, say that there was some clearing-up work to be done, use his authority to stall that purpose. But that's all it would be, a postponement of what seemed maddeningly inevitable.

'Okay,' he said. 'But a word of warning.'

'Oh, yes?' The liquid-dark stare came at him in direct confrontation; one of the long-nailed thumbs hooked into the back pocket of the hipster jeans.

'It comes from Ed.'

'Oh, yes?'

'In regard to Miss Lee. Watch it.'

Kit leaned away. The eyes had become scanners again, hostile, accusing.

'Watch what? What's he talking about?'

Henry shrugged. 'I thought you would know. I'm only the messenger.'

Kit pulled at an ear with traces of dirt in its rim. 'Christ. Now even my personal life is on the line.' He gave Henry a penetrating look, slowly shook his head. 'Anything else?'

'No. That's it.'

Kit pointed a thumb upward. 'In that case – see you tomorrow morning.'

Henry watched him stride off down the corridor, depressed by helplessness. It had been a pretty feeble stab, the strategy of a coward, and though not untrue, he had probably used Ed's name in vain. There was only one remaining hope of escape from the revitalized, upgraded and permanent presence of Kit Cameron . . .

Henry found himself smiling obliquely.

It was a sad and desperate hope that didn't say a lot for the authority of an illustrious organization – but, there it was; for once, he was forced to put his money on that indomitable little guardian of Liza's destiny. If anyone could save them, Liza most of all, it was the one known to the studio as 'the hell-hag'.

'I'm sorry, Kit,' Lizzie called. 'I'm taking off my make-up.'

'I don't care – let me in.' Kit turned the handle of the dressing-room door, opened it, and found himself face to face with Mim Hobbs.

144

' 'Ere,' she said, 'what do you think you're doin'? You 'eard what Lizzie said.'

Kit could never believe his ears when he met with the actuality of Liza's mother, or his eyes. Tonight, her hair was a leaning tower of brass-coloured falls. She wore thick false eyelashes, a silver mini-dress, silver boots to her knees, a huge jewelled medallion on a chain, several assorted rings on her bony-knuckled fingers.

He frowned at her. 'Liza,' he called, 'let me come in.' Over Mim's shoulder, he could see Liza's cream-covered face looking at his reflection in the mirror, her eyes above her smile, like brilliant pools of blue.

'It's all right with me, Mum,' she said. 'Come on in, Kit.'

' 'E can wait,' Mim said, switching her fag from one side of her red mouth to the other. 'Like the others.'

Kit looked about, and became aware that he was not the only one waiting for Liza. He shoved a thin hip against the door jamb, forcing Mim to move back. 'It's me she's got a date with,' he said. 'Right, Liza?'

'No. It ain't right, my friend. Lizzie's got more important plans tonight. She's goin' to a special party.'

'To which I'm escorting her, Mrs. Hobbs.' Kit gave her a flash of his bright teeth. 'Naturally, I'll see that you get a taxi. Liza and I will put you in it, won't we, Liza?' he called.

Lizzie looked at them both in the mirror. 'That all right, Mum?' She went on creaming her face, removing make-up with the tea-towel Mum always provided for the purpose.

Mim turned for a moment, met Lizzie's eyes in the mirror. 'Is that what you want, to send me 'ome by meself, when I've been arst too? Is that what you want, me love?'

'Come on, Mrs. Hobbs. That's blackmail.' Kit pushed her easily aside now, and walking into the small square room, pulled up a straight chair nearby, sat gazing at Lizzie, his dark eyes, caught into the brilliance of the lights, eloquent with new intensity. 'You were stupendous,' he said in a soft, low voice. 'You took everyone by storm, even the old die-hards.'

Lizzie looked at him with a scrubbed face. She seemed no more than twelve. 'I don't know why,' she said. 'I suppose it's all the hard work – since I was two. Mum's training . . .' She turned to Mim, standing with a stiff, uplifted face by the door Kit had thrown shut behind him. 'Don't be daft, Mum,' she said. 'If you feel like that, *of course* I want you to come. You know that.'

'If you say so.' Mim's nostrils were pinched, her plucked eyebrows almost to her hairline. 'I only aim to please.'

'Oh, Mum.' Lizzie smiled at Kit. 'Of course she's coming, Kit. We always go together, to everything. Mum's not just my mum, she's my manager, my agent, my right-hand man – aren't you, Mum?'

Kit pulled at his ear, barely stemming the words of his accelerating impatience, as the two of them grinned in accord.

He got up, patted Mim's shoulder. 'Delighted to have you aboard,' he said, 'absolutely *delighted*.'

'No need to be sarky.' Mim jerked at her shoulder. 'You goin' like that? It's a formal do, you know.'

'Mrs. Hobbs, if appearances concern you to that extent, you'll be pleased to know that this is a Nehru jacket, fashionable, appropriate, and purchased for the occasion over my own dead body.'

Lizzie giggled, as she applied normal make-up, quickly, deftly.

'I don't care what ya call it, you still look more like an 'ippie. I don't un'erstan' you nobs . . .'

'Mrs. Hobbs. I'm neither a hippie, nor a nob. If you insist on stereotyped assumptions, just call me revolting . . .'

'What?'

'From my own class. I much prefer yours, in fact.' He met her hard gaze with a playful smile. It was almost fun,

146

he thought, watching her reach for one of her Cockney barbs, without success.

'Me Gawd – what are you on about? What in the world does Lizzie want with the likes of you, when there's 'alf a dozen proper gents arter 'er?'

'Mum – please.'

'An' I 'ope you ain't got no idea of droppin' me off when the party's done.' Mim eyed him shrewdly. 'Eh?'

Kit tilted his head, stroked his beard with mock humility. 'What a thought; dear, dear.' He raised his head as if inspired. 'But what a good one! Thank you!'

There was a groan of exasperation from Lizzie. 'Pack it in, you two. You'd think I didn't exist. Anyway, I'm ready. Let's go. And, Mum, no deals tonight – give it a rest.'

'She *has* put in a frantic week, Mrs. Hobbs,' Kit added.

'Kit – shut up.' Lizzie straightened the white lace tights that led up her long slim legs to a white lace mini with false satin pockets and long loose sleeves, shrugged into a short white down coat, put on large tinted glasses, gave her thick straight hair and fringe a final push for height. 'Come on, or they'll sweep us out . . .'

'Yum-yum,' Kit said, catching her and kissing her ear above the diamanté hoops, swiftly cupping one breast, sliding a hand to her pertly-compact bottom, 'you're *unbelievably* delicious.'

Lizzie frowned, shook her head at him, indicating Mim who had stopped dead to stare.

'What does it matter?' he said. 'She knows. Don't you, Mim?'

'What do I know?' Mim's eyes were no longer guarding unreined hatred. 'That you're selling your wares bloody fast, that's what. You ain't got no clout in this studio – 'oo d'ya think you're foolin' – 'cept Lizzie?'

Kit laughed softly in triumph. 'That's better,' he said. 'Now we've got it out into the open. It's now completely obvious that you can't bear the fact that your daughter might be in love – it doesn't matter a damn that it's *me*. You're not going to let *anyone* have her, are you?'

Mim's eyebrows were much slower than usual in their rise.

'You think Lizzie's in love with ya, do ya?' Mim clutched at her evening bag like a small, potential weapon. 'That, me friend, is a laugh. I bet you wouldn't dare ask 'er, 'erself, 'ere, in front of me, this very minute.' She stared into his eyes, matching their gleam in unblinking challenge.

'Mum – Kit . . . People can hear you. I'm going on . . .'

Lizzie moved past them, out of the door into the corridor, but Kit was suddenly beside her. He scooped her up into his arms, kissed her on her mouth. 'Tell her,' he said. 'Tell her. Let's get it settled.'

Lizzie drew away, looked up at him, pressed a finger to her lips as if in exploration. 'Oh, Kit – don't. Not this way. I'd *have* to say I don't know . . .'

'You see!' Mim came out to them, closed the door of the dressing-room behind her. 'You got 'er confused, that's all. You'd do be'er to stick with that dolly-bird of Ed Vaughan's.'

Kit almost forgot Liza. As she walked off down the hall, protected by the come-and-go of other people, he straightened from his casual slouch, stood tall and completely immobile, staring at Mim.

Standing her ground, raising her chin so high that her tower of hair seemed to sway, Mim stared back at him.

Both of their faces were relief-maps of full-scale war.

# CHAPTER TWELVE

'Well, darling, we did it.' Kit sat close to Lizzie, as the train pulled out of Waterloo, put his arm through hers, clasped her left hand in his. 'By the time she twigs, we'll be half way to Dorset. Nothing she can do – for once!'

Lizzie stirred uneasily. On the one hand she was excited, on the other, guilty. She was still, after a month of his pursuit, uncertain of what she felt for Kit, afraid of what lay ahead, yet so intrigued and full of anticipation that she knew she could not have said no to going to meet his family, could not have turned back. It was as if she were divided into two people.

'You look terrific, love. They'll think they're going to see this glammed-up star, the way you look on telly – and there you'll be, a fresh-faced girl with natural blonde hair, wearing denims.' He lifted her hand. 'My grandmother's opal and diamond ring is going to look just right on this little finger.' He lifted her ring-finger, gave it a gentle reverent kiss.

Lizzie thought of another ring with an opal, of Robbie. If only he wrote more often, if only he came to London more often, if only she wasn't always rushing from one show or rehearsal to another . . . Yet looking at Kit now, she found him very attractive in a way that was so different that it wasn't like going away from Robbie, not like being unfaithful; even when she was kissing Kit, feeling thrills go through her body, it changed nothing . . .

She looked down at her finger, imagining the ring on it, imagining being properly engaged, not with a little

149

Woolworth ring but with big real gems she could show to everyone and hear them say, 'Oh, how lovely, congratulations . . .'

Her freshly-washed hair, sparkling in the June sun that came muted by dust through the train window, fell forward over her face, and she could not say anything to Kit, neither to deny what he wanted, nor to confirm it. She loved Robbie, always would. The knowledge was like a backdrop to everything that was happening . . .

'God, I hope you like them,' Kit said. 'They'll be like foreigners to you. They are to me. I never would have realized my fate if I hadn't had a chance to cut loose. And, of course, if the Americans hadn't led the way. Thanks to them, one has escaped. I don't suppose you know what I mean, or what I'm talking about – but it doesn't matter.'

Lizzie shook her head, smiled, and turned her gaze to the brown-green undulating countryside. 'Blimey . . .' It was all so beautiful, so much more real! She felt as if she was breaking out of a dark shell, as if she had never ever seen the world she was living in. She was beginning to feel, now, as the train rushed forward with such zest and power past towns, stations, ever-changing scenery, that she was moving into life, ordinary life, as other people lived it . . .

Her eyes felt stretched by her anticipation; it was difficult to keep her lips closed, not to look like an open-mouthed idiot in that image coming back to her in the window.

'I'm not presenting you for approval, darling,' Kit was saying. 'I don't want you to feel for one moment that I give a hoot for what any of them think – I already know how they think, what they think about. They are entirely predictable. All I care about is you, what you think, if you feel you can stand being married into this clan. One could just ignore them – that's the alternative. But I want you to be comfortable, not isolated with me. Understand?'

Lizzie thought she did, but it was new material. Her

thoughts kept sliding back to Mim, to Soho, to Madame, and Mrs. Sterling; to Bert, to Robbie; to the endless rounds of performances since she was born. 'Thank you, Kit,' she said. 'I just can't see what you want *me* for. There must be hundreds of girls better for you than me. I . . . Well, I just don't know anything, do I? And I don't even speak right, yet.'

He looked into her eyes as if she had just made statements of utter enchantment. He seemed not to be able to take his eyes from hers.

Lizzie felt herself swing against the rhythm of the train, dip, somehow drown in those deep dark eyes. Gawd, perhaps she was just as much in love with him as he seemed to be with her! Wouldn't it be loverly – like Eliza's song – if they were really right for each other, despite all Mum's carrying-on? After all, what could she know of feelings like these? Poor Mum . . . No wonder she hated Kit so much, she was fighting for her life, her dream. If I marry Kit, Lizzie thought, that's it, for Mum, curtains . . .

'You're worrying, angel,' Kit said. 'I can feel it. Don't – your mum is tougher than old boots. A survivor. Once we're an accomplished fact, she'll come right round, join us. You'll see. People adapt, Liza, they adjust – when they *have* to.'

Lizzie kept her eyes on his face. She wanted to believe him. 'Mim will have to share your management with me. Eventually she'll *want* to take a back seat. We'll make an unbeatable team, my dearest, unbeatable!'

Lizzie's lips pressed inward. She thought he looked a bit like Christ, like the paintings in the galleries, in the church in Soho Square. Now that he had clean hair, wore a clean white shirt with the collar turned up like a frame for his bearded face, she was overwhelmed by him. Could this splendid bloke *really* want her so much?

Up and down, her feelings went, like the hills going by. Perhaps she was being ridiculous, gullible, naïve, just as

Mum said, the way Henry Marsh hinted, the way all the staff and workers seemed to indicate when they looked at him or spoke to him. *Why* wasn't he liked? It couldn't *just* be the way he used to dress, before he started taking an interest in her . . .

'Suppose I wasn't a singer, suppose I didn't have no . . . any, of this talent, couldn't perform at all? Suppose I was a flop and the critics wrote me off, and there were no more shows, and I was just no-one . . .'

He frowned, put a finger on her pink soft lips. 'Don't be ludicrous, Liza, love. I'd adore you if you were an absolute nonentity, if you'd never sung a note – if you'd never been near an audience. I value people for what they *are* – that's the whole point. Don't you see that at all?'

Her long fair lashes glinted as they lowered. ' 'Course . . . I do, really. Sorry . . .'

'Oh, sweet Liza . . .' He hugged her close to him. 'You must get away from that mother of yours and find out what a wonderful person you are.'

Lizzie lifted her eyebrows, that also glinted now as the train swung round a bend into the strengthening sun. 'Mmmm,' she murmured.

For a while, now, neither of them spoke. Lizzie tucked a leg under her, moved from the weight of his arm, murmuring, 'Hot . . . What weather . . .' and stared out of the window. Kit lit a cigarette, picked up his paper and magazines.

Lizzie knew there were many, many things Kit was interested in that he didn't discuss with her, the state of the world, the Vietnam War, the outcome of the General Election, a man called Mr. Dubcek and the Communist Party, the nuclear bomb that the French people had exploded in the Pacific, the troubles starting in Ireland, all sorts of 'protests' about all sorts of things. He got grim and bitter when he read, when he talked about what he read. She didn't like that, but if she was to consider being married to him, she would have to get used to it . . .

It was so much more fun talking to Robbie. She loved his funny, blunt way of saying things, his cockiness that covered up his need of her, the kind of mateyness and understanding he made her feel when he shared his confidences and hopes with her . . .

Perhaps 'Roots' *would* have been a good name for his group. He was her roots – like Mum was . . .

Lizzie could not put aside the nag of anxiety. Suppose Effie did die, and their escape today while Mum was at the hospital came like another terrible shock when she got back to the flat? Oh, Gawd. Much as she saw what a nuisance Mum could be, and how right Kit was that she had to stand up to her and live her own life, she couldn't just leave her all alone, not with no-one there to comfort her. After all, Alf not being her real father, Mum wouldn't have no-one left of her own – except *her* . . .

'You've gone very quiet,' Kit said, running a finger along her arm. 'Not nervous still?'

Lizzie turned to him. His eyes had the kind of glow that went with the cigarettes he smoked. She knew they were 'grass', could by now recognize the smell; not that it mattered. Mum was barmy to think it did, old-fashioned in spite of her sharp wits. It even made Kit nicer in some way, not so pushy.

'No . . .' She looked into the dark eyes, her image of Mum going floaty and dim, like the fading reflection of a light bulb behind the eyelids.

He threw aside an article on the 'demise of communes', drew her to him, and as if they were alone in the carriage, kissed her on the mouth. 'Christ,' he whispered, 'I can't wait to get you between the sheets.'

As usual, when he spoke like this, Lizzie almost shuddered. What would it be like? She had sort of known, with Robbie, even if they'd never actually done it. But with Kit . . .

153

'Don't worry,' he'd said, when he'd guessed. 'You'll be in safe hands,' and he'd smiled at his own wording.

As his hand covered her breast under the denim jacket, she kept her eyes closed to savour the feel of it . . .

Oh, yes – surely it was all going to be all right.

'Well, we're getting near, Liza – Clagdon's next.'

She opened her eyes quickly, sat up. Beyond the window there was nothing to be seen but the vivid green countryside, a cow or two standing about, hardly pausing in their grass-munching to note the passing train, not a house anywhere, even a barn.

Kit laughed softly. 'I told you – it's hardly a stop, let alone a station.'

When they got off onto the platform, Lizzie looked along it in silent astonishment. It ran for only a short way; both sides of the tracks ended abruptly in fields dotted with yellow dandelions, and buttercups, white daisies. As the train pulled away and rushed off into the distance, there was not a sound except the moo of a cow, the call of invisible birds.

'Cooo . . .' said Lizzie. If it hadn't been for the board saying CLAGDON, she'd have thought it all a play or film.

'Where in hell's Marwick?' Kit threw his cigarette on the cement, kicked it to the tracks. 'Typical.'

Lizzie stood still, drinking in the stillness, the clean, fumeless air, the smell of the meadows, the unbroken blue of the sky. It was like being gently washed, touched with loving hands. 'How lovely . . .' she breathed.

Kit hardly noticed. 'Probably at some horse show or auction – always immersed in the bloody horses.'

How could anything be 'bloody' in a place like this? Lizzie thought, and particularly horses, though she was a bit scared of them up close.

'Ah! At last. And, of course, with the dogs. Be prepared to get covered in slobber and hairs.' He picked up their

154

bags, gave her an off-centre smile. 'Here we go – into the waist-high shit. I wouldn't do this for anyone but you, my love.'

Lizzie did not even try to follow his meaning. As the big, mud-splattered black car wound its way towards them and drew up, she felt the absence of Mim like a missing shell. She had never really faced any situation on her own before, never dealt with other people without her intervention. It was good – yet frightening, almost like doing a performance with Mim nowhere in sight to urge her on, to force her not to cut and run . . .

Suddenly, she was conscious of herself as a person apart from her mother's image of her, apart from making images to match other people's expectations, so that applause and approval were made safe and sure. The fact that Kit said she didn't look like these images today was like dreams she had had of being naked in the street, unable to cover herself . . .

'Don't be shy, Liza,' Kit was saying, 'you're a *star*. Remember – it's what *you* think of *them* that counts.' He gave a jerk of his bearded chin to urge her forward, a wink to make her smile.

Lizzie did what she always did, pulled herself together, got ready to estimate her audience and play to them according to their expectations.

To her surprise, it was not a chauffeur who jumped out of the car, but a large, dark-haired, ruddy-faced man in a checked shirt, baggy tweed jacket and riding breeches. He had the brightest dark eyes and the jolliest smile she had ever seen. There was no need to contrive one of her 'irresistible' smiles; she could not have helped smiling back at him in the same way, as if they already shared an affinity.

'Hello, there,' he called. 'Sorry to be delayed – one of the horses bolted from the van.' As the dogs inside the car barked after him, their heads crowding the half-open window, he strode up to the platform, gave Kit's shoulder an affectionate press, extended his hand to Lizzie. 'Hello, Kit – and this must be Miss Lee. How do you do? Pleasure to meet you.'

Lizzie felt her hand gripped and released in one quick movement, and any uncertainty as to her welcome vanish. 'How do you do?' she said, tossing the glinting fringe from her eyes. 'Did you catch the horse?'

He laughed easily, showing strong yellowed teeth, two or three gold fillings. He didn't talk or act like a nob, Lizzie thought, but who else would have the gold?

'Ah, yes.' He gave her a quick nod, patted his pocket. 'Young Roy's addicted to sugar.'

At the word 'addicted', it seemed to Lizzie that Mr. Cameron's eyes shifted away from Kit, who stood waiting impatiently for the niceties to conclude.

'Let me help you,' Alister Cameron said to his son, reaching for a bag.

Kit shoved off and past him. 'Where's Marwick?' he said.

'Oh holiday – always, in June. You know that.'

'I prefer to forget. Where's Mother?'

'Getting the tea. Priorities. New girl can't master the brew.'

Despite Kit's muttered 'Christ . . .' Lizzie shared his father's smile without knowing what the conspiracy was. As he escorted her to the car, she wanted to put her arm through his; he seemed like Bert somehow, in another version. Such a silly feeling; she would have to control it.

When the dogs' faces withdrew, there was a clear view of another passenger in the back seat of the car, a girl of her own age, with long dark hair, a long, narrow face like Kit's, gold-rimmed glassed, an expression of careful reserve.

'Brenna, our youngest,' Alister Cameron said. 'Miss Lee, dear.' He moved aside for Lizzie to get into the back seat with her.

Brenna nodded. 'Hello.' She lifted a slim tanned hand with dirt under the fingernails. Wearing a shirt similar to her father's but with the sleeves rolled up and blue jeans, she shifted to make room for Lizzie without changing her expression.

Lizzie smiled at her, but she seemed preoccupied with the dogs. 'Do lie down, Martha, Jason – Dad, did you have to bring them? The car smells like a kennels. Kit, shove them onto the floor.'

The blond Labradors, tongues hanging low, but lips lifted with ingratiating grins, continued to monopolize the front seat between Alister Cameron and Kit. Lizzie stifled a smile, it was amazing to see Kit allow them to shoulder him almost to the door, to give him ardent tongue-swipes of welcome.

'They'll be all right, Bren,' he said. He leaned his arm out of the window to accommodate them, swivelled to glance at Lizzie. 'Okay, love?'

'Yes, thanks. What beautiful countryside,' she said, aware that she was guarding against any lapse of grammar. 'I've never been to Dorset before.'

'It is beautiful,' Alister Cameron said. 'At this time of year, it must be the prettiest part of England.' He smiled at her in the rear-view mirror. 'Do you like horses?'

'Oh my God . . .' murmured Kit, as if to himself.

Alister Cameron was only slightly disconcerted. 'Don't mind him. *Do* you?'

'I don't really know. I've never had anything to do with them. I've always lived in the city and been in the theatre. But I love animals so *much*, I'm sure I'd like horses – they look so sweet. I once knew a copper – a policeman – who used to let me pat his horse . . .'

Brenna gave a sudden laugh, almost a grim sound, but she seemed to soften, relax, look at Lizzie directly for the first time. 'I've got a real poppet you can ride, called Jessie. Right, Dad? She won't make a move until you tell her. She's so safe even children ride her.'

'Happens to be ancient and senile,' Kit said. 'But never

157

mind.' He glanced at Lizzie again, winked, then looked at his sister. 'You still mucking out? Why haven't you gone to Art School, got away?'

Brenna frowned, shook her head, put a finger to her lips.

Lizzie felt a kinship with her that she couldn't place. What did Kit want of people? Why shouldn't Brenna want to be in her own home, working with horses, if that was what she liked?

'Yes, Jessie's just the right one for you to start on,' Alister Cameron was saying as he swung the car right, and into a long line of big trees that to Lizzie seemed to go on forever. 'Well, Miss Lee, you'll soon see the house. It's not as grand as it used to be – taxes and upkeep too heavy – but it has Georgian grace, as I'm sure you'll agree.'

Georgian, thought Lizzie; she would look that up in the dictionary as soon as she got home. She should have done so sooner – now she would seem a dunce.

'It's as obsolete as the dodo,' Kit said. 'It should be sold, or turned into a school, or something that serves humanity at large. It is nothing but capitalist indulgence, keeping people like the Camerons in unearned affluence while the rest of the world goes hand . . .'

'What do you mean, unearned?' said his father, almost stopping the car. 'I've worked every day of my life, and what I do keeps *many* people employed. We, your mother and I, have used every penny left us for right and good purposes. You ask the tenants, you ask the help, you ask anyone who works for us – we work together, we produce, we are productive. What more do you want? Don't you, in the long run, come bleating back to us for subsidy? Can you manage without the reliable people, like us, who keep on slogging away, with integrity, paying our bills, employing people in a responsible way? What on earth do you want, Kit – communism?'

Kit stared at him with a smile. 'To argue with you, Father, is like talking into the void. You are beyond ears.

You are set in the cement of obsolescence. You are also treacherous . . .'

'Kit,' said Brenna. 'Please.'

Lizzie lowered her head. In a dim sort of way, she was understanding both Mr. Cameron and Kit. She didn't know anything about it, though she wished she did, wished that her mind wasn't like all that earth before the seeds in it had started to grow – oh, where had she been, what had she been doing all her life that there was nothing sensible or intelligent she could say, or even think about this? She only wanted it to be all right, not to become dark and shadowy, so that this lovely place was dimmed and spoilt . . .

'Son,' said Alister Cameron, 'I understood that this weekend was an occasion to meet your friend, Miss Lee. That, and that alone. Your mother and I have adapted our thoughts to this idea. We greet her. We are pleased she is here. Above all, though it may be impossible for you to accept, we only want what you want for yourself.'

With the sudden sight of the great sprawling pink-brick house surrounded by graceful trees and assorted patterns of colour-splashed flowerbeds, Kit became abruptly silent, his chin sinking against his bare chest in some private reaction and speculation.

Brenna and Alister Cameron turned to Lizzie with the renewed welcome of relief. 'You mustn't be dismayed, my dear,' said Kit's father, with a quick, jaunty smile, 'you know how it is with families – nothing's easy. Many conflicts. Many complexities. The times, inevitable change, one does one's best, you know.'

'I'm sure . . .' Lizzie wanted to hug him the way she had done Bert. He looked so lost, so cuddly. 'Don't worry about me,' she said. 'I'm just so happy to be here.'

'Well . . . Gosh, my dear – we're happy to have you here. Aren't we, Brenna?'

'Yes.' Brenna cast Kit an apprehensive glance, then turned quickly to Lizzie. 'I'll show you round, if you like. I

159

mean, everything. It's really a super place. And I want to hear all about your life – I couldn't believe it when Kit said he was bringing Liza Lee for the weekend. I mean, I saw your special show, and you were absolutely marvellous – even Mummy said so, and she absolutely detests television. We probably seem awfully stupid and dull to you . . .'

'Oh, no!' Lizzie couldn't believe what Brenna was saying. 'Dull! It's me that's dull! Cripes – I've never been anywhere like this, nor met anyone like you!' She stopped her hand creeping to her mouth and pressing it. (Would she never learn? 'When you don't know what you're talking about, me darlin' – keep yer trap shut!')

'It's all relative, I suppose. But I'm sure I'd never find what you do dull. Anyway – those are the stables, as you can see. And the garages. And where we keep the tractors and such.'

'Those,' said Kit, waving a hand towards some gently rising hills behind the house, 'are cows. Mother breeds a certain variety, from which she gets considerable profit.' Kit giggled vaguely, and Lizzie realized the smoke on the train had not yet worn off.

'Not that much,' said his father, with a scowl, as he pulled the car into the manure- and straw-littered brick-walled yard where the big dark eyes of horses could be seen gazing out at them over stable doors. In one corner, a stocky young woman in jeans and shirt was grooming a large sable-coloured horse that pricked up its ears and whinnied as they all got out of the car.

'That's one of the summer help – and that's Jessie,' Brenna said, going over to the animal and nuzzling it. The groom stood back, smiling politely.

Lizzie loved the way Brenna did that. What a great person to know, to have as a friend . . .

'Come and say hello to her,' Brenna called. 'She won't kick you, or anything.'

'Come on, Bren – there's plenty of time for that,' Kit let the dogs out, allowed his father to get the bags and carry them towards the side door of the house. 'Liza – follow me. I want you to go through the front door first, savour the grandeur of Dallord House, built by our forebears.'

'It's not that grand, Miss Lee,' his father called, with a cheery wave, 'only part of my wife's family estate, long-since sold off.'

Kit grunted. 'Details. It's still patently affluent.' He took her hand. 'Note the terraces, the gardeners at work.'

Patting Jessie, Brenna sauntered after them. 'Only two, these days,' she called. 'Mummy does a lot . . .'

'Between horse shows and making additions to the stock . . .'

'Only cook and two maids now, Kit – the Ryans have left, and I don't think Marwick's happy. That's not much for a huge place like this, do you think, Miss Lee?'

'Lizzie,' said Lizzie. 'No one calls me Miss Lee. No, it doesn't seem like a lot, not enough, perhaps.'

'Rot. Half the rooms are shut off in any case . . .'

'Mostly in the winter – and they have to be aired and dusted, or things decay.'

'They should all be in use, by people who have no roof at all.'

'You're hopeless. I don't know why you care what any of us think . . .'

Kit turned to look at her. 'Let's make it clear – I don't.'

Suddenly Brenna said no more.

As they approached the pillared doorway, and Kit opened the great panelled door itself, led her into the huge, high-ceilinged hall, Lizzie also was silent. The quiet, the beauty, the deep glow of polished wood, the vast hangings of silk and velvet, the dimly-seen paintings as they went from one splendid room to another, left her with nothing to say, made all her old terms, like 'Coo' or 'Gawd!' pathetic, even stupid. For another moment, she could see what Kit kept on about – how could any one family own and live in all this? It just didn't seem fair.

'Ancestors galore,' Brenna murmured, perhaps to help Lizzie in her stunned muteness. 'You feel beholden. At least, Mummy and Daddy do – and when Kit isn't inciting me to abandon ship, I do, too. And, actually, though you'd never believe it, so do Meg and Jillie, our older sisters.' She shrugged a shoulder, stuck a piece of straw caught to her sleeve behind her ear. 'Rum, isn't it?'

'You're rum,' said Kit. 'By the time you wake up, you'll be trapped like a mole. Poor old Bren.'

Lizzie felt the same feeling she had for Mr. Cameron; she wanted to slip her arm through Brenna's, show her how she did understand, even if Mim and Effie were as far back as her 'forebears' seemed to go . . . Crikey, she thought, she'd be my sister-in-law if . . .

'Suitably impressed, angel?' Kit draped her shoulders with a possessive arm. 'That's only a taste. Wait till you see the rest.'

'Spare her,' Brenna said, shoving her long dark hair behind her ears. 'Eleven bedrooms, Liza. Four receptions. Servants' quarters. Only four bathrooms for the lot. That's all you need to know. Come on, I'm famished. Up at five this morning to feed and exercise them . . .'

'By them, she means the horses,' Kit said, arching a weary eyebrow at his sister. 'Not to mention various and sundry dogs, cats, some frustrated peacocks . . .'

'Shut up, Kit – you're a supreme pain in the neck. Honestly, Liza – Lizzie – don't you think so?'

The two girls laughed together. At least, thought Lizzie, she didn't ask that unanswerable question – 'What do you *see* in him?' What did any girl see in him? Why did he attract her so much, in such a mysterious way, no different to all the females at the studio who followed him with their eyes, put themselves in his path, vied nauseatingly for his attention? Even at his dirtiest, when he hadn't washed his hair for weeks and smelled, it didn't seem to put them off. In fact, as she had come to notice, they even seemed to prefer him that way. That *was* where she differed: she liked the clean smell of his shirt today, much more than the acrid sweat before he'd suddenly started tidying up . . .

'Here we are,' Kit said, as frenzied barking began at the far end of a big cluttered room where the furniture and carpets had a faded, shabby look and everything, exposed by the sunlight coming through huge, open glass doors, was very obviously in need of dusting.

'Don't be deceived,' Kit said, kissing her quickly before he let her go. 'This is all sheer affectation, the live-in-poverty look of the guilty rich.'

'Do stuff it,' said Brenna. 'It's not in the least true. We've all got to have a place where we can relax and let our hair down. We can't always be keeping the heritage intact.'

'Bullshit.' Kit tugged Lizzie through a badly-scratched oak door. 'Dog claws,' he explained. 'Generations of them.'

As the door swung open, it was the first thing she saw – dogs, all shapes and kinds, lying on mats, ambling about, and kittens . . .

'Well, there you all are! Hello, come on in – sorry I couldn't meet you . . .'

From the huge stoves at the far end of a kitchen so large that even their new flat in Shaftesbury Avenue with a bedroom each for Mim and herself would have fitted into it, a woman came forward, wiping her hands on an apron worn over riding clothes, several dogs trailing behind her.

'This is Liza Lee,' Kit said, without kissing his mother, and with only a nod to acknowledge hers on his cheek. 'Liza – my mother.'

'How do you do, Liza.' Honor Cameron extended her

hand, shook Lizzie's with adequate warmth, but her grey eyes expressed far more, as if she could not entirely suppress instant liking and interest.

Lizzie could not help smiling rather too much, either. She had not expected to meet such an open, natural-looking person; she did not seem at all like a nob, with her grey-streaked sandy-coloured hair worn longish and straight, her broad, weather-beaten face moist with sweat, lipstick eaten off, blue eye-shadow gone patchy, her pale blue shirt sloppily unbuttoned over big breasts in what must be a sagging bra. And her hands – Cor, they were as battered as Mum's used to be before she started having manicures!

'Brennie,' she said, 'give Maria a hand with the tray and scones. She's only just arrived from Spain,' she explained to Kit, 'can't speak a word yet.'

'Why do you keep getting them from Spain?' Kit asked. 'What's wrong with the locals?' There was mockery, if not spite in his tone.

'What locals?' Brenna said, as she moved off to help the plump dark girl at one end of a vast wooden table. 'They don't exist. They go to greener pastures, if you'll excuse the expression.'

'What a terrible bore, what a tragedy!' Kit chuckled, drew Lizzie to him with ostentatious affection. 'Don't you think so, darling? Do you have this kind of trouble? But, of course, you wouldn't. Not a star of your magnitude.'

'I wish you'd declare a truce, Kit,' Honor Cameron said, shaking her head at him. 'We all know your views, only too well – surely you want Liza to enjoy herself.'

Kit gave a quick, falsely chastened nod, lifted a forefinger. 'You're right, I apologize. Where is Dad, then?'

'Here,' said Alister. 'Had to have a word with Matthews about the chickens; some sort of infection, I'm afraid.'

'Let's not discuss it now, dear,' Honor Cameron said, with tart humour. 'Our guest could lose her appetite.'

'Ah,' he said, 'of course.' He had taken off his jacket, but he had it over his arm; and he now put it back on, began to help with the tea things.

'Why swelter, Dad?' Kit asked. 'The ladies won't think the less of you . . .' Kit stopped, held up his hand. 'Truce. Sorry.'

Lizzie gave him a quick smile. He *could* be decent. 'Can I help, or do something?' she asked Mrs. Cameron.

'No, thank you, Liza. You just go and sit down. I've got a cake cooling – if it hasn't collapsed.'

'Mother's cakes. The common touch, you know.' Kit winced as Brenna's foot caught him on the shin.

Lizzie smiled uncertainly. Suddenly, she wanted to pee. She asked Brenna where to go, and everyone began to apologize for not having shown her sooner – 'How thoughtless,' said Honor Cameron. 'Really, children.'

Kit took charge. 'Follow me . . . "Children" – see what I mean?'

'Oh, not *that* one . . .' His father blocked his path. 'It's filled with hunting gear. Upstairs, please.'

Kit backed off. 'My error – come, my love, to the royal bog. I'm sure you'll find it worthy of you.'

Lizzie overcame her shyness with a rather bawdy giggle, followed him up a great wide staircase, along a richly-carpeted hall, past many doors, some closed, some half-open, with glimpses of rolling green lawns, trees, cattle-dotted fields beyond the windows . . .

Suddenly, on a huge canopied bed, she caught sight of her bag. How had that got there, and when?

'Yep. That's your room, angel. Dad must have had instructions. When you're through in there . . .' he nodded to a door on the opposite side of the hall. 'I'll show you. It's not a bad little chamber – room for two.'

She let the insinuation go. She went quickly to the other room, shut the door, almost wetting herself now that relief was near.

165

'Me Gawd!' she gasped as she looked around. 'Royal' was the word! All the trimmings seemed to be in gold or brass, the royal blue tub was big enough to swim in, there were gold and white designs carved into the ceiling, wallpaper that seemed made of velvet, portraits in gold frames hanging from the walls – and deep-piled rose-flowered carpet on the floor.

Could she let herself actually pee? It seemed all wrong. Not that, now, she had a choice. How Mum would laugh when she told her how embarrassed she'd been wiping herself with all the nobby faces looking on.

Bracing herself, she had a quick wash, pushed her fringe straight, went to join Kit.

'There,' he said, leading her into the room that was to be hers. 'Just a peek – we don't want lukewarm tea.'

Lizzie breathed in. Would she ever be able to sleep in such a grand, luxurious place? That embroidered linen on the turned-down bed, the satin quilt . . . !

'Enough. If it cools off, they'll light the fire for you.'

'That was a real fire?'

'Of course. No fakes in country seats, my love.' He grabbed her, kissed her hard on the mouth, putting his tongue to hers.

Lizzie pulled away. This, too, seemed all wrong.

'Not now, not like this?' Kit nodded. 'Only more so, in Dallord House, eh? I know the feeling. Even to masturbate here was profane, courting insanity.'

'Oh, Kit – I like them all so much. You've got a marvellous family.' Lizzie reached up and kissed him in another way, though on the mouth, and looked lovingly into his eyes. 'I'm ever so glad you brought me.'

'Ever so?' He nodded. 'Good, dear. Then we're on target.'

Another time not to question. Some day, when she'd known him well for a long while, she would learn to grasp

166

his meanings, the way she'd learned to read and speak properly at Blatsky's, as if that was a different language.

Tea was the second happiest occasion in her life – the first time she and Robbie had danced in the canteen and he'd proposed – and now, with the tea spread out in delicious variety, the lovely china and silver pot, the dogs all around, snoring or waiting eagerly for scraps, a soft breeze that smelled of flowers and new-cut grass coming through the open glass doors, and everyone chatting and laughing and asking her all about herself and her life, finding it interesting, 'utterly fascinating', and that she'd actually lived, been brought up in *Soho* (they found it too sordid and sinister to walk alone there!), all the incredible training and efforts her mother had made.

'She must be an amazing character,' Honor Cameron said. 'I'd really like to meet her. Do you think you could bring her to visit some time?'

'Would she like horses?' Brenna asked. 'She might, you know.'

'Yes . . .' Lizzie nodded thoughtfully. 'She might. But if she didn't, she'd say so.'

There was a raucous snort from Kit. 'My God, would she! She's a . . .' Again, he stopped, allowing the appreciative laughter to drown his words.

After tea, Lizzie was given the chore of drying dishes, but not of putting them away: there were maids for that, and they liked their own order. Soon, they'd be putting on the dinner, which Honor (Lizzie could now call her that) did not interfere with, didn't dare – but there were masses of other chores to be done, of course; one did one's best to keep up. Lately, she'd had a touch of arthritis . . .

Lizzie went for a walk with Alister, and some of the dogs, to see the cows, while Kit and Brenna played some tennis. Lizzie wanted to hug the cows, and was saddened to think they were sold and sometimes eaten.

'You get used to it,' Alister said, with his cheery smile.

'It's the natural order. We all eat each other in one way or another.'

'Ugh! Do you reckon the foxes don't mind, then, when your hounds go after them?'

He laughed, chucked her under the chin. 'Don't ask questions like that – you sound like Kit.'

She laughed at herself. She was obviously very silly, ignorant, but he made it all right, the way Bert had done. She went close to some of the cows, looked deeply into their huge dark eyes.

'Oh, I love them – and I love it here!' She danced away from him, threw her arms open to the soft green country-side, the great ball of sun that was dripping gold and orange onto everything. 'I could go quite mad with all the animals, with the land, with so much beauty, with such a marvellous family. How could Kit ever want to leave it?'

Alister shook his head slowly. 'Strangely enough, when he was a little boy, he felt like that. Whatever happened to him, was away from here; got worse at university . . . Ah, well – one rolls with the ball, as they say these days. Come, let's see if we can help Honor in the barn.'

That night, after an enormous dinner of roast beef, roast potatoes, fresh vegetables from the garden, a huge apple pie made of apples from their own trees, they all sat round in the big, faded-blue room and, of all things, watched telly. Honor did tapestry work, Alister played patience, Brenna picked tics out of the dogs, plopping the black bodies into a bowl of water so that it turned a dark maroon colour. Kit read and read, plucking at his beard, commenting from time to time, smoking . . .

'You smoking one of those?' asked Brenna, looking up and wrinkling her nose.

'Yes – want one?'

'Don't be stupid. You'll giggle, it's a bore.'

That was what Lizzie thought, but she only watched. If he had more than one, he would certainly come to her room tonight. She wondered if a guest should lock the door.

Luckily, Honor came in when she was getting ready for bed. 'Got everything you need, Liza,' she asked. 'Want a fire, or a hottie?'

'No, thanks. It's warm, and – perfect. If only you knew how wonderful it is to be here!'

Honor put down an armful of towels, sat down in a brocade armchair. 'Liza – Lizzie – may I ask you something?'

'Oh, yes, please . . . I hoped we'd have a chance to talk.' She put a pink voile robe over her short nightgown, curled up on the bed.

'You look too young to be considering anything serious,' Honor said, shoving freckled hands through her hair and smiling in a way that showed her weariness. 'It's that blue ribbon round your hair, I suppose, and no mascara. *Quite* different from your TV look!'

Lizzie nodded. 'Mmmm. I've been wearing make-up since I was a baby. I love to take it off, even if my lashes and brows seem naked – that's what Mim, my mother, says. She can't stand me "bare-faced" – it makes her nervous.'

'Extraordinary. So, tell me, are you thinking of marrying my son? He's made it clear you are.'

Lizzie looked into her direct grey gaze. 'Sort of,' she said. 'Yes.'

Honor nodded. 'You *have* mellowed him. It might not seem so to you as much as to us. He still despises us, but he would never have come home unless he wanted money, certainly not for just a weekend. He actually wants to show you to us. You've wrought a miracle.'

'Really?'

'Absolutely. As far as we're concerned, you're a gift from heaven.'

Lizzie shivered. 'You wouldn't mind? You'd think I was good enough?'

Honor slapped the arm of the chair. 'Good enough!

169

You're much too good, dear. Even somewhat reformed, he's short of what you deserve.'

'You must see things in me that I don't . . .'

'Please.' Honor raised a palm criss-crossed in deep lines. 'I understand that your life and ours are full of contrasts, but it couldn't matter less. I just hope you'll think very carefully about Kit. We try to love him, but he makes it impossible. I wouldn't like it if he made you unhappy, put a blight on your wonderful success, your bright future.'

'Thank you . . . I see what you mean . . .' Lizzie broke into a wry smile. 'I wouldn't expect wonders, but I do think he's changing. And I am awfully – well, I feel a lot for him . . . And . . .' Lizzie felt like lowering her fringe over her eyes, but didn't. 'There'd be you, this family, being part of all this. You see?'

Honor's weary smile became a musing tenderness. 'What a dear girl you are . . . Bless you.' she stood up. 'I'll say goodnight. Sleep well. Alice will bring you tea in the morning, about seven, unless you'd like to sleep in.'

'No, that'd be great. Brenna's going to teach me to ride. I'll probably be hopeless, but I want to try.'

'Good. See you at breakfast.' Honor closed the door softly behind her.

Lizzie turned off the light, slipped deep down between the fresh-smelling white sheets, sank her head into the firm softness of the big white pillow. Oh, yes, she thought. Oh, yes, oh yes. She would tell Kit tomorrow.

She closed her eyes, half-dreamed of a wedding, a white wedding they called it, the kind she'd seen over and over in films, so often read about. She'd wear a beautiful long white dress, a filmy veil, walk up the aisle of a big church, lovely bridesmaids behind her, the music would rise – 'Here Comes The Bride' – Kit would move up beside her, splendid in a formal suit, look down at her with adoring eyes . . .

Those wonderful words would be said by the Minister,

ending: I pronounce you man and wife. She would lift her veil, look up at Kit; he would kiss her so tenderly, lovingly.

After that, the dream became a bit hazy. They would probably have a big reception somewhere, all the Camerons there . . .

She turned over, dug deeper into the pillow. She hadn't fitted Mum into the picture. Mum would be the one to 'give her away', of course. Her hair would be done soft and plain, and she would wear a simple dress, silk, perhaps, blue . . .

Somehow, that part wouldn't come clear.

She sighed without strain. Never mind – that was only a detail. She and Mum were not going to be part of a real family in the real world.

Lizzie smiled, floated . . .

From somewhere in the house she thought she heard the sound of a bell, such as telephones sometimes made when you picked them up to make a call, a small, brief tinkle – and a voice, speaking in a soft, muffled sort of way. It sounded like Kit . . .

But it was probably her imagination . . .

She stretched contentedly, let go . . .

How lovely, deep and quiet the house was, even the animals made no sound . . .

Only a barn owl's soft hoot, at a distance, broke the silence of the countryside. Soho was like an old, fading nightmare.

# CHAPTER THIRTEEN

Mim put out her fag before going into the big ward where all the old crocks and vegetables were kept. She wished her Mum would snuff it, rather than be one of them – that they'd left her to do herself in with the booze instead of keeping her hanging about with these bloody drugs.

It was plain ruddy awful the way Effie looked now, all the spunk gone out of her, just sitting in that wheelchair, her head sunk, the red tint gone out of her Barnet, leaving it like a moth-eaten grey wig. You could never have told that she'd once been a dresser for stars, a person they treated like a friend. Mim wanted to tell all the po-faced nurses who treated Mum like she was a stupid child, how she had more than fifty signed pictures of famous people, had had drinks with the great stars they'd only heard about, got lovely presents from them and even bits of bees to buy herself something or have a fling on the gee-gees.

' 'Ow are yer, Mum?' she asked, drawing up a chair and sitting close to her. Silly bloody question, but you had to say something.

Effie's head shook. Her lids slid upward, her dark eyes that seemed to have lost their ability to focus, straining to meet her daughter's. 'What?' she asked, in a phlegm-clogged whisper.

'Never mind. Do ya know me, at all, love?' Mim put her hand on the bony old claws that were all that were left of Mum's attempt to look like a lady, the endless buffing and filing and clipping of cuticles, and where they had taken

172

away her rings she loved so much, there were only deep grooves under gnarled knuckles.

'Lizzie . . .?' The eyes made a terrible effort, took on a gleam that somehow looked like a smile.

Mim, under a barrage of stares from other oldsters who had nothing better to do, leaned close, as if Effie were deaf, which she wasn't, her ears being about the only part of her the doctors could find nothing wrong with. 'Couldn't come, Mum. Said she was sorry. Sent 'er love.'

Effie managed a slight lift of the head. There was a frown on her thin-skinned, blue-veined forehead.

'No, darlin', nothing' bad – just 'er teeth. 'Ad trouble with 'em. I didn't take 'er to the dentist when she was a kid – like you didn't take me – an' now it ain't good. Lots of big 'oles. Don't show, thank Gawd, but we got to 'ang on to 'er smile, don't we, Mum – part of 'er trade, eh?'

Poor old love, didn't understand a word of it. Drooling now, she was . . . Maybe she was getting fagged out. Mim's smile drooped. 'You all right, darlin'?' she whispered. 'You want anythin'?'

Effie looked past and over the high rise of Mim's new 'bouffant' hair-do into some unseen distance. Her chin trembled, and Mim noticed that there were hairs jutting from it that needed plucking. Not that it mattered . . .

'They feedin' yer all right? You want anythin' special – eels, chips . . . But I reckon Alf brings you those, eh?'

Effie looked out into the ward, into other faces, into the faces of passing nurses, a white-coated doctor moving round with a board in his hand, taking notes, a matron beside him. The whole place looked like some kind of mummy museum . . .

Well, that's it, thought Mim. I don't figure no more. Might as well scarper. She kissed Effie's sunken cheek where the rouge used to go, and it gave her the creeps, like she was kissing a dead person. 'Ta-ta, ol' dear,' she said. 'Next time, I'll bring yer Lizzie – promise.'

She was, of course, nattering to herself. Effie was staring at her own feet, propped on the step of the chair, as if they had nothing to do with her. She hummed a rattling sound, belched softly.

Mim went. At the desk outside, she asked if there was anything to tell her about her mother's 'condition'. They said no, that she was unlikely to last much longer, that was all.

A horrible thought kept coming into her head, as she walked to the tube in the cheerful sunlight. Cripes, it made her feel like a villain . . .

But she wished her mother would hurry up, so she would never have to go there again. It would be a ruddy great relief, it would, and that was the God's truth. She almost looked round to see if she would be struck dead herself, almost looked up. But, as she hopped off the bus and walked towards the little mansion block tucked between shops that was where her and Lizzie's new flat was, even worse thoughts came . . .

What an 'ell of a business it was going to be to get the ol' dear put under ground, what with Lizzie's big new spectacular coming up, all the publicity pictures, rehearsing new songs, meeting the star from the States, clothes and such, it'd be a right chore. Lizzie'd have to have black and they'd have to have some kind of a funeral – and then there was Alf . . .

Poor ol' sod. They'd have to do *something* about him, though Gawd knew what. He didn't have a bleedin' friend in the world, 'cept his boozing pals from the old days, down the East End.

Well, she'd have a word with Lizzie – she'd be back from the tooth-butcher by now. 'Thank 'eavens,' she muttered to herself as she used the posh little staircase up to the second floor, 'that soddin' 'ippie gone off the scene for once. We'll 'ave a bit of peace, 'er an' me!'

The rooms of the furnished flat, which cost them an arm

174

and a leg (but what could you do with climbing so fast?), had a curious hush. 'Lizzie?' Mim called, as she shut the solid wood door behind her. 'Lovey?'

There was not a sound, except for the usual thud and roar of traffic, the thumps of feet from the flat above.

'Now what d'ya think's 'appened to 'er? Don't take no two hours for no pain in no tooth . . .'

Mim smoked cigarettes, drank cups of tea, wandered, paced, read the news, listened to the radio, washed out some clothes, peeled some potatoes, played the piano, ran a few seams of a dress for Lizzie through the machine.

The light diminished, shadows fell. Mim turned on all the lamps, started a little loin of pork she'd picked up for the weekend, opened a bottle of white plonk.

Of course, she was not Lizzie's keeper; the girl could do as she wanted, go anywhere – but it wasn't like her not to say. Christ, she might've had plans of her own. Something that that sarky bastard wouldn't think possible . . .

Mim ate the food she'd prepared in scowling silence. The programmes on telly she ought to have watched, so as to keep her wheels turning for Lizzie, seemed unimportant, too trivial to compete with the ugly suspicion going round in her head . . .

Towards midnight, she rang Harry Org, tried her suspicions on him. 'Whaddya think, 'Arry, ol' cock – I been conned, ain't I? She never went to no den'ist – 'e got 'er to go off with 'im! Right?'

Harry thought about it – but only for a moment. 'Yeah – I think you've been 'ad, ol' girl. 'E's got a real 'old on Lizzie, 'e 'as. Wouldn't put nothin' past 'im.'

'Oh, 'Arry – she don't know nothin' about it – 'e could put 'er in the club – *anythin'*!'

'Now, now, darlin', don't get yerself in a twist till you know for sure. Maybe she's been in an accident, or got in some bother. Maybe you should call the police.'

Mim raised her eyebrows ceiling-wards. 'Now that's a

great 'elp! Ya think I should call the police, eh! An' tell 'em what – that Liza Lee ain't come 'ome to 'er Mum, an' is out late? What kind of nit would they think I was? The kid's near nineteen, 'Arry!'

'Mmmm. There ain't many girls like Lizzie round these days. They'd laugh. Still – if she don't turn up by tomorrer night, you could say she was, missin', like.'

'Liza Lee Missing!' Can't you just see the 'eadlines, 'Arry? Lovely.'

There was a long silence. Mim could tell Harry was trying to think of something by the sound of his breathing. His upper lip, with the little black moustache, would be sucked back against his teeth while the air went in – out . . .

'I'd be'er come over, Mimsie,' he said. 'I'll 'op in the car . . .'

'NO!' Mim snapped the word like a bullet shot down the wire. 'That's the last thing I want – don't come 'ere. I got to sort this out meself, be wai'in'.'

Harry sighed into the mouthpiece. 'As you say – but you should let someone look arter *you* sometimes, ol' girl. I ain't Bertie, but . . .'

'Leave off, 'Arry. You're me mate, me pal. You know that.'

'Yeah. Right. Well – you just give me a bell if you need me – I'll be there like a flash.'

'Ta, ol' cock. G'night.'

Mim stared down from the window into the busy avenue. There was everyone there in the neon-lit darkness – except Lizzie.

'I'll KILL 'im, I swear – I will. I'll 'ave 'is guts fer gar'ers. 'E ain't goin' anywhere ridin' on 'er back. This'll be the last time 'e tries . . .'

At two in the morning, Mim lay down on her bed, still in her white trousers and yellow polka-dot top, and smoked and listened, smoked and listened . . .

176

It was a burning smell that wakened her. There was a round black hole in the pillow. It was the next day. But only a third into it.

Cursing steadily, Mim cleaned up the ashes, had a bath in the neat little tiled bathroom, put on jeans and an orange T-shirt. Never had she missed Lizzie this way. Lizzie was always there – and now she just wasn't. There seemed no point in running through the music, writing letters, or getting on with any bloody thing at all.

Towards evening, it occurred to her to phone Cynthia Sterling; Lizzie did spend more time with her than anyone else . . .

But Cynthia hadn't heard from Lizzie since her last lesson. 'Is it possible she's gone to Rob Grover's gig in Glasgow?'

'Glasgow! Naaah. She don't 'ear from 'im no more . . . 'Ow did *you* know, though?' Mim's voice sharpened.

'Uh . . . I read it somewhere – *Melody Maker*, I think.'

'Ah. Well, ta – she'll probably turn up any minute safe an' sound.'

'I'm sure. Let me know if I can help.'

Mim hung up, pretending she didn't hear that bit. It narked her the way that woman put herself forward with Lizzie, as if she was special, had some inside track. 'After all, it was *me* what got Lizzie singin' in the first place, got 'er singin' out an' makin' 'erself listened to, even if she didn't know all them tricks about breathin' an' "pitch"!'

As night darkened the skies and the lights splashed it again in glowing colours, Mim closed the flower-patterned curtains and moved slowly to the telephone on her cluttered desk. Her brow was lined, her eyebrows tightly-drawn, the cigarette at the corner of her down-turned mouth unlit. Her hand went to the instrument, withdrew, reached again, hovered, withdrew . . .

Cripes. Callin' in coppers fer Lizzie . . .

What a pen-'n'-ink it would make! What would Lizzie 'erself say, feel about it?

'Am I your prisoner, then, Mum?' she'd said, the time she'd decided to go to a disco with Kit and come in after twelve. 'I told you I'd be late. What do you want of me?'

Go easy, she'd thought to herself, then. The girl was right. An' she was such a good kid, never done nothin' mean or wrong in all her life, always workin', doin' what was wanted, what *she* wanted 'er to do . . .

Was 'er girl suddenly changin', influenced by that git, losing 'er morals?

With a little sharp shiver, Mim turned from the idea – whatever happened, Lizzie wouldn't get all 'hotted up' like the girls did these days, doin' it just 'for the kicks' . . .

Would she?

Mim drank a bottle of white wine thinking about it. She sat, head lolling in front of the telly, without actually seeing what was on it. She felt like Effie looked . . .

The next thing she knew, the set was whining to be turned off.

Groaning, muttering, she switched it off; she lay back on the long rose-coloured velvet couch and fell into a heavy sleep.

When the telephone rang, and she sat up to place where she was, the clock said eight. Eight at night, or in the morning?

It was someone at the hospital. Effie had died. She might want to come in and 'talk things over' with Dr. Hale.

Mim felt nothing. There wasn't one little twinge of grief, even when she tried for it. Effie, her dear ol' mum, had 'gone to her rest', as Gran would have said.

She left a note for Lizzie. It now seemed barmy to call the police. If she did not come back by supper time, when people came home from weekends – even rude ones (Kit would have an early call, and Lizzie was due at rehearsal)

– then she *would* call them. No-one could blame her for that, by Gawd.

Dr. Hale, a small, quick-moving man with side-swept wisps of dark hair, seemed relieved that Mim got the matter over without emotion. He said he assumed she had the faith of life after death, very realistic in his view. More people should have it – it would make life a lot easier for the medical profession. Mim nodded. Whatever he was on about, it moved Effie to her rest with unexpected speed; instead of a hole in the ground, why not arrange a cremation? Effie would be put in a bag, sent into the fire, returned to her in a small container of ashes, with which she could do as she liked.

He was sliding his gaze below his glasses to his watch before Mim could even say 'ta, for all . . .'

As she hurried to the lift, she wondered if he would know her if he saw her again. She lit a fag despite the NO SMOKING sign, and hoped he wouldn't, that she'd never be inside this place again.

When she got back to the flat, there were voices . . .

Nerves leaping, she turned the key, walked in. Lizzie *was* there!

And so was that bugger.

'Mum,' said Lizzie, her face freshened by country air, her eyes as radiant as if lit by a blue spot, 'we've got something to tell you!'

'Oh, me gawd . . .' Mim froze. Her handbag slipped slowly off her arm to the floor.

Kit laughed. 'Tell her, darling.'

'We're going to be married, Mum.'

'Married, Mrs. Hobbs. Isn't that smashing?'

Mim averted her eyes. The smile on his face made her sick.

'Lizzie – what're you sayin'?'

'Yes, Mum – it's true. A real wedding, in a church, wedding gown, bridesmaids – the whole bloomin' show! As soon as we can make all the plans.'

When Mim didn't move, Lizzie moved to her quickly and put her arms around her. 'I'm sorry I played a trick on you, Mum. I didn't think you'd want me to go – '

'Actually, I knew you'd try to stop her,' Kit added, putting on a small-boy face to offset his words. 'And, you see, it meant such a lot to us both.'

'I've been in Dorset, Mum, with his family and, oh, they're poppets! You're going to love them!'

'*Poppets!*' muttered Mim. 'Christ, let me get a fag, sit down, gather me wits.'

'Of course, Mum. It must be a shock – but I just, *we* just couldn't wait – could we, Kit?' She looked at him lovingly.

'Absolutely not. You were the first we wanted to tell.'

Mim braved his eyes. Their mutual gaze locked, held. Lizzie saw, but seemed to find they were no longer significant.

Mim took only the time to light the cigarette, to sit on the couch, hunched up at one end in the corner, to bring herself back into function.

'Sorry I can't send up rockets, me darlin',' she said, speaking in a flat, grating slowness. 'This 'as been a day for shocks.'

Lizzie turned from Kit to gaze at her. 'What, Mum? What else?'

'Yer gran'mother died this mornin', Lizzie. Me mum passed away forever. She were all I got left in the world. Me child'ood's gone. There's nothin' be'ind me. I'm on me own.'

Kit cleared his throat, cast a knowing blink at the sad, drawn-down face, the slightly quivering long nose to which, though there was no moisture, Mim kept pressing the back of her hand.

'Mum . . . Oh, Mum!' Lizzie was over to her in one quick movement, down beside her on the couch, holding her in her arms, patting and smoothing the nest of hair, kissing the hard-boned cheek and jaw. 'I'm that sorry – I shouldn't have sprung it on you like that . . . Golly, I should have known – they said it could happen any time. I feel awful I wasn't there . . .'

'It wouldn't have helped much,' Kit said. 'She wasn't recognizing you the last few times, remember?'

Lizzie didn't seem to hear him. 'Tell me all about it, Mum – did she know, was she in pain? What time did she actually . . .?'

'Gawd, Lizzie, don't!' Mim turned her head quickly into Lizzie's shoulder, hid it as if to conceal tears.

Lizzie looked up at Kit, standing tall and watchful in his stand-in-collared white shirt and cotton blazer, his bearded face giving him the wry detachment of a stranger.

'I'll run on,' he said, 'leave you two to your private grief.'

Lizzie's eyes widened with regret, confusion. 'You understand – you don't mind . . .'

'I accept 'tis the proper thing. BUT . . .' He lowered his tone, his bearded chin, gave her a look of unmistakable meaning. 'This shouldn't alter our plans. There's too much set in motion, too many people involved. Right?'

Lizzie gave him a dazed, but reassuring smile 'Of course . . .'

'Aw, Gawd . . .' Mim groaned. 'It's 'it me, Lizzie, 'it me like nuffin' ever 'as . . .'

Lizzie raised her hand to Kit. The opal and diamond ring he'd got Honor to dig out, and they'd all made a little ceremony of when he'd slipped it on her finger, sparkled in the lamplight. 'Ciao . . .' she whispered.

He blew her a kiss. 'See you in the morning.'

He strode to the door, closed it behind him with a snap.


'Mum? Mum darling – please look at me, please stop changing the subject. We've got to talk, clear things up, come to a decision.' Lizzie, in her dolly robe, stopped short in her pacing.

Mim, sitting at her desk, did not change the tight-lipped, permanently busy and pained expression of the past six weeks. 'I know,' she said. 'I can't make up me mind . . . You're goin' so good 'ere, an' there's the 'ope of a Command Performance. On the other 'and – it wouldn't do you no damage to do the U.S. spectacular, no damage at all. An' now there's this Zeke Solway bloke chirpin' about 'Ollywood.' She twisted one side of her mouth. 'If only you'd 'elp by puttin' your mind to it . . .'

Lizzie imitated the twist of her mouth. 'That'd be the day, when I got my say. All I have to do is *look* more interested in one than another, and it'd be the one you snuffed.'

'T'ain't true. It's just that I got to be sure. We can't 'ave you wastin' yer time. We got you so near the top, we can't put no foot wrong now!' Mim nodded sharply to herself.

Lizzie closed her eyes, breathed in, dropped into the rose velvet chair that was part of the three-piece suite. She was beginning to see her mother as Kit saw her, as an ambition-obsessed creature with only one end in view, who would stop at nothing to use *her* to that end. 'She's not thinking of you, darling,' he'd said, 'she's thinking only of herself, her dream. You're not a daughter, a person, you're a *means*. It's time you woke up to it, stood up to her, broke away, did what *you* want to do!'

Yes, thought Lizzie. It was. And she must.

She jumped up, went to the kitchen, made coffee, came back, put a mug beside Mim on the desk, drew up a chair, put her own mug on its broad wooden arm. 'Now, Mum,' she said, pushing her hair completely off her face, 'look at me. I don't want to talk about work – not offers, not shows, not interviewers, not promotion, not rehearsal, photography, techniques, costumes, or any single thing to do with my career. I want you to discuss Kit and me and a date for our marriage . . .'

At the word 'marriage', Mim finally looked up, with a

new lift to her eyebrows. 'I thought that had been put off.'

'You know ruddy well it hasn't. I gave up the idea of a big white wedding, that's all.' Lizzie tried to keep her emotions from bumping up her voice, repeating the thwarted feeling in her chest.

'*I* didn't ask you to do that, did I? What you on about?' Mim reached for the pack of cigarettes by her typewriter, lit one with practised speed, stuck it quickly in her mouth.

It was one of her ways, another, thought Lizzie, of defending herself, of making a wall, or getting prepared to attack. It meant smoke in the eyes, a little screen . . .

'No, Mum, you didn't *ask*. But you *were* in mourning, weren't you? And you wouldn't have attended, would you?'

'You could've gone ahead, ducks. I never said nothin' . . .'

'Not *much*!' Lizzie rolled her eyes.

'Could I 'elp if I were sufferin'? Did I *want* migraine 'eads? Didn't I 'ave 'em when Bertie went? You gone as 'ard-'earted as 'im!'

'Don't start, Mum!' Lizzie felt the impatience in her whole body, like a twitch that made her shift and turn in her chair. To divert it, she sipped at the coffee, plucked at some split ends to her longer-length hair. 'Anyway, you're better now, right?'

'Well . . .' Mim, following suit, sipped her coffee, with her usual sucking sounds. 'Go on, then – what's all this you want to "discuss"?'

'I told you. A date, Mum. As second-best, we want to do it at the Chelsea Registry Office – in about three weeks.'

'Three weeks! You must be jokin'!'

To Lizzie's eyes, Mim's face seemed to turn as grey as a wet dishcloth. It didn't matter how Kit was – there were always these moments when she had only her memories and feelings to go by, that undid the tight knot of resolve, left it dangling and loose . . .

'Or so . . .' Lizzie looked quickly away, biting at a rough cuticle. 'The Camerons would come up, and we'd go on to somewhere like Claridges for a bit of a celebration. We wouldn't need to bother with a honeymoon . . . Kit wants to be the producer on my show, you see.'

Mim stared at her, her eyes seeming to protrude. The edges of her jawbones made little bumps where they clenched. 'So . . .' she said finally, 'you're goin' to let 'im do it, make a right proper monkey of ya. It's bloody marvellous, it is, 'ow 'e does it. It's not as if you 'ad sawdust for brains, neither.'

'I said – don't start!' Lizzie jumped up, sending the coffee slopping over the sides of the mug, the small table swaying on one leg. Going for a sponge, she mopped up the mess, took the sponge back, rinsed it, returned, sat down again. Mum was still sitting, cigarette in mouth, hands about the mug as she did by habit in cold winter weather.

Sorry for her, hating her, loving her, Lizzie leaned forward. 'Mum – look. Maybe I know everything you or other people think of Kit. Maybe I've guessed, put two and two together . . .' Lizzie thought of that telephone bell in the night at Dallord House, of things Kit had said on the train about rising together as a team, forcing Mum off the scene, of the notes she'd seen passing between him and Anna Croft.

'You know? About the others, an' 'ow 'e's usin' ya?'

'Yes.'

'An' you still want to marry the bastard?'

'Yes.' Mim's silence went on so long that Lizzie found it unbearable. 'Oh, come on, Mum! It's not going to make the slightest difference to us, to you and me. He wants me to be a star just as much as you. But, I'll never let him take over your job, honest, I promise. And, he'll have to keep me happy, won't he? I mean, blimey – who's the one with the power, Mum, eh?'

'Cripes . . .' Mim's expression lost its baleful intensity. Some of her old humour seemed to sift through it: 'You surprise me, me darlin'. I'm knocked cold. One thing I don't understand, though – 'ow can you do it, when you don't love 'im? *I* could never go with no man what didn't want me for nothin' but savin' 'is neck.'

'Oh, Mum, it isn't like that – that's not all there is, it's only part. There's good things, too. I don't care what he's done in the past, and I *want* to help him – don't you see?'

Mim creased her mouth into a tight line. The leaven of humour passed from her face like a light going out. 'I wish I could believe that, me love – but so 'elp me. I find it im-bloody-possible. You got somethin' wonky with your thinkin' – maybe it's that nob family. Maybe you got nob-fever – like you used to get when you was a kid with them girls at Blatsky's . . .'

Lizzie took refuge in silence, in the dregs of cold coffee.

'Or you want to get even with that slum-brat what's got 'is Chevvy in the papers with that Society miss – eh?'

Lizzie's heart gave an automatic bump. 'Don't be silly, Mum. I wish Robbie only the best. I'm happy he's doing well, he deserves it. He's got the most talented group there is now, good as the Kinks, more original than the Beatles, or the Stones . . .'

Mim gave a small snort, swiped the cigarette from her mouth and pressed it into a full ashtray. 'Rubbish: that's what they are, that's what they play. An' that Dear'orn girl's on them drugs, leadin' 'im Gawd-knows where.' Mim reached for her glasses. 'Well, now, me pe'al, 'ave we 'ad our discussion? I got some letters to write what needs me full attention.'

'Oh, bloody hell, Mum – leave off.' Lizzie bumped her fist on the corner of the desk. 'Tell me straight – is three weeks from now okay, can we get on with the details?'

Mim blinked, became rigidly still. 'Lizzie, gel – why do ya bovver askin' *me*? Eh? From all what you've told me, you got your mind made up.'

Lizzie's stare was transfixed. An ominous sense of futility stifled her breathing.

'Well, me love – aintcha?' Mim tapped a false nail against the side of the typewriter, dragged in smoke from her cigarette.

'Why do I bother? Because you need to know, don't you? You're the one with the calendars and dates, what I'm doing, where, when . . . Besides, there's a lot of details we'll have to talk about.'

'Is there now? Three weeks, you say – I'll 'ave a look, so's you can get on with it.'

Lizzie's brows rose slowly. 'So's *I* can get on with it . . .'

'I 'aven't got the time, Lizzie. '*E'll* have to 'elp ya . . .'

Lizzie leaned forward, grasped Mim's arm above the elbow.

'Mum? Are you saying you aren't going to come, to be there, for the ceremony?'

Mim lifted her gaze slowly to hers. 'I'm sorry you 'ad to ask that, ol' darlin', 'cause I 'ates to 'urt ya – but, 'ow *could* I? 'Ow could I lend meself to watchin' me very own girl what I worked me 'ole life for, what I loves with all me 'eart, throw 'erself away on no more'n a pimp?'

'Mum! Dammit, that's rotten. It really bloody is.' In the absence of tears, Lizzie's eyes had crystal brilliance.

Mim did not meet them. 'Sorry, me love – it's the way I see it, but I should watch me language. Any'ow, if you got your 'eart set, it don't ma'er a fig if I'm there or not – you just go ahead, me darlin'. 'Ave your big day. Enjoy yerself. 'Oo knows – 'e might change, you might be 'appy as Derby an' Joan. Gawd knows, I '*ope* so . . .'

Lizzie slowly lowered her head; the fringe came down, hung like a curtain between them.

# CHAPTER FOURTEEN

In the following three weeks, Lizzie felt as if she was in a speeded-up film, in which she tore from one place to another in a non-stop sequence that began with jumping out of bed in the morning and ended with falling, exhausted, into bed at night. There was no time to think, no time to examine her feelings. The stray ends of conflicting emotions that floated about in her like dimly-heard messages were crowded out by an unremitting barrage of details.

Although Kit took over a great many of these, such as arrangements for the marriage itself, their two-night honeymoon reservation at the Ritz, the leg-work involved in hunting for a quickly-available flat, she had found herself coping for the first time in her life with what to wear, keeping her work schedule organized while looking at furnishings, fitting in rehearsals – but, above all, facing the unexpected avalanche of press and other media interest that Mim would ordinarily have taken charge of, and which was rapidly turning what she had hoped would be a nice compromise for a white wedding, the little family-style occasion, into a hideous public event.

It had soon become clear, too, as she did interview after interview, that it was not all spontaneous reaction to her growing appeal, the increasing familiarity with her name, that kept the phone ringing, the requests coming. Someone was stirring up the special interest – and it wasn't Mim. Mim, in fact, while she made sure none of her managerial power went to Kit, had kept strictly out of what she called Lizzie's 'funeral'.

The clue had been Kit's irritation as she tried to side-step reporters. 'Don't be silly, sweetheart, we need all the publicity we can get. Loosen up, talk, reveal, give them juicy headlines!'

Well, she hadn't done that, of course; but, even so, there was enough probing into her private life to give her that old turn-and-run feeling. But, just as there had never been an alternative then, there was nothing to do now but carry on. Behind all and every uncertainty was a kind of purring undercurrent, a sense of enchantment that made her immune to them, whatever they were . . .

Mim would not be at the wedding, but – the Camerons would. Honor would be close by as the words were said that locked her into marriage with Kit; as well as Alister, and Brenna, and even the sisters she had never met, Jilly and Meg, with their husbands and children. She would be part of a real family. And there'd be Clagdon, Dallord House, the horses, the dogs, meals around a table, laughter, confidences, belonging . . .

She would be married, and she would have children, and they would all be part of the family . . .

As for Kit, with all his faults, she could still feel that thrill of anticipation, that promise . . . Yes, she wanted him now, wanted to be his wife . . .

At least that, in the midst of the frenzied rush, was clear.

When the day came, a bright sapphire sky held not the slightest interest for the crowd that gathered round the Chelsea Town Hall. Traffic on the King's Road had come to a total halt. Every face was turned to the doors to see the couple emerge.

Many people, caught up in the surge, asked who was causing the commotion, who was being married. 'Liza Lee,' they would be told, 'and her producer at the BBC!' No-one seemed to remember his name, nor did it seem to matter. Bill-boards carried the fact in bold letters: *LIZA LEE MARRIES*.

TV cameramen could be seen hovering, and countless amateur photographers were at the ready. There seemed a prolonged wait, but the excitement was only intensified, and people were beginning to talk to one another, to discuss Liza, her recent shows, her albums, the strange mother they all hoped they'd see.

Inside, in a sedate, parlour-like room with desks and rows of empty chairs, six people surrounded the couple being joined together, Kenneth McKaye Cameron and Elizabeth Hobbs. The groom wore a light grey suit, a white high-necked satin shirt, a white carnation in the lapel of his suit. His long, wavy dark hair was brushed neatly to his shoulders, and his dark beard was tidily clipped to the long narrow contour of his jaw. There was a restrained ecstasy in his dark, deep-set eyes; he was obviously very, very happy, almost unable to wait for the culminating words.

The bride, who wore a knee-length, three-piece, cream-coloured linen suit, a flower-trimmed cream straw hat perched squarely on top of her thick-cut blondish hair, was trembling so hard that the words would hardly leave her shiny coral lips. Her blue eyes had a wide, almost distraught look.

'. . . You are now man and wife . . .'

The dark-suited, middle-aged man had nodded solemnly, then smiled.

'Wheee . . .' said Kit. 'It's done!' He leaned down and crushed Lizzie to him, kissed her on the mouth. 'My wife,' he added, turning to the others.

The others moved in to make their comments, to congratulate, to kiss: they consisted of Henry Marsh (invited by Lizzie), Cynthia Sterling and her husband, Rex, Cliff Patwick, an old mate of Kit's with long tied-back hair and the musty smell of cannabis, and another of Kit's un-met friends, the Honourable Douglas MacEwen (Duggie), who had been with him at Oxford, 'sent down' at the same time, who kept smiling as if with some sly secret knowledge.

Lizzie, still trembling, smiled, mustered appropriate gaiety.

'Well, Mrs. Cameron,' Kit said, draping her with his arm, 'time to face our public.' He started the procession outwards.

'*Why* didn't they come, Kit?' she whispered. 'What could have happened?'

'What's it matter, love – who cares?' He squeezed her arm, looked down at her in adoration. 'Come on, *shine!* Give them romance, something to dream about!'

Lizzie held her hat in place to look up at him, forced a smile. The absence of the Camerons was like a darkness within her, a blight on everything that was taking place. She saw now how much they had influenced her feelings for Kit, how great a part they played, even if in her terms . . .

The knowledge struck through her like a shock, weakening her knees. What had she done? If it wasn't Kit himself she wanted to be married to, then she'd betrayed him, and herself, everyone, even Robbie . . .

Oh, if only the ground would open up and let her drop quickly out of sight!

'Darling, *please!*' Kit jerked her arm this time as they moved towards the doors and steps. 'The cameras are running – this is *it*, the shining moment!'

Lizzie drew in a breath, straightened, brightened her gaze, widened her lips with the smile that had made her famous . . .

The sound from the crowd was like a cheer, hands rose and fluttered, horns tooted, there was a sea of smiling faces, a surge forward against the police cordon, a closing-in of reporters.

Lizzie, as she always did, responded, performed to everyone's delight. She radiated happiness, élan, humorous and affectionate rapport with her public; she broke from restraint to wave, to throw them a kiss, to give them a thumbs-up and a wink for the man beside her . . .

And with Kit looking as if he might devour her at any moment, the retinue behind them and around them looking on in grinning, conspiratorial approval, it was a scene to satisfy everyone, from those who had gathered early and waited, to those passing by and caught up, by force or choice, in the intrigue, the excitement, the knowledge that they were watching news in process. The media, in all forms, were well-fed, replete with excellent shots of the couple, of the talented young British singer illustrating that she was also a romantic in a Permissive Age, chalking up a win for the institution of marriage . . .

Not without reason. The groom, with his dark, Christ-like, off-beat good looks, was a perfect foil for her vital girlishness, a likely justification for her commitment.

'Be happy, Liza, love,' someone called, and there was an outburst of other congratulatory remarks. Confetti and streamers fell all about her and Kit.

'Christ,' she whispered, brushing bits of coloured paper from his hair and beard, 'where's the car?'

'Where *are* you going for your honeymoon?' a reporter, familiar to Lizzie from other occasions, called out with a wink.

'We've told you,' Kit said, leaning across her. 'Nowhere!'

'We've both got to work,' Lizzie added, softening his curtness. Why was he getting so narky suddenly, she wondered? How quickly his moods changed . . .

'Thank God . . . Come on, Liza, let's go . . .' Kit grasped her hand, smiled while she gave a last wave, then signalled to the group; they all moved quickly down the cement steps to the big white Rolls that had drawn up to the kerb.

The crowd stared in awe at the limousine Kit had hired

191

for just that purpose. 'Only the best for Liza Lee,' he'd said at her protest, 'show them you've made it, give them something to talk about.'

As the grey-uniformed chauffeur held open the back door and Kit helped her into the soft-leathered interior, where she sat for a moment in royal splendour, Lizzie's embarrassment was lifted by the wistful thought of Mim . . . How she would have lapped this up; she could just see her waving, nodding, making a real feast of it . . .

Now, she would only read about it, see it on telly . . .

'See you there,' Kit was saying to the others.

Lizzie ducked her head to see them. 'Where's Cynthia?'

'She's there – for God's sake, darling, stop worrying about *people*. We're man and wife now, we've got each other.' He took her hand, patted it, sat back with a benign, preoccupied smile.

Lizzie turned away, watched the crowds gradually slip from view, to be replaced by occasional curious stares as the white Rolls wove its way towards Mayfair. A loneliness she had never know before laid ghostly fingers round her heart . . .

They hadn't really liked and accepted her. They had just been kind for Kit's sake. They'd heard the way she spoke when she wasn't thinking, the bad grammar, the dropped aitches, that coarse giggle like Mim's. They'd thought, how could Kit bring home a common little thing like that? . . . he'd obviously done it only to spite them . . .

They must have noticed, too, the way she ate, that she'd had to watch them to know what was correct – and she probably made an idiot of herself on Brenna's horse . . .

Of *course* there wouldn't be all those lovely weekends and long visits out there, the friendship with Brenna, the feeling of belonging to an affectionate family, Alister a kind of Dad, Honor a kind of mother – not to replace Mum, but more like ordinary mothers . . .

It had all been a ridiculous dream . . .

One she would have to forget. There was no turning back – she and Kit would have to make it in their own way, in their own world, on their own . . .

'Goodness, we're solemn.' Kit drew her chin around so that he could see her eyes. There was a faint trace of irritation in his, despite the glint of his white teeth. 'You *are* going to cheer up, aren't you?' he asked.

Boring, yes, she thought. That's what I'm being. It was like catching a glimpse of herself in a mirror, seeing herself with a stranger's eye. 'Sorry,' she said, breaking into a jaunty smile. 'It's just nerves. The bubbly will fix me up.'

'Ah. Well, there'll be plenty of that. And Cliff and Duggie are good for a giggle. By the way, I didn't have time to tell you that Ed Vaughan's come through with a silver tray – can't be a *bad* sign, eh?'

'Aha – that ought to do the trick with Henry . . .'

Kit nodded. 'Now you're ticking. See what you can glean from Henry when you're dancing. Tell him you want me to produce your Autumn Special, and that's a command.'

'Do they take commands – from anyone?'

He patted her knee. 'Not overtly, my darling, but perhaps subliminally. It's largely up to you.'

Lizzie hung onto her hat as a gust of wind passed between the car windows. 'Gawd – well, I'll do me best, but I'm not Mim, you know.'

'So I've noticed. In fact, you're going to have to explain to me why you don't have a single feature in common with her – you must've looked a lot like your own father.'

'Bertie . . .?' Lizzie smiled, making a dimple in one cheek. 'Not him, neither – either.'

'Hmmm . . .' Kit chuckled. 'You take that as gospel, do you – that Bert's your real father?'

'What do you mean?'

'Oh, nothing. Come on, jolly up, we're arriving. Now, don't forget – throw your weight. I'm your husband. I mean it, sweetheart.'

Lizzie gave him a 'gaminesque' look. 'I know you do. And, I won't forget.'

Kit kissed her quickly but tenderly. 'That's my girl,' he said.

As they rode up in the lift to go to their room, Lizzie leaned against Kit in a smiling haze. 'That was fun, oh, that was fun . . .'

Kit, unsteady himself, held her upright. 'Not bad, not bad at all.'

'Fun, real fun . . .'

'Yes – told you Cliff and Duggie would make you laugh – old mates, knew me when – before I went square – for you . . .'

Lizzie looked up at him, focused his eyes 'Square Kit, looks like Jesus – lots of fun, a real knees-up . . . Wish Mum had been there . . .'

'Glad she wasn't . . .' He grinned to himself, steadied Lizzie. 'How'd'you do with old Hank, eh? Old lech looked as if he was having you on the dance floor . . .'

'Uh?' Lizzie frowned, her blue gaze adrift. 'Who . . .? What?'

He shook her gently. 'Never mind . . . What a treat you gave them, singing your cockney songs – bet no one'd ever thought you could dance like that – *she* taught you, I suppose?'

'An' Robbie – danced lovely with 'im . . .'

'Him. And that's enough about that. No more Rob Grover – understand? You're mine, now – right? Okay?'

Lizzie's head dropped against his shoulder.

'Up, up. We get off here . . .'

Together they walked rapidly, crookedly to the big gold-and-blue flower-filled room with its huge bed, a large tiled bath beyond. Kit closed the door with a foot and half-carried Lizzie towards the bed, where he collapsed beside her.

'Can't do anything, tonight, wife,' he mumbled in her ear. 'Had it, if you know what I mean . . .'

'Go sleep . . .' Lizzie murmured.

'Yes, go sleep. Morning – do it tomorrow . . .'

Lizzie was already asleep, making a delicate snoring sound . . .

Suddenly, as if an inaudible alarm had gone off, Lizzie's eyes opened to a cream-white ceiling stencilled with gold and faintly lit with sun. Her head felt as if someone was beating it with hammers.

Shaking it, blinking past the pain, she lifted its weight, made a survey . . .

There was Kit, sound asleep and snoring, completely dressed. And she, too, fully dressed . . .

In a flash, it was together – they had got drunk, both of them.

Oh, Lord. She lay back with a groan. That was the last thing she'd expected. All evening long, she'd thought about what would happen when they were at last alone. She'd been prepared, determined to please him. He would have to lead her, tell her what to do, but she'd learn, follow, and at last ignorance and virginity would be behind her; she'd be a woman, launched into life on the other side of the fence – where Mum might have kept her from for ever if Kit hadn't stormed her.

She turned to look at him. Even crumpled and open-mouthed, he looked amazingly handsome. His hair was pushed into a ragged fringe and his eyelashes curved darkly against the deep sockets of his eyes. She wanted to kiss him, to run her fingers over his cheeks and down along his long flattened body . . .

How strangely his hands cupped the rise between his legs, inert, protective . . . It made her want to lift his hands and have a look, to see what he had there without him knowing she was looking . . .

If only she wasn't so bloody shy – crikey, Kit would

probably love it if she did that – but she couldn't stand the idea of being forward, going first.

Anyhow, her head hurt too much, and she was faintly sick, more than faintly – in fact, she might have to throw up . . .

Lizzie looked at the clock, blinking against the glare of sky between the golden draperies. Only quarter past seven! Two days of doing nothing stretched ahead, and her awake!

She leaned back for a few moments, closing her eyes to the sudden return of bleakness, to the unpleasant insight that she had *meant* to drink too much, and that it hadn't helped . . .

And worse, that she missed Mim, would have given anything to hear her sure, cocky voice, telling her what to do, what she *had* to do, and to get on with it, to feel her hard little hug that meant she'd done well and was loved for it . . .

'Awake?' said Kit, 'Christ, what happened? I feel as if a bus ran over me with spiked tyres!'

'We got pissed.'

Kit laughed painfully. 'Don't – what on earth time is it?'

She told him, and somehow his groan seemed to lift some of the bleakness, even made her smile. 'Hurts, doesn't it?'

'There's some aspirin in my case – I'll get some coffee sent up.'

'I might have to chuck first . . .'

'Go ahead, get it over.' Kit heaved himself upward, held his head a moment, then walked unsteadily to the suitcase. 'What a mess,' he said. 'Just shoved everything in, post and all . . . Here we are.'

Lizzie took some aspirins from him, padded shoeless to the bathroom, gulped them down with water, but simultaneously threw them back up again. Even so, she felt better, almost well. 'All clear,' she told him, and he followed her in.

An hour later, having consumed a large pot of black coffee, they were sitting back in armchairs, Lizzie in her pink honeymoon negligée and mules, Kit in his briefs (he'd given up pyjamas on leaving home), chatting amiably about life, gossiping about the studio. Kit's remarks no longer carried any innuendos about sex, her body, what he would do to her once they were married. He seemed quite oblivious of her as a female; she might just as well have been one of his male colleagues or friends.

Lizzie was both relieved and apprehensive. Never had her lack of experience left her so inadequate. She kept smiling, making quips – it was worse than getting ready to go on stage unrehearsed. Surely, soon, he would make the move . . .

By noon, he had sent for the papers, read, taken a bath, made some notes in a big exercise book, suggested a place for lunch and what they would do with the rest of the afternoon and evening. 'Fine,' she kept saying, 'lovely.' None of it made any difference; she was already restless for work, to get into the flat and settle it – but . . .

'You're wondering why I don't make love to you, Liza,' he said abruptly, moving to her side as she gazed from a window down at the Piccadilly traffic. 'The truth is, I don't think I'm going to be able to. That's why I got drunk last night – to postpone the inevitable.'

Lizzie turned to look up at him. 'You don't really want me – that way?'

He shook his head, put his arm round her shoulder. 'I want you all right. It's not that easy to explain. I just don't think you're going to want to do what I need done, if you see what I mean.' His gaze into hers was like a small boy's, open with honesty.

'What do you need done?' Lizzie's thoughts went to the books she'd read, the plays she'd seen, the talk she'd heard in theatres. There were all sorts of things men liked to do or have done to them, strange, crazy, really peculiar things – was this what he meant? She tried to keep the dread from her gaze.

'Yes – a kind of set of things, a fantasy sort of; we act it out, together.'

'I see . . .'

He gave her a sideways smile of resignation. 'Don't worry. I wouldn't force it on you.'

'But how do I know if you don't tell me what it is?'

'Hmmm. Good question.' He let her go, patted his pocket and drew out one of his 'joints'. 'Want one?' he asked.

She shook her head.

He lit up, dragged, was silent a moment. 'It would help, sweetheart. Relax you.' He lifted an eyebrow to make his point.

Lizzie breathed in the familiar smell with more than usual distaste. She felt as if she were on a toboggan going down an icy cliff.

'Come on,' he said softly. 'We don't have to go out to lunch, or at all.' He held the cigarette out to her, his deep-set eyes fixed on hers.

'Wouldn't it be better to explain first,' she said, drawing away, going to a large pale-blue brocade couch and sitting rigidly in one corner.

He broke into a soft, hoarse laugh. 'You are so deliciously naïve,' he said. 'It rather turns me on – but I'm afraid it isn't enough.'

'How do you manage – usually?' Lizzie looked down at her carefully-manicured nails, letting her fringe conceal the fear in her eyes.

'Manage?' Kit sank into a French reproduction love-seat, crossed his knees, lifted his face so that it looked more than ever Christ-like. 'I won't go into details, darling – let's just say I do. So – it won't be the end of the world for us, unless a platonic relationship bothers *you* . . .'

'You mean you don't care whether you . . . whether we
. . .?' Lizzie looked up in slow wonder.

'Not that much, to be frank. And I won't mind if
you – well, if you find your fun elsewhere. Just as long as
we stay married.'

The bells that rang in Lizzie's mind did not sound unfa-
miliar, but there was a jangling undertone. To help him in
any way she could seemed only natural, but to be no more
than a means, with no genuine bond at all . . . 'Just so you
can use my name, Kit – haven't you got *any* confidence in
yourself?'

His face turned abruptly. 'Have you, my love – without your mother?'

Lizzie felt the heat rise into her cheeks. She felt his
sharp, hostile stare, could not speak.

'So let's drop the high moral tone, shall we, Liza? Until
such time as we can both stand on our own two feet, let's
at least hold each other up. Right?'

Kit did not seem to notice that she didn't answer. He sat
smoking, head tilted as if listening to a voice in his mind,
every now and then a smile forming and withdrawing
from his neat, strong mouth.

Lizzie was numb, her every thought stumbling into confused dead ends. Vaguely, as if from a distance, she heard
the rattle of hunger in her stomach; the urge to leap up and
simply take off came, and went . . .

'Liza – look,' Kit said suddenly. 'What you were saying
about explaining . . . Maybe it *is* a good idea. Suppose
you *didn't* mind, suppose it actually worked out between
us! That'd be the answer, wouldn't it, satisfy us all?'

Before Lizzie could answer, he had gone to his suitcase.
'Just put these on, darling,' he said. 'That's how it begins.
It'll seem silly to you – but it won't to me. Then go lie on
the bed on top of the clothes.'

Lizzie did not move, but could not help a curious look at
the items of clothing he had thrown on the bed – what

seemed an old-fashioned camisole, some long knickers with elastic at the knees, some black wool stockings . . .

'Gawd!' she muttered. 'You really must be joking!'

'Aw, don't say that . . .' Kit pouted, shifted his shoulders, 'they're very important.'

'Maybe, but no thanks.' Lizzie reached for some newspapers left scattered on the floor beside her.

'Oh, Liza, please – not now you've got me started . . .' He came over to her, squatted beside her, looking appealingly into her eyes. 'Let me *tell* you – it's as if you're my mother, you see – I catch you undressing, and then . . .'

'Oh, no – oh, Gawd, Kit – let me alone!'

Lizzie jumped up, practically knocking him over. 'I'm getting out of here,' she said. 'I can't breathe!'

'Come back – come back, do you hear. Do as I tell you, Liza, or you'll be sorry.'

Lizzie was like a deaf person. She put on her clothes with resolute speed, forgetting that she bared her body to him for the first time. It was no longer the least bit relevant that each had bodies, one male, one female; she yearned only for fresh air, freedom from the sight of him . . .

'Damn you, damn you, Liza. Why did you tell me to tell you? Why did you let me get started?'

The frenzy in his voice startled but did not stop her. She shoved the brush through her hair, threw the brush down, moved quickly to the door.

'Where are you going?' Kit called.

'I don't know . . .'

'When will you be back?'

Lizzie didn't answer – but suddenly, as she reached for the big gilt doorhandle, she felt the squeeze of his arms wind round her like a steel vice.

'You're not going anywhere, Mummy,' Kit whispered in her ear. 'You're going to put on those clothes and then take them off, in the dark, and I'm going to watch through the curtains, and then I'm going to fuck you . . .'

Lizzie struggled with every bit of strength she could muster, but she could hardly move in the vice-like grip as he dragged her towards the bed. She heard her own screaming, but it seemed muffled, and she was somehow enmeshed in her clothes, being undressed, shoved bodily into folds of cotton and sateen, her legs into the rough feel of wool . . .

'Stop it, leave me alone, you're mad . . .'

Her strangled gasps were drowned in his heavy breathing. 'You're very stupid, Liza – it's fun, it's wonderful . . . Anna loves it . . .! It makes me big, it makes me hard – you'll see . . .!'

It was while he was saying this that, for just a moment, he let up, lifted his hands – Lizzie twisted, turned, was out of his grasp, running . . .

The next thing she knew was a great blasting thud on her jaw. The room, Kit's blood-red face, rotated, spun, went black.

She came to in dim silence. Somewhere, a clock was ticking like hurrying feet. She raised her head. As the memory of what had happened came sliding back into focus, Lizzie appraised the situation in cautious fear . . .

But, after a moment, it seemed certain that she was alone, that Kit was not there. She drew in a long, quivering breath, struggled from the bed . . .

It was then she noticed that she was still wearing the strange garments, but half-ripped off, and that a sticky substance with an acrid smell covered her from the waist to the top of her thighs.

She made a moaning sound of distaste, protest, sank back for a moment in despair.

But she could not lie there forever. Life went on.

Getting up, she bathed until every inch of her was fresh and clean again, washed her hair and rinsed it three times, cleaned her teeth, rinsed her mouth several times over.

At last, she felt moderately detached, ready to face the world.

Before she left the room, having cleared it of every trace of herself, she cast one last curious glance at Kit's suitcase, still open and spilling its contents onto a wooden trestle.

Pausing, she walked over to it, peered in, ran her hands this way and that through the contents. Under a cleaner's bag holding a shirt and jeans, lay an envelope. It was marked First Class, Urgent, and addressed to Mr. and Mrs. Kenneth Cameron.

It would not, she thought, be prying to open it . . .

'Dear Liza and Kit,' it said, in clear, round handwriting. 'I'm writing on behalf of the family to wish you every happiness in your marriage which will, by now, have taken place. We were very sorry you decided not to invite us as I think all of us would have been glad to be there. I must be frank and tell you that there is considerable regret here, as well as some deep hurt, that you excluded us. We cannot believe it was you, Liza, who wanted this, and you will always be welcome at Dallords, even if Kit, as he implied in his brief note, never wants to come here again. As for you, Kit, I feel the way you used us to influence Liza was utterly beastly. I'd better stop now before I make an absolute ass of myself. Your "also-ran", Brenna.'

For the first time in her life, Lizzie broke down into sobs.

After she had recovered from them sufficiently to go out into the world she slipped the letter into her handbag, and walked from the room without a backward look.

# CHAPTER FIFTEEN

'Aw, me darlin', me baby, me li'l' one.' Mim's hard arms rocked her so long and so hard that Lizzie was getting limp.

'All right, Mum, all right. I love you, I'm sorry, and thank you for having me back. I need my head examined. I don't know anything about anything, and I'll never go against you again.'

'Don't be a twit! 'Course you will. You'll grow up an' see what's what. Only, for now, we've got to get this bugger sorted out so 'e don't bother you no more.'

'No barneys, Mum.' Lizzie held her by the shoulders, looked sternly into glinting eyes. 'Understood? I don't hate him, I can't. It must be terrible to be so – well, muddled . . .'

'You goin' to tell me just what 'e done?' Mim interrupted her to point out the supper she'd been making. ' 'Ere, sit yerself down an' 'ave a nice kipper an' some tea. I want to 'ear the lot.'

'Well, you won't, Mum,' Lizzie moved in a trance to the familiar smell, hunger and relief to be home dimming the ache in her jaw, her weariness and confusion. 'Not from me, at least.'

Mim put an apron on over her plaid trousers, lit a cigarette, fussed round Lizzie like a waitress with a special customer.

'Sit down, Mum,' Lizzie said, between gulps of brown-black tea and salty fish. 'I'll tell you most of what's happened, but not the *lot* – never.'

Mim's eyebrows gathered across her nose. ' 'Ow we going to explain them bruises, then, eh? An' suppose you're in the club?'

'The bruises aren't bad. You can cover them with make-up. I don't know whether or not I could be pregnant – but if I don't get the "curse" on time, you can take me to that woman you know down Bale Street.'

'Me Gawd – you 'ave grown up sudden. Well, I never.' For a moment, Mim forgot her outrage to gaze at Lizzie in awe and wonder. 'You'll never know, me darlin', 'ow I missed you, like it were a terrible black 'ole inside me . . .'

'Mum – I missed you, too – honest.' Lizzie was surprised to find the hardness of Mim's hand under her own a comfort. 'What you been doing with yourself, anyhow? Hope you got a chance to rest, have a bit of fun with Harry.'

'What!' Mim plonked her sharp elbows on the table. 'You jokin'? Near got you a contrac' for 'Ollywood, ain't I. Wrote just like the nobs. An' – wait till you 'ear this – got meself enrolled in a school to learn to talk proper like you.'

Lizzie swallowed a piece of kipper, slowly put down her knife and fork. 'Mum?' Her eyes widened into Mim's, gleamed with suspicion. 'You *knew* I'd be back, didn't you? You'd got it all worked out. Knew you'd win, eh.'

Mim dropped her gaze with wry modesty. 'Not as 'ow I'd admit, darlin' – an' not so soon, but . . .'

Lizzie pressed her lips, shook her head. 'What chance I got, Mum?' she said, unconsciously lapsing into a little girl's voice. 'You're a fox, you are.'

Mim grinned, winked. 'No-one puts nothin' over on Mim 'Obbs, me duck. You'll see – even them moguls out there'll 'ave to watch it.'

Lizzie gazed into her shrewdly puckered face with the cigarette jutting almost straight up from the side of her mouth. 'I don't doubt it,' she murmured, with a wise, tender smile. 'I wouldn't want to tangle with you myself!'

Mim smiled back. 'I'm so 'appy – Gawd, I could blub. It's up to the stars an' away we go, eh? I got so many plans. D'ya wanna see yer press cuttin's, all the post what come, 'ear the song . . .?' Mim was already leaping to her feet.

'Oy – hold on, Mum, hold on. You've got to let me sleep first. I'm wiped out, deep-down wiped out – you know?'

'Oh, of course, me poor lamb . . . You sleep till the cows come 'ome – yer bed's all made up with nice sheets, just wai'in' for yer.'

'Thanks, Mum.'

Lizzie went to the small, pink wallpapered room, feeling the full weight of the last few weeks, the last two days, begin to drag her downward into a kind of stupor. Oh, how good the small neat bed felt, like a little life-raft in the middle of a great dark sea . . .

'There, me love.' Mim's greasy lips brushed Lizzie's forehead, rough fingers smoothed back her hair. Lizzie drew in a long, deep sigh . . .

'Mum . . .' she murmured, as her eyelids descended like small lead curtains. 'Bertie *was* my real father, wasn't he?'

'Why, 'course! Why d'ya ask, me pe'al?'

Something in Mim's tone made Lizzie fight the weight of her lids, open her eyes. 'You sound funny . . .' She struggled to lift her head, to focus Mim's alertly tilted head, to see the expression in her eyes.

'What's up with you, Lizzie, love – someone been sayin' thin's – that bastard . . .?'

'No . . . But I don't look like you much, and I don't look like he did . . .' Lizzie's attention blurred, returned. 'You'd tell me, wouldn't you, the truth . . .?'

'I'll fix that bugger proper!'

Lizzie's eyes opened fully, saw the scowl, the anger. It was as if a window suddenly opened in her mind, letting in a real blast of light. 'He wasn't,' she said. 'Bertie wasn't my real father. Mum, don't lie to me.'

Mim seemed to back away. The protest in her face was like a mime. ' 'Oo said I was lyin', an' why would I do that, eh? Come on, you got yerself in a right ol' swivet – just close your minces an' . . .

'Who was he, then, Mum?' Lizzie sat up, plumped the pillow behind her, folded her arms across her chest. 'Come on, I got to know. I won't shut up till you tell me.'

'There's nothin' to tell – poor ol' Bertie, if 'e could 'ear you now – after all 'e done for ya, 'ow much 'e loved 'is Miss Cuddles . . .'

'MUM!'

Mim blinked. Her lips pinched. For a moment, it seemd she might revert to her old tactics of handling Lizzie as if she were still just a child untouched by the outside world; but the frown on Lizzie's face, the intensity of the blue gaze seemed to daunt her. She lowered her chin; the cigarette jerked, finally came to rest. 'It should never 'ave 'appened,' she said, her tinny voice flattened to a drone. 'But it did, me love, it did. I were only a kid – seventeen, in the chorus of *Kiss Me Kate* . . . An' 'e – well, 'e were lovely . . .'

Lizzie thought her heart had stopped beating. As Mim talked on, the story gradually unfolding, she felt her face crumple, her eyes fill. 'So that's why I look the way I do . . .'

' 'Ang on – you *do* 'ave a bit of me chin, an' some of me expressions – an' all me talents . . .'

'And American . . .' Lizzie looked off into some invisible distance, her eyes dreamy. 'I'm half American . . .'

'Well . . . Bertie did take you on, you know. You were really 'is . . .'

'I loved Bertie – but it's not the same, is it?' Lizzie's eyes came back to Mim's. 'Oh, Mum – I want to meet him, to *know* him!'

Mim grunted, dragged on the cigarette without touching it. 'Not a prayer, ol' darlin' – don't even know 'is name. 'E was goin' back to the States next day – never 'eard another peep. 'E probably never remembered me name, neither. It was just one of them thin's what 'appens in life. You got to forget all about it, Lizzie-girl. It won't do you no good. We got to get on with our lives, the two of us, stick together, make it come out right an' shinin'. That's the song I done – "Together". The ti'le ain't original, but it don't ma'er.'

Lizzie looked at her, seeing her as if for the very first time. She saw the jaunty, cheeky little chorus girl with her brassy curls and East End humour tearing about London in a flashy sportscar with this tall, blond, handsome young American, having a ball, having the time of her life . . .

And the brave, no-tears, no-regret way she'd said goodbye to him in the dawn in a great hotel . . .

What a truly amazing character her mother was, marrying old Bertie to give her child a name, then devoting herself to nothing but bringing her up, training her, sacrificing herself entirely to her child's success, with no thought for her own needs, her own life . . .

'Oh, Mum, darling.' She reached for her, pressed her forehead to hers. 'I'm sorry I made such a problem for you. I'll try to make it all up to you, I'll be anything you want. I'll get to the very top – I will, I *promise!*'

Mim's nose quivered. She ducked her head. When she lifted it again, she had a stern look. 'No more sop – you got to rest, I got work to do.' Nodding briskly, Mim got up, left the room, closed the door behind her.

Lizzie lay for a few moments, arms behind her head, wrapped in a brand new kind of sensation, almost a glow . . .

She had a father, big and tall, blond, blue-eyed like herself – what was he like? What did he do? What kind of things would he be interested in? What sort of business would he be in? Or perhaps he was an artist, a musician, a writer . . .

Was he married? Did he have other children? What would he do, say, feel, if he knew he had a daughter in England? Suppose they met – would he like her? Would they be able to talk together, go for walks, get to know each other as father and daughter . . .?

She began to dream of all kinds of ways they might meet, the surprise, the gladness . . .

The faint shadow of other possibilities, that he might not want to know, that he was *not* a nice person, that he might avoid her, shut her out, deny all connection – even that he might be ill, long-since dead, she turned away, refused . . .

She *would* see him. They *would* love each other. Some time she would like to tell Robbie about him. Robbie, who had nobody of his own, would understand how she felt, what a difference it made . . .

She fell asleep, the image of a man, somewhere, who was her own father, looming large behind her lids, blotting out all other thoughts, dreams, feelings.

# CHAPTER SIXTEEN

'Well, me darlin', it won't be long now. Best freshen up for the photographers. Put yer false lashes back on.'

'Surely not just for landing, Mum – nobody'll be there at this time.'

' 'Course they will, silly. You're a big name, you're news. Like the Beatles were when they got 'ere.'

'That's different, Mum. I'm only a female singer, going to do one spot on one television show, as a guest!' Lizzie leaned back, closed Mim's sharp-boned little face from view, tried to recapture for a few more moments the delicious sensation she'd had while dozing . . .

She had somehow got free of her body, herself, the plane, and seemed to be floating and flying outside, tumbling about on the clouds, spiralling upward and downward with such swift, effortless ease that it made her laugh with joy. She, who was Lizzie yet not Lizzie, could do anything she wanted just by wishing it, and she knew that if she really wanted to, she could simply take off into that horizonless blue beyond the clouds, travel onwards in complete freedom for ever and ever . . .

The song she'd sung as a little girl came back to her, and she was singing 'Somewhere Over the Rainbow', her voice trilling in great sweet waves as she flew and floated away, away . . .

And then Mim had spoken in her ear, and just like that, without even a movement, she was back in the seat beside her.

'There'll be a big bloody queue for the loos, love . . .'

'All right – another five minutes – why don't you go first?'

'Well, if you're goin' to be shirty, I *will*!'

Lizzie had to smile to herself as Mim shoved her way past other passengers, using her elbows and scowling brows to clear the way; but, of course, the spell was broken – and even with Mim gone, in the peaceful, droning calmness with eyes tightly closed, Lizzie could not recapture that blissful liberation . . .

Instead, she found herself going back over the events of the last two years, trying to remember their sequence, to wonder how she had got from there to here with so much speed and so little light . . .

Mim's plans had not gone smoothly. The man in Hollywood, while interested, had financial and technical problems to sort out before a definite offer could be made. A musical in New York had decided to make its cast all-black, ruling out Lizzie as the star. The producer of the Ed Sullivan TV show for CBS in New York hoped to feature her on one of their programmes, but apparently they were having 'unsettling' times due to the shift of interest to 'talk shows'. At last, after clashes with Mim over money and terms, CBS had 'won' Lizzie for their Percy Cosmo show. It made no difference to Lizzie herself – she simply went on, worked hard, rehearsed hard, practised hard, sang to the best of her ability; the venue, the time, were unimportant.

Kit had been fired suddenly, without warning, not specifically for the nasty rumours and lies he spread about her, including that she was 'too kinky even for him', that 'under all that sweetness was a vicious little sadist', but because it gave Ed Vaughan and Henry Marsh the excuse for which they'd been waiting for so long.

She had not said goodbye to him or seen him again and, when she visited the Camerons one weekend, she found that they knew no more of him than she did. There was only one clue: Anna Croft had also disappeared, and a girl at the studio who knew her thought she and Kit had gone to some ashram in California, which struck Lizzie as another of his flights from psychiatry.

The Autumn Special had gone well: Mim's 'Together', the rousing lyric given a rock beat by the famous song-writer, Tusker Jennings, had not only become a hit song, number 1 in the charts, but a kind of theme song: wherever she appeared, it was always a winner.

Tusker, who'd got the art of dealing with the 'hell-hag' (with blatant flattery and much hugging), also stepped in to write 'Lovable', and a revised version of 'Stars Over Soho' with a beautiful minor wail to it that Lizzie, in black satin with black lace stockings, had sung leaning against a lamppost, her hair lit up the same colour as the low-hanging moon, with all the theatres and cafés and porno shops sug-gested in a neon-lighted silhouetted backdrop, a chorus of passers-by joining her in muted refrain.

'It's all due to my clever little Mum,' Lizzie would say to the press, to the people who praised the number, re-praised Lizzie's 'ever-developing interpretations and vocal versatil-ity'. Why did they never seem to believe her? Why did they resent Mim's being with her, always trying to brush her off, talk around her as if she weren't there? Mim was looking marvellous these days, too, with her toned-down hair or nice flattering wigs, and she had taken Lizzie's protest to heart about 'the rotten old fag' always in her mouth and now smoked Gauloise cigarettes in a gold holder, with an air of style and panache that was amusing but quite impres-sive . . .

Lizzie found it more and more annoying when Mum was ignored, or treated like an object in the way. 'Don't you bloody do that,' she'd burst out one night at an opening they'd gone to (presided over by the Queen Mum), and tug-ged Mim round in front of her so that the photographers had had to take shots of Mim too, if they wanted *her*.

Those stunned looks still warmed the old cockles – *but*, it had started a new trend in write-ups – like: 'Is Liza Lee a split personality – not just the radiant, self-effacing lovable of "Lovable"?' one reporter had written in the *News of the World*; 'but someone else as well, someone quite unpredictable and mysterious that none of us know at all?'

'What a load of old codswallop.' Mim had said. 'Just because you show a bit of guts, spit back – and so you should. Gawd knows, they got to be kept in their place, the cheeky bastards.'

Even so, Lizzie tried not to lose her cool again. When they tried their 'in depth' approach to her and Mim's relationship, she would answer in smiling unflappable patience. 'We love each other, we're a team.' It baffled them, totally.

As for Robbie, she'd had a letter via Cynthia that she treasured, read again and again. He told her he loved and played her albums. He could hardly believe they'd actually been sweethearts. 'To think you'd have married *me* – blimey. I wonder what would have become of us, eh? Maybe we'd have been as happy as bears in a blanket – but I "hae me doots", Lizzykins. I ain't what I was. I'm on the stuff and I can't get off. Luckily, it don't seem to matter to the fans, and don't hurt the music none. We're off Stateside soon, for a tour. I'm trying to write some decent things for the changing market, experiment, so to speak. We got to be a commercial success this time or go bust. I wish I could lay eyes on you, baby. Sorry about your marriage – I didn't like his looks in the picture as you come out of the Registry Office, a right phoney creep – you looking scared out of your wits, me poor lamb. Your Mum must have broke her seams. Never mind, one day you'll find your Prince Charming – wish I could have been him – but you're better off without Rob Grover (wonder what me real name was, eh?). I can't even do take-offs no more, can't even recognize meself in the

212

mirror . . . Well, sing your heart out, sweet Lizzie, give pleasure to this sad old world. See you on the screen, hear you on the waves and discs. Think of me – I dream of Lizzie with the light brown hair – and great blue minces – and everything else . . . G'night, Gawd bless you. Robbie.'

Oh, how the tears had come – all she'd saved, held back since her first smack from Mim.

Right after that, she remembered that strange, lightning-struck feeling when she missed her monthly, when it could mean only one thing, that she had a baby starting inside her . . . Oh, the wonder of it! Even if it was Kit's, it had a special life of its own. She could let it grow within her, give birth to it, be a mother, love it and care for it, bring it up . . .

Where? How? She'd had the most inane dream about *that*. She would tell the Camerons. They would take her in, along with the baby, become its family, help her to give it a good life, surrounded by love, growing up with animals, the countryside . . .

She, in turn, would help Honor and Alister run Dallords, muck in with everything, become strong, efficient, indispensable to them all. Robbie might some day come there, to rest, recuperate, and he would love the little – boy? girl? it didn't matter – and they would marry and have other children. He would use the piano in the music room to compose, she would help with lyrics, they'd have a music school in the summers, in the big barn . . .

'Well, thank 'eavens we've caught it early,' Mim had said, becoming rough with her in her panic, practically shoving her into the green Mini and rushing her off to old Mrs. Podinska who, though she'd grown senile, remembered Effie's kid from Bale Street days, had kept her skill and been able to prod out the clot with a catheter. Lizzie had bled a frightening amount, felt weak and deeply depressed, but other than a greenish pallor under her freckles, showed no *outward* signs of suffering, having turned a very sharp corner of her life.

Following that was a general blur of shows and concerts. Hammersmith, Birmingham, Manchester, more TV appearances, through which Mim moved with tireless energy, supervised the lighting, the acoustics, the transport, the endless details and unexpected problems of production, balancing the resentment and hostility she raised with grudging respect. When Lizzie was bothered by headaches or colds, or just plain inertia, Mim alternately cosseted and drove her, never allowed her to sag . . .

Which was not a bad thing. For Lizzie suspected that, left to her own devices, she might be overcome by laziness, or a detachment that bordered on ungrateful indifference. She loved to please people, loved the people she pleased, enjoyed the giving and the receiving, the performance and the applause; but the applause was really for Mim, made her happy because it made Mim happy. The two couldn't be separated – Mim = applause, applause = Mim; it had been that way ever since she could remember . . .

Sometimes, she longed to bring herself right into the heart of it all, connect directly – but there was some sort of veil there, a vague mist – and, anything, almost anything at all, distracted her . . .

Anyhow, the months had moved on like in movies where the pages of a calendar flick over to show the passing of time. She'd had Asian 'flu and missed her very first performances, three in a row. Mim had paced up and down, up and down, waiting for her to open her eyes. Every time she did, she would sit quickly down beside her and say 'Better, are we? Want to get up – 'ave a nice cuppa strong black tea?' Poor Mim, she had suffered more than herself, and she couldn't blame her – it had cost everyone a lot of lost money; there were no understudies for Liza

214

Lee, a horrid feeling, like a pressure between the ribs . . .

A rather nice time, after that, with Danny Jones in the picture. For some reason, Mim didn't mind him taking her out. Danny looked like a fashion dummy in the window of a menswear shop, correct pin-stripe suits, mousey hair worn neat and short, granny-style metal glasses. In fact, he was an executive with Pia Records, very influential in the music world, admired Lizzie's talent unreservedly. Danny respected Mim's rules, brought her home from suppers in expensive restaurants by midnight, helped her from his beautiful Mercedes, kissed her hand. 'Sleep well. Take care,' he'd say, 'my dearest Liza.' He wanted to marry her.

This part she hadn't confided in Mim. It was the only way to keep Danny from being scuttled – and she was enjoying the feeling he gave her of being wanted – and respected. Though how she would ever be able to tell for sure about what a man might really be like, she didn't know. That part of it still made her shudder. On the other hand, she couldn't stop there, never taking another risk. Sometimes she wished Danny were *not* so correct – she was almost fond enough of him to – well, at least *explore* something closer. Cor blimey, here she was, twenty-one, and not even started! What *hadn't* happened was almost more frightening than what *had*! It was time, more than time, to get into life, into the living of it!

But of course, the event that stood out the most over these last years, was one that still gave her a twinge of sadness, of loss . . .

The maid hadn't turned up that day, and while Mim was typing and telephoning in the living room, she'd decided to make herself useful by making the beds. There, under Mim's pillow, was a torn-out page of a magazine. Beside one picture on it, was a pencilled 'X'. The picture was of a tall man with a rather pudgy chin, a paunchy middle. He was raising a tweed cap and grinning at a jockey on a horse. The caption under the picture said: 'Rocky Middleton's famous "Camelot" romps home again. Best season ever for the Kentucky breeder, pictured here with his wife, the erstwhile Mrs. Jemima Farmington of the Severn Valley clan of that name.'

Lizzie's heart had pumped up a storm. Was it *him* – her father? Why else would Mim have X'ed the picture? Mum got all the American magazines, but for show-biz news, *not* for Society's doings, horse-racing!

In the end, she found it too difficult to hold a lid on her excitement, her hopes. She'd revealed her find, confronted her.

'Why did I 'ide it if it weren't 'im?' Mim looked like a child caught stealing. 'Well, darlin' – just so's you wouldn't look the way you look now – all goo and sop, breakin' me 'eart. I 'ad to make sure, didn't I? Couldn't go arse-over-tip, could we? I mean, I ain't laid eyes on the bloke for over twenty years . . .'

'Well, Mum – did you? Look into it? What did you find out?'

Mim shrugged, her expression sour. 'It ain't 'im.'

'How do you *know*?'

''Cause I 'ad 'Arry look 'im up, didn't I? Goes to the editor, he does, finds out all about the gent. Seems 'e was in Korea with General MacArthur at that time. *Couldn't* 'ave been 'im.'

Lizzie felt her hopes seep out like the air from a balloon. She felt sorry, too, for the way she had jumped on Mum – after all, she must be just as keen to know who the father of her child was – and just as disappointed to find this man wasn't him. She decided it was best not to mention the subject again.

Perhaps some day, somewhere, somehow, she'd find him . . .

Meanwhile – America. First, the TV stint – then west to Hollywood to do the modern version of *Nymph Errant*,

216

a thirties play Mim remembered, with Gertrude Lawrence in it, about a girl who does everything she can to plunge into life and lose her virginity, but is always thwarted – so that she finally returns to the gardener's boy who loved her in the first place, and he takes it. According to what Zeke Solway had told Mim, the new story would make tongue-in-cheek excursions through the so-called Permissive Age, would be a 'spoof' of the no-holds-barred, liberated sex of the sixties and today. 'The Little Brit', as the American papers had named her, was the one and only natural for the part; Mim had made a very 'sensible' deal with Mervnick Pictures, Inc. The great Benny Sebastian was to direct her (whoever *he* was, Lizzie had thought, but not said) . . .

'Right you are, me darlin' – 'op to. You don't want to be caught in the bog when they say fasten your ruddy seat belts!'

Lizzie looked up. Her mother's familiar face was wreathed in grim excitement. 'America, Lizzie,' she said. 'Well, they ain't seen nothin' yet. Yanks, 'ere comes the greatest warbler of 'em all – Liza Lee 'erself, in person!'

Lizzie sighed, stretched, drew her overnight bag from under her seat. 'Better remember the aitches, Mum – they might not understand you.' She smiled, winked, patted the knobbly shoulder, went to get ready.

Waiting for Liza Lee with the crowd at the barrier, a large, frowning man in a light tan suit suddenly became an amiably smiling man in dark glasses that glinted with bright October sun. 'There she is, Harv. Stands out like a beacon. Look at that walk, those legs, the peekaboo hairdo – straight from Swinging London!'

'Simmer down, Fred – who's the hatchet-face with her?' Another man, in a similar suit in grey flannel, retained his frown, pushed irritably at the knot of his floral silk tie.

'You know,' said a young woman in a beige trouser suit,

dark glasses pressed up on the top of her long dark hair. 'Her. The dragon. And everywhere that Lizzie went . . .'

'Brother,' said Harv,' she looks like a man in drag.'

'Maybe she is,' said Fred. 'The bowed legs give her away.'

The two men laughed.

'Orders from Percy are to play it cool, lay on the charm – without the mom on your side, it's trouble all the way.'

'Bullshit, Ruth. Percy's a coward, we all know that.'

'Only when it comes to women. The battle-axe variety.'

'Must have had a bad experience in his childhood.'

'Yeah – being born!'

They all laughed together, then fell silent to watch Lizzie and Mim with their porter and luggage approach. When they were close enough to be seen by them, the group began to wave, smile.

'There we are,' said Mim. 'Now, don't say a lot of stupid things, just show 'em your minces, give 'em a penny-a – I'll do the talkin'.'

'Yes, ma'am,' Lizzie said through closed teeth.

'None of your lip, neither.' Mim settled her light blue cape over her green plaid suit with the authority of Burberry's label behind her, of every stitch on her bought without reference to expense, the aura of barrows gone for ever, even her teeth resplendently crowned or replaced with new, beyond reproach.

'I don't see any press, or welcoming mob,' Lizzie said, forgetting her own appearance, oblivious of whether she was wearing a Quant, Feraut, or Mim-special, only that there was something different in the air here, a quickened pace, some sort of exhilaration that came from the louder, more exuberant sound of American voices.

'Well, I do, ducks. What do you think all that kerfuffle's about down there, eh?'

'Hmmm . . .' Lizzie cast an unconvinced glance to a large crowd of young people at the far end by the exit doors but, just in case, began to brace up, prepare to turn on the 'Little Brit' act. Looking beyond them, to the sea of huge cars and taxis (that were yellow instead of black) glinting blindingly in the afternoon sun, she had a moment of almost unbearable excitement. Oh, if only she could dissolve and vanish, somehow disconnect from all she was here to do and be, and experience this new world, first-hand, alone!

'Shove back yer 'air,' Mim muttered. 'Lift yer chin. Pay attention.'

Lizzie wrenched from the nudging elbow, but obeyed. By the time they reached the outstretched hands, were drowned in an effusion of welcome, solicitude and identification, reality overwhelmed her; beaming radiantly, she threw herself into matching the expectations of an executive producer, the head of the promotion department, an assistant Mr. Cosmo sent to see that she was made comfortable, and *au fait* with her schedule.

'You're just as cute as they said you were,' Harv told her, as they gathered up the luggage; 'that's a real cute accent you got.'

'Yeah,' said Fred, his irritability changed to boyishly open flirtation. 'It's different to when you sing. You're going to make a big hit with our people. Hope you don't mind interviews, radio spots, things like that.'

' 'Course she don't,' said Mim; 'it's what she's used to, ain't it?'

The others looked at her as she moved briskly along, resisting the back-seat role unconsciously assigned her. ' 'Ere,' she said to Ruth, 'who are *they*?' She lifted her chin towards the milling noisy group outside. 'They wai'in' fer Lizzie?'

'Uh – no, Mrs. Hobbs. We didn't want to expose Liza to that sort of thing before she'd recovered from her jet-lag – that bunch is waiting to see a British rock group going home. Say, you must know Rob Grover . . .'

Lizzie stopped dead. 'Rob Grover!'

People tripped over them as they all stopped to look at Lizzie's open mouth, stunned blue gaze. 'That's right,' said Ruth, half-smiling. 'Friend of yours, Liza?'

Lizzie was not there to answer. Shoving her bags and coats at Mim, she was off and running, her soft pink dress riding up to show her long thin legs like white scissors, her hair waving outward like a pale brown nimbus.

'Lizzie!' Mim shouted, her voice turned upward with a tinny vibration that could be heard clearly above the general noise, even the loud drone of the announcements, but not by its target.

Lizzie ran on, was swallowed from view.

'Now what's all that about, Mrs. Hobbs?' asked Harvey Lehman.

'What's it look like – done a moody, ain't she? 'Ere – you take all this gear – an' do me a favour, will yer?'

'Why, yes, of course . . .' They all looked at her grim face with the fierce brows drawn into a line, dumb with wonder.

'Don't move an inch. Right?'

'Okay,' said Ruth.

'Sure,' said the other two.

With that, Mim, too, was off, with the muscular sprint of a trained athlete; the ruthless determination of a cop in pursuit. Bags flew from hands, luggage crash-landed, Coke bottles were jerked from mouths, a toddler lost its balance and fell with loud screams, an elderly man lost his cane, groups were torn apart, sent staggering . . .

Lizzie's frenzy reached its peak when she saw him, finally actually saw him . . .

'Robbie,' she screamed, 'Robbie, Robbie . . .!'

But he was totally surrounded by a great motley crowd of teenagers and young people screaming louder than she did, shoving autograph albums at him, practically tearing his clothes.

At one moment, she thought he heard her – he stopped, looked about in a dazed sort of way. His hair was very long and scruffy, his familiar dark-blue eyes puffed and dark-circled, his wide fixed grin inanely benign.

She cupped her mouth with her hands, drew in a huge breath. 'Robbie!' she shouted with all the force of her long-trained vocal chords.

Again, he seemed to pause, to hear something above and beyond the surrounding clamour.

Lizzie pushed, shoved, but she lacked Mim's technique and was equally pushed and shoved back . . .

Suddenly, someone else was blocking her view, a short, whitish-blonde girl in a green fur coat, who took hold of Robbie's arm with a firm, possessive grip and made him move on . . .

Louisa Dearborn!

Lizzie watched him lift a hand in farewell to the crowds, look down lovingly on the girl, allow himself to be hurried onward to, through, the gates, disappear . . .

She stood a moment, paralysed in frustration, loss, sadness. It was as if not a day had gone by; she loved him still – so *much* . . .

'Lizzie – what in bloody 'ell do you think you're doin?'

The rasp of Mim's voice behind her brought her awake, brought her back. 'It was Robbie,' she said, her eyes still moist, her voice sunk to a whisper.

'Blimey – I wouldn't 'ave guessed. What were you going to do about it – take off with 'im?'

Lizzie looked into the sharp, glinting gaze. 'How did you guess?' She turned, began to stride back, forcing Mim to half-run to keep up.

When they got back to the three waiting people, Lizzie had recovered her sense of occasion. 'Sorry,' she said, with her wry, appealing smile. 'He was one of my best mates. It was so amazing, him being here – I just couldn't help it . . .'

'That's okay,' Ruth said. 'Long as you're still with us.'

The others nodded, laughed supportively.

'Well,' said Harv, 'best make tracks. We got a lot of plans for you.'

'That we have,' said Fred Gold. 'How long do you intend to stay in the Big Apple, Liza – don't mind if I call you that?'

'If you like, by my real . . .' Lizzie began, but Mim cut in. 'Long enough to do 'er job – then we're off to 'Ollywood.'

'You are!' said Ruth. 'Really?'

'We are. Lizzie got the lead role in a new Sebastian film. No title yet, but I got a few to suggest.' Mim nodded curtly.

Ruth looked at Mim, as did the other two, resignation beginning to edge their reluctant inclusion. 'I guess you kind of manage your daughter, huh?' Fred asked.

'That's right, mate. I'm her agent, manager, trainer, songwriter, costumier, you name it, I'm it.' Mim gave a short grating laugh, to which the others responded with grunts in their throats.

Lizzie was glad of the respite from their attention. She was suddenly very, very tired . . .

Almost too tired to appreciate the wonders of the great towering city of Manhattan through which they bore her and Mim to a hotel called the St. Regis, 'just off Madison Avenue', passing en route the huge, dark glass building of the studio, the 'black rock', they called it, just so she could see where she would be singing. She nodded sleepily when they told her they would pick her up again at seven, for dinner with Percy Cosmo and various other people she would be working with. Ruth suggested she be ready, because the chauffeur would have to park if she wasn't and Percy hated to be kept waiting.

'We'll be ready,' Mim said. 'I never let 'er be late, do I, darlin'?'

Lizzie shook her head. 'Never.'

'Oh, yes, of course, Mrs. Hobbs – naturally, you're invited, too. Right, Fred? Right, Harv?' Ruth smiled brightly.

'Well, of *course*!' Mim gave them a dismissive nod, shut the door of the big, rose-and-mint-green suite on their smiling faces. 'It'll be nice to 'ave a bit of a kip, won't it, me pe'al? You didn't 'alf give me a turn at the airport. Don't know what you want running after that drug-addict – I told you 'e weren't good enough for ya – right from the start, didn't I? An' I was right, wasn't I? Like I was right about the other bugger.'

Mim, hanging away clothes, organizing music and papers, hardly noticed that Lizzie, who had flung herself onto one of the satin-covered twin beds just as she was, hadn't answered. ('Why ever should we want two rooms?' Mim had said in her letter to the studio management.)

'Nope, you wouldn't take no prizes for judgin' the opposite sex, me darlin'. You best listen to me. Gawd knows, I ain't much to look at, but I know a good man when I sees one – take Bertie – weren't none better! Take 'Arry – well, 'e ain't pretty, but 'e'd give me the shirt off 'is back, an' for no more'n a bit of slap an' tickle, know what I mean?'

Mim paused, went to peer down at Lizzie. 'Aw, bless me if you ain't popped off. Well, we 'ave been pushin' it a bit – an' we got a bigger push 'ere – in the Big Apple.'

Mim took the cover from her bed and draped it over Lizzie, kissed her forehead, tip-toed away. Whistling 'Stars Over Soho' in a soft rasp under her breath, Mim took off her clothes, ran a tub, sank into the foam, sighed deeply. 'Beats Bale Street of a Friday!' she observed, with a grin. 'Only the best for Lizzie an' Mim 'Obbs . . .

'Oy – 'old on. She's right, you know, cheeky li'le sod – I do 'ave to watch me aitches. Well; she could do it, so can I! Mim *Hobbs*. Me name is Mim *Hobbs* . . .

Lizzie rolled onto her side, dug deeper into the soft pillow. The dreams of floating and flying she had had on the plane were changed now to long, long corridors of open doors, each door, as she approached, closing gently and firmly in her face. But, at last, at last, there was one that opened – she pushed through, quickly, holding it in case it should spring shut – and there, facing her, gazing at her with a radiant face and smile, was herself, singing so loudly, forcefully and clearly that it drowned her in sound, bashed at her senses till she moaned, covered her ears, turned and ran, ran for her very life . . .

# CHAPTER SEVENTEEN

'Well, Liza, thanks for leaving your pool to be with us today,' said Zeke Solway, as Lizzie and Mim were ushered into his huge, air-conditioned office in Los Angeles. 'You settled in okay, everything to your liking?' A short, stocky man with a red hairpiece that contrasted with his very dark eyes, he came round the front of his big desk to pump her hand warmly, hold it between his own with paternal fervour.

'Oh, yes, Mr. Solway – it's all . . . fantastic!' Lizzie's eyes, in her already lightly-tanned face, seemed bluer than ever, matching her short, pale-blue dress. 'I never dreamed of anything like this . . .'

'It'll do,' said Mim, choosing one of the bigger leather chairs and placing a cigarette into her gold holder, 'for *starters.*'

'Mum – leave off . . .'

'What do you mean, Mrs. Hobbs?' Zeke Solway waited for Lizzie to take one of the bamboo armchairs from the prepared circle of chairs, then returned to his own, a startled, half-amused smile forming on his wide mouth. 'What's missing?'

Mim lit her cigarette with a slim gold lighter, then leaned back. With her hair twisted sideways into an emerald-green scarf, her orange trouser suit, freshly-plucked and blackened eyebrows, vivid cherry lips, she made a surrealist clash with the pastels of the décor. Her smile was shrewd. 'Yeah – well, from what I understand these days in 'Ollywood – *Hollywood* – your stars are your bread and butter. Without 'em, you got nothin'. So, it's first you got Liza Lee, then the rest of the "package", that's what you call it, the directors, the producers, cameraman, designer, composer, writer, of course. Right, Zeke?'

'Well, yeah – something like that. But . . . I mean, Liza's not yet . . .'

'What about these perks I 'ears so much about, eh? Like spending money, 'er own trailer, 'er own make-up person, 'airdresser, massyer . . .?'

'You do all *that*, Mum . . .'

' 'Ush. Then you should 'ire *me*, put *me* on the payroll – see what I mean?' Mim waved her cigarette at him in triumph.

Zeke Solway shook his head as though something buzzed in it. Leaning back, he sighed deeply. 'There's something you gotta understand, Mrs. Hobbs – Liza's not *that* big a star. Not *yet*. What you've been reading about happens after a movie's been a smash, when a star's name ensures millions and is worth millions. Like Streisand, Newman, McQueen, MacGraw – our Liza has gotten a big name on television – but for motion pictures she's an unknown quantity, a gamble, maybe an educated risk . . .'

'She ain't no such thing, an' you know it! I couldn't 'ave got 'er a percentage of the profits if she were a gamble, ol' mate.'

'Mum – *please*.' Lizzie leaned forward, pushed at her sun-bleached hair, but neither Mim nor Zeke Solway seemed aware she was there.

'Maybe you don't want to remember that you took a lower salary – not that it couldn't turn out in her favour. No, dear lady, what you got in me is a one-time agent nose on an executive producer's face. I did some hustling to get Liza into this in the first place. To be honest with you, there was some opposition. What worked was the writer

226

himself, Adam Levine, liking the idea of Liza for the picture!'

'Really?' said Lizzie. 'Adam Levine, the playwright? Cor, we did his plays at Blatsky's, *Armistice, The Calendar, Beyond The Hill* . . . Madame Irayna said he was a "voice of our times" . . .'

Zeke Solway gave her a vague but benign nod. 'Then you read the script, you like it?'

Lizzie sat back, staring at him blankly.

'Ah, she ain't 'ad a chance yet, Zeke,' Mim said. 'I been readin' it meself. So far, I don't like it no better than Ralph Gordon's – in fact, I don't think neither of 'em's got it right. If you ask me, it's all too arty-crafty, no big laughs like what Gertie would 'ave got.'

Lizzie stood up, walked to the window, stood with her hands on her hips looking out between the big slats of blond pine. Anger lifted the golden hairs on her arms, made the nerves in her teeth vibrate. Out there, indescribably beautiful, lay a great exotic world, a city as foreign to London as New York, equally full of new and amazing sights, sounds, possible experiences. As in New York, she had seen practically nothing of it except in fast rides in a chauffeur-driven 'limo', various big offices where 'meetings' of one sort or another took place with endless discussions that seemed in a foreign language and lead nowhere *exact*. She would be asked her opinion, but Mim always answered. She would be taken out to dinner, but Mim was always along . . .

In New York, she had managed to go up inside the Statue of Liberty, to go to the top of the Empire State Building, through the Rockefeller Center, round Manhattan in a boat, to a succession of expensive restaurants that all looked alike. And Mim had been with her, and all the people she met and worked with would smile at her, ask her questions, and Mim would explain. On the night of her actual performance, Mim almost did it for her; she took the rehearsals, took over with Percy Cosmo himself, and though at one time it looked as if the production staff would rise up and bodily remove her, they didn't, and Mim remained, urging her on, clapping loudest of all when the songs went over all right and talking to all the newsmen afterwards on her behalf.

On the radio shows where she was interviewed, Mim briefed her, winked and nodded her encouragement. At one interview Lizzie found herself frozen, dried-up. 'Look,' she said to the nice smiling American woman whose show it was. 'The absolute truth about me is that I'm my mother's project – she's trained me, worked herself to the bone for me, watched over every detail of my career – it's really *her* show – I just do the singing.' They had thought that 'very *cute*' – everyone should be so honest – but 'much too modest. We think you're just terific, and I'm sure all my listeners will agree that you have a glorious future. *Thank* you, Liza Lee, and the best of luck in all that you do!'

Without the sound of applause, Lizzie felt inert, dissociated. Only Mim's face told her that she had done well, that she was pleased. Yet, an empty, uncertain sensation hovered in her, like memory, or nostalgia . . .

For just an hour of her stay in New York, there was a sudden break in their schedule when Mim had a facial at Elizabeth Arden's salon on Fifth Avenue, and while her head was wrapped in towels, Lizzie found herself taking off like a fugitive.

Jostling along with the crowds, she shook off her identity like an invisible cloak and strode along looking up at the great towering buildings, looking into the shop windows, gazing into people's faces, getting a feel of America, Americans . . .

Just think, she was actually half a one. Somewhere in this vast continent, there was an American man who was her father. Mum could say, would say, no more than that he had been a 'big, tall bloke with curly blond hair and blue eyes, a fair complexion, a real charmer'. Pushed further, 'nagged' she'd called it, she'd say 'like as not he'd 'opped his perch years ago. So give it a rest.'

Still, it was a good feeling, to know there was more to her than only Mim, reasons for things she felt and did, thought about, was interested in . . .

In fact, she was so little like her that if she hadn't known better she wouldn't believe Mim was really her own mother – though there *was* something similar in the way they moved their bodies when they danced, something that was not only her copying and following, that was in the natural way their legs and arms moved.

She had a longer big toe on her right foot just like Mum's, too, and kind of squashy, bendy thumbs (Robbie said that meant 'passion'!). Then, in certain lights, by half-closing her eyes and looking sideways at herself in the mirror, Lizzie had to admit there was a 'carved-out', granite look to her chin. By gritting her teeth, clenching her jaw, she could almost see her mother's face in her own. If her hair and eyes had been darker . . . Oh, Gawd, yes – probably as she got older, as the moisture went out of her skin, she might come to look a lot like her!

Lizzie pushed the guilty feeling from her, as if it were a betrayal – flipped to another idea, far more convincing, that they could be nothing but mother and daughter, the way they laughed at the same things. Mum could always set her off – there was such a predictable sauce in her points of view, and Mum always saw through pretensions and attitudes, could curl her up with recognition. Of course, you could say that that was because of Mum's influence from the very beginning . . .

Suppose she had not been born in Soho, lived there with Mim and Bert, but had been born here, in America, and lived with her father, never knowing who her *mother* was . . . ?

It was all very mysterious, trying to figure out who and what you were, what you had been born with, what you became by conditioning . . . Hard enough for anyone to sort out, probably not much use in trying . . .

And yet . . .

If she were on her own, could get away . . .

'Liza, honey,' Zeke Solway was saying. 'Let's get you in on this. Did you hear what your mother said? Well, it's not strictly kosher to inject an outside voice – in fact, I cannot remember one instance when a star's mother had a say – except maybe Ginger Rogers' mom . . .'

'I remember – I saw a picture of them taken together.' said Lizzie, her eye brightening as she moved back to her chair. 'They looked so alike, so perky and smiling – it was an old fan magazine Mum had – right Mum? They were a great team, just like us.'

Both Zeke Solway and Mim looked at her, each in their individual ways struck by the dazzling beauty that could suddenly come to life in her face.

'That's right, me darlin',' Mim said, her smile showing the newly-crowned teeth, little flashes of gold.

Zeke Solway cleared his throat. 'Uh, yeah, well – what I'm trying to say here, Liza, is that, since you did not read the story and do not have any of your own ideas, maybe it wouldn't *hurt* to let your mother talk with Adam . . .'

'Let? Zeke, me ol' chum – you ain't got no way to stop me!'

This was one of those times Lizzie felt like laughing, but she restrained it to a smile. 'It's fine,' she said, shrugging. 'I wouldn't know what to say anyway, and Mum takes care of *all* the details.' She crossed her long, lightly-tanned legs, sat back.

'Okay, okay – I think I get the drift. When I talked to you two in London, I maybe didn't realize . . .'

'Realize – what?' Mim's lips prepared to pinch.

'Uh – well, let's say I got no precedent.' He laughed to himself, looked at his watch. 'Anyway – we'll see how it goes. One thing for sure – if we don't get it right this time, even Adam can't save us; they'll *all* walk, which means we won't have a picture to make.'

'I'll bloody well sue you.' Mim sat up, ground her cigarette butt into the centre of a Royal Doulton souvenir bowl. 'Lizzie ain't wastin' a year of 'er life while you ruddy moguls chase yer tails an' play 'ide an' seek – she's got other things to do. I already 'ad to turn down a Broadway musical for 'er – an' she could a done a Command Performance, like as not, for the Queen, Zeke – the *Queen of England*!' Mim's gaze was like a bolt of amber fire aimed with lethal force at an enemy.

Zeke Solway's gaze faltered. 'I know how you feel . . . I'm sorry to hear that . . . I'm sure things'll work out . . .'

Lizzie could hardly stifle her protest. How could Mum make up such things, go so far. 'You'll only bugger it up – for *yourself*!' she wanted to scream out. But all she could do was to stare at her in rigid silence.

Suddenly, a buzzer went on Zeke Solway's desk. He held up a hand, before he answered the inter-com, implying a truce. 'All here? Sure, show them in.' He got up, cast a glance at the flinty-faced mother, the reproachful eyes of the daughter. 'Look,' he offered. 'Let's take the optimistic view, huh? Can't hurt.'

Not waiting for a response, he went quickly to the door, started shaking hands with the four men and one woman who filed in.

'Great that you could all make it. Let's hope this'll be the last of these pow-wows. You've all met Liza Lee, of course, and her mother, Mrs. Hobbs . . .'

There was a general nod, a smile for Lizzie that stiffened somewhat as it reached Mim. One man deferred.

'Except you, Adam – let me introduce you.' Zeke Solway took the arm of an exceptionally tall man with a

231

scholar's hunch to his wide shoulders, led him to Lizzie. 'Liza Lee, our star – Adam Levine, our writer.'

Lizzie jumped up. 'How do you do?' she said, reaching out a hand.

'How do *you* do? This is a pleasure.' He kissed her hand.

Lizzie's left cheek dimpled. 'Yes – it is. Thanks.' How gauche she still was, she thought, only even more so with this famous sophisticated-looking man with the crinkled grey hair, deeply-seamed face and horn-rimmed glasses, behind which keen grey eyes seemed to penetrate to her very thoughts. She was instantly afraid of him, yet compelled to stupid reverence. Blimey – all those deep, clever, witty things he wrote, all the wise observations of human behaviour seemed to convey themselves to her in his one long-held glance. She remembered from reading about him that he had been married three times, that women 'suffered from his unpredictable moods, his sudden switch from worship to contempt, from tender understanding to cruel cynicism. How terrifying it would be to get involved with him – yet, how exciting and thrilling, like a dangerous adventure – and to surrender to him, be held deep within his confident wisdom, to be wanted by him, if even for a short while . . .'

She hardly heard the niceties, the small talk that preceded the taking of chairs, the beginning of this meeting with the director, the cameraman, the production designer, another producer of some kind, Zeke Solway, her mother, Adam Levine . . .

All she was aware of was the terrible beating of her heart, the sensation of Adam's eyes whenever they looked in her direction, seeming to linger on hers, to be absorbing her, whole, into his knowingness, his silent speculation. Of course, she was probably imagining it all, making it up from romantic novels. He was probably thinking, Oh, Christ, what have we got here? How am I going to let my

232

work be contaminated by this naïve, unschooled kid whose only claim to fame is – *singing*?

'Yes,' he was actually saying. 'I think I've come up with something viable. But I'm not wedded to any particular scene, so if there are any suggestions . . .' He crossed his long, thin legs in the light cream trousers he wore with a blue cotton blazer, sat back with big slender hands resting easily on the chair arms, so obviously relaxed and confident of himself that it made everyone else in the room appear to twitch, to have compulsive mannerisms.

'What I like,' said Benny Sebastian, the director, 'is the building of moments. That's what we can work with, and what the others didn't create. A picture is only as good as its great moments.'

'Glad to hear you say that,' said Adam Levine. 'The story of this girl is basically a series of episodes. She goes from one attempt to lose her virginity to another – but this can easily lapse into farce. What I've seen here, and attempted to do, is to give it irony, significance.'

'I think you've succeeded,' said Morris Lloyd, the cameraman every female star always wanted, and Mim had learned to demand. 'From my point of view, there's great possibility to interpolate this visually.'

'And the scenes, particularly the one on the train – and, yeah, the beginning and end, in the garden – they're delightful, full of scope for special effects.' Ferdy Gunther nodded to the others for agreement, and got it.

'The dialogue is economical, without being so terse that no-one understands it before something else is said and it's too late – which most of the clever writers stick you with,' said Zeke Solway, beginning to release his ingratiation for a sincere earnestness. 'Now, the only thing is that Mrs. Hobbs has some ideas. She speaks, of course, for Liza . . .'

'Why can't Liza speak for herself?' said Sylvia Pressman, one of the few respected female producers in the business, according to Zeke Solway. 'We want the star's own viewpoint, don't we?'

Lizzie, caught with thoughts light years away, cast Mim a quick 'S.O.S.' look. 'Mum's the judge,' she said quickly. 'Mum knows the play. Her mum, you see, my grandmother, was a dresser for Gertrude Lawrence . . .'

'Really?' Adam Levine looked at Mim with sudden sharp interest. 'That's fascinating. And what are your objections?'

'Yeah, well.' Mim swept a forefinger over each eyebrow as if clearing her vision, blinked knowledgeably at Adam as if he were the only person in the room. 'I don't know nothin' about what you want to say, like – what price virginity an' all that lark – but Gertie weren't sig . . . nif . . . Well, you know what I mean. Gertie, she sang these songs, "Experiment" and such – an' she was *naughty*; she gave you a big laugh, not a *lesson*. See what I'm sayin'?'

The circle of faces about them shifted like spectators in a tennis match, from the small, almost grotesque little woman with the Cockney accent to the dignified, scholarly man with the thoughtfully tilted face and shrewd gaze.

Lizzie was aware of them all, like subjects in a painting within the framework of softly-tinted walls; the director, a strong, handsome man with a bush of black hair seeming to sprout from his chest at the open neck of his checked shirt; the cameraman, lean and angular, with a thin, beaked nose, long grey hair, wearing a short-sleeved safari suit; the production designer, a big man with a wide smile, long bleached hair tucked back behind his large ears, wearing tennis clothes; another kind of producer (Mum had learned the ranks, but *she* never could), a big woman with close-cropped black hair, large, amber-tinted glasses, a too-tight pink jersey and trousers . . .

And in there, the more familiar face of Zeke – and

Mum . . . Mum, a flash of green-and-white light, a riveting point of focus . . .

But also, as if she were double, could be both *in* and looking *at* the picture at the same time – was herself, the one they called Liza Lee, the star, the supposed centre of all the group's combined skills and efforts . . .

How really peculiar, she thought. That's me. I know that because it's like the pictures they've taken. I have this straight-cut hair, almost blond, very thick, and it sort of swings around my face as I move. I have very blue eyes, and when I smile there are these little squeeze lines round them. My nose is short, so short that the make-up people run a line down over it to stop it from looking turned-up. I am not tall, but I am not short. I sit very straight, the way I was trained, and my legs are long and thin, and so are my arms. I look at people in a friendly, direct way, and seem to be taking an intelligent interest in what they are saying.

But I'm not, really, that person. I don't even know who that person is – she is made up, she is Mim's, her mother's . . .

I can see a long row of little hers that go back to Soho and Bertie and doing endless auditions, going to Miss Tina's, and Madame Blatsky's, doing her 'bit', dancing, singing, performing, in front of thousands of watching people . . .

Then there was the Lizzie with Robbie, Kit . . .

Who were *they*? They seemed separate. They looked like the others, but also like strangers, recognizable, but unrelated . . .

And how did they connect with this person sitting here – this Lizzie, or Liza? How could there be so many, yet none of them quite this one – and this one, not quite any of them? Were any of them real? *Was* there a real one? Were they all an illusion of a someone, a mirage held together by a name, Liza Lee . . .?

Lizzie's eyes roved from face to face, then back to the whole picture . . .

But something had shifted, something had changed . . .

She was no longer in it. She had *disappeared.*

Her hands clenched. Panic dilated her eyes, quickened her breathing. What was happening, where had she gone?

Then suddenly, the measured authoritative voice of Adam Levine came to her like a reaching hand, drew her back into solidity; and his knowing gaze, no longer frightening, seemed to reassure, to protect, to be a kind of anchoring . . .

'I take your points, Mrs. Hobbs. But I'm reasonably sure that Liza, with her particular style – innocence with a sly edge – will more than leaven the cerebral content,' Adam Levine, while speaking to Mim, drew all attention to Lizzie with his considered nod.

In a moment, there followed murmurs of accord.

Mim, not appeased, cut off, lapsed into watchful silence, one sandalled, purple-nailed foot jerking with impatience.

Lizzie could not have told what the rest of the discussion was about. Vaguely she understood that there was a long haul ahead, that the picture would be part of her life for some months to come. She no longer cared what it entailed, or what she would have to do. Just as long as Adam Levine was there . . .

'Well,' said Zeke Solway. 'Looks like we got the show on the road at last. Next thing you know we'll have a shooting schedule.'

Everyone rose. Tension evaporated, there was a lot of small talk, shoulder thumping, plans to meet soon socially, the laughter of camaraderie, some forced, some real, like people setting out together for the moon.

Adam Levine lingered by Lizzie. 'Can we have dinner some evening?' he asked. 'I think we ought to get to know each other.'

236

'Lizzie's got a lot to do, evenings, Mr. Levine,' Mim said, moving up between them. 'Why don't you stop off at the 'ouse after work – we'll make you a real English cuppa, won't we, darlin'?'

'I'd love to have dinner with you,' Lizzie said. She pushed back her fringe, looked into his eyes.

He pressed his glasses into place on his long, down-curved nose, looked at her over their tops. 'Tomorrow?' There's a place out toward Malibu . . .'

Lizzie nodded.

'I'll pick you up about seven.'

Lizzie nodded again.

They all filed out, went back into the world of sunshine, palms, white buildings with flashing windows, fumes, cars, limos.

'Well, I never,' Mim said, as she walked with Lizzie towards their beckoning chauffeur. 'The cheek of 'im. A bloke old enough to be your dad. I saw the way 'e looked at ya – ol' lech. I 'ope you're not goin' to let 'im use this getting-to-know-you lark. You ask me, you 'adn't ought to see 'im alone. Any'ow, not first off.'

Lizzie said nothing. She smiled at Mim, as she got in beside her. Poor old darling, she thought. How awful it must be to be so dependent on her – to have nothing else. She must be very kind to her, let her down gently . . .

After all, she owed her so much, loved her so much. It was funny – all her anger had gone; she didn't remember what it was about.

'Don't worry, Mum,' she said, putting her arm through hers, 'everything's under control, everything's going to be all right.'

# CHAPTER EIGHTEEN

At long last the shot was set up. It was to be a very simple one well within the limits of the tight budget: a fake apple tree in a fake garden with fake grass, a spread blanket, a picnic basket, a metal bike helmet. Sound would produce birdsong, a distant church bell to show it was Sunday morning in the small, New England town. The only real things would be Lizzie and her co-star, Glen Wyatt. Lizzie was to lie on the blanket and entice him from his apple-picking to lie beside her. The whole scene would be over in a few moments – if all went well. By now everyone knew it would not be Liza's fault if it didn't. Glen Wyatt was another matter. Since Liza unwittingly stole every one of their mutual scenes, he might be trying to steal this one back, particularly since it was his last until much later in the (as yet untitled) picture.

Glen Wyatt rose from his chair, stretched, tucked his check shirt tightly into his tight jeans, allowed his tanned, handsome young face to be blotted, patted, his thick brown hair and his eyebrows to be brushed smooth, and strolled to the tree, mounted the ladder, keeping his eyes averted from the lights.

'The grass blade . . .' the script girl called, and the make-up assistant came up to him quickly, with an apologetic smile.

Glen, considered the sexiest male actor of the moment, though as yet only as a result of his role in the famous television series *Dollar Man*, nodded, winked, stuck the long strand of plastic grass into his mouth. Amusement trickled through the small regiment of technicians settling in for the take.

'Well,' said Lizzie, reluctantly letting go of Adam's hand and getting up from her chair, ''ere goes nothin'. You'll hang about, won't you?'

Adam looked up at her in sober enchantment. 'I guess so.'

'You'd bloody better.' She leaned down, pressed her forehead to his, seeming oblivious to the unflagging curiosity aroused by their every move, her teasing smile as secret as if they had been alone.

Adam was far from oblivious, but he was too far on the way to paying the price for his besotted state to turn back. His kiss was more perfunctory, but equally committed. 'You don't need me on this. Seduce him with your eagerness, your lust to *know*.'

Her smile, when she stood up from him, straight and braced for action, was like a small rainbow in her face. 'You sure . . .? You might be sorry.'

'Art before heart, dear.'

She gave his hand a last squeeze and was about to move off when Mim sprang from her chair on the other side of Adam's. 'Oy,' she whispered, 'your tits ain't goin' to pop out the sides, are they?' She lowered her huge, harlequin-shaped glasses to inspect the scrap of a sleeveless vest Lizzie wore with frayed jean hot-pants, her gaze triggered with protest.

'They're taped, Mum – not to worry.' Lizzie gave her a jaunty wink and proceeded towards the blanket and picnic basket.

Mim returned to her seat and she and Adam both watched Lizzie as she stretched herself out on her side, raised up on one elbow, closed her brilliantly-lit blue eyes a moment against the blazing onslaught, in which stray tendrils of strawberry blond hair dangled from an upsweep like glints of fire. Her skin, wherever it was

239

exposed, gleamed a magnolia whiteness, and in the midst of all that concentrated attention and growing stillness, she seemed over-radiant, vulnerable and isolated at the same time. Glen Wyatt looked down at her with something between hostility and dread. Neither of them would have anything to say in this shot but, somehow, in this little British singer there lurked an endless fund of unexpected and unerring nuance, prompted by her Jewish 'Professor Higgins'. But he couldn't work up a hearty dislike of Liza, any more than he could have hated Eliza Doolittle – it was just his goddam luck to get stuck with a winner, a budding superstar on his first big break!

Lizzie managed an upward smile of encouragement through half-closed eyes, and drew the motorbike helmet that lay beside the basket up across her face like a fan against the heat.

'She's sweatin',' Mim muttered to Adam. 'Nervous as a cat. You done it again with all that dirty talk. Play it saucy, she should, like it was darin', like Gertie done it.'

'That was the thirties, Mrs. Hobbs – this is meant to be the sixties. That's the whole point.'

'Bloody cheek, I calls it, monkeying about with the original. I just wish the whole blinkin' thing was over and done with, and Lizzie and me was on our way to Broadway.'

'Ssh . . .' Adam said softly, raising his gaunt chin towards Benny Sebastian, folding his arms to indicate his withdrawal.

'Thanks very much, and by your leave.' Christ, how she hated this high-and-mighty old bastard with his smarmy, wise-owl expression, his snobby, bookish talk. A right traitor, Lizzie was being, forcing him down her throat just when everything was comin' up biggest roses ever, not only letting him take over her life, but run it lock-stock-and-barrel. Being *kind* to her mum, treating her like an affectionate old dog. Not a harsh word, only that bloody

240

awful smile, like that Italian painting they drew moustaches on. It was yes Mum, no Mum, kissing her, whirling her round in a dance, never listening, buying her ruddy great presents, never really telling her anything, saying, 'Oh, I'm so happy, Mum, so happy. That's what you want me to be – and when we're married, Adam and I, you can live with us and always be a part of my life, and I'll make all those hard years up to you. Maybe I'll have a baby – if Adam will let me, because, after all, he's already got children, and even a grandchild – you'll be a grandmother. We'll have lots of friends, and you can go back home and visit and maybe Harry will want to marry you . . .'

'Whoa, whoa,' she kept saying, but Lizzie didn't have ears, even cloth ones these days; all she thought of, spoke of, cared about was Adam Levine. Little did the sod know where this disgusting carry-on with twenty-one-year-old Lizzie was going to end: Lizzie was not going to be his prize protégée, his performing genius – not on your sweet mellie. She knew something he didn't, and it made her split a gut to think about. It would be her trump card: Lizzie was going to give up performing the moment she married the man. She had told it to her in gleeful confidence. 'I'm just going to be a wife, Mum – at last. I'm going to be his companion, run his home, make him happy!'

What then, Mr. Fancy Intellectual, Mr. Superior Brain! How will you like that, eh?

As Benny Sebastian called, 'Go, Liza!', Mim cast Adam a glance of such venom that her eyes seemed to come at him like marbles, white and vibrating from the blackness of her brows.

He sat straighter in the leather-back chair, drew himself into a stony fortress of non-reaction. It seemed incredible to him now that he had been fascinated at first by this sharp-tongued little Cockney. He'd automatically researched her knowledge of East End London in war-

241

time, her illuminating flashes of early theatrical lore, listened to her handling of language with immense interest, comparing it to that of Brooklyn where he'd been born and raised till he got a scholarship and went away to school, followed by college and degrees that had erased all but a deliberate usage for humorous effect. He had seen at once the situation with Liza, knew intuitively, without it being spelled out, what she had done to the girl, would continue to do to her if she wasn't rescued, quickly, urgently. Yet he hadn't really understood at all the lethal complexity of her hold on Liza, or the deadly power of her almost barbaric persistence.

Good God, he had almost been frightened off when he began to catch on – but, of course, what had happened to him with Liza had power, too – the power of a miracle.

In his late fifties, he had thought never again to feel *the enchantment*. There was no other way to describe it. Outside all logic, beyond all words of description – a feeling, a combination of feelings that moved through all the senses, took over the mind, thrilled through the body just as if it had never been wearied, sated, half-depleted. All the direst clichés applied to him – revived youth, renewed interest in fitness and vigour, in the ordinary everyday pleasures of being alive. The world looked good again. For the first time in a decade he saw hope for it, for the possibility of a better future for the human race. Holding Liza, he felt surges of protective masculinity he had failed to muster for any of his ex-wives or even his own children. She had given him back the optimism of his salad days, when he thought to be a published playwright was what he had been born for, the only true happiness, and that he would achieve it through absolute single-minded dedication. With the optimism, ambition soared to new heights: with Liza in his life to love and to be loved by, he would turn out a play that changed the thinking of mankind, not just for a few months or years, but irrevocably, forever . . .

The immortal aspects, always potential and intimated in his previous work, would now emerge and solidify. He would be a contributor to the ultimate self-enlightenment of the human species!

He moved with involuntary delight at the way Liza was urging the only-too-knowledgeable young man down to her with eloquent outstretched arms, nodded with approval at the mixture of hunger and excited anticipation she conveyed with yearning eyes, seductive but reassuring smile . . . Yes, good girl, that would certainly put this horny guy, scheduled to go to college, wanting no complications with a local virgin, into critical conflict . . .

'See what you done,' whispered Mim, with a nudge; 'looks a right tart!'

Adam showed no sign of hearing, but a nerve twitched in his left eye and the thought-grooved line between his greying brows became a black strip. There were times when his irritation with this woman was savage. If she had not been Liza's mother, he could at least verbally annihilate her on her own level. Lately, he was not optimistic about his control. Unlike the rest of the company, he was not resigned to her as the bitter pill of having Liza . . .

If only his connection with the picture had not lost power he might have found a way of banishing her without at the same time losing Liza . . .

No, he must be careful, hang on. It was not just Mim Hobbs who wanted him gone. Now that his stint as writer was done, he was completely *de trop*. The six months of painstaking effort on an assignment he'd accepted because alimony, taxes and his long list of dependants had made him vulnerable to immediate money, had been taken over from him as if he'd never existed. Everyone, from Benny Sebastian himself to the script girl, had more to say in the shooting than he did. Without saying it, the implication was clear: he, Adam Levine, for all his reputation and status, was in the way . . .

And not only because he continued to haunt the set!

Adam ran a thumb along the creases beside his wide, thin mouth, pressed at the wedding ring from his most recent marriage where it was grooved under a slightly arthritic knuckle, Mim's rasping accusation echoing in his head from their last 'argy-bargy' . . .

'If you gave a tinker's for Lizzie, you'd stop 'oggin' 'er to yourself. 'Ow's she goin' to be a romantic 'Ollywood star 'idin' 'erself away with a man old enough to be her father?'

Publicity obviously agreed. A brief, torrid affair they might have managed, but her passionate commitment at the very moment of launching her as a 'British Bardot who can sing' would be a killer. 'Look, Adam,' Zeke Solway had come right out and said, 'don't let us keep you from your real work. We can always call you, fly you out if we need you.' And Benny had stopped acknowledging the wonders of Liza's improvement, looked over his head or past him when he spoke to her, as if he had become invisible. It was galling, demeaning. 'No, don't go, don't leave me – *please*!' Liza's panic was hardly justification for renting the house in Malibu . . .

It was a joke to think that he could get on with his work out here, without his books of reference, his files, his familiar chaos of papers, the feel of his old typing chair and huge, specially-designed desk, the view from his study of white birch woods and the willow-banked Connecticut river below the sloping lawns, the presence of his companionable cats and the ministering of his staff who knew his every working need by heart; he couldn't settle down for an hour, his theme had drifted from his mind, he couldn't recapture or even focus its original meaning to him, let alone produce copy . . .

'Good, Liza; good, Glen. Cut. Print!'

Adam blinked, pushed at his glasses, at the sides of his longish, greying hair. He felt his pulse quicken, his blood heat as if she were the first woman he had ever desired.

Here she came – as if she glowed, was lit up like the sun itself, inflaming him to almost insupportable love . . .

How could he possibly leave her!

'How was it, darling?' She rushed to him, sat down, looked into his eyes as if he was the only reality in the world. 'Was I all right?'

'You were . . .' He kissed her nose. 'Just right.' He pressed her bare knee, she put her hand over his.

'Christ . . .' muttered Mim. She already felt *like* a spare po, now she *was* a spare po. What was she supposed to do – sit there simpering like a bleedin' idiot while they mooned and carried on? Obscene, it was – this dried old prune and her lovely Lizzie . . .

'Well,' she said, 'I don't know about you two, but there ain't nothin' goin' to be happenin' till they set up for the close-ups – ruddy great bore. I'm for a bit of kip – Lizzie, 'ow about you?' She stood up, shook down her new fringe ('bang', they called it here) so that it mingled with her eyebrows in a ragged curtain above the lens-enlarged sharpness of her gaze. With her stark white ear-rings, nautical striped T-shirt and bell-bottom white slacks worn with rope wedges that added four precarious inches to her height, she drew more eyes to her than Liza or Adam.

'You go ahead, Mum,' Lizzie said quickly, 'that's a good idea.'

Adam rising tall, thin, dignified by his wry solemnity, twined an arm about her, as she did him.

'Whatcher you goin' to do, then? You don't have to do nothin' afore the close-ups . . .' Mim looked sharply from one to the other.

Adam's smile was a message only to Lizzie. 'We need some air. I might give her another driving lesson.'

'That's right.' Lizzie looked up at him as if he had spoken words of incomparable wisdom. 'I've got to drive in the next scene.'

Mim grunted. 'You got a proper instructor for that. No need 'im teachin' you.'

'But I'd *rather* he did. He's so good at it, and I feel safer with him.' Lizzie gave Adam another of her adoring upward glances.

Mim felt nausea in her gut. 'I'll speak to Benny hisself about it, I will.'

'Mum – please. It's all settled.' Lizzie moved from Adam's arm to give her a quick hug. 'Not to worry, we'll be careful.'

'Like 'ell you will . . .'

Suddenly aware of the growing attention of the staff and crew, Lizzie stood back and took Adam's hand. 'See you later then, Mum.'

' 'Ang on,' Mim said, raising her chin at Adam. 'Maybe I'll come along, make sure . . .'

Adam stared down at her, one brow slightly raised. 'I think not,' he said. 'Liza and I would like to be alone.'

Mim looked up, into the thick lenses of his glasses, seeing her own face reflected there. But she also saw the grey light of his eyes. It was like the pebbles on Brighton beach on a cold winter's morning.

She clamped her lips, stood still, watched them link arms and move off past the technicians reassembling the set, past various groups in conference at its periphery. She saw Lizzie wave and smile to Benny and Morris Lloyd, to Ferdy Gunther and Sylvia Pressman, even to Glen Wyatt. Everyone smiled and waved back – at her. Not, Mim noted with a twinge of triumph, at *him*. 'You just wait, Mr. Big-Wig Levine,' she muttered under her breath, 'you got a real surprise comin', you 'ave.'

'All right, Benny, all right. I'll do it.'

Lizzie turned her face away from her director so that he would not see the anger in her eyes. Going to this Hollywood party with Glen wasn't just for the publicity, and she knew it. They were trying to show that she and Adam were not tied, that she was free and available, and to scotch the rumours that she and Adam were planning to marry, might already be married.

'Thanks, dear,' Benny said. 'It'll be a great party, too – the kind you should be going to all the time. Publicity would also like you to go to Billie Oliver's poolside lunch at the Beverly Hills, and be seen having dinner every now and then at some of our famous restaurants with various big stars, the details of which they'll arrange. It's a matter of making the local and national news. I'm sure you'll agree we've got to do everything we can to bring people into the theatres. If we don't, the picture can be a wipe-out, lose the millions that went into it.'

Benny patted Lizzie's shoulder, walked away from her to another part of the set, got behind the lights. Lizzie could tell, by the way he rubbed his swarthy face and shook his bush of dark hair as if it had been in his eyes, that he had disliked laying it on the line to her, that he had been forced out of his niche with its myriad claims and responsibilities by urgent demand.

She felt guilty, ashamed. Walking back for her next scene, she played it with extra care and effort, not only remembering Adam's coaching, but putting some of her own touches in it – like the time she had teased Robbie until he had almost taken her, and it fitted with the picture because now she had run off to become a groupie with a rock band – only no-one wanted to take her virginity . . .

That night, after a long, mournful talk with Adam, who said he would use the time to try to work, Lizzie allowed Mim to help her dress. It felt wrong, like being unfaithful – and oh, how she missed him already!

'Like old times, you and me goin' gaddin' together,' Mim said, tugging Lizzie's white silk jersey dress into its draped gathers on one hip, settling its long side-slit so that a bare tanned leg was in plain sight. 'Mind you, I'd just as soon you and Glen didn't want me along.'

Lizzie's eyebrows lifted to the fringe of her platinum-dyed hair. 'Who said we wanted you, Mum? You saw to it you were included, didn't you?' She prodded her, winked. 'Eh?'

'I did not.' Mim drew her bony jaw to her neck like a retreating turtle. 'It was the studio what asked me.' She adjusted the wide sleeves of her brocade caftan, the clips of her long 'crystal rain' earrings. 'Seems *I'm* in the news, too.'

'Oh, yes? What now?' Lizzie's blue eyes held something close to ennui in their fond tolerance.

'They got this article on you and me, 'ow we came up from nowhere, 'ow I made you into a great star with me own bare 'ands, so to speak.' Mim showed her efficient new teeth with sudden coyness. 'Makes a change, don't it? Me, gettin' credit.'

Lizzie was torn between suspicion and concurrence. 'It does, and you deserve it, Mum – but why, how . . .?'

'I rung 'em up, didn't I. Told 'em a few 'ome truths.' The crystal rain vibrated to her nod of self-approval.

Lizzie shoved back her long, middle-centred fringe the better to see her. 'Like what, Mum?'

'Oh, nothin'.' Mim moved off to study herself in the variously angled mirrors covering one wall of the huge, luxuriously furnished bedroom.

'Mum – come off it. Like what?' Lizzie picked up her white furs, followed her, stood behind.

'I got fed up, darlin', if you want to know – everyone always avoidin' me, actin' like I wasn't there, makin' theirselves talk to me, as if I 'ad foul breath or smelly armpits . . .'

'Aw, Mum, that's not true. They're just not used to doing business with the mothers of the stars. We're very unusual – you heard what Zeke said, right in the beginning . . .'

'Right!' Mim whirled round to face her, hands on her

248

jutting hip bones. 'That's what I told 'em. 'Ow unusual we
are. 'Ow it all 'appened! 'Ow it's about time they took
notice of yours truly!'

Lizzie looked away, looked out the windows where the
light-dotted hills made rose-mauve shadows against the
turquoise horizon. 'Oh, Mum, I'm not sure . . . I know
how you feel, but it's so personal, so private.' Lizzie gave a
shudder. The contents of her life turned out for public
inspection . . . That, together with all the rest of this
phoney nonsense . . . 'I wish you wouldn't,' she murmured, 'I just wish you wouldn't . . .'

'What – you, too?' Mim's face seemed to twist from
protest to shocked pain.

Lizzie stared at her a moment, feeling the twinge of
some deep oppression that seemed to cut her off from the
reality of the moment. She could see her reflection in the
mirrors, but it seemed to have nothing to do with her; and
Mim, too, was no longer familiar, but someone remote
and unconnected. It was like that day in Zeke's office,
only without Adam's voice to bring her back . . .

'You want to get rid of me, too, Lizzie? You want me to
scarper now you got to the top and got 'is nibs to 'elp ya?
That it?'

'Oh, Mum, Mum.' Lizzie went to her, took her in her
arms. 'You know I didn't mean that. You know how much
I love and appreciate you. Even when I tease, I don't mean
to hurt you. You know that!'

Mim's body was stiff for only a moment. "Course I do,
me petal, course I do. Don't know what got into me.' She
drew back her head to look into Lizzie's misted eyes. 'So
you don't mind, eh? You won't be narked if I tell 'em a bit
about meself . . .?'

Lizzie shook her head. 'Tell them what you like, Mum. I
don't suppose any of it matters.' She let her go, smiled,
righted one of the earrings that almost obscured Mim's
lean jaw.

'You *are* a public figure, you know, love.'

Lizzie let her have the last word with a nod.

There was a knock on the door. 'Mr. Wyatt's here, Miss Lee.' The grey-haired maid, casting an approving eye on both of them. 'My, you look gorgeous – like sisters.'

'G'arn,' Mim said, 'you just *'ad* a raise.'

The woman laughed heartily as she withdrew.

'Come on, Mum.' Lizzie slung the furs over her shoulders, checked the clasp of the diamond bracelet Adam had insisted on giving her for her twenty-first birthday, took up her satin bag from Neiman-Marcus.

'You look a treat,' Mim said. 'A real 'Ollywood star.'

Lizzie almost said, 'I don't feel like one, and I wish Adam was here,' but didn't.

Glen Wyatt wore a frilled evening shirt with his dinner jacket, and looked so handsome as he greeted them and helped them into his new red Porsche, that both Lizzie and Mim had to stare.

He laughed. 'Used to seeing me in the jeans, huh? I do have other aspects.'

'Yes,' said Lizzie. If only she weren't so completely in love with Adam, her heart would surely be jumping. He had some special kind of charm to his features that singled him out from the thousands of other handsome men she had seen in Hollywood. And now that some more scenes had been written in for him, and the sullen look that detracted from his appeal had gone, he would most certainly be among the chief attention-getters.

'Glad you could come, too,' he said to Mim, as he slid behind the wheel.

Lizzie was impressed that he could swallow back his aversion to the extent that Mim actually believed him.

'Some people got manners,' Mim said. 'Others – not namin' names, ain't.'

Glen understood as well as Lizzie: Adam would hardly welcome Mim's company on this, or any other night. It was Glen's chance to get a foot in the door, and Mim would open it further. For some time now, he had kept his growing lust for Liza under wraps. The scenes he did with her hadn't helped, and it was becoming a real problem to disguise the swelling mound of his crotch at the sight of her tits and pert little ass. What did they think he was made of, straw and sawdust, as she wiggled and pressed and thrust herself at him?

Anyhow, with a bit of luck and deft manoeuvring, he might get this grotesque old battle-axe to be his ally. 'Hey, Mrs. Hobbs,' he said, glancing past the white, perfumed lusciousness of Liza. 'There's someone I want you to meet tonight, someone who's been wanting to meet you ever since you came out here . . .'

'Me?' Mim's nose wrinkled at the bridge. 'You mean for the papers, like tonight?'

'No, no – purely socially. He's a great guy, used to run a circus back East. They've been using him for background research on a Barnum and Bailey picture.'

'Mmm,' murmured Lizzie, eyeing Mim meaningfully. 'Fancies you.'

'Get on.' Mim nudged her sharply. 'Sounds fishy.'

'No, honest, Mrs. Hobbs. You'll see.'

Glen drove furiously through the fading light, enjoying the hair-raising near-misses, the sudden braking, and the bursts of renewed speed. Adam Levine would never drive like this. But Liza was young, she needed thrills, risks, some life in the raw (like Sabina in the picture, like the song 'Experiment' that she sang so knowingly) – and by God, she'd get that tonight!

'Hey, Liza,' he said, grinning. 'Want to take the wheel?'

Lizzie's eyes widened, her lips pressed. She looked at Mim. 'I wouldn't mind, actually . . .'

'Don't you *dare*,' said Mim. 'And you, young gent, watch how you go, 'ear?' She cast Glen a look so sharp with command that his grin widened engagingly to the ears.

'Don't have much faith in your daughter, huh? Well, okay, I'll take it easy. We're almost there anyway.' He gestured towards the looming mansion in the heights of Beverly Hills. 'Used to be some great early star's hangout, forget whose – but they never had parties like *Sammy's*. No-one knows where he gets his money, but he's sure got it – and he sure spends it!'

Mim sat up straighter, peered with belligerent appraisal at the immense mansion they approached from a long tree-lined drive. 'Looks 'oppin all right,' she said with considered approval. 'Like you expect. Like what Lizzie and me should've been at, *if* it weren't for some I won't name.'

'Leave off, Mum – we're here now, aren't we?' (For better or worse, Lizzie thought, with a familiar signal from her bladder. Crikey – she'd never seen so many lighted windows, heard such a din of rock music even in a disco . . .!)

'See what I mean?' Glen gestured to the masses of cars, the parking attendants, the swarms of people to be seen inside, spilling to the terraces and around the edges of a great lighted pool, glimpsed towards the rear. 'There'll be eats like you've never experienced, liquor without end, drugs on the house . . .'

'Drugs!' Mim's voice was like a bark.

'Yes, ma'am. You name it.' Glen winked at Lizzie, making her a conspirator in shocking their elder. 'Just keep your eyes and ears open, Mrs. Hobbs. You'll get an education.'

'Well, I never. I 'ope you don't 'ave any ideas of educatin' Lizzie. I'll 'ave you chopped, I will. One word to Zeke . . .'

'Oh, Zeke'll be here. Gathering clients, dropping names of stars he's signed. How do you think I made it into films? Being here! Sammy Fielder's is the mecca of Hollywood gossip, Hollywood deals. Orgies are only a sideshow . . .'

'Orgies!'

'Mum, do shut up. You wanted to come, I didn't –
either way there's no turning back.' As Glen turned off the
motor and jumped out, Lizzie shouldered the furs, shook
back the flossy blond hair she endured for her next scene
in the picture. (Adam, oh, Adam, I *ache* for you. My arms
feel so *empty*. If only you'd said 'don't go' – oh, darling,
I wouldn't have, not for anyone, for anything!)

'Okay, you two. Into battle.' Glen moved between
them, clipped an arm of each into his own. 'Family touch.
This should ring the register.' He lowered his head, as they
started into the blazing lights, the blazing din, raised his
voice: 'The press are mixed in with the guests, anyone you
want pointed out, anyone you want to meet, just ask me.'

'First off,' said Mim, surveying the crowded halls, the
huge staircase where people sat, the jungle of dancers in a
vast room to the right. 'I want to 'ave this interview,
before everyone's elephant's . . .'

'Huh?'

'Drunk,' Lizzie interpreted.

'Ah. Uh-huh. Good thinking, Mrs. H. Oppenheim,
wasn't it, Russ Oppenheim. I know the guy – and I'll find
him for you when you've dumped your things upstairs.'

'You'll wait?' Lizzie asked, a plea in her eyes.

'Sure. That's what I'm here for.' He dared his first move,
pressed her arm to his, pecked her cheek.

Lizzie was reassured, though it came to her that Glen
was not going to be all business. The idea of it, of anyone
other than Adam touching her in more than a casual way,
gave her a shiver of aversion. She would have to maintain
her distance with Glen, without risking his support. After
all, without him, this whole ordeal would be a waste of
time. To think that she and Adam could now be strolling
the beach, or listening to his lovely classical music, or
reading plays or poetry together . . .

Lord, how wonderful it all was, being with him, learning from him. Instead of being here in this jungle of

shouting, laughing, gyrating strangers, he might be cooking one of his delicious meals, showing her how to use garlic and spices, teaching her how to judge different wines, discussing the ideas of great philosophers in a way that made her think about them, use her mind as she had never used it before. It was all so new to her, so exciting. She never wanted to stop exploring now – she wanted to look into all the big questions of life, see if she could think out at least some answers for herself, come back at him with more than just nods, mmms and ahs so he could be genuinely interested . . .

Sometimes he was. His face would light up. 'That's good, dear,' he'd say, 'perceptive, observant.' She'd feel happier than when the largest audience applauded.

And then, he always wanted her to sing for him, even to dance. He'd sit back, gazing at her in that calm way that she'd come to know was deep pleasure. That's why she did it; she'd just as soon have forgotten all that . . .

But she saw that it made him want her, too. And *his* wanting *her* was very important. Much as he adored her, their love-making might just end with long-drawn-out cuddling, his just holding her, loving her with words that were beautiful in themselves. He wrote poetry about her body, her face, her eyes, her skin, her mouth, her voice, and every part of her, speaking it aloud as they lay there so close as to feel like one person . . .

She knew so little about making love. In fact, nothing.

'In actuality, you're the virgin of our story,' Adam had said.

'I suppose so – yes . . . Please teach me, darling.'

Well, he had. And in a way that warmed her to a passion she could hardly believe – was it bad to feel so aroused by him all the time? What would Mum have said, if she knew what was under her innocent looks?

The trouble was, that though Adam felt just the same way, having taught her, he could not always 'enter' her.

The word 'enter' was his. She knew others used the work 'fuck' – she had never heard another word in the English language used so much out here in Hollywood. She'd got used to it, but she still didn't like it – why, she didn't know.

Anyway, Adam knew how to please her. And sometimes, when she had moved him mentally, and pleased him with something she wore, or the way she laughed or touched his hand, he would be hard and fierce and take her so forcefully that she could imagine it was like being raped.

Oh, Lord – who could want anything more? She'd found her man, she was the luckiest woman alive . . .

'Lizzie – come on, what's up!' Mim tugged at her elbow. 'You poorly or somethin'?'

'Sorry – it's the noise, likely. Murder, isn't it?'

'A bloody racket. I don't like the look of things. Stick with me, and Glen.'

'Don't *worry*. Like glue.'

Lizzie followed Mim's determined tread up the stair, winding round the people, to a large gold-and-white bedroom filled with gossiping women in exotic and uniformly expensive clothes, adjusting wigs and hair-dos, false eyelashes, falsies.

'I have to pee, Mum,' Lizzie whispered, after she had thrown their furs on a king-sized satin-covered bed, already piled so high that minks, ermines, sables and fitch merged in an amorphous mass.

'Ditto,' said Mim. 'Pays off.'

Squatting in the big marble and gold bathroom, with all its ornate fittings and huge sunken tub, Lizzie was reminded of Dallord House, the day she'd been too awed by their bathroom to pee. It felt that way again, much too grand. Would she ever be comfortable in huge great homes; would wealth ever be real to her . . .?

Adam said that his house, though spacious, was far

from grand. It had been built by a famous modern architect to fit against the side of a hill, to blend with the trees and woods. Unlike these show places out here, he told her, it was natural 'clapboard' and could hardly be seen until you came up close. It had a high porch set up on stilts running all round it, and the main rooms had ceiling-to-floor windows so you were right among the trees, could see squirrels leaping about and birds looking in at you . . . In bed, you could imagine the house didn't exist at all, that you were sleeping right out in the woods . . .

How lovely it sounded. She could hardly wait to get there. If only this picture would hurry up and end. It seemed to have dragged on forever. She had had no idea how slow the whole process was, how many things could hold up shooting – not just actors acting temperamental or forgetting their lines, as she had thought, but having dental or marital problems, or the weather would let everything down, and some *ideas* didn't work out and had to be reconstructed, and then there was the interminable wait for sets to be changed and re-lighted to look the same. Only the first day had been really exciting; from then on it seemed mostly waiting, filling in time. And when you did get working, it was exhausting in a draining kind of way, and if it hadn't been for Mim, for Adam, she would have been tempted to take off, scarper for the horizon . . .

'Hey . . .' someone said, pounding on the door, 'you died in there, honey?'

Lizzie leaped back into the present. She must have a good stiff drink, she thought, something to help her belt up and cope. 'Think of it as a job, dear,' Adam had urged, 'we all have functional chores to perform in the line of duty.'

That was *not* what she'd hoped he'd say. But what *had* she hoped . . .?

She opened the door, smiled into a familiar face – me Gawd, she'd been keeping Belinda Wood waiting! Next to

Streisand, the biggest star in Hollywood these days!
'Sorry . . .' she murmured.

But the big-breasted red-head simply pushed past her,
her huge dark eyes strangely glazed. Adam was right, she
must stop saying 'sorry'. It might be polite in England, he
said, but here it's taken for ingratiation, and you, my love,
have no reason to ingratiate yourself with anyone – least
of all 'film folk' – most of whom are scum.

She braced her bare shoulders, tilted her chin, moved
briskly to where Mim, her small face gathered and
pinched with distaste, waited. 'What cats!' she whispered.
'You never 'eard the like of their language, the things they
say about men and such, like it was over the fence.'

'What kind of things?'

'Lor', ain't nothin' for your ears.'

Lizzie took her arm. 'Come on, Mum – I'm a big girl. I
know about the birds and bees.'

'I wouldn't let it pass me tongue. You just take me word.'

Lizzie laughed. 'You always had a dirty mind.'

Mim gave her a sharp look, but seeing no insinuation in
Lizzie's expression, dammed a retort.

They picked their way down the big stairs, back into the
rising thunder of amplified rock. To Lizzie's relief, Glen
was waiting, though a dark-haired girl looked up as they
approached, then slipped off into the crowd. Well, of
course, there would be someone, plenty of someones in his
life, she thought. She really didn't want to know. She was
beginning to discover that she had absolutely no basic
interest in show-business people – yet there was nothing
to compare them to, since she had never known any other
kind, other than the Camerons. Adam was different, only
on the edge of the business, and he didn't mix with them
much socially. His friends were in all sorts of things in the
ordinary world. It would be such a relief to be with them,
get to know them.

'I've located your guy,' Glen said to Mim, putting an

arm around her as well as Lizzie. 'And Eddie, your fan. Who do you want to meet first?' His grin was flirtatious, served to put Mim on the map with the people around them who were beginning to note and recognize who the three of them were . . .

Sammy Fielder himself was suddenly materializing from a mixed group of celebrities. It surprised Lizzie to see he was no taller than Mim, with a very dark skin and a smile like white light.

'Greetings, Liza, angel!' He kissed her hand. 'You grace my humble abode with your beauty. Are you happy, is this ugly prince taking care of you? Have you found the victuals, the libation, the needs of your psyche?'

Lizzie shrugged, dimpled. What an extraordinary character – she could hear herself describing him to Adam, 'looked just like a miniature Sydney Poitier with a voice like a Jewish comedian taking off an English nob, chest bare to the waist, mass of gold chains.'

'You must meet everyone, everyone – many more to come – night's young. So this is the famous *Mrs.* Hobbs – welcome, welcome, dear lady – you must find us all very crude . . .'

'Crude?' Mim made a comic face. 'That's a laugh. I ain't exactly royalty. Ever 'eard of Cockneys?'

'A Cockney! How delightful. You must sing us one of your wonderful songs! That one about a barrel – please, you must promise!'

He actually kissed Mim on the cheek, too speedily for any reaction, and after a quick, conspiratorial pat of Lizzie's arm, a hurried 'have a ball, darling, we all love you', bustled off to a noisy group coming in the front door.

'A fag, of course,' said Glen. 'You'll see some of his boys around the place, a kind of harem, if you'll pardon the expression.'

'Cor,' said Mim. 'Ought to be whipped.'

'Yeah, that, too.' Glen winked at Lizzie, and Lizzie had to laugh. Mim could be so solemn. Sometimes she could be a real prude. Funny – in other ways, nothing shocked her . . .

They all moved on into a large room at the back of the house where, suddenly, there was almost a silence, just a few people sitting round in big deep chairs or at a circular black leather bar, drinking and talking in a quiet, serious way. The contrast made Lizzie blink.

'This is what Sammy calls his Club Room,' Glen said, smiling amiably about, 'strictly for business.'

'Ah,' said a pick-faced, red-haired man, jumping up and coming over to meet them with eager, outstretched hands. 'Mrs. Hobbs and Miss Lee. Glad to meet you – no doubt Zeke mentioned me?'

' 'Course,' said Mim. 'It's why I come.'

'We'll leave you two,' said Glen, grasping Lizzie's arm. 'Have a good rap. See you later.'

'Oy.' Mim grabbed at Lizzie. 'Where'll you be, eh?'

'Safe with me, Mrs. Hobbs – Scout's honour.' Glen dimpled as nicely as Lizzie, far to the left of his mouth, a quirk which counted heavily for his popularity in *Dollar Man*.

'Whatever's a Scout?' Mim's nostrils pinched.

'Boy Scouts, Mum – you know. Baden Powell, all that.'

Lizzie grinned, her face creasing the way it had as a little girl.

'Go on with you.' Mim shook her head. 'Just you come back and fetch me in an 'alf 'our. Shouldn't take more, not that much to tell.'

'I dunno,' said Russ Oppenheim, reaching in his pocket for a notebook, 'depends. It'd be great if Liza – Miss Lee – would get in on this.'

'No thanks,' Lizzie said quickly.

'She's here to have fun tonight,' Glen put in, sliding an arm around her waist. 'With me. That right, Liza?'

'Right.' Lizzie looked at him in perky response.

The journalist gave them a sharp, analytical glance. 'Oh, yeah?'

By now, thought Glen, they had been noted by a good sampling of the customers – and, as Sammy had said, 'the night is young'.

He urged her away, a possessive, knowing grin ensuring that they made a telling exit.

'What now?' asked Lizzie.

'Don't look so resigned, darling – you're supposed to be nuts about me, remember.'

'Sorry . . .'

'Okay. We're going to plunge into the fray now. You're going to dance with me like you could eat me whole. Shouldn't be hard, just act like Sabina.' Glen tightened his grip on her slim waist, let his hand accidentally brush her breast – untaped tonight, yet! Christ, he was already horny. He'd have to go easy, particularly with Pammy barely restraining a threat to give that British whore a poke in the eye!

At the arched entrance to the huge, Spanish-style room, Lizzie faltered. From closer range, the great swarm of frenzied jerking dancers had the impact of coming upon a jungle of savages working themselves up for war; the looks on their faces had a ferocious intensity, and the heavy, reverberating beat of the music seemed their ultimate incitement.

'What's wrong, honey? You do this stuff better than any of them.'

'I'm out of practice . . .' Lord, how could she go in there! Oh, Adam, darling – why didn't you stop me? Why didn't you say it wasn't necessary, that nothing mattered in the world but – love . . .?

'Well, you shouldn't be – it's criminal . . .'

'What is?'

'Never mind . . . Come on, little Liza – let's go!'

Suddenly Lizzie knew it was useless to think of Adam (though he could still remember the twist if he didn't swivel too vigorously for his old back problem). With one quick look at the band, all of the five sweatily absorbed in making what she knew was fabulous rock sound, and the singer's Jagger-style look and gyrations reminding her with acute nostalgia of Robbie – she was galvanized into the mood with such abruptness that Glen was all but left behind.

Lizzie was in there, her shoulders, hips, arms, legs, feet moving in seemingly wild but precisely controlled rhythm, her face rapt with aggressive enjoyment, her hair spilling backwards, forwards, round to each side like spinning light.

'Yeah, baby!' said Glen, pocketing his bow tie, undoing his jacket, 'let's show 'em!' He moved with her, not to be outdone, reverting to his pre-fame days in Ohio when he was known in his gang as 'Pelvis the Second'.

'Ever hear of Rob Grover?' Lizzie asked, between gasps of breath.

'Sure, great. Know him?'

'I was his girl.'

'No, kidding! What happened?' Glen angled closer, the better to hear this new light on Liza.

Lizzie shrugged without pausing. 'Don't know.' She actually didn't, she thought. It had seemed impossible that they would ever be apart, but they were, and only now and then, since Adam, did it hurt any more.

'Did you love him?'

'Yes. We were dancing just like this, when he proposed. We were too young, though . . .'

'Liza, hey, baby, you can't cry *now*!' Glen's handsome face tilted furtively – were the tears standing in those great blue eyes noted . . . ?

'Don't be soft – as if I *would*.' Lizzie pressed her lips, shook her head at him, increased her momentum.

'Say – can I borrow her, Glen?' A man about her own age, with long curly dark hair, wearing a full white satin blouse and black satin trousers, started moving into Glen's place. He had dark, staring eyes that reminded Lizzie of Kit, and he had a smell she recognized, that also hung like an invisible cloud in the room.

'Jesus, you're lovely, just as you look on TV,' he said, before Glen had actually withdrawn, muttering 'Only for a minute, she's with me.'

Lizzie continued to dance, neither smiling nor unsmiling. 'Who are you?' she asked.

'You wouldn't know – Dan Ace, talk-show producer. I hear rumours you're great in the picture, that you'll take off like a rocket.'

'Who says?' Lizzie leaned back, her eyebrows raised, bumped each slim hip, each shoulder.

'It gets around. Hollywood's a small place. Is it true you've split with Adam Levine?' Dan Ace's dancing was not his strong point; he struggled with the last steps he'd learned, trying even harder not to get swept away from her by the crowd.

Glen, scowling, jostled, waited.

'I don't talk about my private life,' Lizzie said.

'Come on, I'm not going to put it on the air . . .'

Like bloody hell, thought Lizzie, looking at Glen from under her fringe.

'People want to know what you're *really* like.' He winked, lurched closer to her. 'When that old bat's not guarding you, huh? Huh?' He giggled. 'Honest, tell me – I won't tell anyone. Bet you're some scorcher. You'd have to be for Adam Levine to . . .'

Lizzie stopped dancing, smiled over to Glen, and he came over so forcefully that Dan Ace stepped back, falling over one couple, getting kicked by another.

'I'm sorry, Glen,' she said, 'but this isn't going to work – I can't go through with it. Could you please take me home?'

'Wait, hey – steady on, you can't let one jerk bother you, honey. Let's get some champagne – and meet up with all the people who want to meet you.'

'I don't see anyone *I* want to meet.'

'That's not the point – we're trying to make history, remember?' Glen held her arm in a tight grip, preventing her from moving off without him.

'It's not the kind of history I'm interested in making.' Lizzie gently disentangled her arm, met his eyes in softened appeal. 'Look, Glen, I'm awfully grateful, honestly. If I'm letting you down, I'll try to make it up to you in the picture – but you must understand. I mean, it doesn't take much imagination to know what the rest of this party's going to be like.'

'It doesn't?' Glen felt a jolt of uncertainty. Perhaps *he* didn't have a clue about this girl, either. 'What *do* you imagine?'

'They'll be stoned, running about naked, having sex in all available places and ways. The pool will be filled with them. Wives will be looking for husbands, husbands for wives – it'll be one great sodden mass of drugged and drunken humanity . . .'

'Liza! Where'd you learn all that – not from *experience!*'

'You don't have to experience things to imagine them – any actor knows that!' Lizzie did not stop walking. She was not about to tell him that Adam had given her a graphic run-down of what to expect of a Fielder party (the decent, mature element of Hollywood wouldn't be caught dead there!), or that she'd even used some of his words.

'Come on, honey – at least have some food, a couple of drinks. We'll get your mother and Eddie . . .' Glen followed, kept up, with the dogged persistence of a man about to have his ego, image and claim to Liza reduced to ashes.

Lizzie looked about for the room where they'd left Mim. A flickering montage of faces and bodies intervened, varying from tanned and glossy, spectacularly casual,

263

cosmetically grotesque to the desperately undistinguished . . .

Suddenly Lizzie could not make her way, even with a more civilized version of Mum's elbow technique . . .

Smiles and voices were coming at her – she was stopped, trapped.

'Liza Lee – gee, you're cuter than in your photos . . .'

'I heard you on the Cosmo show – you were terrific!'

'Gee – you and Glen Wyatt. Wow! Has to be a winner!'

'Hey – you gonna sing for us tonight?'

'Yes, yes, yes . . .'

' "Together" – sing it for us, please!'

'I couldn't . . .' Lizzie swung a radiant, professional smile from face to face. 'Not tonight.'

'Why not? Why not?'

'I don't think I'm allowed . . .'

'Sure you are, Liza,' said Glen, joining the chant with new hope. 'This is a private party – you can do anything.'

' 'Course you can,' said Sammy coming up, taking charge, 'no one says no to Sammy Fielder. Come on, beautiful one – I'll announce you myself!' He tucked her hand into his ringed, cushiony palm, tugged.

'I'd rather not.' Lizzie attempted a not-too-ungracious resistance, smiling as she drew back, but the cry for her to sing gathered momentum, increased the crowd, reached the attention of dancers beyond, caused them to pause, stare expectantly . . .

How many times had she felt this way, she thought, not *wanting* to sing, not *wanting* to be thrust into the spotlight to perform, her heart just not in it . . . why was it any different this time?

'Come on, Liza – sing, sing, sing!'

No, no – no, no, *no*! She wanted to scream. Please let me alone, let me go!

'Lizzie, me darlin' – so 'ere you are. Eddie and Russ and me's been lookin' for ya – 'ang on, what's this – they want you to *sing*?' Mim's thin, boney face seemed to plump, her eyes to spark, her eyebrows to wing apart. She moved forward like a mother-bird in full attack. 'Right, stand back everyone – let 'er breathe, for Gawd's sake. Where's the leader – I'll 'ave to clue 'im in.'

In amused shock, all eyes turned to the strange little figure pushing their host aside as if he were beneath contempt. 'Come on, lovey . . .' She nodded to Lizzie, began elbowing her way through the crowd towards the bandstand at the far end of the huge room.

All the dancers slowed, came to a stop. There was a short hush, then a steady clapping . . .

For just one suspended moment, before Lizzie followed, her body seemed to have left her, to have rushed away and out into the night . . .

It still might . . .

When she hovered, though, the applauders, further galvanized by her modesty, her 'British reserve', intensified their clapping.

Mim looked back, frowning. 'Come on, ducks . . . don't keep the customers waitin'.'

'Well, this is sure a scoop, fella,' a voice said nearby.

In a revolving mist, Lizzie was aware of Glen's satisfied nod to the journalist – and, somewhere close enough to emerge in tandem, the large, round, grinning man with a black hairpiece like a quiff – and the ginger head and freckled face of Zeke Solway . . .

She felt her breath squeeze, her hands turn cold, her knees limp. There was an old tug of hope that she might faint, simply and neatly pass out.

But, of course, she didn't.

And Mim briefed the musicians, and the band played full steam, getting all the keys and rhythms right – and Lizzie, as usual, 'sang her heart out', as the papers often described her performance. She was dynamic, radiant, inspired. She brought them all into the second chorus of

265

'Ready Heart' and 'Together', and they shouted and stomped for a repeat of 'Stars Over Soho' – and then, still unrequited, they begged for all the current popular songs – and she ended up doing some Beach Boys' songs with the bandleader, who was so like Mick Jagger that he could have *been* Robbie . . .

Finally, with the entire party who were still on their feet gathered in force, and to Sammy Fielder's mike-amplified command, Mim got up beside her and together they belted out 'I've Got A Lovely Bunch of Coconuts,' 'Roll Out the Barrel' and 'Knees Up, Mother Brown'.

They would have had Lizzie back after that for even more. It was what Judy Garland would have done, sing on and on as long as her voice held out, but Lizzie, with a wide-armed gesture, brilliant smile, kisses blown this way and that, was suddenly gone.

Even Mim could not track the speed with which Lizzie plunged through the applauding crowd, became a receding figure, vanished.

Out in the darkness, Lizzie looked wildly about. How could she get to Malibu? It was one thing to escape, another to get anywhere in this vast place in the breaking of dawn . . .

There was no other way.

She circled the masses of parked cars – there it was. Dear God, let there be a key in it . . .

There was.

# CHAPTER NINETEEN

Adam did his best. He sat himself down, he brought all his papers and books together, he cleared his consciousness, focused his thinking on the theme that had intrigued and challenged him with such urgency, such excitement and force . . .

The typewriter seemed to wait, to demand, and finally to accuse. Creative guilt mounted in proportion to the emptiness of his mind.

He got up yet again, made another cup of coffee, wandered about the room, went to the porch and looked out at the sea, watched the waves, the rhythm of the tide, the changing skies. There was yawning nullity in their effect. Beauty, nature, those reliable goads to artistic response, had no power of rescue.

Whenever the telephone rang, instead of swearing, he strode to it in eager relief. First, it was his agent in New York, telling him the promising news of a backer. Then his first wife who had not received her alimony cheque. After which, in turn, his younger son, who wanted to drop out of college and take a year abroad, and would he talk to Mom about it and get her off his back – and finally Helena, who wondered when he was coming home; despite the business of her law practice, she was feeling deprived.

All of these, the still empty page in the typewriter, a gradual tightening of every nerve in his body, the whisper of a migraine, kept Liza like a beacon in his awareness.

Sprawling in first one of the great leather chairs and

then another, he rubbed and rubbed at his face, his head, as if he could somehow rub clarity into his brain. He wanted her so much – yet what good was he doing her, what good would he do her? Tonight was only the first open sign of warfare between him and the studio. Even if it didn't achieve its aim this time, there would be an unbroken assault. Liza would suffer for his obsession. It wasn't fair to her: he was not even an adequate lover. He'd taught her how to make love, then couldn't always get an erection. He'd been so spoiled by women, and most of all Helena, who catered to him with so little in return. It was difficult to understand what they saw in him. Helena had called him a Jewish George Sanders, which was nonsense, of course.

But whatever he seemed to have for them, it had been unremitting, allowing him no respite. He could hardly remember when he was not either married, engaged or living with someone. Women didn't even seem to care when he was married; it never stopped their approach.

And, charming it had all been. There were so many types of women to love, each with something distinctive, something to learn from and add to his perceptions . . .

The complications and complexities, both legal and financial, had eventually worn him down. His ardour had slipped. His preoccupation with his work had quietly taken over his physical drive. Helena soldiered on (still did!), more his companion than his lover, and there was no doubt he was extremely comfortable with her. Helena wasn't pretty; she was solid and matronly, with frankly Jewish features, a cap of hair like a monk's, a hearty laugh and a very shrewd intelligence. Even when he was with Liza, he still told Helena things in his mind. She was like a reference point in his diminishing virility.

But, he *loved* Liza. He adored her. Whenever he saw her bright face, the big blue eyes, the swing of vibrant blond hair, the warm, unaffected smile that dimpled her lovely mouth, he came as close to worship as in any church. If he could name any sense of God in a real way, it would be holding her close, listening to her sweet, hoarse little voice confiding her thoughts, telling her his own and hearing them as new in her wonderful receptivity.

Oh, God! How could he possibly give her up, let her go? She was his. She belonged to him. They had been meant to meet at this time, to be the salvation each of the other!

He jumped at the sound of his own groan, poured a brandy. What would she be doing now – dancing with that plastic young man, hero of the seventies' female, a modern brand half-Joe-College, half-amoral exploiter . . . getting led into what nauseating charade . . .?

But, perhaps, it would grow on her, the change from their quiet times, almost entirely alone except for a few occasions with some of his friends, mostly established couples, literary people, intellectuals caught up in the movie game, or the bigger stars who flew in from homes in other parts of the country to do a picture, flew out again when it was done.

Liza had always seemed content; on the other hand, there was a lot of fun and humour in her, the energy of youth unused in generally older company. Would she be letting off steam tonight, be trying her newly acquired sexual wings on her co-star?

Adam's mouth twitched. It was so obvious the guy had the hots for her – it would give him a legitimate chance . . .

If the mother could be placated. Though would that be necessary – wouldn't Mim Hobbs more than welcome the intervention of Glen Wyatt?

Another brandy felt indicated. It had been a long time since jealousy twisted his gut.

But it did now.

He kept looking at the various clocks in the house, as if they could tell him something to ease it . . .

Damned if he was going to lapse into the cliché of drink. Hangovers, he'd long since graduated from, he told himself in Jewish wryness. So forget work. Take a sleeping pill and go to bed. She'd call him, or he'd call her, in the morning.

At two o'clock, he was still roaming the house, his eyes stark behind his glasses. He felt troubled, deeply, deeply troubled . . .

At last, as the clock struck three, he knew what it was, and what he had to do. He stopped wrestling with himself. It was clear, precise, unequivocal.

He would leave. He would break with Liza, now, before it became messy, impossible, a disaster for them both.

A stinging came to his eyes. He already yearned, knew how the months ahead would feel. He would probably have to abandon the play. He might even have some kind of a breakdown . . .

But – it had to be done.

He sighed heavily, nodded, got into his pyjamas, went to bed. There was no question of sleeping, but he would lie there till it was time to get up, make plans, start to set them in motion.

In spite of himself, he must have fallen into some form of sleep – he was awakened by the feel of a soft body melting into his . . .

'Darling – please hold me. Hold me tight.'

He groaned. 'Oh, dearest love . . .'

There was no question of his making love: he had never been very potent even in his youth. It was beyond happiness, an ecstasy without description. 'I love you, I love you,' he repeated.

Liza was satisfied, happy, too. She lay beside him, arms wound so tightly about him that he smiled at her strength.

'It was a hideous party,' she said. 'I hated every moment of it. You must never make me do such a thing again.' She told him everything that had happened, how she had ended up having to sing and sing . . .

270

'*That* wasn't a bad thing, though,' he murmured. 'They must have enjoyed hearing you in person. Won't do you any harm at all . . .'

'I wish I never had to do another performance for the rest of my life.'

'You say that, dearest – but you'd have to. You're much too good to give it up. You wouldn't be able to live with yourself if you did. That's the truth about talent, real talent.'

'You're wrong – about me, anyway.' Lizzie became suddenly quiet, as if she had decided to keep something else to herself.

Adam turned away, looked at the bedside clock. 'I'm going to make us some coffee, my love – and *then* I want to have a serious talk with you. A very serious talk.'

Adam did not enjoy the quiet, hopeful smile that lighted Liza's face and mascara-smudged blue eyes. It didn't make it any easier, when he told her as gently as he could, what he had decided.

What he was *not* prepared for, was her reaction. He had known it would be dramatic and traumatic. He had suffered through female hysteria many times, and knew that with Liza it would be that much more heart-rending to cope with . . .

But he had never expected her to say that she would take her life. Even while he talked, argued, explained, it dawned on him fully for the first time that he had become her father-figure, the American father she yearned for, her security, as well as her lover.

He found himself saying, 'What about Mim, your mum, who loves you as herself? You have her, and you have the most wonderful career a girl could wish for, a whole life ahead – many men will love you. You'll marry one of them, perhaps more, have children. I'll fade into memory . . .'

The worst part was that she had not cried – and now

she merely turned her face into the pillow and was still.

'Dear heart – Liza, my love . . .' He looked at her help-
lessly, his face drawn, his tan a coating over grey; had she
looked up at him right now, she'd have seen an even older
man, the difference between them more apparent than
ever. But she didn't – and presently she got up, walked to
the bathroom and began a shower.

He followed her, saw the water cascade over her slim,
beautifully shaped body, down over her thick hair, flat-
tening it against her skull so that drips ran down her uptilted
face like the tears she hadn't shed.

What was she thinking? What was she going to do?

He suddenly didn't know her. Fear stabbed at him.

Moving slowly, he threw aside his robe and stepped in
with her, held her in a panicked embrace. The feel of her, as
she stood close in his locked arms, the water coming
steadily down over them in a warm flood, was sweetness
pierced with pain . . .

'I love you so . . . Oh, my little Liza, my love, my love.'

She looked up into his eyes, larger and clearer than when
behind his glasses. 'I only want you in all the world,' she
said, in the flat tone his experience recognized as the onset
of depression.

'Liza, dear – look at me. Really look. In a few years I'll be
grizzly, elderly. You need a young man, red-blooded, passionate, enthusiastic, worthy of your very special talents!'

'Cobblers!' Liza pursed her lips at him, opened her eyes in
sudden blazing protest. 'That's *your* idea – not mine! I'm a
perfectly ordinary female trained to do tricks, like a dog.
I'm fed up to the back teeth with being called talented. If you
loved me, you'd love me for myself – and . . .'

There was a silence, with only the rush of water to break
it. 'Yes,' said Adam. 'And?' At least she was sparkling with
life, feeling again.

'Nothing.' Wet lashes curtained any expression in her
eyes.

'Speak your mind, Liza,' Adam urged, 'please.'

'It's no use. You won't be interested . . .'

He shook her with force. 'Try me.'

She remained silent, pulled away.

He helped her into a large towel, wrapped her in it. But she moved away again. 'I'll get dressed . . .' she murmured.

Adam got out, patted himself dry, got into jockey shorts, a clean shirt. 'Do you want me to drive you home?'

Lizzie got some jeans and a striped T-shirt from the closets that Adam had assigned for her use. Without looking in the mirror, she tied her hair back in a white ribbon. 'I'd better see if she's all right . . .'

'I'll drive you. I suppose Glen will be looking for his car. And you'll be due on the set . . .'

She shrugged.

Adam finished dressing, the worry in his face gathering it into hard creases. For Liza not to care, not to be concerned about what she'd done, or her work, was more than alarming.

Before they left the big rambling 'cottage' in the Malibu Colony, Adam paused by the door, drew Liza to him. 'Look, dearest, if it will help I won't go immediately. I'll try to hang on till the movie's finished – you can do all the publicity stints necessary, but I'll be here for you, loving you.'

Lizzie looked at him as if through a deep layer of gauze, as if she could hardly get him into focus. Her eyes were dull with sadness. 'No, thanks, Adam.'

As she pushed on, Adam felt the most cataclysmic moment of his life was upon him: he could escape it if he wanted to, but did he want to?

'Dear?' he said, drawing her back from the onslaught of sun into the salty cool of a shadow. 'What is it you want of me? What would make you happy again?'

She looked at him a long time, her mouth seeming to

273

form a word then abandoning it, her eyes so large that they drowned the rest of her face as they had when she was a little girl. 'Happy?'

'Yes, darling, happy.' His smile was wry, pleading.

'Only to marry you,' she said, dully. 'To be your wife.'

He took her slowly into his arms, rested his lean jaw on the top of her head for what seemed a long time.

'Done,' he said, at last. 'Done. But you must promise to finish the picture first. And tell no-one. Least of all Mim.'

She didn't answer, couldn't. Tears poured down her cheeks; her throat was closed.

# CHAPTER TWENTY

As she sat by the pool, drying off her leathery skin and red polka-dot bikini, Mim chewed thoughtfully on her cigarette holder and kept a sharp eye on Lizzie.

'Great party,' said Eddie O'Reilly, lounging beside her like a furless Great Dane, gazing at her with fond eyes from under his slipped hairpiece. 'You sure know how to organize things, Mims. Wish I'd had you around when I was running the circus. I never had the right woman, know what I mean? All they ever wanted were the diamonds.'

'Ain't nothin' wrong with diamonds,' Mim murmured. 'Any'ow, *they* must 'ave been the kind of birds you fancied.'

He grinned at one side of his big, fleshy mouth. 'You think so, huh? You're a shrewd little dame, just as I figured. When are you goin' to Acapulco with me? We could make it a honeymoon, if you want, if you say the word.' He tugged his inadequate black trunks a bit higher towards the white over-hang of his belly, as if to better present himself.

'Leave off, Eddie, will you?' Mim gestured irritably with a sun-baked, cerise-nailed hand. 'I got things on me mind.'

Eddie blinked in her direction. 'You shouldn't worry about Liza, Mims – looks like she's doing mighty well for herself, mighty well.' His sage nod wobbled his chins.

'Yeah – I know. That's just it . . .'

Watching the way her high thin eyebrows drew together (making her look like an old Marlene Dietrich

275

photo, he thought, only with more character), Eddie knew it was time to shut his mouth. If he was to grab this feisty little woman before someone else did, he would have to watch his every 'p' and 'q'. She was like dealing with one of the high-strung circus ponies that had to be tamed before you could get it into the string. He leaned back on his elbows, joined her in watching her Lizzie . . .

Look at her now, thought Mim. So *happy*. Laughing and making her dimples, chatting away with everyone like she loved them all, loved being in Hollywood, loved the whole movie colony, loved being in pictures, loved being a star with all the lark that went with it, loved giving parties and having her house filled with people, even if she hardly knew their names . . .

And look at her with Glen Wyatt, flirting like a tart, paying no mind to Pamela Shaw, the girl who'd played his sister-in-law in *Dollar Man*, but used to be his girl! And ruffling Benny's hair, and actually hugging back all the members of the company who kept hugging her, and . . . 'ang on, who was that she was running over to like he was her long-lost . . .?

'Me Gawd . . .' she muttered.

'Uh?' said Eddie, alertly.

She shook her head. Eddie subsided again. The composer bloke, eh? Adam Levine no sooner out of her sight on his business in the East, than she's latched onto this dishy type, who'd just come onto the picture to do the music . . .

Quick work, me gel. Hmm.

'Get us a shandy, old dear,' she said to Eddie. 'And fetch me 'andbag off the desk in me office.'

Eddie hauled himself up as fast as possible. ' 'Andbag, huh. You mean purse.' He winked down at her, dug her bony hip with a large pink toe.

'Get on with you.' She pinched his toe, winked back.

He lumbered off, and Mim lit a fresh cigarette, the

better to think without his bulky presence. It was all very peculiar. First off, Lizzie comes home after the time she run out on the party in Glen's car, doesn't say nothing about what she's been doing, looks like 'ell but acts all gooey. She says she and Adam have come to 'an understanding'. So now, it would be 'so serious', and she'll feel better about 'co-operating with the studio' and getting out and about . . .

And sudden as that – there's Lizzie going to lunch at *Chez Vous* with other female stars, wives of producers and directors, playing tennis and golf with them, and being seen with Glen like she was in love with him, giving interviews, acting all sunny and friendly and sociable, and loving *me* as if I was the moon and the stars of her life . . .

Hmmm.

And when old pi-jaw comes to the set, nothing like as often, he acts more like a Jew uncle or brother, laughs at me jokes. They don't even hold hands no more . . .

Hmmm.

'Mind if I have a word, Mim?'

Mim peered up through mascara-burdened lashes, into the sun-blurred face of Zeke Solway.

'Be me guest.' She reached for her dark glasses, put them on, tucked her sun-flaked legs under her in the lotus-position she'd learned at a yoga class.

Zeke, a Hawaiian shirt over his trunks, heaved himself down beside her. 'Look,' he said, 'you know Liza won't talk business, but what's all this about a Broadway musical you've had up your sleeve? You never told me it was a deal.'

'What's she been tellin' you, then?' Mim's sharp glance was only suggested by the tilt of the big sunglasses.

'*She* doesn't tell anyone anything. She only says – "ask Mim – she takes care of all that stuff". That stuff meaning what? That she doesn't give a damn – or that she hasn't got any mind of her own?'

Mim wiggled a finger at him. 'Na, then – none of your sauce. My girl knows I know what's best, and what's more, 'ow to go about it. Can you imagine Lizzie puttin' 'erself forward, doin' bargains with 'ustlers like you?'

Zeke smiled grimly. 'Okay. But you haven't answered my question. Why not level with me? How am I gonna talk with these guys who want to put money up for her next movie, if all the time you got this deal fixed back east?'

Mim's gaze wandered from him to where Lizzie was strolling towards the house with the music bloke. Not just strolling – but hand in hand for everyone to see! What was she playing at – what was her game? It didn't make no sense – one minute in love to her eyeballs with the old bluebeard playwright, the next anyone's gel, loving them all . . .?

'What you say?' She became aware that Zeke's voice had a nasty push to it, that he was narked. 'I was just thinkin'.'

'I gotta have a straight answer, gotta know, Mim. Do *you* want these guys to back down, take their investment elsewhere? I mean, if you think it's that easy to . . .'

Mim drew in air through her teeth. 'That's what it *is*, me friend, easy – now she's proved 'erself. Only stars make pictures – you said it yourself. You say Liza will do it – the millions will come.'

Zeke shook his head. 'You sure do learn fast, I'll grant you that.' He looked at her in grudging respect, forcing his eyes to accept what they wanted to reject. 'Still and all – what's the answer, Mim?'

Mim lifted her chin, as clearly, from the interior of the big, rambling Monterey house, came the sounds of Lizzie singing to the exploratory chords of the Steinway – one of the investments she had made with Lizzie's amassing money, 'as a bit of a nest egg' (which could be added to their Mercedes and Porsche, their furs and jewels when they moved on).

'Rehearsing,' said Zeke, 'improves the shining hour; I got to hand it to her . . .'

'That's 'er trainin'',' murmured Mim, but her mind had left the moment, had wandered back to the time she and Eddie had gone fishing in the dusk at Malibu – who should they see coming down the beach, wrapped up in each other so close they were like one figure, but ' 'is nibs' and her girl. Laughing so soft and low as they went on, letting the water lap their bare feet, talking their heads off in that way she'd heard them do back in the beginning – 'discussing life, Mum', she'd called all that drone of high-falutin' words . . .

'Well, all right, Mim – have it your own way. I hoped we could work together on this . . .'

Mim blinked. 'Aw, come off it, Zeke – I ain't 'oldin' out on ya. I just don't know meself yet. There's things I got to think about . . .'

'Like what?' Zeke spread his sunburned forearms. 'Spell it out.'

Mim chewed on her empty gold holder. She was not about to be squeezed into a corner. She wasn't ready. Something wasn't smelling right. Only when she knew what it was would she make the decision between the Leoffler and Hartz musical, which would take Lizzie to the east coast of America, and the next picture, which would keep her here in the west.

'Zeke, me friend, tell you what I'll do – soon as I make up me mind, you'll be the first to know. 'Ow's that?'

Zeke gave a heavy grunt. 'Not good enough. Maybe you'd better find yourself another agent for Liza, Mim. There doesn't seem to be room for the two of us. Either I'm handling her, or you are.' He folded his arms, looked straight into her glasses as if he could see through them.

Mim's mouth pleated. She looked away, watched the

swimmers, the guests sitting at the umbrella-shadowed tables laughing and talking, the bronzed young man in white trunks doing another fancy dive into the sparkling turquoise pool. Over the sounds of splashing water, tinkling ice, birdsong on the high, spiky trees, rattling dishes, the quick passing roar of a silver flashing plane, came the sound of the theme of *Maiden Voyage*, and then, yet again, with lilting, buoyant clarity, the familiar voice of her girl . . .

She gave a sudden shift, undid the lotus, stretched out her legs and arms. 'I 'ate to say this, Zeke, but there ain't no choice. No one 'andles Lizzie – only me. You want Liza Lee, you 'ave to go through yours truly. If that ain't clear by now, you need your noggin looked at.' She slid her glasses down, stared at him.

Zeke's sun-reddened face went slowly redder. 'Okay,' he said. 'Okay. We'll leave it like that – for *now*.' He got up, nodded curtly, moved off.

'Couldn't find your 'andbag, Mimsie. Wasn't in your office. Know where you left it? In the downstairs powder room – loo. Anyway, here it is – and your beer and lemonade – ugh.' Eddie gave her the items, sank down again beside her. 'What did Zeke want?' he asked, sipping his ice-jammed highball.

'None of your beeswax, me love.' Mim gave him one of her sharp-elbow nudges in the middle of his tyre waist. 'You know what I want you to do for me next?'

He grinned happily. 'What? Anything, name it.'

'I want you to drive yourself out to a certain 'ouse in the Malibu Colony . . . Eh?'

The glee of conspiracy tipped his hairpiece further forward. 'Eh-heh, yeah . . .?'

'Get yourself inside, like a burglar, so no one sees ya.' Mim edged a little closer to him, put her sharp jaw next to his plump one. 'I want you to go through 'is desk, like you was Raffles . . .'

'Who?'

'Never mind. Just do it quiet – if you *can*, you big lump . . .'

'Mimsie . . .' Eddie's mouth turned down into the folds of his chin. 'I *am* on a diet. I *have* lost six pounds . . .'

'Belt up – I was only larkin'. Any'ow – listen careful. I want you to see what you can find about 'im and Lizzie . . .'

'Like what?' Eddie's brow furrowed thickly.

'Cripes – use your loaf, what do you think? Letters, love letters, things like that . . .' Mim's thin eyebrows managed to meet.

'I don't get it. Read them? Why? That isn't like you, that's sort of sneaky, isn't it? I'm not sure, Mimsie . . .'

Mim drew smartly away, reached for her sandals. 'If that's what you think, Eddie O'Reilly . . .'

His hand reached out to her, pulled her back. 'Mimsie – I'm sorry . . . Don't scowl at me. You must have your reasons – of course I'll do it. Tell me exactly what you're trying to find out.'

'Plans, Eddie. I want to know if they've got some plans they ain't tellin'. You just look out for anything what says about when the picture's done – see what I mean?'

Eddie's brow remained in furrows. 'Plans for what, Mimsie?'

Mim put her hand to her head, hit it. 'Gawd, you're thicker than an outside wall. I don't know 'ow you manage to get out of bed in the mornin'!'

Eddie became solemn. 'I did run a very large circus, you know. A large organization. No-one ever said I was stupid before . . .' Eddie looked at his toes in a stern way.

'Well, I'm sayin' it now. Don't you get mè drift at all? Look 'ere – ' Mim edged closer again. 'Say you was Lizzie, and you loved this old five-to-two more than you loved singin' or bein' in pictures or anything and all you wanted to do was get married to 'im – right?'

'Mmm.' Eddie listened intently, one finger on one lip.

'Right. Now suppose everyone was against it, including your mum what is the closest thing in the world to you. And suppose this old cove says 'e'll get out of your road till the picture's done, so's you can do everythin' the studio wants, and put the old girl, and all the rest, off. Then, when it's done – you just say ta-ta, tell your mum you're ever so sorry about the trick you played, and ask 'er ever so nice to come to the wedding . . .'

'Wedding?' Eddie's small dark eyes opened to their widest. 'Jesus. Is that what you think, Mimsie?'

'I didn't say I thought it, Eddie. I just said I want you to nose about a bit. It's dead certain I ain't goin' to get it out of Lizzie!'

Eddie nodded slowly. 'She did change mighty sudden-like. Now you mention it, she don't seem in character. I thought it was because she was free, and maybe enjoying her power like they all do. I never saw one where it didn't go to their head . . .'

'We won't 'ave a sermon, Eddie.' Mim swallowed back her shandy, took a Gauloise from her handbag, lit it, took a drag. 'Now,' she said, her flat tone sharp with business. 'If there's nothin' and I'm barkin' up the wrong tree – fair enough. I'll push the deal through with L and H. If I'm right, then I'll sign her up with Zeke's money boys.'

Eddie nodded sagely. 'But is your signature enough?'

'Don't be daft – we sign together. As usual.'

'How can you be sure she will? She's just as likely to say no to both, isn't she?'

'Ah, that's me boy – now you're using your nous.' Mim's nod was accompanied by a poke at his lower tyre where he was the most ticklish. 'That's what she'd do – if.' Mim drew back dramatically.

'If?' Eddie's chins all but vibrated.

'If. I, me friend, 'appen to 'ave what is known as a trump card.'

'You do? You gonna tell me?'

'No – I am not goin' to tell you. You take me for a loon?'

'I wouldn't say anything. You can trust me, can't you?'

'You're 'uman, ain't you?' Mim flicked her cigarette end into the bushes. 'You goin' to get started, then?'

'What – now? This minute?'

'Why not? I ain't got no time to waste – none at all.'

'Shouldn't it be dark?'

'Naa. If anyone notices, you just pretend you're elephant's goin' in the wrong 'ouse. 'Sides – Belinda Wood's never 'ome, next door – and there's no other neighbours in sight.'

Eddie looked longingly at the heightening momentum of the party. 'We haven't had our dance yet . . .'

'Silly sod – there ain't goin' to *be* no dancin'. Only food, and maybe tennis.'

'Yeah? Oh, well.' He helped Mim up, and got their things together. 'I was gonna take a picture of you today, in your bikini,' he said, scooping up his camera.

'Another time, darlin'.' Mim gave him an encouraging wink.

Mollified, Eddie moved along with her towards the house.

'You'll say goodbye to Lizzie all smarmy and nice, tell her you've got to meet your old auntie at the airport, and that you'll be back later. I'll tell her, if she thinks to ask, that you and me is 'avin' dinner. If you got somethin' to show me, you'll wait till we're alone. Right? You got it?'

'Of course I've got it, Mimsie. I just wish it weren't something like this you asked me to do. I only hope it's worth it.'

'It is. Would you want to see Liza Lee's career go down the drainpipe, like it never was?'

Eddie shook his head, ambled dutifully along beside her across the table- and chair-strewn patio with its flower-laden bushes and great tubs of ornate plants into the cool, lemon-wax-smelling interior of the house.

In the great white bamboo furnished 'fun room', Lizzie and Max Glasser were still at the piano, surrounded by smiling listeners with glasses in their hands. 'Come on in, Mrs. Hobbs,' Morris Lloyd called, 'we've got an open rehearsal here – isn't it great?'

Mim, shrugged into her big striped towel, gave an acknowledging nod. ' 'Op to,' she whispered to Eddie, 'get 'er while they're pausin'.'

Eddie, pink with the effort of his charade, said what he had to say to Liza, was smiled on affectionately, even given a quick kiss – and the worst was over: they all returned to the music, Eddie forgotten, and even Mim.

No-one seemed to notice them whisper at the door to the wide, shallow steps, and only the cook's Alsatian looked up from his doze on the front lawn as Eddie got into his car, started it up, drove off.

Mim drew in a slow, deep breath, turned and went back inside.

'Come on, Mum,' Lizzie said, as she came through from the breakfast room, her head wound in a blue bandanna, no make-up on her face, wearing her jeans and pale blue T-shirt, 'let's go – I've got to be made-up and on the set by seven, you know that!'

Mim, still in her Chinese-red robe, sauntered into the hall, her hair in huge rollers, a thick layer of cream all over her small, gaunt face. 'I ain't comin' with you this mornin', love.'

'You're not?' Lizzie's mouth made a startled 'O'. 'Aren't you well?'

'I ain't never been fitter, me darlin'. I'm just goin' to take it easy like, 'ave a swim and such.'

Lizzie shouldered a huge canvas bag. 'That's a good idea – but I don't believe a word of it. I think you and

284

Eddie are up to something. Well, more power to you, Mummy. You two are a natural, as they say here.' Lizzie threw her a kiss. 'So – ta-ta, then. See you when I get here.'

Mim moved over to her. 'You're wrong, you know. Matter of fact, I got business.'

'Business?' Lizzie's rounded eyes were innocent, a match for the bandanna.

Mim noted the alarm in them from long experience. She wondered how she had been fooled for even five minutes, let alone nearly three months – but then, Lizzie had become an actress now. Madame Irayna had been right about *that* . . .

'Yeah – business. Appointment with some investors at Zeke's office. You know – that movie deal for you. After all, me petal, we can't 'ave you doin' nothin' at the peak of your career, can we?'

'I thought you were planning the musical . . .' Lizzie's voice had a breathlessness that suddenly made her seem a kid again; almost, but not quite, melting Mim's resolve – no time for that nonsense, she told herself, this kid's a young woman now, and about to do us both in for her stupid obsession with the old Jew boy.

'I was, ducky, I was. But I've got to keep me 'ead – you're about to be a superstar. You got to pick up the ball and keep runnin', see. You're what they call "hot property" now. We go east, we don't do the movie, who knows what might 'appen. You ain't that big *yet*. Once you got the ball in your 'ands, then nothin' ain't going to stop you – *you'll* be namin' your terms, goin' to the moon. You know how much the big stars make these days?'

'Oh, Mum, pack it in. You're like a record with the needle stuck these days. Or, maybe you always were, and I'm just seeing it. Anyway – I may have put on a good act for the sake of the picture, but I'm just not interested in staying out here; I'm not cut out for it. It's all like a great second-hand dream. I may not know what I want – but it's not this.'

Lizzie reached her arms about Mim. 'Oh, I do appreciate it from your point of view, and you know how much I've always wanted to please you . . .'

'BUT?' said Mim, saliva spraying from her teeth.

Lizzie frowned. 'What are you on about, Mum?'

'But now you don't give a tuppenny-'apenny 'oot, eh?'

Lizzie sighed, looked at the big sunburst clock on the wall. 'I *must* go.'

'No – you just tell me what *you're* on about. You don't want to be in pictures, but you don't mind bein' in the musical, is that it?'

If she knew her Lizzie, Mim thought, then what she was doin' was squirmin', deep down in her innards. 'You want me to ring 'em up and say yes, Liza will do *Where Angels Dare*, thank you very much?'

Lizzie's eyelashes, pale as they were without make-up, were visibly fluttering, first up then down, like clusters of moths. 'I . . . well . . . oh, Mum, I'm just not ready to do anything at all just now. Just put them off, let me have a little *time!*'

'Why? What do you plan to do with your "little time" – say no to all offers, 'ang about till people forget you?'

'Mum – you exaggerate. Lots of performers take holidays.'

'Do you want a short holiday? Is that what you mean, darlin? Two, three weeks, a month – of course I could arrange that. Everyone would understand – we could go to Palm Springs or maybe Mexico . . .'

Lizzie's face was stiff with anger. 'I don't love you when you go on like this, Mum – I don't even like you. You're pushing at me all the time like a . . . like a keeper, like a gaoler – I can't breathe! Please, please, get off my back!'

Mim sucked in air. Her eyes were larger than Lizzie's, twice as dilated. 'So that's how you feel about me, is it? Now we've got the truth. All this fussin' over me like I was your lovin' best friend, tellin' everyone 'ow close we was,

286

'ow you owed everythin' to me – that was a load of old cods. You don't love me – you *ate* me!' Mim's voice rose until it broke apart like a shattered plate; her eyes gleamed with tears.

Lizzie's animation drained on the instant. She stared at a wall, her eyes glazed. 'Mum,' she said finally, through clenched teeth, 'I do *not* hate you. I love you. I just want some space. That's all – some *space*.' She turned to her slowly, reached out a hand. 'Look – I must go, Mum – let's talk later. Let's try to sort things out when there's no rush. Eh?'

Mim drew back from her implied hug, her kiss of truce.

'I want to know, Miss 'Igh-and-mighty . . .'

'Leave off, Mum – goodbye.' Lizzie started out the door.

'I want you to know,' Mim called out after her, 'that I know just what you're up to. You want to wait till tonight to sort that out?'

Lizzie faltered, stopped, but did not turn around. 'Tell me what you mean, Mum,' she said.

'I know you're plannin' to marry your old Jew. I know that's why you don't want to sign no movie out 'ere. I know that's why you don't even want to do the show . . . 'Cause you just want to be a *wife* – right? Like what you said in the beginning, when you used to tell me everythin' – right?'

Lizzie turned slowly around to face her. The smooth, tanned skin of her face was greyish-beige. Her breasts, under the T-shirt, had a quick up-and-down movement. 'That's not true,' she said, but her voice had no momentum, as if she had repeated a learned phrase.

'We both know it *is*, me darlin'.' Mim drew the brilliant, bird-embroidered robe across her flat chest. 'You're plannin' to give up everythin' we ever worked for, what I spent me whole life at – before you've even 'ad a bid from 'Er Majesty! All for a man old enough to be your father, because that's what he is to you, your old man what you never seen. I ain't all straw between me ears. And you'll wake up to it, and 'e'll get tired of you, because you ain't ever goin' to be 'is steam – and you expect me to stand by like a ruddy spectator and let it 'appen.'

Lizzie could no longer meet the fierce gaze, the eyebrow-gathered scowl; she looked instead at her bare, ringless, trembling hands, the hands of Sabina the virgin, who she played so well it seemed there was no separation between them.

'I'm sorry you've found out now, Mum,' she said. 'I was going to tell you as soon as the picture was done . . .'

'Yeah – and invite me to the weddin'. Thank ye kindly.'

'Mum . . .'

'Don't "Mum" me. And don't ever again call me "Mummy" – it'd make me puke. I ain't finished with you, young Miss. If you think I'm goin' to shut me trap and take a back seat while you ruin your life, you've got another great big think comin'.'

Lizzie's gaze was almost pitiful in its stark apprehension. 'What do you think you're goin' to do, Mum? There isn't anything you can . . .'

'There isn't, isn't there?' Mim patted the top of her rollers, put her hands on her hips. 'That's where you're mistaken, me gel.' She stood closer to Lizzie, caught up her eyes in a locked gaze. 'Bet you ain't ever told 'im you're givin' up, not takin' the show or the movie, 'ave you?'

Lizzie's gaze was trapped. She looked as if she did not know how to retrieve it. 'That's really none of your business, Mum. I don't intend to discuss it with you.'

'You don't, eh? Well, me clever little pigeon, I intend to discuss it with 'im. See? I intend to tell Monsewer Adam Levine that thanks to 'im, Liza Lee is throwin' in the sponge – at the 'eight of 'er career, that she's goin' to become a dear little 'ousewife and darn 'is socks and make 'is tea, and 'ave 'is kids – which 'e wants another of like a 'ole in the 'ead.'

Lizzie was quite still. Outside, the chauffeur was about to mount the steps. The Spanish maid looked again at the clock and frowned. 'Mum . . .' Lizzie's voice was less than a whisper. 'You wouldn't.'

'Oh no? I bloody well would – with bells on. And then – do you think he'd want to marry you? Eh? Does 'e want another little wifie – ain't he got enough to pay 'is alimony to? Would he want to be the one to make the wonderful Liza give up her 'ole career, 'im who's lived 'is life, who only wants me little girl to rev up his old motor with?'

Lizzie pressed her hands to her face. 'That's enough!'

There was a brief silence in the big, cool hall between the many great rooms, as if it had become a kind of cul-de-sac of time.

'Mum,' said Lizzie at last, 'I'm going to marry Adam. If you don't understand how much we love each other, it can't be helped. And if you want to tell him what I've not told him yet, but planned to soon – then you must do it. And – I'll understand. But . . .'

Lizzie looked up, looked into Mim's eyes. 'I just wish you wouldn't, Mum.'

She turned quickly away, ran down the steps, got into the car.

# CHAPTER TWENTY-ONE

Adam looked with wry pleasure at the grim, reluctant face of his bride-to-be's mother, juxtaposed among his relatives gathered in the living room of his home for the wedding. The cliché phrase 'fish out of water' had never been more apt. What could have impelled the little woman to wear a hat like a man's boater, banded in gypsy-coloured ribbons that dangled downward to her jutting nose, or that strange long dress like a white nightgown trimmed with ostrich feathers? ('It's Quant's new thirties look for the seventies' she'd told Lizzie. 'I want to look smart so you can be proud of me – after all, I'm the only relative *you'll* 'ave!': which was too true for Lizzie to argue.)

He had been clear in the option he had given her: 'You are welcome to come, Mrs. Hobbs, but we will also understand completely if you'd rather not.' He'd been blunt about the obvious: that all but a few present would be of the Jewish faith, that he'd been married to one gentile, so that two of his children were half-and-half. Because of this, they would be married by a liberal rabbi friend. No, Lizzie would not have to become a Jew, he had told Mim, finding himself roaring with laughter at her so-predictable outburst, not minding her any more, free of her entirely with the gaining of Liza . . .

His thoughts slipped happily through the walls between them to the big bedroom among the trees where Lizzie would be getting ready. The enchantment was still there, intensified now by possession – how precious, infinitely precious she was to him! He would do his best to treasure her, to take charge of his many perversities, his alternately insatiable ego and black self-doubt, his compulsion to play cat-and-mouse games with people of lesser intellect, his inclination to use whoever was closest to him at the time as a whipping boy for all his unresolved childhood traumas and current dissatisfactions. Dear God, he thought, if you exist, help me to honour her youth, her vulnerability, her trust . . .!

With these sentiments, he felt he had already married her, but, of course, to her, the ceremony itself was vital – he would go through it, for her sake, as if he had never gone through it before. He would act as if he came new to marriage, as if this was his one and only *heartfelt* set of vows.

He excused himself from his ushers, guests, relatives, closest friends (Helena amongst them), to go and check on his appearance. Despite all the ice-cold water he had splashed on his face this morning, last night's celebration had left him with deep bags under his eyes. He stood before the mirror in the guest room in stark contemplation of not only this fact – but that there was no mitigation of his age in the expert cut of his Brooks Brothers light tan suit, the blending Christian Dior tie, the fresh crispness of his cream-coloured shirt. His face was seamed and his neck irrefutably scrawny. Under the suit, he could see as if visible the pucker of his leanness, the retreat of moisture and elasticity from his skin . . .

Appalled at his sudden panic, he forced cheer to his expression, set his glasses straight, showed himself a more presentable image – Adam Levine, the distinguished playwright, charmingly erudite, satirical, Helena's kind of Jewish George Sanders in appearance.

Better. Perhaps he was unduly harsh on himself. Perhaps Liza wasn't cheating herself so much as showing precocious maturity of perception. She'd had a wide range of choice of younger men, extraordinarily attractive and often intelligent men of more than usual variety – and she'd preferred him.

Forget the nag of being a father-figure. Forget that time was an enemy. Remember only that many rare and wonderful marriages had been made of the June-December union.

Suddenly, he felt so happy that he could hardly move. His Liza, his dearest love, was handing him a brand new life: he could hardly wait for the words to be spoken, to be on the way to Paris as – man and wife.

Mim saw Adam coming back into the room, and thought: he's actually smackin' his lips, like a ruddy lion about to devour 'is kill . . .

And it's me very own darlin' who's the lamb. I could cut 'im up in little pieces, I could, and stamp on 'em. No – that's too quick. I'd like to 'ang 'im up somewhere and torture 'im slowly, maybe burnin' 'im with 'ot irons . . .

Mim met the polite smile of a long-nosed, blue-rinsed lady standing beside her, with an icy stare. Now which one of Mr. Shylock's tribe was this old cow? Cripes, you could 'ardly count them. Enough to drown poor Lizzie. 'Ow was she ever goin' to cope? All them kids, too. Askin' 'er to accept all his previous wives, like they were friends. 'It's what I want, Mum,' the soppy girl kept sayin', stars poppin' out of 'er eyes. 'They're all part of *him*, don't you see?' She saw all right. Her Lizzie was took, a proper gull.

'Time to assemble,' someone called, and Mim found herself moving forward to the place where she was to take part in the slaughter – to give her daughter away to the old five-to-two.

She braced up, put on a po face, went like a stiff walking doll to her position. The awful music struck up, the funeral march. 'Ere goes everythin', she thought. 'Er life, my life, just like she'd said to Eddie – down the drainpipe. Gone, all those long hard years, the work, the sacrifice, the strugglin' and the inchin' up that ladder to the top – all gone in one hour . . .

'Don't worry, Mrs. Hobbs,' he'd said, 'I don't. Lizzie won't be able to stay away from show business for long. You'll see. It's her life, it's what she is: her very blood. Just give her a bit of time to enjoy playing the role of house-wife. Let her explore. She'll be that better an actress, that better an interpreter of lyrics. She'll have expanded, grown, gained dimension. So, you just relax. Bide your time. And, there'll always be shows and spots for her talent.'

Stupid sod. He'd got right up her nose with his pi-jaw sermon, smilin' down on 'er just like he was Jesus, even puttin' his arm around 'er shoulder – which she'd been right smart to shake off . . .

'Here she comes – oh, *my*, isn't she beautiful!'

Mim turned, thought her heart would come out of her chest . . .

Lizzie shook so much she could hardly make her legs hold her up, and her bouquet fluttered in her hand like a vibrator. Even her lips wouldn't stop trembling as she attempted the right kind of smile. The silly part of it was that she wasn't in the least frightened or awed. She loved all the faces looking towards her as she came through the log-laced archway into the huge room that overlooked the river, loved the sight of the people who were to become part of her life, loved the sight of her beloved husband-to-be . . .

And that was really it. She loved him so much she could not really believe this was happening. She couldn't believe he was really going to marry her, commit himself to her, make her his wife, promise to stay with her forever . . .

Her marriage to Kit, which had flashed into her thoughts as she dressed, seemed a complete and absolute mockery, a farce she had played out. What could have been in her mind to let him use her like that? Why had she been so desperate? Because yes, she *had* known in her heart that it couldn't work. There was a mystery there – but this was no time to try to solve it.

Worse was the last vision of Robbie, looking back at her over his shoulder, seeming to see her, then hustled on in his daze, unsure – an unfinished feeling, a lingering unease . . .

Yes, she had loved Robbie, too, she thought, as she dipped her head to let Adam's sister Ruth put a garland of real white roses in her hair. But it was different, so different that it had nothing at all to do with today, with her feelings for Adam. It could exist separately, all by itself, without having to be lost or extinguished. Adam, of course, would understand, would not want her to deny any love she had felt for someone else at another time. She would have to live up to that in not wanting him to deny any of *his* old loves. The past was the past. Now she was going forward into a new and wonderful life.

Please God, she had said silently, as she took the bouquet from Ruth, who bent her dark head to kiss her in loving acceptance of their new relationship, let me match up to this wonderful man, keep him content and happy, supply him with all his needs from a woman. Help me to develop myself as a person, so I am not just a performer, so that I am more than a good pair of lungs, a pretty face, a sexy body – so I am as Mum said but meant in another way – 'a real someone'!

It was when she actually met Adam's eyes, that Lizzie tripped slightly, swayed, nearly fell . . .

'She's so nervous, poor dear,' said the woman beside Mim.

'So would you be, dearie,' Mim muttered.

Lord, thought Lizzie, how the room spins . . . all the smiling expectant faces, like the audiences she had always known, only this one very special, expecting far, far more from her than any past performance – could she do it?

Would she make it to the place where Adam joined her?

The music seemed more like the background to old plays and movies she had seen since she was a little girl – always roles, roles, life in one, unending series of performances . . .

All her life second-hand, living her mum's dreams – a second-hand dream . . .

Adam's elderly dad gripped her elbow – and then, like a jolt of reality, the coarse, hard feel of her mother's touch – and all was well.

Adam moved up, tall, dignified, stern: only *she* knew that he was smiling. She felt her lips relax, felt her legs strengthen, felt her fingers loosen on the bouquet, to hold it lightly, without tremor . . .

Lizzie lost awareness of her mother's tightly-pressed mouth, the fierce, betrayed look of her dark eyes, was aware only of the solid presence of Adam beside her – she did not dare to look at him yet, for the delicious sweetness of the moment pressed at the back of her eyes, would spill at the least contact . . .

Somehow, they got through the words. Adam's voice was firm, almost buoyant: it was as if he told them all in no uncertain way that this was IT. So – he's made many mistakes, messed up a lot of lives, shown himself to be riddled with human frailties – but now, at least, he was on the beam. This girl beside him was the one he'd never found, the missing 'true' love . . .

'I will,' he said, and it vibrated round the room like the sound of 'Amen'.

'I will,' whispered Lizzie.

'You are now man and wife!' said the rabbi in solemn emphasis, and for good measure repeated it in Hebrew.

At last Lizzie confronted Adam fully, met his surrendered gaze, lifted her lips to his.

Strangely, it was only in the middle of the wild and jolly festivities that followed that Lizzie noticed her mother was missing. At first she thought she was simply out of sight somewhere – then, just as she and Adam drew together by the table to cut the big cake, it became apparent that Mim had gone.

'Did she leave any word?' Lizzie asked, her smile fading, a pang of guilt almost destroying this ultimate moment.

No, no-one had spoken to her. No-one had seen her go.

'Don't worry, dear,' Adam said. 'I'm sure she'll be in touch.' He put his arm round her waist, pressed her to his side.

How like her to do it this way, Lizzie thought: so that she *would* worry – so that if it were *possible* to upset her happiness, this would succeed, give her the last word, the edge of triumph. But – Adam was right, and Mum wouldn't win, not ever again.

# CHAPTER TWENTY-TWO

'Are you all right, darling? Want some more coffee, tea, something to nibble on – or maybe a Coke, or a whisky?'

Lizzie hovered by the door of Adam's study, feeling melted in a way that had nothing to do with the summer heat, that came always with the sight of his bent head, wide, hunched shoulders, long beaky nose, the deep seams beside his mouth. She yearned to go to him, kiss him, smell the sun-sweet freshness of the shirt she had both washed and ironed for him, nuzzle the sideburns he complained were hurrying his old age by turning silver, but which she loved. After six months, she still could not believe he was her husband, her own to adore without fear or apology.

It made no difference that he did not look up, that his grunt was indecipherable. She hadn't really expected anything of him at this deadline stage of his writing, and was by now quite used to the intensity of his concentration. 'I think I could set off a fire-cracker beside him,' she had confided to Helena, a neighbour and old friend of Adam's, 'and it wouldn't make him stir!' Helena had nodded. 'It's the secret of his genius, dear. Drove the rest away – but you're much too clever.'

Not clever, Lizzie thought, smiling to herself, noting how much everything needed dusting but that she would have to wait to get in here till he was finished. She was anything but clever; but she did respect him for it, even envied it in some ways. Because much as she read these days, tried to learn things and carry through ideas to form intelligent conclusions, had Adam been anywhere in sight or reach, nothing else would have seemed as important as his nearness. That, she supposed, would always be the difference between them: she lived for him, he lived for his work and her in that order. The lovely thing, though, was that they could share his work. She could read his play with genuine interest, and he seemed to appreciate, even to need her comments. Often, she read the lines for him, changing her voice from role to role, and he said he found this extremely useful.

Eventually, of course, if she *kept* standing there, he would begin to feel her presence; the echo of her question would reach into his awareness. But then he would be trying to conceal irritability, impatience. He would answer, smile, reach for her and make some loving remark or inquire about what she was doing . . .

But – his train of thought would be broken. He might have difficulty getting it back, it might cause him to lose precious time . . .

It was best to withdraw quickly before that could happen. There was no lack of things to do, to keep her busy. Life had never been so full. She had Ruth as a special friend, Helena for advice and wisdom, neighbours who were endlessly friendly and helpful, the Club to go for swimming, tennis, golf, picnics, and just plain chatter. She could not get over how interested everyone in Stoneyvale, Connecticut was in her – at first, she thought it was because she was Adam's newest wife, understandable curiosity, and she felt she was constantly being compared and had to match up to her predecessors. But after a while, she realized that it was her own background, her reputation as a performer, her Englishness that made them vie for her company.

'You're a novelty, a celebrity,' Helena explained. 'You liven up the hum-drum round, give éclat to parties.'

Lizzie wasn't sure how to feel about it. *She* wanted to be

like *them* – but they wouldn't let her. They listened to everything she said with ready smiles, or laughter, took up her sayings – and were forever asking her to present prizes, open fêtes, sing for their charities, organize musical shows for the schools.

But even if they hadn't always been after her to perform, to attend their cocktail, lunch and dinner parties, Lizzie would have been hard-pressed to keep up with their expectations of her as Adam's wife. He was the most talked-about male in the community, had for some time been their biggest bachelor-catch, was considered the most fascinating, the most difficult and elusive. Lizzie watched how the women gravitated to him, attempted to amuse, interest, attract him, as though they could not quite give up, give him over to her. She thought that perhaps they did not believe she'd last, that Adam would end his days with someone so much younger, so alien to their culture.

She felt it herself, and often asked: am I just a diversion, a novelty to him? Did I come along at a time when he was jaded, wearied with people familiar to him, with predictable relationships?

It crept into her mind at odd times, like a faint chill, that she might not be *able* to hold his interest. Yet, there was no tangible sign that he was the least bit bored. At the same parties where he was courted for his status and 'charisma' (a word she'd recently picked up and taken on), he would never let her stray too far, take her hand, hold her by him like a wordless denial of any hopes the others might have of creating a wedge.

'The way he looks at you,' Helena observed, 'must grate in the throats of our hopeful divorcees and predatory housewives like ground glass.'

Lizzie felt herself rapidly blossoming, developing ordinary repartee that had nothing to do with the TV or movie she happened to be in, making observations with new confidence. She hoped that if she stuck at it, eventually people would stop thinking of her and calling her 'the little Brit', and asking her to perform. Perhaps some day, they would just pay no particular attention to her at all. She could then run the house, pick up the cleaning and meet the train when Adam spent days in the city, just like the rest of them . . .

One day, now that she was no longer taking the pill (without mentioning this fact to Adam – not because she wanted to deceive him, but because she didn't want to worry him just now, and once the play was finished and delivered, he'd have time to think about it – for she was certain he would be, despite what Mim thought, and *said*), she'd have the thrill of being pregnant with his baby, their baby! The joy of this idea was too much to contemplate. She could hardly wait . . .

Meanwhile, as by far the most popular couple in Stoneyvale, life was beautiful for them, their future magical, just like her name! Filled with love for him that made her eyes radiant, she smiled, drew the door gently shut . . .

. . . Adam blinked, drew in a breath, shut his eyes, rubbed his face slowly. He had, of course, been perfectly aware Liza was there. He felt mean and guilty for pretending to be oblivious – but it had been sheer self-protection. It was not just his time he was forced to guard these days, but the excess of her devotion. She could never quite leave him alone, as if she still felt he might disappear, was only a dream. Nothing he did or said was able to convince her that he was not going anywhere, and was as real as bread and taxes. Had he looked up, acknowledged her, he would have had to play out a reassuring scene of undying love. Which, no matter how much he matched her intensity with his, would fall short: there simply was no way he could relax her, set her mind at rest . . .

Against his own inclination and desire – because he did in fact love her as much as she wanted him to – he found himself longing for his old space. There were times he felt like fleeing the house and setting off down the road through the woods that led to Helena's – not for anything heavier than a long quiet talk, or maybe no talk at all – just to find his old shape, the sense of inner freedom he seemed to be losing.

He got up and wandered to his window, stared at the rapidly moving river that forever carried with it the driftwood of where it had been. His life seemed to be rushing past like that – and there was still so much to be done, to be accomplished. The play was not going as well as it ought to be. The dialogue tended to be limp where it needed to be incisive. His ideas did not crystallize, but remained murky and blocked. Could it be that he was having the famous but unknown to him 'writer's block'?

His shoulders hunched upward as if to dismiss the possibility from his mental ears. That was too easy. It was much more than that . . .

He wandered over to one of the book-lined walls, took down a battered copy of Emerson's *Essays*. More likely, he thought, it was some point of required growth in himself from which he was allowing himself to be diverted . . .

Ah, here were the words: 'Each man has his own vocation. The talent is the call. There is one direction in which all space is open to him . . . This talent and this call depend on his organization, or the mode in which the general soul incarnates itself in him. He inclines to do something which is easy to him and good when it is done, but which no other man can do. He has no rival. For the more truly he consults his own powers, the more difference will his work exhibit from the work of any other. When he is true and faithful his ambition is exactly proportioned to his powers. The height of the pinnacle is determined by the breadth of the base.'

He snapped the book shut, and replaced it. That was it in a nutshell. He was drifting away from himself, imitating, detracting from 'the breadth of his base' by his preoccupation with Liza – succumbing to her preoccupation with him . . .

*If only she'd get back to her own work!* He had been so sure that by now she'd be restless, bored with the dead-end routine of domesticity. He had been even surer that she'd turn tail and run from the claustrophobic rounds of community life, the semi-incestuous shuffling and re-shuffling of the same cast at every social function. But she hadn't. She'd loved it, thrived on it, wanted nothing else!

He sat down, leaned back in his large adjustable chair, pushed the wheels away from the desk and put his feet up on it. He felt like smoking again, but resisted . . .

By God, the mother had been right. It was so obvious, but he hadn't seen it, that *she* would know Liza far better than *he*. When she had accused him of annihilating Liza's career, he had been so complacently certain of his better judgement – but that's just about what was happening. He simply could not interest her in going back, in at least going into New York to talk to Leoffler and Hartz . . .

Mim's frenzy that she should was doubled by the fact that Art Leoffler had had a heart attack, so that the whole show had had to be delayed, waiting for lyrics to the songs. There was still time, Mim had written, phoned – even begged *him* to do something about it. 'They still want 'er, Mr. Levine,' she'd said, still refusing to acknowledge their relationship by calling him Adam. 'They don't want nobody else. Liza Lee is the only one, they say, to carry the songs, who 'as the looks and sex appeal for the lead. It's a criminal waste, Mr. Levine – don't you see?'

He couldn't help but agree. But Liza had taken it all wrong, had been sure he wanted to send her away from him. She had that same wounded, apprehensive look as when he had tried to say goodbye to her in Malibu, the look she had when she spoke of taking her life . . .

Forced to let the subject drop, he could find no way to

re-introduce it, except in moments of accord and happiness, when he lyricized on how fine it would be if they were both involved with their separate careers, how much her public wanted her, and what fun it would be to go to her opening night, instead of her just tagging along with him to his openings.

'I'm so proud of you when you get out there and sock it to them, darling,' he had said. And it was the truth. It was Liza as a performer that had captured him, caught his imagination, commanded his respect . . .

Without this superb dimension, the concept of her was beginning to pale; and, horrible to admit, to stir him less than he dared to face.

He looked at the papers strewn on his desk, the page in the typewriter, and felt one of his oncoming lethargies. The big leather couch across the room looked more and more inviting – perhaps just an hour's doze wouldn't hurt . . .

So much for the drive of ambition!

He stretched himself upward. At the far end of the desk was a small pile of Liza's mail, which, because she had no interest in it, she left alongside his each day. Idly, his eye wandered to it . . . What was that from Mervnick Pictures Inc.? She hadn't mentioned anything . . .

He picked up the letter, read: 'Dear Liza, you will be pleased to hear that, after considerable delay at the distribution end, *Maiden Voyage* will be opening at the Paramount on September 8, and we hope that you and Mim and Adam will attend a party we are having afterwards at the Waldorf-Astoria. All advance intelligence is that we have a gold mine, that we have sneaked in with an international winner.

'Please let me know how many tickets you want and if we can expect to see you. We certainly hope so, for while we wish you all the happiness in the world in your marriage, we do miss "the sunshine of your smile".'

It was signed 'Zeke' – and a postscript said: 'Any time you change your mind, we'll have a movie ready and waiting for you – terms that will satisfy even Mim! Z.S.'

Adam jumped up and snapped his fingers. Jesus Christ, this was too much. Not a word out of her, the letter cast aside as if it had been as expendable as a circular!

A hot feeling moved through his entire body, entered his head like fire. He felt stifled, without breath. Liza was not only procrastinating, deferring, she had no intention whatsoever of *ever* going back into show business. She was through with it. What he had, from here to eternity, was a wife nearly thirty years younger, one who he could not always promise to satisfy sexually, one who wanted a baby (that was only too obvious, too!), one whose mind was growing, but at its best had only moderate potential to intrigue him for the long haul . . .

Adam jumped up and walked about as he had done that night at Malibu, as if the blinkers were off, as if the enchantment showed up like the last trail of a sunset on grey dusk . . .

It wasn't that he didn't love her . . .

It was more a question of who he was loving. Who *was* Liza, without her radiant singing personality, her powerful renditions of songs that made her stand apart as a performer, her subtle interpretations as a fresh young actress, the wonderful way she moved her young body for the delight of audiences? Who was she when she wasn't pleasing audiences, throwing out her arms, her kisses for the thunder of applause, or the approval of the TV or movie company?

He pressed his forehead in desperation. The awful truth was that all three of his wives had had just as much as she, as women, as females. They had all been intelligent, pretty, willing to try – and far more suited to being just wives.

'Okay . . .' he muttered, 'okay.' Since it was useless to

confront Liza, he'd have to take their welfare into his own hands, act for her on her behalf.

He threw the letter back on the heap, sat down, picked up the phone, dialled the number Mim Hobbs had given him.

Down in the huge kitchen that thrilled Lizzie with its gleaming built-in equipment, the biggest fridge she had ever seen, where the sun shone in on the hanging copper pans, the red brick floor, the white circular bar that divided it from the breakfast room with its multi-coloured bottles and glasses and big coloured TV, she suddenly paused to realize that she was not entirely sure of this dish she was making for tonight's dinner party . . .

She wiped her hands on her chef's apron, went quickly to the red telephone on the sparkling white wall over the bar. She could only hope Bea Godfrey was home to give her the recipe again. How dim of her not to have listened more carefully, she was so hopeless at making things up the way real cooks could . . .

'We can't be good at everything, Liz,' Bea had said. 'Me, I can't hold a tune, and I love to dance but oh-my-feet, you know. The reason I can cook is because I came from a big family and had to help my mom, who was a wizard. First thing I wanted to do when Chuck finally married me was get into the kitchen and make like her – never look at a typewriter or shorthand book again as long as I lived. Just like you don't want to sing – quite a pair, you and me, huh?'

Lizzie grinned to herself, imagining the solidly-built woman with short dark hair and humorous, growly voice who was becoming the best friend she'd ever had. What fun, in their own special way, they had together! They must have been the only two wives in Stoneyvale who got their 'kicks' from meeting up in the supermarket and comparing notes on prices and value as they piled up their trolleys, who actually got high on the challenges and demands of running a home, tending their husbands' needs exhaustively and to exhaustion.

'Don't ever tell anyone,' Bea said once, as they suddenly decided to drive her two children to the beach for the day, taking a picnic, 'but I even love being stuck with the kids without help.'

Lizzie, holding the baby Godfrey on her knees, laughed happily. 'I'd love it, too,' she said.

'We, my dear Liz,' said Bea, 'are freaks.'

While the children crawled, cried, got covered in sand, made endless requests and created an unending assortment of minor and major crises, Bea talked about herself and at the same time gave Lizzie instruction in how to change 'diapers', give the baby a bottle, burp him, help the older one build sand castles, divert attention from the howls of protest. On her own, Lizzie saw how to make them still and calm with very brief, softly-sung lullabies.

'You're a natural, Liz,' Bea said. 'You oughta have a raft of 'em.'

'I'd like to,' said Lizzie.

'Better not waste time. I *couldn't*: by the time Chuck was divorced (and by-the-by, *she* split, after all his guilt-trip – started her own business, would you believe). I was near forty. I was pregnant a month after the wedding!'

Their laughter made the children gurgle and smile.

'What did Chuck have to say?' Lizzie asked.

'He was for it. I'd been his secretary, and part-time wife for so long, he said, that I deserved a reward! *His* kids, of course, were out of high school. That's what *she'd* been waiting for – to get out of the house and into the labour market!'

'So I suppose it's what you've never had you want most.'

'That's right, Liz. The others don't see it, but it's what makes you appreciate this place, the life here . . .'

'Adam calls it "Exurbia",' Lizzie said. 'Can't understand

why I love it . . . Oh, Bea, the houses are so big and wonderfully equipped, the shops so clean and orderly and full of all the good things one could ever want, and everyone's so well-dressed and well-fed, the schools are so big and prosperous-looking, the cars are so new and plentiful . . . He should have seen Soho, or where Mum was born and brought up . . .'

'Tell me about it, Liz.'

She and Bea had talked for hours, then and on many, many occasions when they went about their furtively joyous domestic rounds. It mystified Adam that she was trying so hard to adapt to the humdrum, and when she said, one night, ecstatically, that she was *determined* to adjust to the American way of life, he looked at her a long time over the top of his glasses, seemed about to comment, but didn't, went on with his reading.

Well, it hadn't stopped her. He must love it, too, she had thought, or he wouldn't be here, living so comfortably in this house he'd had built for himself in the woods. She would just go on keeping him happy, be happy making him happy. It seemed only natural to creep off now and then to Bea's church with her, to kneel beside her and say thank you . . .

'Yeah – hello,' someone was saying, as Lizzie reached to press out Bea's telephone number. 'No, sir, Mrs. Hobbs isn't here. Want to leave a message?'

Lizzie's eyes widened. Adam . . . ringing *Mum*? For some reason, her heart seemed to rocket about in her chest, completely out of control. She would never have listened in to Adam talking to anyone else – but now she could not help herself . . .

'Do you know when she might be back?' came Adam's voice, with its usual firmness.

'Just a moment . . .'

There was a pause. Lizzie could hear Adam's breathing on the connection.

'Who is this, please?' came another voice on the wire.

'Mr. Levine. Her son-in-law.'

'Ah, yes . . . Well, Mr. Levine, she's left word for your wife if she should call. Mrs. Hobbs can be reached at the Park-Lexington Nursing Home. We care keeping her rooms here at the hotel until her return.'

Lizzie put a hand over her mouth to stifle a gasp.

'Thank you. Oh – by the way . . . Are you able to tell me if it's anything serious?'

The woman's voice sounded guarded. 'Just a rest, I think. That's all we've been told.'

'I see. Thanks again. Goodbye.'

Lizzie heard the click, followed by the hollow silence of disconnection. Quietly, carefully, she hung up.

For what seemed like minutes, she stood holding onto the counter, her entire body limp with shock. She could not remember what she had been going to do. It was as if she was waking up from a joyous dream to a terrible reality . . .

Perhaps he had only called Mum out of guilt, out of pity, the way she had from time to time, not as often as she would have if Mum hadn't made it so difficult and painful with her misery, her diatribes, her pleading, her threats, the accusation that Lizzie was killing her off . . .

Perhaps there was something he wanted to ask her about the postponed show, or for news of Art Leoffler, whom he'd known for years . . .

Or perhaps he wanted to plan a surprise, something for her twenty-second birthday . . . Except this was the wrong time of year for *that* . . .

Lizzie's perspiration turned cold on her body. Her hands, that had melted the pastry dough with their warmth, were now blue-fingered.

What did Adam really want with Mum? Why would he ring her up without mentioning it, when he usually avoided any direct contact, only spoke to her if there was no way to escape?

In fact, Lizzie remembered the time when he actually disguised his voice, pretended to be a servant answering.

Lizzie's hands now pressed the top of her thighs, holding on as she so often had to before a big performance . . .

Something was dreadfully, horribly wrong!

Why wouldn't her heart stop pounding? What was it she suspected? Why did she somehow *know* . . .?

A small 'ping' told her that the phone in Adam's study was again in use. Her hand moved slowly to it, drew back. How could she spy on her darling, her love – whatever he was doing – why couldn't she completely trust him, turn away in faith that he would never act in any way that was not loving, for her good . . .?

For her good!

Lizzie's hair swung forward in guilty panic, then back from her face in resolve. Quickly, she picked up the phone.

'Is it possible to speak to Mrs. Mim Hobbs?'

Was there a furtive sound in Adam's deep tone?

Lizzie dug her fingernails into her palms, pressed her lips tight.

'I'll see,' someone said. 'Who is it calling?'

Adam gave his name, explained.

There was a long pause. Lizzie heard the gardener begin to mow the sloping lawns at the back of the house. The smell of the blueberry muffins she was making for Adam told her they were at the browning stage. Car tyres crunched on the rocky driveway, signalling the arrival of Delia to help with the preparations for tonight . . .

'I'm putting you through, Mr. Levine, but please don't talk for long, Mrs. Hobbs is very tired.'

Lizzie shut her eyes. Oh, God, Mum – what's happened?

' 'Ello! Mr. Playwright 'isself, is it? What you want, then? Somethin' wrong with me girl?'

'No, Mrs. Hobbs – don't be alarmed. I called the hotel

and they told me you were here. Liza's fine and well. But I do want to speak to you about her – if you're up to it.'

'Well, I ain't dyin'. I come in 'ere 'cause I needed lookin' after. I told Lizzie, but she ain't got the time, 'as she. I could die in that 'otel room. I mean it don't matter it's big and posh and 'as its own loo, if there ain't no-one to talk to. I know she don't care about me, don't love me no more now she's got you, but she could at least . . .'

'Mrs. Hobbs – are you actually ill?'

'Ill! 'Course I'm ill. Pains in me stomach, pains in me legs, pains in me chest, pains in me 'ead – you name it, I got pains in it. Me 'ole self is a pain!'

'May I come and see you, have a talk with you?'

Lizzie leaned against the wall, slid slowly to the floor, clutched the earpiece with hands pressed white.

'You – come to see me? Well, I never.' Mim's voice grew strangely free of its throaty dirge. 'What you want to see *me* about, then?'

'Something, some*one*, dear to both of us. Apart from owing you an apology, I feel we can help each other to help her. What do you say?'

There was a short silence. Lizzie held her breath.

'You could knock me over with a feather, you could. Wonders will never cease. Right – you're on. When will you be 'ere?'

'What are your visiting hours?'

'Oh, it ain't that kind of place – you can come any old time you like. They cost you a fortune, but they treat you like a royal.'

'Tomorrow. I've got an appointment for lunch with my agent, and I'll come up there right after. Okay?'

'Okay! Crikey – I can't wait to 'ear what's on your mind.'

'You take care. Get well. See you tomorrow. So long, Mrs. Hobbs.'

When the sound of disconnection came this time, Lizzie

310

stayed where she was. When Delia, black and shining in her white uniform came in, the blueberry muffins were burning, and Lizzie looked up at her as if she were blind.

'You all right, ma'am?' Delia asked. Some of her ladies did drink a martini or two during the day – you could never tell for sure . . . But Mrs. Levine . . .?

Lizzie drew herself up, stood for a moment to steady herself. 'I'm fine, thank you, Delia,' she said, 'I just felt a bit faint for a moment – must be the heat.'

'That's just what it is,' said Delia, showing a spread of white teeth. 'Engine was boiling, had to stop and get water for it. Now – what do you want me to do first?'

'Take over here, Delia. Clean up, beat me four eggs, put the muffins to cool, make some iced tea . . . I'll be back down in a moment.'

What in the world was she doing? thought Lizzie as she moved with trance-like steps from the kitchen, out through the big main room, across the wooden platform that led to Adam's study . . .

She did what she never did, opened the door without knocking. Adam was sitting as she had left him before, his long back hunched, his glasses down his nose, his head bent to his work.

'Darling,' she said. 'There's something I need to ask you . . .'

'Yes?' He looked around, cleared his scowl, smiled.

'Remember you asked me if I wanted to go in with you tomorrow, spend the afternoon with you, and perhaps have dinner and go to a show? May I change my mind and say, yes?'

Adam was still. He bent his head to peer at her more closely over the top of his glasses. 'Ah, my dearest – I'm sorry to say my plans have altered. I've got a meeting with one of the backers after lunch, and a P.E.N. committee meeting after that. That should bring me home for a latish dinner.'

Lizzie stared at him. Her eyes were large, round, sad. She knew now, for sure. Everything *had* changed.

'Don't be disappointed, angel. There'll be other times, lots of other times . . .' Adam smiled his most reassuring smile.

Lizzie looked at him long and hard, nodded, closed the door.

# CHAPTER TWENTY-THREE

Mim was pleased with "is nibs'. She had to give him his
due – he *did* care, and he *did* want Lizzie to accept L and
H's offer. He saw now that she'd been right, that Lizzie
wasn't about to go back into show business. He even
admitted that he knew for a fact that Lizzie had gone off
the pill – and he even admitted that he'd let her think he
didn't know. He didn't like to hurt the girl, but now he was
desperate: Lizzie the housewife was just what she'd
warned him it would be like, a bore, and the man couldn't
face it . . .

Come to her, he had, her who he couldn't stand, come
crawling. 'Let's cook up a plan,' he said. 'Let's see what we
can do to get her committed to the musical. Once back,' he
said, 'she'll get the taste of it again.'

'Why don't you talk to her yourself?' she asked him.

'Don't you think I *have*, Mrs. Hobbs?'

'Aah, for Gawd's sake, call me Mim!'

'You call me Adam,' he said, right smart.

'You're on,' she said.

What a day, what a defeat for Mr. Shakespeare!

'Anyhow, what did Lizzie *say* to you, *Adam*?'

'You know how stubborn she can be, Mim. Changed
the subject, turned away, didn't answer – or, if she did,
something like "Oh, Adam, I'm so *happy* – maybe later
. . ." *It was always maybe later*.'

She knew just what the man meant. Lizzie was not the
blue-eyed little lamb she looked. She could be as bloody-
minded as anyone, and often was. BUT – there were

ways. She and Adam had had quite a chin. By the time he left, she almost liked the four-by-two. Not that she wouldn't get him out of the way as soon as she got Lizzie back in the business. Several of the offers that had been stalled could be set going again. Another rumour had floated to her, via Harry, that Lizzie's name had been mentioned as a possible candidate for the Royal Command Performance. Harry kept his ears to the ground, which meant in the pubs of Soho where everyone connected to the management might be letting things slip.

Mim got out of bed, signed herself out of the nursing home, returned to the hotel, got her hair and face restored, bought a shocking-pink pants suit, and made an appointment to see Art Leoffler.

He was a short, dreamy-eyed man with a long face and fine thin black hair he swung over to one side of his head. Although they both knew he despised being put in the position of dealing with her, he contrived a charming smile, did not blink at her foot-high bouffant red hair, the grey shadows where eyebrows had been plucked to leave two thin black arcs, or the clashing orange of her side-crooked mouth with the jutting cigarette holder.

'My goodness,' he said, 'you're looking well. Great. I hope you're going to have some news for me. Sit down, Mrs. Hobbs.'

Mim sat forward in the too-big leather and chrome armchair. 'Look,' she said, 'it ain't nothin' certain, but Adam and me – that's Adam Levine . . .'

He nodded. 'Yeah, yeah,' pushed at the paperweight on his desk.

"Im and me *both* wants 'er to sign up. We think if you ring 'er up yourself, and ask 'er to give you an answer real quick, she'll maybe do it. You see?'

He sat back, frowned. 'Can't you two talk to her yourselves? I mean, I'm not in the habit of chasing after people – usually I can't beat them off with sticks . . .'

'Mr. Leoffler – she won't talk to us, she won't listen . . .'

'Then she obviously doesn't want the part. Much as I'd like to have Liza, I wouldn't try to force it on her.'

Mim leaned forward and slapped the edge of the desk. 'But she's got to be saved from 'erself, Mr. Leoffler – don't you see? If she don't come in to your show, she's goin' to stop at 'ome bakin' cakes, 'avin' kids Adam don't even want, throwin' all 'er best years out the window . . .'

He sat up, rearranged his shoulders. 'You mean, it isn't something else she prefers to do, like another movie or a TV show back in England? She's not just playing footsies? You're not just going for a bigger percentage?'

'Aw, come on – think I'd be 'ere 'at-in-' and, beggin'? 'Course there's other things she could do – but she don't want to. She's puttin' 'erself out to pasture, Mr. Leoffler, at the age of twenty-two!'

'Phew. That's terrible. If that's true . . .'

'On the Bible, Mr. Leoffler – would I lie to you?'

He looked at her with one eyebrow curled. 'I wouldn't put it past you – but somehow I'm inclined to believe you now.'

Mim threw up her orange-nailed hands. 'You've got to! This is life or death!'

His mouth twitched. 'Well . . . but, I do agree with you – it'd be a damned shame . . .'

'A catastrophe, more like it.' Mim was so wrought up that she forgot there was no cigarette in the holder, dragged in air, swallowed bubbles, coughed.

'Water?' Art Leoffler offered her his glass.

Mim shook her head. 'I'm not meself. I wish you'd do this, honest.' To her own surprise, she could feel the sting of tears, blinked them back quickly before they smudged her mascara.

Art Leoffler was silent. He placed the tips of his long fingers together and gazed out of his window at the geometrical Manhattan skyline. 'I've never considered anyone could sing our songs like Liza . . .' he murmured. 'The costumes would look great on her. She'd make a beautiful foil for Tom Jurgen. She'd have an edge on anyone else we've got in mind with her dancing – I can just see her out there, holding the audience in the palms of her hands – Liza Lee, the cute, appealing, talented girl from England, sexier than Julie Andrews, than Petula Clark . . . Yes, yes Mrs. Hobbs, I would certainly hate to think of her giving up, and perhaps we could try again to persuade her, to lure her back.' He nodded. 'One thing . . .'

'Yeah?' One of Mim's eyes opened wider than the other.

'Are you absolutely *sure* this is what Adam wants?'

Mim reeled back. 'You doubt me word again – per'aps you want to get 'imself on the 'phone, check me credentials?'

Art Leoffler put up his hand. 'Sorry, sorry . . . It's just that where marital problems are concerned I stay clear: you can never tell what goes between a man and his wife, and it's their prerogative to louse things up without interference.' He looked at the skyline again. 'Yup,' he murmured, 'that's sure the truth . . .'

'Eh?'

He shook his head. 'Talking to myself. Well, okay – let's see what we've got here. I'll have Liza contacted, see what can be done.' He put down his hands, used them to hoist himself up, stretched one out to her. 'Thanks, Mrs. Hobbs – we'll be in touch.'

Mim got up, shouldered a large straw handbag with a splash of embroidered flowers, given to her by Eddie on their brief holiday in Acapulco, every moment of which she'd been poorly, and let her hand be shaken. 'This "we'll see" bit – you are goin' to do it, you ain't chickenin' out?'

'It has to be discussed. But I'm sure my organization will agree to this follow-up – after all, it's only that, isn't it?' He gave her a one-sided smile, escorted her to the door.

'When will you do it, when will you let me know?' Mim

blocked the way with the handbag, a wave of her holder.

'Soon – on both counts. Goodbye, now, Mrs. Hobbs.'

The Yanks had this way of saying 'goodbye, now', Mim thought, that was nothing short of a boot out the door. 'You remember this, Mr. Leoffler – it's what you stands to win – me, I'm only a bleedin' pawn in the game.'

He broke into a chuckle, but his hand on her arm had an insistence, and behind them the telephone was ringing – in front of them, faces looked in at them from the outer office. The limit of his time for her was already exceeded.

Her head high, Mim walked out, gave the receptionist a cheery nod, the curious waiting people who looked up at her a pitying smile, closed the outer door with a hard snap.

'That'll do it,' she said to herself, almost skipping to the elevators. 'Me darlin' will be the biggest 'it Broadway ever 'ad. And me and Adam will be out there cheerin' our 'eads off. Thank you, Gawd, you're a chum.'

Everything turned out just as Mim and Adam planned – except for one thing. Lizzie. It wasn't that she actually refused Art's persuasion, wasn't flattered, tempted . . .

She just didn't *want* to go back into performing. Even locally, she was beginning to pull back, much to the disappointment of their civic-minded friends. In fact, this very morning, at their brunch Red Cross meeting at Bea's house, the women had looked at her almost accusingly.

One by one, they had all spoken up.

'You're so *good*, Liza,' said Sophie Weinberg, who had once been in summer stock, but was now an overweight matron with four children, a den mother, a school meals volunteer, and anything else that helped make up for not having become an actress. 'How can you stand not being up there, wowing them?'

'I mean *anyone* can make Adam's chicken soup! Even Delia!' said Mary Parsons, who was known locally for her amazing figure after three children, including a set of robust twins.

Everybody laughed, because strangely enough, whenever Adam wasn't well, he asked for chicken soup, and Lizzie had learned to make it to his Jewish mother's complete approval – a fact that she had foolishly crowed about at a cocktail party, thinking it was a great plus to her housewifely accomplishments.

'And they *have*,' said Fanny Drake, in her side-of-the-mouth drawl that so amused the group.

Lizzie felt the colour coming to her cheeks. She felt such an idiot at times. Would she, could she, ever be anything but an oddity in this community?

'Personally,' said Vicky Ainsworth, 'I think Adam would be a helluva lot happier if you were to leave him to stew in his own juice – he's not exactly your helpless male. Seems I can remember him managing pretty damn well . . .' She grinned around slyly, her broad-boned, deeply tanned face with the sky-blue eyes, the whole framed in tightly-drawn-back platinum hair, implying some secret knowledge that made the others look quickly into their coffee cups.

He's had an affair with her, thought Lizzie. Who knew *what* Adam had done before she came all breathlessly new to the scene, assuming her role with such ardour? It became hard to look them all in the eyes now . . .

'Look, everyone,' she'd suddenly said, jumping up with one of her sunniest smiles, 'I'll do it this time. Count me in. But please don't cast me in the role of your local star performer any more. I'm sorry if you don't understand – I don't myself. But that's the way I *feel*. I want to live a private life.'

In the silence, with all eyes staring at her in astonishment, she had tucked her shirt firmly into her jeans, picked up her beach bag filled with knitting, tossed back her long hair and waved a smiling goodbye.

Jumping into her Pontiac station wagon, she had driven at top speed down the winding lanes and main highway to her house, Adam's house, she thought now, with a nasty lump in her throat.

As she drove up under the stilts into one of the garages, she saw that his car was out. She did not want to think where he was: he made it clearer every week that he had to do what he wanted to do. He might want to think, to be on his own, to drive, go to the beach, drop in on one of his friends, take in a movie . . .

Or, Lizzie thought, in spite of her best intentions, stroll down to Helena's . . .

More and more, this is what he did.

She tried to think generously about it: she, too, liked Helena. One couldn't help liking such a forthright, kindly person. And Helena had a brain, a great big intellect with which Adam could commune, was used to communing. He needed her, he said, as 'feedback' – no more. The kind of love he felt for her, Lizzie, was not in any way to be compared. Or, she *used* to say, 'jeopardized' . . .

Lately, he had added, 'If you keep on like this, dearest, foisting this domestic jazz on me when I don't need or want it, refusing to use your God-given talent, to take up a lifetime opportunity to star in a Leoffler–Hartz musical in New York, just in order to fritter your time away like any run-of-the-mill suburban housewife, then you *could* have something to worry about!'

Lizzie pinched her lips, picked up her bag, walked resolutely into the house. If there was one thing she was not going to do, it was to play into the hands of Adam and Mum. Little did they know that she knew their game. That the offer from Art Leoffler was genuine, she didn't question – but, she was not about to be *bludgeoned* into being a performer. Let Adam go to Helena, let Mum wind herself up in her endless little plots and connivances, her barrage of pleas and accusations – it would do neither of them a bit of good.

'I have a right to my life, too, Adam,' she would say tonight as they sipped their inevitable pre-dinner martinis (martini was only a kind of drink at home – here it was gin in which you put a little dash of vermouth, served ice-cold, with an olive!), and Adam got his little 'edge-on' which he claimed improved his appetite (they all claimed that as the excuse for getting pissed), but also became more talkative and approachable.

'If I'm happier not being on the stage,' she would say, really confronting him this time, 'why try to force me, why not just leave me alone? Perhaps, as you once said, I really will get restless. Why isn't that soon enough?'

She would give him tit-for-tat in whatever argument he brought up. She was fighting already.

Unfortunately, Adam did not come home to dinner.

The food went slowly dry, the candles burned low, the house fell silent and the night insects turned on their cacophony out in the dark surrounding woods.

Lizzie sat for a long time letting the dusk deepen and finally close the house in. She thought of ringing Helena, then resisted. No, she would say nothing. This was a test.

She turned on the television, curled up on a large black-and-white couch, watched until the late show, and then the late-late show, her ears like antennae for the sound of a car . . .

At last the television show ended. She fell asleep where she was . . .

When she awakened, her pink linen dress was a mass of wrinkles, her legs contracted in cramps, her neck and head aching, her mouth dry, and her eyes stinging.

It was dawn. The sun was coming up behind the trees, streaking the river with golden light. Birds were trilling furiously all round the house and Adam's little band of stray cats were looking in at her for their morning feed.

After a moment, focusing the situation, Lizzie sighed. Adam had stayed away all night for the first time. Without ringing, without explaining, leaving her with a cooked dinner to spoil . . .

And yet . . . No. That wasn't like him, surely . . .?

She leaped up. My God, he might have been in an accident – something awful might have happened to him . . .

That was more likely. How could she have been so suspicious, so self-pitying?

She rushed to the telephone connection in the far end of the room, pressed out Helena's number.

'Yes?' said Helena, in her calm manner. 'Oh, hello, my dear – what can I do for you?'

'It's Adam, Helena – he hasn't come home. I'm so worried something terrible's happened to him. Did he come there? Do you know if he started for home?'

'Liza, Liza, stop there. Adam's perfectly all right. Do you want to speak to him?'

Lizzie's face had never felt stiffer, been so drained of blood. She could barely stand up to wait for his voice.

'Hi,' said Adam, with a remote, almost amused detachment. 'Sorry, dear. I didn't mean to frighten you – but Helena and I got rapping into the early hours – you know how it is. I'm afraid, as you would say, that I also got drunk on her Spanish wine. She was kind enough to let me stay . . .'

'Adam! You must have known I'd be scared shitless . . .'

He laughed heartily down the wire. 'You're getting the lingo, old top.'

Lizzie frowned. She had never heard Adam like this. Not a note of remorse, almost mocking.

'You there?' he said. 'Don't make a drama, dear. Unless you need to. Which I'd understand much better than your needing to . . . Savvy? Oh dear, you don't . . . You'll have to forgive me, waves of the Spanish still hitting the brainwaves.'

To her horror, Lizzie could hear Helen's grudging but explosive laughter. She hung up.

When Adam came home, later in the morning, he made no further apology, but went straight to the bathroom, showered, got himself some breakfast, waving off Lizzie's automatic attempt to help, and went straight to his study, where he stayed until evening. When he emerged, he changed his clothes, said he would not be home for dinner, and went off in his car.

Lizzie watched him go, watched until the car was out of sight and only a small cloud of dust hung in the distance where he'd been. The big empty house loomed behind her, around her, all about her, like a great echoless shell. She roamed about, feeling like a kind of ghost, like a figment of her own imagination.

What was she doing here? Why was she in this house, this place, this country? What *had* happened to her, what *was* happening to her? What had come of all the love she and Adam had felt for each other, that she still wanted to feel? What was to happen to them now?

She felt bereft, stripped of any familiar reality.

Who was there to turn to now? – certainly not Helena. Nor truly, any of the others. They were all only members of a play that worked itself out around her . . .

She was nowhere. Lost.

And, yes, she thought, as she stared at her white, big-eyed face reflected in one of the tall glass walls, in her heart she knew it was only the beginning, knew with a deadly certainty that her Adam could be cruel beyond her ability to conceive or withstand. What she had read about him so long ago, what Mum had warned her of, was the truth of what lay ahead.

Tears came into her eyes but did not fall. Oh, if only she didn't love him so much, in spite of everything – if only she could just say what-the-bloody-hell, pack up her things and go! She could even imagine herself doing it, taking every trace of herself from this big house of his, which she had tried, but could never make her own, leave a terse, dramatic note: 'Thanks for nothing, Adam. But I do wish you good luck with your play. Liza.'

Of course, he would love that. It was what he wanted, what he was trying to make her do. He and Mim would simply congratulate themselves.

She shook her head with sudden vigour. No – she would not make it that easy. She was not through yet.

With more than a touch of Mim's resolute lift to her chin, she went quickly to Adam's study, sat down in his chair at his typewriter, put into it a top page, carbon, and copy page, started to type with as much speed as her hunt-and-peck method allowed:

'Dear Art, I'm very sorry to have to turn down your kind and generous offer to appear in your new musical. I have given it a great deal of thought, and am very, very grateful and flattered that you have given me such a wonderful opportunity and waited so long for my answer, but I'm afraid I'm unlikely to return to show business. I don't share either my husband's or mother's enthusiasm for my talent. I believe that I have only been performing to command, not out of my own desire to succeed. I'm glad I've met with approval and pleased a lot of people, most of all my dear mum who has put so much of her life into mine. But the bare fact of the matter is that I am happier out of the limelight, happier just being a married woman – married, as you know, to one of the most talented and valuable men in the world.

'I do hope you understand and will forgive me for having wasted your time, and I wish you every kind of success with your new show. I shall try to come with Adam to your first night. With warmest regards, Liza Lee.'

There, she thought, with satisfaction: done. And, in the business-like way she had learned from Mim ('always make a copy of everythin'; I do. When you deal with bandits, you got to look slippy').

In case she weakened, changed her mind, lost her momentum, Lizzie addressed the envelope, sealed it, stamped it with Adam's franking machine . . .

Then, with artful care, she put the copy onto her end of his huge teak desk, onto her pile of post, where it must catch his eye, just as the letter from Mervnick Pictures had, with its disastrous results.

Sorry, darling, she thought. I hate games, but you started them, you forced me to play.

# CHAPTER TWENTY-FOUR

On the opening night of Adam's play, *Until Such Time*, people kept saying that Liza Lee, as she moved into the theatre beside him, had never looked lovelier. She wore pure white, her long blond hair side-swept, a gardenia over one ear. Adam, in his immaculate evening clothes, seemed more of a stern and solemn father beside her radiant youth, her soft, sexy manner and smile – but, then that was intriguing, too. Liza so obviously adored him, and the way he looked down at her, in its dignified ambiguousness, created a mystique of implied power.

'What a couple!' someone observed loudly, as they took their seats in a front box, and everyone was looking up at them, Liza still clinging to Adam's arm, Adam still acknowledging her with unsmiling solicitude.

'Did that suit you, dear?' Adam asked, as he disengaged himself from her arm. 'Have you made your point?'

Lizzie looked into his cold eyes. 'Adam . . . please, not tonight. I'm so proud of you . . .'

Adam's large lids descended with ennui. 'Yes, my dear – I know. Would that I could say the same of you.' He turned his gaze to the packed house below, nodded to critics he knew, to people who waved up to him.

Lizzie sat straight, her bright freckled face and blue eyes seeming to be filled with inner radiance. No matter how Adam treated her, she was determined no-one would know they weren't happy, that he not only didn't love her any more, but was acutely bored with her, capable of showing it at any moment . . .

'Your smile is inane, Liza,' he whispered.

'Sorry . . .'

'Sorry, sorry.' Adam shoved at his glasses, ran his hand around his chin, drew himself as far away from her as physically possible.

Lizzie felt stabs of fear in her stomach. She had managed to withstand some ghastly moments of rejection, had completely lost face in the community, yet up to last night had not succumbed to complete defeat . . .

For a start, Adam's family and relatives still influenced him; the idea of yet another divorce would bring a storm of protest from his mother, from all of them. Even his children, though grown and leading quite separate lives, would find this quick end to 'the great love of his life' the last straw in their already disturbed relationships with him. It was, after all, no matter how he might justify it to the world, another failure – and Adam had tired of failures.

So, to that extent, Lizzie had a little wedge that kept the door open . . .

She had tried everything she could think of to please, to fit in with whatever he wanted to do, to accept whatever he inflicted on her, just as long as he let her stay. Since he could not exactly walk out of his own house, his only hope, that she would come to the end of her tether and leave, was frustrated by her continuing presence – and effort.

Last night, she had tried desperately hard to arouse him, to bring him back to her in their old loving way. She didn't mind what she had to do, she had read books and manuals, gone to a therapist in New York to get advice – all this, added to the urgency of her lingering love, must surely succeed . . .

'Christ!' he had groaned suddenly, as she covered him with her body, with her soft kisses, her caressing tongue, 'will you for God's sake leave me alone? Don't you see I can't make it? You just don't turn me on, girl. Do you want me to spell it out more clearly than that?'

She had had no alternative than to stop. In fact, he had thrust her off almost violently, turned himself away, dug his head into his pillow.

The hurt of it wouldn't allow her to be quiet, to let him just drop away into sleep. 'Please, Adam, can we talk?' she said, leaning up on one elbow, still unable to stem the love she felt, the longing to touch his averted face, to stroke his dear head . . .

'Talk?' Adam grunted. 'Why do women always want to talk? Either something is, or it isn't.'

'You did love me?'

'Oh, hell. Yes, I *did* love you. But it was an image, child, an image. Perhaps if you'd gone back – it could have been salvaged. Now, that's all I want to say. I've got an opening tomorrow, if you remember.'

There was nothing to do but shut up, close-back and swallow the last of her hopes.

And so there it was, plain, cold, unchangeable. He would not divorce her. He would do his best to make her divorce him. Meanwhile, the play . . .

It was almost too predictable – as the curtain fell on the first act, there was an electric atmosphere in the theatre, the emanation of a sure success. Lizzie could see the jaw muscles in Adam's face stop clamping, the relaxation of his mouth and frown.

'It's marvellous, Adam,' she said, 'a real winner.'

He gazed at her as if she were not there. His eyes roved downward, towards the centre of the stalls . . .

Lizzie saw her, then: Helena, with her gay, fill-in escort, who also looked up in conspiratorial message to Adam.

Adam rose. 'I suppose you'll want to tag along,' he said.

Lizzie bit at her bottom lip. 'That's all right. I'll just stay here.'

His relief was unhidden.

Lizzie used the time to line up at the loo, to repair her lipstick, brush out her hair. Women looked at her with frank admiration. Some of them smiled in recognition of who she was, not only as Adam Levine's wife, but in her own right.

Adam came back into the box, actually smiling – but his smile faded immediately he saw Lizzie sitting there, waiting. She said nothing. At least he was still here.

But at the party afterwards, at the Pierre, she could no longer say this. Naturally, with all the congratulations and celebration of an assured success, Adam *would* be taken up, surrounded – and it wasn't unusual that he would wander away to his friends, or join all kinds of people; it *was* his night.

Hardly anyone noticed that Lizzie was left out of it all, that she wandered about alone, that he did not even get her her food, or come back to see if she wanted a drink.

Lizzie inflicted herself on a few people in an effort to offset her abandonment, reached hard for things to say, laughed and smiled appreciatively at whatever called for it, and was so successful in seeming happy, at ease, filled with joy for Adam's triumph, that no-one even saw the total fear and defeat in her eyes . . .

Or, finally, to notice that she finally slipped away, left . . .

The taxi driver who took her to Mim's hotel thought he recognized her. 'Ain't you Liza Lee, the singer? Yeah – I knew it. I seen you on TV – and I seen you in that movie . . . What was it called?'

'*Maiden Voyage*.'

'That's right. Gee – you were great. What're you doin' now?'

'Nothing.' Lizzie's lips would hardly move.

'Nothin'! Geez – that's a shame. You'd think there'd be a lot of work around for someone like you. Guess it's because you're British, huh?'

That was a good one, thought Lizzie.

Mum, of course asleep, was startled out of her mind, she said. '*But* get right up 'ere, darlin',' she added, 'I'll put the kettle on.'

Going up in the big gilded elevator, Lizzie had to smile. 'Put the kettle on' – as if nothing had ever happened, nothing had changed. And thank God for *that*!

Mim answered the knock at once. She was wearing her Chinese robe. Her hair was wound up in huge rollers, her face lathered in cold cream. The familiarity of it swept Lizzie with unexpected emotion. She stood rigidly a moment, fighting it off, resisting the lump in her throat.

'Me old darlin',' Mim said, reaching out her arms.

Before she knew what she was doing, Lizzie was in them, feeling their muscular grip like a coming home she didn't want yet couldn't deny. 'Oh, Mum, Mum!'

'Lizzie, Lizzie, me little Miss Cuddles – what's up, eh? There, there, come an' sit down, tell your old Mum all about it.'

Shaking her head, Lizzie let her grasp her hand, lead her to a large brocade sofa in the richly-furnished suite. 'Never all, Mum. You know that. Just why I'm here *now*.'

'Right, right. 'Course, I ain't one to pry. All's I know is me girl's in awful bad trouble or she'd never 'ave come to the one she been runnin' away from.'

Lizzie threw off her ermine stole, sank into a cushion, leaned back wearily. The cup of tea Mim brought her with a ceremonious flourish looked suddenly very good, tasted even better.

'Well?' said Mim, settling herself beside her, taking her tea with a noisy gulp, then setting down the cup the better to listen.

'Adam and I are through, Mum,' said Lizzie. 'It's all over.'

'You don't say. I'm sorry to 'ear that.'

Lizzie smiled wanly. 'Oh, Mum, leave it out. Be yourself.'

'Whatever can she mean?' Mim gave a large, nose-wrinkling sniff.

'I happen to know that you connived with Adam to get me back to work . . .'

'What? I'll 'ave you know that . . .'

'I heard you on the extension. Adam admitted it, anyway, so give over. It doesn't matter any more. It's irrelevant.'

'What does that mean?' Mim eyed her alertly, mouth pinched.

'It means that he didn't want me to go back for *my* sake, but for *his*.'

'For 'is! I thought 'e'd given up, that you'd won and everythin' was nice as pie.'

'Well, you're wrong, Mum.' Lizzie took the gardenia from her ear, threw it on the big, mirrored coffee table, held back a threatening flood of misery. 'Without my glamour, he couldn't care for me. I was just a female, not a very interesting one even compared to his other wives. The novelty of my accent wore off. He didn't find me funny or endearing. My love for him became a nuisance, an embarrassment. He escaped to Helena, ignored me at parties, flirted with anyone at hand. The more I tried, the more I clung, the harder I played his game, the crueller he got. The only reason I'm still with him, why I could go to the opening with him, was that *he* doesn't want to be the one to get the divorce . . .'

'Divorce!' Mim started back as if she'd been struck. 'The Jew bastard wants to *divorce* ya!'

'Me to divorce him, Mum.'

Mim scowled with eyebrows partially grown back into line. 'You mean 'e'll let you go – just like that, without no fight nor nothin'?'

'That's about it. Just so long as everyone knows *I* wanted it, *I* gave up, *I* left. So the sympathy stays with him, you see.'

There was a silence between them. Fifth Avenue traffic sounds wafted in the window open above the central heating, an American innovation Mim had never been able to come to terms with. A fire-engine siren screamed louder and louder, then faded into a thin, dying wail.

Mim's expressions changed like a series of little masks, from shock, to outrage, to protest, to dawning inspiration, and finally to wide-toothed pleasure. 'Lizzie, me petal – what are we *waitin'* for!' She grabbed up Lizzie's hands, shook them up and down with excitement. 'You're free – FREE! There ain't nothin' to stop us!'

'Mum . . .'

'I mean it, love – look 'ere . . .' She jumped up, went to a gilt escritoire, picked up a thick folder, opened it and let the papers in it float down like falling leaves. 'Offers, me pet. 'Ollywood Bowl, places in Chicago, Dallas, all over the bleedin' country – TV shows, record companies, pictures, other musicals . . .'

'What happened to the Leoffler and Hartz show?' Lizzie murmured, feeling a faint, hazy stir of response.

'Didn't you 'ear? Art Leoffler 'ad another attack – a "massive coronary" they calls it. 'E might still kick the bucket. Why? You might want to do it, 'stead of the others?' Mim could hardly contain the frenzy of hope.

'I didn't say anything like that. Calm down, Mum. I came for comfort, not to be attacked. I've had enough of that, enough for a lifetime . . .'

'Sorry, old mate. I got meself carried off proper. 'Ave some more tea. Want a digestive? Got some with chocolate on.'

'No thanks, Mum.' Lizzie was suddenly aware of all the cases strewn about, of coats lying over the chairs down the far end of the room. 'What's all that?' she asked. 'You goin' somewhere?'

Mim made a grimace. 'I was, me darlin'. I was.' She sat

down, forced back her excitement, made an effort with her tea.

'Come on, out with it – where were you off to?'

Mim pressed her lips a moment. Then she drew in a grim breath. 'Well, I might as well tell you as not – 'ome. I was goin' to throw in the sponge and 'op it.'

'You were!' Lizzie felt a tug of bleakness. 'What about Eddie?'

Mim shrugged. 'Oh, 'im. 'E weren't a bad cove – but we 'ad a barney. 'E's scarpered.'

'Oh, Mum – why did you have a barney? He *adores* you . . .'

'Did. Past tense, ducks. I just ain't interested in all that sex lark. Not at my age, with my old corpse.'

'Mum – you're only forty years old. That's nothing. It's positively young. Why, women out in Stoneyvale were having second batches of children . . .'

'Please. I don't want to 'ear about 'em. Maybe they never 'ad to eat muck when they were young, or live 'and to mouth in the slums. And Gawd knows I weren't *never* your prize-winnin' beauty! No, I'll settle for me old mate, 'Arry – who likes me for me brains!' Mim broke into a metallic chuckle.

'Seriously, then, Mum – what were you going to do back in England?'

Mim stared down into her cup. 'Good question, old dear. I don't rightly know. Twiddle me thumbs. Watch the goggle box. Wait for 'em to come and put me in a wooden box.'

'Mummy!' Lizzie reached out, grasped her into a hug.

Mim pushed her off a bit. 'Well, might 'ave a go with Alf, back 'is business – you know, more chish and fip shops . . .'

'But you hate the smell of fish!'

Suddenly they were both laughing, rocking each other in a hilarious burst of nostalgia and shared memories.

332

'Maybe I'll come with you, Mum,' Lizzie said, when they had quietened down and wiped their eyes. 'You've made me feel homesick.' Perhaps that's what's been wrong with me all the time, she thought. Perhaps that was what was missing, that made her seem absent from herself. In one of Adam's books on psychiatry, she'd read the term 'self-alienation' and took it to mean being an alien, far from home . . .

'Come 'ome, Lizzie, back to old Blighty – you would?'

'Why not? I might find work there – don't you think? With you behind me?'

Mim's face was too tightly wreathed in smiling lines to speak.

Lizzie took her hand. 'But, Mum, we'll have to work things out for a while. It'll take a bit of time. Would you be willing to hang on, wait?'

'Oh, me darlin' – would I ever?' Mim sat back, assumed a look of efficiency. 'First off, I'll move from 'ere to a cheaper 'otel. No sense pourin' out our 'ard-earned savin's. I can be gettin' back into me 'arness, startin' the balls rollin' – eh?'

'Terrific, Mum.'

'Oy, watch it, you're gettin' a Yank accent there, Miss Lee.'

'That's okay. Instead of "little Brit", I'll be Miss Middle Atlantic!' Lizzie raised her eyebrows, rolled her eyes.

Mim patted her hand in beaming approval. 'That's me gel, me old Lizzie. Darlin' – there won't be nothin' to stop us now. And, I don't think we should be in too much of an 'urry to go 'ome, neither. Let's do some of these big things 'ere first. That way we get your name up real 'uge – when we go 'ome, we'll be that much nearer the invite.'

'The invite!'

Mim winked. 'From 'Er Royal 'Ighness, of course.'

'Mum – really.' Lizzie shook her head at her. 'No-one could say you didn't stick to your guns. When you have a dream – you have a dream.'

'Right. And it'll come true – you just wait and see!'

Lizzie nodded. 'If you say so . . .'

Once Adam was sure Lizzie was going to leave him and his life could start over in peace, he was again his supportive and reasonable self. He co-operated completely in their legal arrangements, and agreed to a quick divorce procedure in Juarez, over the border from El Paso in Mexico. He even took Lizzie to the airport, hugged her goodbye, said he was sorry, but glad she'd come to her own rescue. When she was her 'own person', stopped demeaning herself, had back her 'self-respect', he said, he felt the old attraction – too bad it was all too late . . .

Torn with mixed emotions, Lizzie had waved, smiled, boarded the plane. If Mim hadn't been beside her, she might easily have got off again, run back to him.

'Well, that's that,' Mim said, settling upright in her seat and fastening her seat belt. 'And good riddance.'

Lizzie was thankful that the legalities were over within a matter of hours. They had spent one night in the hotel in El Paso, sped over the border to Juarez, met the lawyer, gone to a court building, waited a few minutes, been escorted to the attorney who questioned Lizzie, asked her to sign several documents (as Elizabeth Hobbs). The lawyer handed them to Mim to sign as witness, they had all shaken hands and left.

Outside, the lawyer had said goodbye, and Mim and Lizzie went back over the border to their hotel, checked out, boarded their plane and been in Los Angeles in no time at all. There, Lizzie had sung at the Hollywood Bowl, just missing Robbie by a day, to her deep disappointment, then travelled on to their tour of six cities, in all of which Lizzie sang to enormous audiences with huge success.

Returning to New York, they found that Hartz had a new partner and the show was resuscitated, and Mim re-offered them 'Liza Lee' for the lead.

Lizzie was extremely nervous to begin with, but as the beautiful costumes were fitted, as she grew easy in the lyrics and melodies, the dances and dialogue, became accustomed to the leading man's quirks and moods, familiar with the cast and hands, she lost much of her fear and shyness. It was, of course, mainly Mim who kept her motivated. More often than anyone knew, she had the old urge to bolt. Singing alone, she would suddenly recede from herself, have to re-orient herself in where she was, who she was.

If only it wasn't all so much of a strain, if only she could truly *enjoy* her success. It seemed horribly ungrateful – not just to Mim, or the people out there who got pleasure from her performance, but to all those who put their money on her, trusted her to deliver. If only she could relax, relax, relax, *be* what she seemed . . .

'You're doin' just lovely, Lizzie love,' Mim rasped in her ear at the final rehearsal. 'There ain't nothin' to take the place of proper trainin', is there?'

'S'pose so, Mum.'

Judging from the audience reaction to *Where Angels Dare*, the rave reviews of the critics, Mum was right. Lizzie found herself the biggest star on Broadway, and awoke to the fact that the show could run indefinitely.

'We should have taken the movie, Mum,' she said, as the weeks went by. 'I can't do this every night, and twice with matinées . . .'

' 'Course you can, my love. It'll come second nature, like a regular job.'

Lizzie subsided into a dream that had no end. Mim moved them to a spacious Park Avenue apartment, hired maids, bought a Jaguar for Lizzie to drive on weekends to their cottage in Southampton, invested in a mink coat for each of them, and started following the stock market. Lizzie went to yoga class, slept, read, watched TV, sometimes bicycled in Central Park – and did her performances.

Rescue came in a strange way – one night she simply

stopped singing: when she opened her mouth, no voice came out. They had to halt the performance. She was rushed to the hospital.

'Nothing organically wrong,' the doctor said, after many tests. 'The girl needs a rest. Simple as that. She should not perform for at least a month.'

'A month!' said Mim, 'that's bloody stupid. She's the star of the show.'

'I am aware of that, Mrs. Hobbs,' the doctor said, with a quiet sigh. 'Nevertheless.'

Max Hartz had a private conversation with the same doctor, a man with a big name at Memorial. 'If it's not organic, what good's a rest going to do?' he asked.

The bearded man with a face something like Adam's shrugged. 'Maybe a psychiatrist?'

Max Hartz, a huge man with permanently rumpled grey hair and clothes, looked furtively at Mim. 'Sssh . . .' he breathed.

The result was that Lizzie's understudy, Judy McClain, went on. The receipts fell off; in a very short space of time the show was in trouble.

'I can't – not yet, Mum,' Lizzie pleaded, as she lounged in beach chairs, slept on the sand, stayed in bed for hours on end. 'Give me a break.'

'A break, me love! Don't you know your month is up? You want to ruin the show?'

Lizzie stared at her as if not able to comprehend. 'I do wish I cared more . . .'

Mim's frustation turned to anger. 'That's gratitude for you. What do you want of me, ducks – that I should just let you turn into a vegetable out 'ere in this Godforsaken 'ole?'

'Just time, Mum.' Lizzie had almost drowned in her own yawns. Her tiredness seemed to come from a bottomless pit inside herself, she went to bed tired, got up tired, stayed tired all day. Nothing interested her, nothing whatever.

*Where Angels Dare* was suddenly revived by replacing

Lizzie with Goodgie Barnes, another English girl with far less of a vocal range, but an adequate competence and considerable charm. That was the way the critics described her, and while Mim burst apart at the seams with fury, Lizzie was infinitely relieved.

They broke her contract, and during the time Mim was going in and out to see lawyers and sue, Lizzie found that there was something to be said after all for being alive . . .

She went swimming, made friends with a young life-guard and walked miles with him along the beautiful beaches, gathering driftwood and shells.

'Well,' said Mim, coming home one evening with the worn look Lizzie hadn't seen since she was waiting on table and cleaning out loos . . . 'I've got us a movie. A real beaut. You're goin' to love this.'

'Oh, Mum, no. I'm better – but a movie! And I hate it out there, you know that . . .'

'This ain't, as you say, "out there" – me petal. You just sit down, let me get you a nice little snort of somethin', and I'll tell you all about it.'

They sat together under an umbrella table on the big wooden porch, drinks and nuts, cheese and crackers set between them in festive array.

'Cheers!' said Mim, raising her glass, amazingly restored and altered in appearance from a grim little woman in crumpled city clothes to a cockily-grinning little woman in purple short-shorts and top that showed almost every inch of her leathery anatomy.

'Cheers . . .' Lizzie swung her neglected hair away from her eyes, waited in wry anticipation.

'Rome,' said Mim. ''Ere's to Rome.'

'*Rome*?'

'You wouldn't believe it – I didn't think nothin' of this batty letter come in the post, askin' you to meet with a bloke called Sheldon Albright whilst 'e was in New York . . .'

Lizzie's interest flickered. 'The multi-millionaire wonder-boy? Made it all himself before he was thirty?'

'Eh – 'ow do you know about 'im?' Mim, thrown off, gave her a look of sharpness someone else would have mistaken for suspicion.

'I read it, Mum. Everyone knows about him. He buys up failing businesses, parlays his investments, doesn't know how to spend all his money, or what he wants. There's always some ruddy great article about him.'

'You're joshin'. Well, blimey. Any'ow, just for a lark, I answers 'im, signs your name and goes to see what 'e's got on 'is mind.' Mim gulped her drink, lit a cigarette, took a deep drag, piling up the dramatic effect. 'Well, me love – seems 'e's backing a film to be made in Rome and wants *you* for 'is star. Big money. International release. A good story, darlin', good songs – quick before 'e could change 'is, I said "you're on, Mr. Albright". Did he need to see you? he asked, and I said no, you were restin' out 'ere – I'd see that you put your signature on the dotted line . . .'

'You *didn't*. Damn, Mum – honestly, this is too much . . .'

'G'arn – you're up to it now. We leave next week. 'E's left me a big cheque for our expenses, real generous. We tell 'im when we're goin' to arrive – and 'e'll meet us 'isself. 'Ow do you like that for starters? Biggest 'otel in Rome, anythin' you want laid on. Ain't it great? Give us a penny-a, me lovely. This gets us back to Europe – what we wanted. It's 'eaven-sent.'

Lizzie was so quiet, that Mim's eyes gradually narrowed, watched through the smoke of her cigarette with shrewd question. 'What's up, Liz-me-love?' she said, finally.

'I won't do it, Mum. That's all.'

Mim looked at the stern, set face, the straight, direct gaze of blue eyes, and for just a moment her own faltered. 'You won't?'

'That's right. I won't.'

Mim waved her cigarette holder. 'But why, me darlin' – why?'

'I don't know. I only know that I don't want to.'

Mim chuckled. 'You sound like little Lizzie, four years old.'

'Perhaps that's what I am – four years old. All I know is, I can't do it.'

In the silence, the water lapped at the shoreline, bathers ran into the shadow-greyed waves, their faces bobbing like pale moons. Somewhere in the distance a foghorn blasted, and nearby a dog began a steady bark at some invisible threat.

Mim's face had a stiffness of fear. 'What *do* you want to do, me little one? Eh? Just give up? Waste the lot?'

Lizzie felt her mind contract, dodge from her grasp. 'No . . .' Her voice seemed to waver on a current of air. 'No . . .'

'I think you're just moonin' over that nasty lot you married. It ain't been easy – I know that. I ain't so 'ard-'earted as I seem. I got feelings. I know what you must 'ave been through with 'im. Best that you get your mind took off – best to get back over there and work real 'ard. It's Italy, love – all romantic, different kind of people, different weather, different food – you'll forget all about 'im . . . And you'll make a wonderful movie, me petal, you'll show all the world – 'Er Majesty beside!'

'How long will it take?' said Lizzie, her voice sunk to almost a whisper.

'Not long, ducks, not long – no more than a year . . .'

'A year . . .' Lizzie wished she could think what that meant, other than she would be over twenty-five when it was done. Where had time gone – why did she feel she had never even *begun* her life?

# CHAPTER TWENTY-FIVE

Sheldon Albright had begun to wonder how he could get through each day. His wide-open, ruddy face and brilliant curly blond hair, his tall, lean, restlessly energetic body still emanated the enthusiasm and drive with which he had bulldozed his competitors and all forms of legal impedimenta in his path to wealth, but what had been his passionate resolve had turned to inertia, and the blinding computer-like brilliance of his brain to sluggish disinterest.

As he drove through the lush Italian countryside towards the airport to meet his new star, Liza Lee, he wondered if there was another woman left on the face of the earth that could lift his pall of satiety. It wasn't a matter of not wanting to meet someone he could love enough to marry – in fact, getting married was the only adventure that appealed to him now – it was the stultifying logistics of his situation. Because of his money, because of his exceptional skill at amassing it, he had found that no girl he met ever refused to sleep with him.

The result was that he had no opportunity to yearn, to pursue; his every whim was met. He had had by now girls of every nationality, build and variety. They had used every technique to please and ensnare him, and for a long time he had fallen into their hands, become sex-obsessed, substituted all earlier ideals and values for the sheer stimulation of his penis. That's what it amounted to, was not even worthy of a leer.

He honked back at the irate Italian motorists who did

not understand the slow casualness of his driving. In some ways he was dreading meeting such a volatile, sexy, beautiful little dish as Liza Lee. He would probably fancy her in person as much as he fancied her for the role of Diane. Unless she had taken a lover since her divorce from the American playwright, she would probably be free, available and interested, and he would find himself in another situation he didn't really want.

He would play it cool: though this sometimes had a reverse effect on women, turning them into cunning, indefatigable pursuers.

Anyway, the important thing was to make a good picture, to keep her happy until it was in the can . . .

He drew in a breath of the fresh, rushing breeze, savoured the strong Italian sunlight on his face, the vibrating power of the new sky-blue Jaguar. He was glad he'd got away from Britain. Perhaps this new venture would revive him, banish the ennui. There was only one sour note – the manager-mother. How to dispense with her? There would hopefully be advantages in her not speaking a word of the language, not knowing the country. It shouldn't be *too* difficult to trim her sails. After all, he'd brought down some of the world's most audacious bargainers . . .

He broke into a grim chuckle thinking of her at their meeting in New York – how fearlessly she'd pressed for the best possible deal for her 'Lizzie', forced him to increase the money, improve the terms, add guarantees – even refused to commit her to a second picture. Liza Lee certainly had effective representation there! 'If I were an actor,' he'd said to her, 'I'd let you be my agent any time.' Instead of laughing, she'd said, 'I'm not in the business – only for me own girl. No-one's goin' to put anythin' over on 'er and live to tell.'

He wouldn't admit to anyone that little Mrs. Hobbs had forced his hand as no industrialist competitor had ever done. It was a good joke – but not to be repeated.

Watching for the arrival of the Alitalia plane, Sheldon (or Sheldy) Albright felt a slight lift to his boredom. Liza Lee was a bright bit of casting, his own inspiration after seeing her in *Maiden Voyage*. She was perfect for the part of the young English singer on a nostalgic visit to the little village that had sheltered and saved her father's life in World War II, and would be very convincing when the earthquake threatened to kill them all and she led them away with her singing, keeping them free of fear until they could be rescued. She would also be a striking contrast for Vincente di Riccoli in the love scenes. Yes, this picture could take off, add to his tax troubles rather than reducing them . . .

Ah, there they were . . .

My God, she was fabulous! You could have Bardot, Deneuve, even Monroe – they didn't come tastier than this little bird, with her straight-edged swing of blondish hair, jaunty breasts, long slim legs, radiant face, and eyes so blue he could see them from yards away! And there was something else to her, too, that conveyed itself like adrenalin to his senses – a person in there, not just a show-biz type, something besides the undeniable talent that had made her world famous, a look of interest, seeking . . .

Look at the way the mother, peering about with shrewd glances, alert for attack or defence as the case might call for, had to tug on her as she stopped to stare at a mother nursing an infant . . .

What a smile!

Beware, he told himself – first impressions. You might be reading into her something you hope for . . .

He strode up to the two figures, one in a pale pink suit, a white scarf thrown round her throat that fluttered as she swung along, the other in an orange coat and what was obviously a wig of almost the same colour, earrings dangling beside her sallow, sharp-boned, long-nosed face.

He put out his big freckled hand to the younger one. 'Liza Lee?'

She nodded, took his hand. 'You must be Mr. Albright . . .

Her smile was magnetic, he thought. It brought a responsive one from him without effort. 'I am. Welcome to Rome. And – you, too, Mrs. Hobbs – nice to see you again.'

Mim allowed him a brief shake. She was far more interested in their luggage, and why no-one else was meeting Lizzie and where were the photographers, the press . . .

He shook his head. 'Not the way we're doing this, my friend. Enough of that later. Right now, let's just get you settled in your hotel.'

'I can't wait,' said Lizzie. 'We made a stop-over in London to take care of a few things and ran into the press, and we've hardly been to bed.'

'Well . . . It'll be siesta time anyway – so we can all kip without loss.'

'Siesta time. What's that?' said Mim, looking him up and down as if she were assessing him all over again, now that he could hardly take his eyes off Lizzie.

He explained to them both. Lizzie was wide-eyed with surprise and interest, not only about that, but about everything she saw and he told her on the twenty-odd-mile drive into the city. She did not mention the film, her role, what would be expected of her, seemed only to be looking out at the world as if she wanted to grab it to her with both her hands, to absorb it with her eyes, her mind . . .

Sheldy had not felt such a reprieve from himself in many months. 'There's nothing much for you to do, Miss Lee,' he said, 'other than report in and meet your director and so on, for at least a couple of days. I'd be delighted to show you the sights.' (He could hardly believe he was offering to suffer the Rome-for-tourists scene again; he'd

343

even refused his mother on her recent visit – sent his secretary with her.)

Lizzie raised her fine smooth eyebrows at him. 'You would? Oh, how wonderful! We'd love that, wouldn't we, Mum?'

'I daresay. But I 'ope it don't cause no problems at the studio.'

'Absolutely not, Mrs. Hobbs.' Sheldy dipped his curly blond head at her, dazzled her with his open-faced charm: or, at least, thought he did. The blank stare she gave him was like a slap.

'I so seldom get a chance to see where I am,' Lizzie confided. 'It's to the studio, theatre, whatever, then bed.'

'That's the way it is when you got a big job to do, a big name,' Mim said, tartly. 'You don't get to the top muckin' about.'

'I'm sure you don't.' Sheldy nodded vigorously. 'Eye on the ball – my motto, too.'

'Got you where you are, didn't it?' Mim confirmed, with a warning glance into Lizzie's smiling face.

Lizzie's smiled faltered.

'There's no question here, Mrs. Hobbs,' Sheldy said quickly, adroitly avoiding the frenzied push of traffic as they neared the centre of the city, honking back at those who honked and shouted comments in rapid Italian at him. 'Would I risk my own profit?' (And, or, time-wasting involvement, he added to himself.)

'Don't suppose you would, Mr. Albright.' Mim gazed about, narrowed her eyes at the tall blocks of flats that vied with ancient buildings and obvious slums. 'Strange sort of place, this; thought it would be more romantic-like.'

'Wait, Mum,' Lizzie said. 'Lots of cities are like this when you first drive into them . . .'

'Most,' agreed Sheldy. 'Don't worry – there'll be plenty of romance in the Eternal City. I'll try to be a good guide.'

'You're very kind.' Lizzie looked at him with open and direct interest.

Sheldy wondered what she was seeing, concluding about him. He could not remember when he had so much wanted approval. It was almost amusing, would have flattened his reputation of not giving a fig for what anyone, under any circumstances, thought of him. In one of his famous predictive flashes with which, in business, he had leap-frogged seemingly impossible hurdles to achieve 'miracles' of gain, he saw her as the girl he might want to marry, to be the mother of his children, the one to run his big houses and always be on hand for him as companion and reference point . . .

Sliding his eyes over her firm face and jaw-line, his equally good instincts told him that it might not be that simple. This career of hers . . . He might need to give her leeway at first, appear to want her to keep on with it, wean her gradually, subtly, so that she hardly realized, hardly missed it . . .

'Is this our hotel? It's lovely,' she said. 'isn't it, Mum?'

'It's one of the oldest and best. I've got you two of their best suites . . .'

'Two?' said Mim sharply. 'Why two? Lizzie and me share, don't we, darlin'? - always 'ave.'

'That's all right, Mr. Albright - that's fine and thank you.' Lizzie kept her face averted from Mim.

'Stupid,' muttered Mim. 'Waste. Never mind, we'll spend most of our time in *one,* any'ow.'

Sheldy noticed that Liza knew when to be silent. What a strange and curious relationship. He wondered how it happened, wanted to know more, to learn all about *Liza Lee* . . .

As he gave their luggage over to the porter, made sure of their reservations, led them to the big, ornate lifts, made plans to take them to dinner, said *'arrivederci'* with his most charming and appealing smile, he could not believe this was Sheldon Albright, the astute, the phenomenal, the wizard-brain, the up-to-the-gills with life's pleasures and treasures, the jaundiced Sheldon Albright who knew of nothing or no-one who could not be outwitted or bought with money . . .

Striding away from them, he actually bumped into people as he looked back over his shoulder for a last glimpse of that lovely, radiant face . . .

And, driving back to his big, bougainvillaea-covered villa purchased for his stay in Rome, he almost got lost.

Was this, then, love?

'*Grazie*,' said Lizzie, as she paid off the taxi. Walking briskly through the golden morning towards the steps of St. Peter's basilica where Sheldy would be waiting, she felt odd, almost strange, to be on her own. It happened so seldom. Between Mum, the studio people, Sheldy, she was alone only when she had a bath. Even then, Mum was likely to be outside the door, talking to her through it, waiting for her to come out, then following her about while she dressed; 'When else can I get a word in edgeways with you, me darlin', sort out what we're goin' to do next?' she'd argue when Lizzie complained.

As for Sheldy, his presence was non-stop. He had ideas for her every moment when she wasn't working. If it wasn't sight-seeing every famed aspect of Rome, it was places for lunch, dinner, shopping – he never stopped buying her things, beautiful dresses he thought would suit her, a fur coat, a breathtaking negligée, a bracelet or necklace, an art treasure, something funny to make her laugh, like the big furry bear that looked a bit like an enlarged Freddie, great baskets of fruit, huge boxes of sweets, and flowers – flowers, every day, enough to crowd their suite at the hotel and give off a permanent fragrance that overcame even the fabulous perfumes he sent . . .

When she'd had to admit to him that it was all 'a bit much', and please, she didn't really want any more gifts – he'd sighed. 'You'll have to forgive me, darling Liza,' he'd said. 'I'm using the only tactics I know, the only ones I've seen work with everyone else. Things just don't do it for you, do they? You can't be bought. And that just makes me love you more.'

She was sorry she'd said anything, because she *did* appreciate him, did like his generous, big-handed approach to life. He was the opposite of Adam, who had been strict and business-like with money, given so little himself. Sheldy might be called an 'entrepreneur' behind his back, but he was as kind as he was brash. In fact, without even trying, she was liking him more and more. Their brief, stolen conversations, Mum always with them, gave her glimpses of a person she could feel easy and comfortable with, who wouldn't want her to be more intellectual than she was, who didn't seem star-struck by her performing, hardly mentioned it outside its connection with the film, who seemed genuinely interested in her . . .

Yes, it would be wonderful to be alone with him today, even if it was only for a few hours, and she *was* glad she'd finally simply run out on Mum, depressed as she was these days. He'd been amazingly patient with Mum – 'After all, if it's to be a merger, she comes with the deal, right?' – and no-one else had ever tried so hard to keep the peace with her, get on her right side, to understand her feelings . . .

'But there comes a time, Liza,' he'd said, finally, 'when enough's enough. I'm going not-so-quietly mad – you must know that. Please, please, while they don't need you . . . God knows when there'll be another opportunity before the end of the picture. Then, I'm frightened she'll bear you off and close me out . . .'

'Don't be silly,' she'd said. 'Mum couldn't close you out. Not if I wanted to see you. People overrate her power.'

He had shaken his head. 'I don't know . . .'

Well, he was quite wrong – yet she knew what he meant. Mum had been increasingly impossible lately. She moaned, protested, grizzled. She'd made the wrong choice, she said. She hated the foreigners, couldn't speak their ruddy language and wasn't about to learn it. She didn't give a fig for Roman culture, despised spaghetti, thought they were all round the bend the way they went to sleep in the afternoon, they should all be locked up and lose their licences for the way they drove – and rude! One of them had called her the equivalent of a 'dead 'en!'

'Thank you kindly,' she said to every suggestion Sheldy made, no matter how thoughtful and tactful, 'I'll just 'ang about with you and me girl.'

Each day she had sat doggedly through the shooting, following every movement with sharp, watchful glances, pushing herself into whatever was going on or being said with such ferocity that she was sometimes sworn at in voluble Italian, with nil effect. 'What are they on about, then?' she'd ask Lizzie. 'Silly sods.'

It had been somewhat easier to lose her on location. Most of the film, luckily, had been shot in and around Contina, close to the famous Mount Vesuvius, which had once erupted to destroy the famous city of Pompeii. Only a minimal amount of the story had been done in the sprawling studio in the suburbs of Rome, and sometimes Vittorio Bertolucci, the director who'd made several famous Italian films, would contrive little plots to capture Mim's attention elsewhere. He found her infuriating, but, he said, mothers were mothers, you have to keep them appeased for having had you.

Lizzie was grateful to him, and they got along very well, despite their language differences. He had a sensitive way of communicating with her, seemed to convey with his warm, dark eyes what he did not put into words. He sensed her occasional lapses of attention, brought her back from her 'reveries' – which were actually moments when she stepped away from herself, as she had in Zeke's office – with a gently repeated command.

'She is a lovely girl, this Liza,' she heard him say once to his assistant, 'but not quite with us – except when she sings, eh?'

Yes – when she sang, all was always well. Even Vincente di Riccoli, who was stiff in their love scenes, unbent and smiled when she sang. Thank goodness she could still do it, that it came through, dissolved barriers . . .

There was just one thing that singing didn't solve – the sudden urge, just before she was to begin, to run to the loo. How stupid she felt when she had to hold up production. She didn't need to speak Italian to recognize the jokes that ran round the studio. Her heartbeat would skip, her face go pink.

Sheldy had asked her about it, suggested she see a doctor. 'Probably a weak bladder,' he'd said, sensibly.

She had told him it was a very old complaint, had started when she was a little child hardly able to walk, when she had been made to do 'her bit' by Mum.

He had frowned, wanted to know more . . .

Today, he would probably ask about that, and a lot of other things.

There he was, his curly blond hair blazing with sunlight, his face creased with pleasure at the sight of her. She tugged at the floppy-brimmed pink hat she'd bought to shield her eyes, smiled at him from under it as she hurried forward.

He gave her a restrained version of his 'bear-hug'. 'You made it. What did she say?'

'She was still asleep.'

'Coward.'

Lizzie dimpled. 'I know.'

He took her bare arm, noted her floaty pink voile with approval. 'Just the way I like a girl to look,' he said. 'And you smell just right. I'm very sensitive to skins, you know – yours smells of . . . How *do* you describe skin smells?'

Lizzie laughed. She'd had the same thought herself. 'You can't.'

They walked inside, mingled with the tourists, heard the spiel of guides in different languages, moved on. They had already gone through the basilica and many of the chapels, gazed on 'La Pietà' – today, they were headed for the lift to the roof, where there was a coffee bar.

Here, they were able to look down on Bernini's St. Peter's Square, feel the height and vastness of the church and all its approaches, and yet appreciate the human touch nearby, the steaming coffee and little saffron-and-white sandwiches (the papal colours).

'No-one will find us here,' Sheldy said, sitting close to her at a tiny table. 'Not even Mim.'

'Poor Mum – she won't know what to do with herself. She hates being shut up in the room, and she won't go out . . .'

'But she could. It wouldn't hurt her. After all, Liza, she must expect you to have some privacy, some life of your own.'

Lizzie nodded, looked into his bright, inquiring gaze. 'I've not done too well at that. She is dead scared I'll go off again and throw away everything she's worked for, I've accomplished.'

'Do you think you might?' He gave her a teasing smile as he ordered their sandwiches and coffee.

'I don't think I could. If you knew her as I know her – if you'd seen what she did, and how important this dream is to her, you'd understand.'

'But, Liza, darling Liza, it's *her* dream, not *yours*.'

She cast him a quick glance. 'How do you know that?'

He pinched her cheek lightly. 'Ah, you admit it. I think you could be perfectly happy without it – and with me.'

350

'Is that so, Mr. Albright? Well.'

'Look at it this way. You won't want to sing forever. You'll surely want children. Married to me, you can sing or not sing – and you can have children.'

'Mmmm.' Lizzie's gaze wandered to some passing nuns. 'I might want to be one of those.'

'Nonsense. I've seen the way you look at *children*.'

'Seriously. Or go to college, get some education, do something solid and real with myself, be of some use, some service to others.'

'You can still do that, and be married to me and have my babies.'

'I don't even know you, Sheldy. I really knew Robbie, but I didn't know Kit, and I didn't know Adam. I must know the next person in my life.'

'That makes sense. Let's get started knowing each other right now. Let's talk and talk and talk – and then let's go walking – and, at some time, you must decide whether or not you'll let me make love to you.'

He put his arm around her, and she leaned into it, looking deeply into his eyes. 'What is it you see in me? Where is the person you say you fell in love with on sight? What is she, who is she?'

He chuckled. 'That's the mystery, isn't it? Can anyone explain it? You are – you.'

'But you see a "you" that I don't . . .'

'Ah, Liza, do any of us see anyone we don't put there? I just recognized you as my dream, someone I'd been looking for, waiting for without knowing it. I was miserable that day – bored rigid with life. And then, just like that, there was this lovely, lovely person – Liza Lee.'

Lizzie was still. She looked at him for a long time without speaking. 'I want to know you,' she said finally. 'I would love to love you, if . . .'

He put a finger on her lips. 'That's all I need. Let's start from the beginning. And, oh, by the way . . .'

He released her to reach into the pocket of his light grey suit. 'I brought this along – in case.'

Lizzie's eyes opened wide, blue, astonished. There, in a small black velvet box lay the most exquisite pear-shaped diamond ring she had ever seen.

'Don't say anything,' he said. 'Yet.'

# CHAPTER TWENTY-SIX

'It is lovely, Mum – you must admit it's beautiful . . .'
Lizzie held out her finger with the ring on it once more, as
if in its sheer brilliance and perfection it might force a
truce between them.

Mim, in the beige satin underwear Lizzie had bought
her for her forty-third birthday, placed her hands on her
jutting hip-bones and looked at the ring as if it had a bad
smell. 'Me Gawd – I never thought *you'd* go for the bees-
and-honey! You got your own. We don't need 'is – probably got in phoney deals . . .'

'Mum!' Lizzie dropped her hand, continued to dress,
quickly, urgently, so as to be ready when Sheldy got back
from Switzerland, where he'd gone to look into his francs.
'You've got to stop calling him a crook, inferring he's a
villain!'

'I didn't say crook . . .'

'As good as. Outwitting, quick-thinking, foresight,
daring – that's what's made Sheldy rich, not shady deals.
And I want you to know I admire him for what he's done.
He's an incredible person.'

'Leave off, Lizzie – I can't stomach no more praises –
it's the same record every time you fancy a bloke. No 'alf
measures. You can't just know 'em, 'ave a good time –
you got to put your 'ead in the noose the 'ole way. You'd
think you'd 'ave learned your lesson . . .'

Lizzie walked into the panelled dressing room, out of
range, where she finished dressing, putting on a royal blue
knitted hat and bulky sweater coat for the sudden turn of

weather. 'See you at the studio, Mum,' she said, planting a firm, quick kiss on Mim's stonily-set face. 'And don't worry so much – we're not going to do anything drastic. Who knows, we may never get married. It's just a trial. Honest, Mum – that's the truth. I wouldn't fool you.'

'Hmm. You've been known to, me girl . . .'

'You just leave me be, Mum, and maybe you won't make me have to, eh?'

Lizzie swung past her and out the door, closing it with a finality that left Mim standing there, mouth clamped.

Lighting up a cigarette, she took in a deep drag of smoke, went to the big curved windows and gazed down at the wide city street with its steady rush of darting cars and lumbering buses. She had to do some bloody hard thinking to get Lizzie past this one – at the moment, short of shooting him, she couldn't come up with anything. The bloke was like a ruddy great wall. He took whatever you said to him and came back smiling. She couldn't even make him fight. Even when she'd called him a fly-by-night, he'd only winked at her, said 'We'll see about that.'

He had a lot of sly ways, too, like when Lizzie wasn't there or listening, talking about his big houses and how he couldn't wait for Lizzie to see them. And he kept saying things like, 'Isn't she wonderful, Mim – wasn't that super?' as if he already had joint ownership and they shared her like a piece of property.

Mim grunted. Even cheekier was his way of telling her things like 'She's very grateful, you know. She's always saying how much she appreciates you,' as if she was second and outside and had to be told by him, who was first and on the inside!

Who the bleedin' 'ell did he think he was, anyhow? She'd known Cockney lads like him, full of theirselves, pushing their way up in the world with nothing but brass. Who was he? The son of a shopkeeper, wormed his way into university 'not looking at my books till an hour before exams', looking down on people for being 'plod-ders' . . .

He needed a good kick up the arse. Which, if only she were a man, she'd be happy to give him . . .

As it was – well, short of putting poison in his food, what?

Mim turned from the window, paced slowly about the big, ornate room which she had come to detest. She felt as if she'd been trapped in a huge gilded cage with no way out, nothing to do . . .

She couldn't understand a ruddy word anyone said on the Italian television, so it was no use sitting in front of that. In the end, there was only the desk, with its pile of post, her typewriter, the telephone . . .

Here, only here, was there any hope.

'Don't sign me up for anything, anything at all for a while, Mum,' Lizzie had said, with a firmness that was almost hard, not like her at all, *his* influence, of course. 'Sheldy and I want to take a holiday, go somewhere on our own, look at property, things like that.'

'Oh, yes . . .' she'd said, 'and what am I supposed to do, sit on me thumbs, tell 'em all to stuff their offers?'

'No, Mum. I'll be back. I only want a break. No-one performs *all* the time.'

'Yes, they ruddy do – if they don't want to fade out. You always got newcomers – there's that girl Paddy Andrews, sings like a machine, big tits . . .'

'More power to her.'

'I don't believe I'm 'earin' this.'

'Mum – don't be so melodramatic. Everyone has to have a holiday some time. You should have one yourself. You've got much too thin. Why don't you and Harry . . .'

''Arry, 'Arry, 'Arry.' Mim could feel the name boil-up in her head. 'Whenever you don't want me, you stick me on 'im. 'Ow do you know 'e's even with us? 'E could 'ave 'opped 'is perch long since.'

'Well – someone. You should make a woman friend.'

Mim had stared at her. Great ripples of fear had gone up and down her, a feeling like being kicked in the stomach had kept her silent.

And the same fear was suddenly with her now . . .

Gawd – it was happening, really happening. Not like her going off with Kit, or even the Jew – because she'd always been sure she'd get her back, in time . . .

This one, with his girlish curls and big open face, was likely the end of the road, no turning back. Lizzie, the little idiot, would go off and have his kids, get herself fat and matronly, and when he got back to playing the field, she wouldn't even care . . .

Whatever happened to Liza Lee? people would say. She was fantastic, a true star . . .

Oh, she lives in the country now, married to that tycoon, and has a raft of children, you wouldn't know her to look at . . .

Shame. Waste, really. She could have gone on for years and years, what with the movies . . .

'Bugger!' said Mim, slumping into the desk chair.

For a while she sat inertly, staring at some vast religious painting with lots of fat women and bearded men and angels floating about. Crikey, how she yearned for home. How she longed for kippers, chips, English tea . . .

And for Lizzie to be out there, doing her bit, with herself standing by, helping, egging her on . . .

Mim's black-wigged head (short cut, Italian style), came to rest on the typewriter, hit the metal in a slow hard beat. All the desperate moments of her life swamped over her in a great blackness, like being inside a grave . . .

It had all come to nothing. Lizzie's Command Performance would never come. Her dream was at an end.

Mim felt with disgust the wetness of the tears that slid between the metal and her face. There was no longer any reason to go on living. It'd be a pleasure, in fact, to bow out – leave them to it, the pair of them . . .

She raised her head, drew in a long hard sniff. What she'd do was disappear . . .

Wouldn't even leave a note. Let 'em look, go bonkers . . .

She pinched her mouth, nodded. That's the ticket, no ta-ta, no explainin'. Just take your suitcase and . . .

Scarper.

Right!

Mim stood up, went to the dressing room, brought out her luggage, threw it on the bed, and began to pack.

When she was all ready, dressed in a suit and plaid mac, her own hair tied into a sombre black scarf, no jewellery except the fancy watch Lizzie had bought her last Christmas, Mim went to the desk and hovered there a moment in indecision.

Should she take all the business folders, the correspondence, the addresses and telephone numbers accumulated with such care over the years, her precious typewriter – or leave them all behind? Which would hit them worse, worry them most?

She wanted them to suffer, suffer like bloody hell, suffer the way they'd made her suffer!

Suddenly the telephone was ringing. She hated the very sound of Italian telephones . . .

Should she pick it up, or let it ring?

Her mouth twitched – suppose it was something about Lizzie, something wrong . . .

None of this would be much bloomin' use if it *was*.

' 'Ello?' she said, keeping the flat edge to her curiosity.

'A call for you, Mrs. 'Obbs,' a voice said with a heavy Italian accent. '*Momento* . . .'

Mim scowled at her dismal, unmade-up face in the mirror across the room. Well, who cared how you were dressed when they fished you out of the river, or dragged you from under a car? Maybe she'd leave everything behind – what did she need with suitcases, clothes?

'Hello, Mrs. Hobbs? This is David Pendy. Did you get my letter? We've been hoping to hear from you . . .'

Mim could hardly focus the name; she was already wandering along by that river they called Tiger, something like that . . . 'David Pendy?'

'Hello, yes – you know, BBC.'

'Oh, me Gawd, yeah . . . yeah, we did get your letter – about the big special, eh?'

'That's right, only we'd hoped for another *show*, another Liza Lee Show. Frankly, her name's that much bigger now, and we're prepared to talk better terms.'

'You are?' Mim's eyebrows rose in a straight, wavy line high above her lifted nose. 'Like 'ow much?'

David Pendy laughed. 'You don't change, Mrs. Hobbs. Can we not discuss that after you've indicated whether or not Liza would be interested? Has she finished the picture?'

'Naa . . . they had weather trouble – they got rotten weather 'ere . . .'

'Really? You surprise me . . .'

'It'll be done soon, though. Only Lizzie's got 'erself engaged like – she wants an *'oliday*.'

'Oh.' David Pendy's disappointment came clearly despite the fuzz on the line. 'Could you not persuade her to defer?'

'I ain't been able to persuade 'er of nothin', David. She's gone on this bloke. Me 'eart's broke.'

'Oh, dear. What a pity!'

'We got lots of things – they want 'er for a movie in 'Ollywood; Australia wants 'er; they want 'er for a concert tour of the U.S.; Japan's been arter 'er . . .'

'I'm sure . . . Liza's really made it. When one thinks back to that night at Madame Blatsky's – what a way she's come! And she deserves it.'

'Now she's throwin' it all away . . .' Mim's voice dragged to a rasping halt.

'Are you there?' said David Pendy. 'Mrs. Hobbs? Look, are you sure of all this? You've always kept her on the mark so well – can't you manage this for us? It'd put her back on home territory, and we've got in mind a person who'll agree to come on the show with her that should not only make a great combination, but please her . . .'

'Oh, yes . . . Who's that, then?' Mim's eyebrow-line hovered, one eye opened wider than the other.

'Remember that same night, the boy impersonator, who went on to become a big rock star?' David Pendy's tone had an almost sly undertone.

'You don't mean . . .'

'I do, Mim. Rob Grover. How about that?'

'Naa – we don't want the likes of 'im . . .' Suddenly Mim's voice stopped. She felt her heart lurch in a way that seemed to kick her ribs, then crush her breath. "Ey – 'ang on . . . Robbie, eh?'

'That's right. We only got him because of her – I mean, he is contingent on Liza's acceptance. It's an exciting prospect, don't you think? Bound to succeed.'

'Yeah . . .' Mim's eyebrows descended, her other eye opened, her mouth drew into a strange double curve at both sides. 'Robbie Grover . . .'

The silence Mim left was so long that David Pendy coughed, cleared his throat, finally said, 'Well? I'm terribly sorry, but they're waiting for me, and the other line's . . .'

'I'll do it,' said Mim. 'I'll do it.'

There was an intake of breath on the wire. 'Ah,' said David Pendy. 'Well. I'm chuffed, I really am. How shall we leave it, then? Shall I call you, or you call me? Shall I send a contract?'

Mim pressed her hand to her mouth. There was another short silence while the wheels of her mind did their familiar sort-out. 'Yeah. Right you are. Send a contract.'

'Thank you. Thanks a lot, Mrs. Hobbs. This is much

appreciated. Talk to you soon. The best of luck – and give my love to Liza.'

Mim put the receiver back on its hook almost gently.

Crikey, she thought, sometimes there seemed to be someone up there after all, someone who could be on *her* side. Good old Gran had been right – only this time she hadn't even had to light a candle.

She went to the suitcases, put them back on the bed, unpacked them, changed into her new purple trouser suit, put the black wig back on, and went downstairs to find a taxi to take her to the studio. She wouldn't even be late.

'Darling,' Lizzie said, 'it won't make the least difference. I promise!'

Sheldy had been dubious, very. Some of his breezy assurance diminished. 'You loved this one,' he said. 'You haven't yet decided whether you love me.'

'I loved Robbie a very long time ago – when I was a kid, Sheldy. And, anyway, you're wrong – I do love you. Not the way you want me to – not yet. But it's coming. Don't let's spoil it with imaginary problems. Please?'

As she rehearsed the new show, Lizzie thought back to that conversation with Sheldy. She had really meant it. They had become closer once they had slept together. Sheldy was a happy surprise after Adam. *He* did all the work, was so turned on by her that she had only to respond – and, it was lovely. She had discovered sex itself – not just the wanting and arousal she'd felt for Adam, but the working side of it that could be improved, made so satisfactory that one could feel relaxed and elated for hours afterwards . . .

It was funny. She'd never been much interested in her own body. She made no connection with the effect it had on men. Now, she was very conscious of her movements, of the feel of herself in relation to a man – namely, Sheldy. Adam had been practised, an 'adept', he called himself – but Sheldy was wildly enthusiastic. There were times when he already had an erection when he met her. It was almost embarrassing, but exciting, too . . .

Dear, darling Sheldy – there was no question in her mind that they would marry. She kept wearing his ring, despite Mum's insistence that it was too flashy and would put people off . . .

In fact, the reverse had proved to be true. The press made big meals of their romance, Sheldy's self-made millions, her fame in show business; they were photographed everywhere they went, and neither of them held back or pussy-footed with the 'just good friends' routine that Mum insisted on in *her* interviews. 'The ring's just a gift,' Mim said to one newspaper reporter, 'don't mean anything serious. Liza ain't got no thought of marryin' 'erself off to no-one. She's got a show to do, and performin' is 'er life.'

Lizzie had to admit that for a moment, back in Rome, when Mum had confronted her with the contract, she'd actually felt close to abandoning her mother, to simply running out on her for ever and ever. She could still feel the urge . . .

And yet . . . Mum had been right again. Despite Sheldy's dismay, the idea of appearing with Robbie had sent currents of conflict through her. Sheldy had never said she *shouldn't* go on performing, wouldn't have, but she knew in her heart that his hopes were set on her weakening on their holiday in Hawaii, letting it all slide as they married and set up their homes . . .

Finally, after a battle with Mum in the old style, she had agreed, and forgiven her. The idea of appearing with Robbie had superseded all the ends-and-means. She looked forward to it with genuine pleasure. It would be like a glorious fantasy come true.

'Rob should be arriving any time now, Liza,' David Pendy told her, as Lizzie went through her dialogue, business and songs as the technicalities of the production took shape around her.

When Robbie did not show for the third time, they began to work around his spots, and have everything in order for the last minute.

Lizzie's anticipation grew to near obsession. Living with Mim in a Grosvenor Square flat, seeing Sheldy every spare moment, she was growing tense. Dark circles appeared under her large, anxious blue eyes, and she blinked more than usual.

Sheldy took it personally, accused her of still being in love with Rob Grover. Mim acted in a furtive manner, offering endless cups of tea in comfort and compensation . . .

Still Robbie did not turn up.

'We'll have to make a substitution,' David Pendy said, and they hired another rock group called the Vibes, who were close competitors of Rob's group.

Lizzie's spirits drooped. She forgot words, lost portions of the lyrics, dried up twice in the final run-through, and seemed to herself to have no hold on what she was doing, or over her bladder . . .

'Come on, me love,' Mim urged, 'there ain't nothin' to be scared of – they're only people, and you sang to thousands of 'em without an 'itch.'

'Oh, Mum,' Lizzie said. 'I don't know what's happening to me. I've never felt like this, Mum . . .'

It was Mim's answer, spoken in last-minute desperation, that jolted Lizzie into realization . . .

'You got *me*, me love – and that *fiancé* of yours . . .'

*Mum*, bringing up *Sheldy*?

Lizzie's eyes, made up for her performance, huge with eye-shadow and mascara, even bluer under the lights, opened wide into her mother's.

'Robbie isn't coming, is he?' she said in a near whisper. 'You *knew*.'

Mim gulped, went grey-white. 'What you on about?'

'Mum?' Lizzie's knuckles tapped the boney chin. 'Mum?'

Mim shook her head. 'No, me darlin' – he ain't.'

'Why? Did you stop him, pull some trick?'

Mim spread her sallow, red-nailed hands. 'No, honest, I didn't 'ave nothin' to do with it – 'e's wiped out on drugs, love, Gawd's truth.'

The crew was waiting for her, time was up. Lizzie could barely tear her gaze from the naked, protesting stare. 'Drugs?'

'That's right. I didn't want to worry you, petal – see?'

'Do the others know?'

Mim nodded. 'They just found out.'

'Who told them – you?'

Mim brought up a shoulder. 'I 'ad to – didn't I?'

'Miss Lee!'

'Come on, Liza . . .'

Mim quickly withdrew. Lizzie looked after her, then drew a great breath – moved into the arena of action.

As she opened her mouth to sing, the thought flickered through her mind that she was now obliged to perform for at least another *year*. Even if she married Sheldy – there was no way out.


'But I was hoping you'd come with us, Mim,' Sheldy said, as he arrived to collect Lizzie to see the 'pied-à-terre' he wanted them to move into when they married, 'give us your expert opinion.'

Mim cocked an eye at him. With his gold eyebrows raised high, his ruddy, open face lighted by the late autumn sun beaming in from the tall windows of the Grosvenor Square flat, his big bulky-crowned smile of affection and respect, she could almost believe him. Clever neddy, he was, using her to get the noose tied round Lizzie. 'Aw, I ain't dressed,' she said, pulling her feather-trimmed robe over her scrawny chest. 'Besides, I got an appointment with this bloke from Mervnick Pictures, over from the States 'e is, special to sign up Lizzie.'

Lizzie, in a mint green, fur-trimmed coat Sheldy had brought her back from the couturier in Paris whose flourishing business he had backed when it was failing, her hair shining and a bright coral lipstick heightening her new 'pale blond' look, spoke up with sudden urgency. 'No, Mum, no – I told you I don't want any more commitments . . .'

'You mean never?' Mim's eyes narrowed, her head tilted parrot-fashion, alert, ready for battle.

'I didn't say that. It's just . . .' Lizzie looked away past both their watchful faces. 'I'm tired. I've told you . . .'

'But you'll 'ave time for a nice rest – like you 'ad in our cottage in the . . .'

'No, Mum. You mustn't tie me up, you'll have to put them off.' The dark circles under Lizzie's eyes, well-covered with a white undercoat, pressed through in mauve shadows.

"Ow can I put them off?' Mim began.

'Let's change the subject,' Sheldy said quickly, firmly. 'Come on, Mim, jump into your clothes, Liza can give me a cuppa – right, darling?'

Lizzie shrugged.

'Well, then . . .' Mim gave a considered nod. Maybe she should take his hint. There was more than sawdust between his ears. If he could use her, she could use him. 'I'll only be a tick,' she said.

Lizzie took off her coat, went to the kitchen. 'This is stewed, Sheldy,' she said, as he followed her, loomed behind her, ready, as he always was, to put his arms around her. 'I'd better make fresh.'

'Lord, no – it was only a ploy. Just put some hot water in it. Here, I'll do it.'

Lizzie nodded vaguely. Her eyes had a strained, faraway look. 'I made a mess of rehearsal yesterday,' she said. 'Everyone was upset. I forgot everything – they're really worried now.' She turned to him, looked up into his eyes. 'Oh, darling, what do you think is happening? What's wrong with me?'

He put down the kettle, wrapped her in his arms. 'Nothing, nothing's wrong with you, my angel. It's just as you said – you're tired. You've been at this for years and years. That's why you've got to get away, marry me – to hell with Hawaii, we'll go on a world cruise, take a year, *longer*. When we come back, you can think again. And don't worry about your mother – she's a resourceful old girl. Take my word, whatever she threatens will happen to her, just know it *won't*.'

Lizzie gazed at him with longing and hope. 'If only I could be sure as you are. I couldn't bear it if anything awful happened to her, and it was my fault.'

He smiled tenderly. 'I understand that. And you can be sure I'll always provide for her, include her in our life. I don't even have to play-act so much any more – I'm getting used to her. She's not unlike my mother's sister, Auntie Annie – she came from the East End, too.'

Lizzie drew away, blinking as if there were tears in her eyes, though none was visible. 'I wish we weren't going to see this flat today, you know . . .'

'What?' Sheldy's eager sincerity had an anxious edge. 'I thought you were keen . . .'

Lizzie walked to the iron-grilled window, beyond which was a conclave of pigeons waiting expectantly for crumbs, and she lifted her hand to them, murmuring, 'In a minute, chaps . . .'

'What *is* wrong, sweetheart,' Sheldy said.

'If only I knew.' Lizzie turned to face him, her hands plucking at the low white collar of her blouse. 'I don't want to let you down, but . . .'

'Well, 'ere's 'er ladyship, smart as a pin, don't you

think?' Mim appeared in the doorway dressed in a mannish black suit with shirt and tie, her perm-kinked brass hair pressed to her skull by a white bowler. 'Straight out of *Vogue* and twice as chipper,' what?'

Neither of them could help smiling.

They resumed departure, set off into the crisp bright day.

Lizzie walked between them along the street to Sheldy's dark green Mercedes. Each took an arm, as if she needed both propelling and protection.

'Please . . .' she said, shaking her head. 'I seem to be out of breath or something . . .'

They released her, giving each other an inquiring glance over her head.

'I'll sit in the back,' Lizzie said.

'No such thing.' Mim stood back. 'With me so skinny, we can all three fit – right, Sheldy?'

'Perhaps it would be better if you sat in the back, Mim,' Sheldy said, with his big smile and firm voice.

Mim gave a stoical, good-natured nod. 'Anythin' to oblige.'

As they started into the busy London traffic, they made note of a protest taking place around the American Embassy. 'It's them skin'eads,' Mim said knowledgeably, and for the first time that day, Lizzie laughed. 'Oh, Mum,' she said, 'you do get things twisted.' She turned round, gave her a look of wonder, tinged with nostalgic fondness. 'We should show Sheldy where we used to live, don't you think?'

Mim enjoyed the laugh, even if she didn't know how she'd got it; now she was confused. 'What's that got to do with the price of eggs?' she asked.

'Soho?' said Sheldy, glancing in the rear-view mirror at Mim. 'Yes, that would be interesting. Let's do it after. Perhaps we could have lunch around there. I know a place, excellent food.'

'Why not?' said Mim.

Lizzie lapsed into silence.

'I see you got the papers – didn't 'ave time to read 'em this mornin'. Anythin' in about Lizzie?' Mim flicked open the *Financial Times* with a disdain of its contents, her eye going to where it had been folded open . . .

' 'Ey – me Gawd, look at this! Why didn't you say somethin', old friend!' Mim leaned forward, all-but planting her chin on the back of the seat between them, screwing up her eyes to read without her glasses. 'Listen to this, me petal . . .

'Don't bother, Mum,' Lizzie said. 'They're always rubbish.'

'I agree. Why don't we give her a rest, Mim.'

Mim's head jerked backwards as if they had left their minds. She pushed up the bowler, the better to see the fine print on the Entertainment page. 'No-one don't need publicity like *this* . . .'

' "The popularity of Lize Lee 'as soared this last year. There is somethin' new in 'er voice, a greater maturity that at the same time does not ob . . . obscure 'er youthful vibrance . . ." What's that mean?'

'Don't bother, Mim – we're almost there. It's right on the Embankment, Liza, old and historical. You'll be able to look out on the river, watch the boats . . .'

'Yes?' Lizzie sat up a little. 'Sounds good.'

' "The audiences," read Mim, "love 'er. The television was turned on faithfully for 'er shows, according to the ratings. Apparently she 'as developed a tremendous rapport with the feelin's and emotions of 'er listeners. Without any quibble . . ." What's that?'

'Mum – never mind! And do take that cigarette out of your mouth and stop blowing smoke over us!'

Mim did not hear. ' "Whatever – from critics or press – she is now accepted as England's foremost star of light entertainment." 'Ear that! "And no matter 'ow famous or powerful, few would refuse to appear readily on 'er show – she knows just 'ow to introduce the 'ighest of ranks with ease and grace . . . The delightful Liza Lee is at 'er peak – long may she reign!" '

Mim threw the paper over into Lizzie's lap, thumped on the seat-back. 'Ee! Crikey! Bloomin' 'ell – if that don't take the cake. Wait till Zeke sees *this* – I'll be uppin' our terms sky-high. Aw, me love – I'm that proud of you!'

'Here we are,' Sheldy said, touching Lizzie's arm.

Lizzie seemed to wake from a sleep. 'Oh . . . lovely house!'

'Isn't it? Do you like it, really like it? Do you, Mim?'

Mim looked at the red-brick Georgian house in frowning reluctance. Hadn't they heard a word she said?

' 'Course I like it,' she said, ' 'oo wouldn't? But I thought you said "pied-à-terre" – ain't that French for a sort of place to 'ang your 'at? You must 'ave a lot of 'ats.'

Sheldy smiled at Lizzie, turned off the motor, 'Only the best for my darling,' he said.

Lizzie smiled as if she heard his voice from a distance.

As they went in and through the vast empty rooms, their footsteps and voices echoing back to them, Lizzie shook her head in growing amazement. 'Servants' quarters? Five bedrooms? Dining room you could skate in – why, Sheldy? It gives me chills to think about running it . . .'

'You won't have to do a thing, darling – that's the point of the separate flat for the housekeeper and her husband. They'll look after the whole thing!' Sheldy threw out his big arms in expansive emphasis. 'Entertaining won't be any problem at all. We can walk out of the place any time and travel. While we're in another house, this will just be ticking along, waiting. Practical, don't you see!'

Lizzie drew in a quiet breath. 'I feel very peculiar,' she said.

'You do? You don't like it?' Sheldy went to her, drew her up to him, looked into her eyes. 'Just say – we'll forget about this. You can pick out something yourself, something that appeals to you – whatever you like I'll like – just as long as we're together . . .'

'Excuse me,' said Mim, 'but 'aven't you forgotten somethin', Sheldon Albright?'

They both turned to look at her, standing in the middle of the immense, cathedral-ceilinged living room, her hands on her hips, her shoulder bag like a tourist's pack shrinking her height.

'What's that, Mim?' Sheldy was reddening strangely. His Adam's apple jerked, one eyelid twitched.

Ho-ho, thought Mim, I've got 'im on the run. 'E knows and I know can't both of us win. And I, Lizzie's own mum, ain't goin' to lose!

She walked forward in the high wedge shoes that gave her an extra three inches. 'Lizzie can't go nowhere till the last show's done. Lizzie ain't goin' to 'ave no time to play bleedin' 'ostess to your tycoons – and can't you twig the fact she don't want to get married, don't want to marry you! You're drivin' 'er off 'er nut with your push, push, push. You ain't never let 'er draw breath – now this ruddy great place is one thing over the top.'

'Mum!'

'Well, it's true. She's too kind 'earted to tell you 'erself. No – it's me what gets the blame, isn't it? Wantin' 'er to work, to do what she does best – me what's makin' 'er "tired".'

'Liza?' Sheldy took her hand, held it against his chest.

Lizzie shook her head, smiled at him in pleading dismay. 'What can I say? I've never known how to shut her up, and I don't know now.'

'Just tell me if it's true. Is it how you feel about me?'

'Cripes – you don't think she's goin' to admit it, do you?'

'Tell me, Liza – if you tell me to ignore her, I can. No hard feelings.'

Lizzie leaned her head against his shoulder. 'Ignore her,' she said. 'And let's go.'

'All right,' he said softly. 'I see you don't want to make up your mind today. This can wait – and so can I.' He shot Mim a look of guarded victory.

Mim frowned hard. Something had gone wrong, got out of hand. Why did she feel she had shot her bolt, that Lizzie, although she hadn't been able to speak out, had somehow kicked her in the bum? Black fear clamped her mouth, dilated her eyes.

They left the building in silence. Sheldy locked the big oak front door behind him, pocketed the key. They walked along the paved garden, shut the gate, went to the car. Sheldy helped Lizzie in, locked in her seatbelt, let Mim fend for herself.

They did not go to Soho, or to lunch. In a flat tone, Lizzie asked to be taken home. She wanted to be left alone a while. She hoped he would understand, she would ring him up later.

'Of course, my darling. We'll have a quiet dinner somewhere.'

Mim watched them kiss goodbye at the door, whisper a moment. The misery, like a clammy shadow, engulfed her . . .

'*Please*, Mum', Lizzie said, taking off her coat, her shoes, as she moved past towards her bedroom, 'don't disturb me. Not for *anything*.'

Mim kept quiet. Any power she had had with her girl was gone. The pain of it was unbearable . . .

'What about the post?' she asked, her voice uncharacteristically muted. 'Don't want to know?'

'No, Mum. Everything can wait.' Her words trailed, were lost in a long, deep yawning.

' 'Ere – 'ang on, what's this?'

In the pile of mail stacked on the floor below the big brass letterbox, one particular envelope seemed to jut out as if lighted up . . .

That beautiful posh stationery . . .

Mim pounced on it, her hand a grasping claw. Throwing her bowler from her head as if it obstructed her view, she tore the letter open.

Not a letter. Something stiff . . .

' 'Ang on.'Ang on, Lizzie love, 'alf a mo' . . .'

She drew out the card, stared.

'Oh, me Gawd, me livin' Christ . . .'

Lizzie paused, turned. 'What, Mum – someone's died?'

Mim shook her head. The words wouldn't come. Silently, tears pouring down her cheeks, she handed it up to Lizzie.

What she held in her hands was a scroll, its borders like braided ribbons, in the centre, surrounded by a crown and shields, a portrait of the Queen. The words below said: 'Patrons, Her Majesty the Queen, Her Majesty Queen Elizabeth the Queen Mother . . .'

And below that, they said, 'we the undersigned tender our sincere congratulations to . . . (in handwriting)

*Liza Lee*

'as being one of the representative Artistes selected to appear before

HER MAJESTY THE QUEEN

on the occasion of the

ROYAL VARIETY PERFORMANCE

held at the

LONDON PALLADIUM ON

MONDAY, NOVEMBER 10th, 1979

the performance being in aid of the Entertainment Artistes' Benevolent Fund.'

It was signed by the President, Vice President and General Secretary.

Lizzie sank slowly to the floor beside Mim. 'Oh, Mum . . . oh, Mum, Mum, Mum . . .' She wrapped her in her arms, rocked her, held her face close to hers so their tears mingled.

*     *     *

Surprisingly, in the months that followed, Mim had been able to accept Sheldy, and even played his game with him of being future in-laws. She was impatient for 'the royal occasion' yet permanently ecstatic – 'over the moon', in her words.

Sheldy moderated his campaign, increased his stays abroad, allowed himself to be tied up in new ventures, dropped the subject of a 'pied-à-terre', or even a definite date for a wedding. He seemed to accept that if there was any hope at all of Liza marrying him, it certainly would not be before the Command Performance. After – he might step up his attack, even provide a threat or two of his own: after all, a man couldn't hang round forever, and now that he'd had a taste of permanency and stability, he wouldn't be settling for predatory bachelorhood again.

In this liberated atmosphere, Lizzie felt a big weight lift. There was only one lingering pressure, and that didn't go away, didn't let up . . .

. . . the fear of losing her voice. And worse, of floating so far away from herself as she started to perform, that she might not be able to get back.

Mim was of no help. If anything, discussing it with her made it increase. 'Nerves is natural. All performers 'ave 'em. You ask any of 'em – it don't get no better with the years. It's a sign you're good; the better you are, the worse you get the willies.'

She longed to be able to talk about it to someone who wouldn't tell her to see a psychiatrist, or make it public at this time. With what lay ahead it could be fodder for the tabloids, disastrous for her career . . .

Which, now, was her unavoidable destiny. Never, for any reason on earth, would she jeopardize the culmination of Mim's dream: it would be a form of murder.

She *did* think of going to Cynthia Sterling – but that was all so long ago – and thoughts of Robbie came and went, too, always with the feeling that he would help *if* . . .

The word on him was depressingly consistent: missed and cancelled concerts, arrest, court cases, pictures of a distorted Robbie, bloated lips, swollen eyes with black puffs under them, giving *up-yours* gestures to the police, the public that had adored him, and always that frowzy-headed blonde with the short leather skirt and jacket, her eyes as bad as his . . .

Robbie would know all about floating away from oneself – that was certain. And would he even remember her, except in dreams, perhaps nightmares?

If only *she* could help *him*. What a pair they had turned out to be. Would anyone have guessed that dear, funny Robbie would make such a total down-trip of his life!

And she – only better by a hair – by dint of Mim!

Sometimes, tempted to confide more in Sheldy, she caught herself just in time. He was wonderful in so many ways – but in the subtleties, where material things, physical things, lost their exactness, couldn't be precisely worded, he seemed to turn off, as if there was a barrier to his comprehension beyond which he refused to, or could not, go.

Strangely, she once thought of Kit. She'd run into him on the King's Road one day. The only thing the same about him was the beard. He wore a long saffron robe and greeted her with pressed hands and a low nod. He urged her to come to his 'ashram' south of the river, run by a guru whose name she would surely know . . .

But she didn't. It sounded interesting, though, and she'd taken some literature he'd handed to her and said she might pay a visit some time. How soft his voice had become, how gentle his eyes. Could he have changed so much?

When she'd told Mim, Mim grunted. 'Probably the same bastard under them robes. They do it to get out of earnin' a livin'.'

Predictable. Yet, perhaps it had influenced her a bit *not* to look him up . . .

And then, there was Adam. Would he have understood, known what was wrong? Would Helena's death in a car crash have softened him?

Musing about that, between performances, Lizzie had decided writing to him wasn't much use. And even if she'd seen him in person, he would probably turn it all into an intellectual tract, perhaps make a play out of it.

She wished she had been able to make close friends in her life, but it had never seemed possible – Mim had been her friend, her whole life; everyone, everything else had come and gone.

Ah, well . . .

Lizzie at her dressing-room mirror, turned a fond look on the hovering little figure of her mother, who, now that she was fully re-instated in her supervisory role, was busy checking the lyric of the new song she'd written for Lizzie, one that she hoped might be sung on THE NIGHT. Thank God, she thought, that all this has actually materialized. How dreadful if it never had. Poor Mum . . .

How she would have suffered! And – she'd almost done it to her – so many times, given up, betrayed her, let her down. If it hadn't been so powerful a dream, it would have collapsed years ago, and *she* would have caused the collapse. Lord, what an escape.

Brushing her hair into its smooth line, so much her trademark by now that she never thought of wearing it another way any more, Lizzie considered her own face in the mirror. It looked back at her like a stranger's. Liza Lee, the singer, she said under her breath.

'What's that?' said Mim, looking up sharply.

'Nothing, Mum – humming.'

'Happy, eh?' The sharpness turned into a knowing smile.

It didn't matter that she didn't answer – Mim wouldn't have had it another way. 'You should be ready, me love,' she said. 'You got to be word-perfect on this. You need more colour, too – *lots* more, chucks.'

As Lizzie complied with rouge, she wondered if Mum realized that this was her twenty-seventh year. There was no difference between the way she talked to her now, and when she was four . . .

Funny how four always stuck in her mind. Was that the year she'd met Robbie, when Mum had said she was five?

'Up straight with the shoulders,' Mim said. 'Let's see your teeth – cameras picked up somethin' on the front ones the other night . . .'

'I remember. Lipstick – from *your* kiss, when you should have been scarce.'

Mim chuckled. 'Missed, didn't I? Got excited.' She moved closer, out of the range of an actor in the next cubicle. 'Speakin' of that, don't forget the loo.'

'As if I would.'

Lizzie stood up, wriggled into the black tank top to go with her stretch-pants rehearsal outfit. 'I hate these,' she said, 'but they're better than the old leotards.'

'None of your sauce. 'Ow's your underarms?'

'Sweaty. Worse than ever . . .'

' 'Ere – let's put more of this deodorant what I got.' Mim grabbed up her big bag, fished in it, brought out a tubular bottle.

'Mum – whenever did you get it?'

'In the lunch hour, whilst you was gabbin' with Pendy.'

'You're something.'

Suddenly Lizzie felt curiously close to her mother, as if *knowing* that she would make her dream come true had finally merged them. For a moment, the floaty feeling took a different turn – instead of her own body, her own face, she had Mum's, *was* Mum!

Thank the Lord, minds were one's own and no-one else could see her thoughts, read her feelings . . .

Suppose she was mad?

'Time, Miss Lee,' said a young woman with long dark hair, 'Studio Five B.'

The weeks and months moved on. Lizzie did several concerts, a short film, had a brief, abortive holiday in Venice with Sheldy where he forgot his resolve and pestered her from day to night about a date, and she could hardly wait to get back to practising and rehearsing.

Her nerves were increasingly jumpy. She had one nightmare after another about opening her mouth to sing, the Queen watching from her box, and no sound coming out. She would wake up gasping, her throat bone-dry, her heart bumping wildly in her chest.

Mim would come padding in, take her in her thin hard arms, comfort her, make her tea. 'Don't worry yourself like this, me dear one,' she'd say, 'when the time comes, you'll knock 'em dead. You always 'ave, ain't you?'

'There's the first time . . .'

'Not for you. You, me little petunia, are like death and taxes. You and me together saw to that, we worked like . . . coloureds. See, ain't I improvin'?'

Lizzie had to laugh. It was too mad not to be funny. She'd gone back to sleep, and just as Mim said, whenever she actually began to sing, it was always all right. No matter how close it came to *not* being. She was like clockwork, one interviewer had said, 'You wind her up and she goes, perfect every time.'

But even clocks broke down . . .

At last the actual rehearsal began for the royal performance. The list of participants was enough to give anyone cold feet, even the most intrepid veteran: Carol Channing, Yul Brynner, Les Dawson, James Galway, Red Buttons, Elaine Stritch, among the many; Marti Caine, the English National Opera Chorus, Gemma Craven, Jim Davidson, Bernie Clifton, Bill Haley in the long line of top performers . . .

How *could* they have chosen her? The image they had of her had nothing to do with her – 'that radiant, dynamic star of film, television and stage, that favourite of the young and old alike, whose voice reaches into every heart, sets everyone to dancing, reminiscing, singing with her, or just plain listening to that powerfully enchanting voice, will make her royal début . . .'

Nonsense. She was a pale blob of shadow, of shapeless energy. Her voice was not even her own – it came from a set of vocal chords set in motion by music . . . They could fail – she would be exposed!

When the weekend for the royal show finally arrived, even Mim seemed frantic as the performers began to assemble for rehearsals, where they were taken back and forth by coach from their Shaftesbury Theatre base to the Palladium. She got in everyone's way demanding answers to her anxious questions, making sure none of 'Miss Liza Lee's' rights of position were overlooked.

'My God,' a member of management commented, 'she's worse than her reputation. Can't something be done?' There was some effort by a stage manager, so royally ignored by Mim that it was not repeated.

Lizzie, over-awed at the assemblage of great names and familiar faces from all over the world, the way everyone met, talked, laughed, cracked jokes with such apparent ease, for once was so deeply embarrassed by her mother that she felt like hiding, walking away, pretending not to know her . . .

Oh, the guilt of it – when everything Mum was doing was for *her* benefit. It was true she might not have got the band to understand her special counter-rhythm in 'Together' without Mum's intervention, or got the lighting right for 'Stars Over Soho' without Mum's 'Oy!' to the lighting crew, and it was even truer that she would have forgotten the new lyric of Mum's 'Dream Girl' if Mum hadn't prompted her loudly from the wings.

Drinking coffee, sharing sandwiches with her fellow performers, Lizzie found herself wishing Mum wouldn't interrupt or correct. They were so funny, interesting, full of stories about themselves, and there was comfort in their confessions that they too, had had sleepless nights, were paralysed with nerves. When Bill Haley rehearsed his 'Rock Around the Clock', Lizzie could not sit still – oh, if only she could just be a listener, be the audience instead of having to perform, what fun this occasion would be . . .

' 'Orrible music,' Mum had whispered. 'Don't understand 'Er Majesty askin' 'im!'

Lizzie had nudged her. 'Sssh – for God's sake, Mum – you'll be heard.'

'So . . .? I'm entitled to me opinion.'

Lizzie had looked around, her face hot. 'In private, yes.'

'What's eatin' you, then?' Mum had nudged her back. 'No need for nerves, me love – *you're* goin' to be the 'it of *this* Command Performance. You're the best of the lot – by miles!'

Lizzie looked at her. The ferocity in her eyes had the glitter of triumph, of abandoned jubilation. Lizzie had felt a deep shiver pass through her body, raise goose-bumps on her arms, freeze her lips.

And, as the final arrangements took form about her, the immensity of the organization and details, from the disciplining and briefing of programme sellers, stewards, front-of-house and security staff, transport, hotels, dressing-room space for all the 'artistes', co-ordination of television cameras and vehicles, operation of scenery, wardrobe, catering, band rehearsals, floral arrangements for the Royal Box, the colossal efforts of supervision of those responsible for bringing it all together in harmonious accord, Lizzie's nerves tensed proportionately.

'I can't do it,' she kept saying to Mim. She said it hourly, like a prayer, she muttered it in her sleep, woke up screaming it . . .

On the Sunday before THE MONDAY, Lizzie grabbed Mim's arm as the overture was run through and one by one people were bouncing onto the stage in final rehearsal, doing their acts – Lizzie's soon to come.

'Mum – prepare yourself. I'm not going to make it.'

Mim broke into a complacent, carefree grin. "Course you are,' she said, patting her on the behind, 'you got no alternative now, 'ave you – the *Queen* and all?'

Lizzie's breath vanished. There was a wet scalding sensation between her legs . . .

'I'm wetting myself . . .'

'Never mind – too late – get out there!' Mim had given her a sharp push.

Lizzie, later, couldn't remember moving out to the middle of that vast stage. Everyone had been so encouraging afterwards, saying how good she was, that they wished their nerves would be so well hidden. She could only remember laughing in a stupid way, giggling, falling into various people's arms to feel their reassurance. She'd forgiven Mum, who knew her so much better than she knew herself.

Yes – as theatre people always said – on the night it *was* all right.

With Her Majesty there, her earrings and brilliant gown glittering from the shadows, the faces of her party smiling down expectantly, Lizzie's voice had come from somewhere, burst from her in vibrant force. From a kind of memory file that seemed detached from her head, the words and melodies flicked into place just in time, and, somehow, in the right order. Her smiles and gestures were as reliable as if programmed by computer. Despite a fine coat of sweat all over her face and body, her heart had continued to keep her going, its pounding lost in the sounds of music. Coming to the end of 'Dream Girl', a feeling of peace had warmed her. She had got through. She could open her arms, lift them above her head, bow to the

Queen, throw kisses as she walked briskly off in her gold twenties' dress. The applause vibrated in her like waves of thunder . . .

Approving faces surrounded her. She was patted, kissed, smiled on . . .

And Mim kept hugging her with those steel-band arms so that it was hard to recover her breath. 'I *did* it for you, Mum,' she murmured dazedly. 'I did it for you.'

'You did, me darlin' love, you did. And I was right, wasn't I – you *were* a big 'it. Did you see 'er face?'

Lizzie nodded.

And she saw it again, the beaming approval when they all went on stage together to take their final bows. Of *course*, she hadn't been the outstanding hit Mum made out – Bill Haley had been that, and quite rightly – but it was lovely to see Her Majesty so pleased with them all.

'Now,' Mim whispered, 'quick-like, let's get you ready to greet her.'

. . . Unexpectedly, the cold feeling again, the freeze of nerves . . .

If only she could go home now, not have to stand up there, find something sensible to say . . .

'Don't fret, lovey,' Mim said, 'I'll be there, so will Sheldy. And never forget – the royals go to the loo just like ordinary people – they ain't no different to you and me. Just be your charmin' self.'

As they all stood in order, waiting for the Queen to come along and pause by each one, shake hands, say a few words, Lizzie had the sudden urge to look behind her, to the left, to the right . . .

It was a strange, compelling feeling, a bit like her old urge to run before she performed, only much, much stronger . . .

A band of bright, wavy light passed across her mind, and she saw the approaching face of the Queen in a large kind of aura . . .

Does *she* always want to do this? she thought. Does she always want to perform? Isn't she *always* doing a Command Performance?

How stupid, Lizzie thought, to imagine the Queen was looking right into her eyes, one Elizabeth facing another, hearing what she was thinking, a wistful, compassionate sharing in her blue gaze . . .

But of course it wasn't the Queen looking like that, it was her own reflection . . .

She must turn right around and see it in the mirrors, see it for herself . . .

Was she moving or not moving? Who was that beside her looking so joyously, so ingratiatingly at the Queen that her mouth was too small for all her gold-glinting teeth – and that big man with gold curly hair like a prince in the fairy-tale books, who was he?

Lizzie didn't really want to know any longer – only wanted to disappear like Alice in Wonderland into the glass . . .

Good that they opened, because she couldn't have got through like Alice . . .

. . . People, people everywhere . . . Looking at her. Why?

Lizzie walked faster and faster, faster and faster, till she was running. It seemed important to run, to keep running . . .

Why did they blow horns at her, didn't they see her? Had she become invisible?

That would be nice. Yes, she *was* invisible. She could see out, but they couldn't see in. She could see them, but they couldn't see her . . .

What a huge place this was, with glass ceilings as high as the sky, people hurrying, hurrying, and a smell she knew – oily. Trains coming in, going out, great huge blackboards with white letters that made puzzles you could sit and try to figure out . . .

Good to sit down, sit on a hard bench. No one could see her. Pigeons came up to her – they could see her. They wanted food, and she didn't have any, but some crusts were being thrown down. How they hopped and fluttered after them.

Except for one, who was having such a hard struggle . . .

Oh, no – oh, dear, his poor thin little legs were tied together – he could hardly hop, he was always too late to get a crust – and he just kept trying and trying . . .

She could help him, if only he would be still . . .

He didn't understand, only looked at her questioningly.

Lizzie got up and ran around looking for someone who might help. Nobody had time to listen, or if they did, they only shrugged, looked at her pityingly. A woman pushing a big broom stopped to listen a moment, then said, angrily, 'They're not supposed to come into the station – nobody should feed them, the filthy things.'

Lizzie put her hand over her mouth. She went back to the bench. The other pigeons had gone, only the tied-up one was left, still trying to hop its way to the crumbs . . .

Lizzie put her head down into her hands and wept, wept.

When they found her, finally, Mim, Sheldy, the police, the press, Lizzie looked up with a mascara-smeared, tear-stained face, her blue eyes a total blank.

'Lizzie,' said Mim, 'what in the world you doin'?'

Lizzie looked at her. 'Eh?'

'Liza?' said Sheldy. 'What's wrong, darling?'

'Wrong?' said Lizzie. 'Who are you?'

Faces surrounded her. Masses of them. They swam past, waved over and around her. She could not imagine why, what it was they wanted of her . . .

Strong arms grasped her, too strong to resist. She was

moved along, put into some kind of a conveyance.

The last words she heard were: 'That's Liza Lee, the singer – had some kind of breakdown . . .'

Liza Lee?, she thought. The name didn't ring a bell.

# CHAPTER TWENTY-SEVEN

The Bronson Clinic in Belgravia, where Lizzie was taken at Sheldy's insistence, looked more like one of the embassies in the Square. For the first two weeks after her admission, a knot of reporters and cameramen, the morbidly curious, were generally to be seen hanging about the front steps waiting hopefully for informative clues that could be made into news.

There had been no dearth of it, with all the important visitors that came and went, the constant appearance of the mother and millionaire fiancé. But lately, only the mother seemed regular; after the great bold headlines, the endless articles that analysed the situation, gave so-called inside glimpses and facts of a 'very private person, strangely remote from her public image', that had a field-day with gossip and spice, a kind of silence had fallen, an anti-climax of action.

Sometimes, when it rained or the wintry wind bent low the potted trees out front, there would be nobody there at all. A faint pall of gloom seemed to hover, unrelieved by the coming and going of the staff, occasional visitors, the by now dully familiar little figure of the mother, with her stony face and hostile stare. Nothing more was to be got out of *her*, one reporter observed to some colleagues, except comments unfit to print.

Inside the big house that had once been the grand home of an illustrious family, there was deep quiet, the gleam of polished wood and floors, a smell of wax and some pervading chemical in odious blend. Here, there were no starched coats as there had been in the hospital where Lizzie had first been taken. The staff were all dressed in their own clothes, conservative and beyond type-casting. There were no rooms of confinement on the many spacious floors, only variously assigned bedrooms – equipped with bells, private bathrooms, instantly-answered telephones – furnished with antiques and offering a neutral, unobtrusive elegance.

Patients were allowed to bring their own possessions, add personal touches, and the flowers that were brought to them were placed in attractive vases and kept watered. Television sets were available, and of course radios, videos, anything that would help to make the patient as happy and occupied as possible.

Meals could be brought to the room, or served in the big dining room downstairs, with its many white-cloth-covered tables, its great chandelier, decorative flower arrangements. There was a communal room for sitting about, reading, talking, playing cards or other games. There were more helpers than there were patients, and only an upward glance brought attention.

It was like a glorified hotel, yet a centre of caring that tried bravely to honour its high cost.

Doctor Frederick Bronson, who gave the place its name, had started off his career as a straightforward psychiatrist dealing with any and all forms of mental disturbance, but gradually his interest had fastened on the curious subtleties of lost identity, the processes involved in a memory black-out, the amazing and baffling techniques of human 'opt-out' when the going got beyond control or endurance. Amnesia had a maddening syndrome of self-refusal, self-obliteration, of infinite stubbornness that would die before it yielded up self-concealment to recognition. Often, he would wonder how he had allowed himself to specialize in such a complex game of detection, such a mysterious interplay of pursuit and withdrawal, of one

385

human bent on rescue, the other on escape.

If he hadn't, to his own surprise, succeeded so often in finally effecting the rescue, he might long ago have gone back to the somehow simpler manifestations of madness: even violence could be less thwarting than the facsimile of sanity . . .

Take Liza Lee for instance . . .

When she knocked and came in this morning, she would look tidy and fresh, pretty and smiling. She would be genuinely pleased to see him. He knew she liked him, trusted him. She would notice his tie and shirt, ask about his wife and children, perhaps chat amiably about some television programme she'd watched, even ask his opinion on the political situation, did he think the Labour party would survive . . .?

She would accept a cup of tea from Miss Lister, tuck back her straight hair and sip the tea appreciatively. 'Always like a cuppa,' she would say, totally unware of slipping into her mother's idiom, 'it warms the cockles.'

He would smile as if he hadn't heard it before. Leaning back in his big leather chair, which to his dismay he was more than filling these days, despite his aversion to playing the lived-in, avuncular role, he called out to her now to come in . . .

. . . and, it was just as he knew it would be, as it had been for the past four months. He eyed her without optimism, as she took the tea, her small-talk over, and waited for his questions.

'Well, Dorothy,' he began, having long-since deferred to her rejection of any connection with the name Liza Lee. 'I've got a bit of a surprise for you today.'

'You have? Oh, good!' Lizzie's blue eyes were surrounded in the little smile-lines he could not help but find endearing. With the emergence of freckles from her sun-lamp treatment, she looked almost child-like.

He restrained a nod to himself – yes, each week she *was*

becoming more ingenuous, more child-like. He might just be getting somewhere – yet he must avoid definite hope.

'Your – friend – Mim, has been able to obtain a clip from a film made in Hollywood. We would like to run it for you in the lounge.'

Lizzie's eyes rounded. 'If it's something to do with that person, Liza Lee again, please don't bother, Dr. Bronson. Really, the fact that she looks like me, moves like me, sounds like me doesn't *make* her me. Whatever you persist in thinking, I am not Liza Lee, never was, never will be . . .'

Dr. Bronson put up a hand. 'I'm not saying you are her – you know I don't do that any more. I'm merely hoping that watching the film might trigger off some old associations of your own.'

Lizzie ran a finger under the polo-neck of her blue jumper. 'You're trying to trick me again. You want me to give up and say okay, that's who I am. But I'm not going to, no matter how many *facts* you show me. I'm sorry I don't know who I really am; I'd like to know that as much as you would, and I'm working very hard with all your suggestions – but I don't want to see the film, it won't do any good.'

'Your friends say that Liza Lee never liked to watch herself in films even when she was very successful, that it gave her what she called an "eerie feeling" . . .'

'What do you mean when she was very successful, Dr. Bronson? Isn't she any more?' Lizzie tilted her head with interest.

'She disappeared, Dorothy, you know that. The same day you did, the very same time and hour – just as she was about to greet the Queen . . .'

'Oh, dear. I'm sorry about that.'

Dr. Bronson kept his big, gentle features at rest, his hands still on the desk. It was what she always said. 'Strange, though, Dorothy, don't you think?'

Lizzie spread her hands, looked at her unpolished pink nails. 'A big coincidence, I admit. Looking alike, all that.'

'All right.' Dr. Bronson offered her some more tea.

'No, ta.'

'Dorothy – Lizzie was also born in Soho, in the very same flat as you, by the very same mother. Did I tell you that?'

Lizzie nodded. 'Yeah – like a bleedin' record.'

Dr. Bronson suppressed a smile. 'Your mother . . .'

'She is not my mother. She is not my friend. I never seen 'er before.' Lizzie folded her arms across her chest, looked at him in solemn yet alert denial.

She's screaming for help, he thought. What more can I do?

'Dr. Bronson . . .'

His big nostrils noved a little. 'Yes, dear?'

'That woman . . . You promised you wouldn't let her come 'ere no more. Why do you?'

'She's your . . . She's a very determined lady, Dorothy.'

'That's no skin off my nose, is it? And that man with all the curls – why you keep lettin' 'im come?'

More and more of the idiom, he thought – was there something going on? Perhaps he should choose a risk, make a push. 'He's engaged to you. We've got the ring in the safe. He pays for you to be here. His name is Sheldon Albright.'

'Yeah . . .? Why would he do that? I ain't got no ring from anyone.'

'Dorothy – let me ask you these things *again*. How do you think you came here? What do you think you were doing in Charing Cross station? You've seen the dress you were wearing – why was it very special and why were you wearing it? If the card in your handbag wasn't *your* invitation to do a command performance, why was it in there? Why did Mrs. Hobbs come after you, and your . . .

388

Mr. Albright, and the police? And why did everyone say you were Liza Lee, even the other performers, the production staff of the Palladium? And – why is there a passport with your picture in it, and why do you speak with a Cockney accent when I question you – and like an upper-class person when I leave you alone?'

'Stop! Stop! Stop!' Lizzie covered her ears. 'I'm sick and tired of it. I 'ate her, this Liza Lee, wherever she is. If I didn't look so like 'er, you'd leave me alone, I could 'ave peace!'

'Take your hands down and listen, Dorothy. If there was any alternative information, any other thread of connection you could offer, we could go on pursuing it together. I only want to find your identity, for you to be free to live . . .'

'I'm sorry, I'm sorry – you want me to make somethin' up, tell you all kinds of lies, pretend to remember things just so you can get me off your 'ands, get rid of me!'

Ah. Emotion. Protest. At last. 'I'm sure you know that isn't true. I want you off my hands, yes – but through the truth. Now – I want you to see this film. You'll see just how like her you are . . .'

Lizzie shook her head. 'Don't want to. She *ain't* me.'

He heaved himself up, buttoned his grey jacket over his thickening waist, smoothed back strands of grey hair. 'Come, my dear, it's part of the treatment, which is why you're here as my patient.'

Lizzie tightened her arms, hugged herself away from him. 'I'm no-one's patient,' she said. 'I'm just here for a rest, till I remember things.'

'Come.'

So suddenly that he had no time to react, Lizzie was past him, out of the door, headed for the stairs . . .

Blinking, shaking his head, Dr. Bronson pressed a bell at the side of his desk.

In a few moments, they brought her back, kindly,

firmly, but with enough force to ensure that she stayed. They apologized to her, smiled encouragingly, left, closing the door with a metallic click.

'All right, dear,' Dr. Bronson said, 'we'll forget about the film today. We'll just look through these photo albums and scrap books of publicity clippings, just sit side-by-side over here and look at them together.' He tucked the albums under one arm, took her by the elbow, led her gently to a large black leather couch where daylight streamed in through bay windows.

Lizzie bit her lips into a stiff line. 'You're goin' to try and make me say I'm 'er again.'

'No, no – but we must see if something stirs for you.' His smile was kind; he did not intentionally sound paternal, but he did feel a fatherly rush of concern for this poor disturbed young woman who had never known her real father, whose mother found nothing untoward or significant in the fact, who seemed unable to apprehend or recall the the slightest explanation for Liza's breakdown. 'It beats me, Doc,' she'd said. 'Done me level best for the girl all me life. Worked me arse off to get 'er where she is. Put 'er before meself. Took the 'urts and knocks she give me when she went off and married blokes that could only make 'er un'appy – took 'er back, loved 'er with all me 'eart, sacrificed me 'ole life to 'er. Naa – I don't think you'll find your answers with me, Doc – most likely it's that fella calls 'imself 'er fiancé. Wore 'er out, he has – and, of course, all the excitement singin' for 'Er Majesty . . .'

'Where'd you get these?' Lizzie asked, as he opened and spread the pages of photographs between them. 'They must belong to 'er!'

'Of course they do. But I didn't steal them – they were lent. By a friend.'

'Oh, 'er.'

'That's right.' ('Anythin' to oblige,' she'd said. 'Though if she don't know me, 'ow's she goin' to know 'erself?')

'We'll start here,' said Dr. Bronson. 'This seems to be the first snap – perhaps there was no camera in the family – this is in costume at a Miss Bettina's Theatrical School, a little girl with lots and lots of wiry-looking curls, a lot of make-up, doing some kind of a dance with a top hat and cane, bows on her shoes, little cape . . .'

'I can see. You don't have to describe it. She looks ridiculous – she can't be more than four or five!'

'That's what I'd say. These seem to be more of the same period, the same troupe. Now we have another school – Madame Irayna Blatsky – oh yes, I've heard of that, very famous, made lots of stars. Several of Liza here, playing different parts, in all kinds of different costumes, lots of hair still, and make-up . . . and this tall, thin boy making disdainful faces – looks familiar . . .'

Lizzie looked a little longer at Robbie. Something in her gaze flickered – or so Dr. Bronson thought, until she quickly turned away and gazed out of the window.

'Come back,' he said. 'Look at these . . .'

Slowly he turned the pages of Liza's progression: graduation at Blatsky's, her first television spot, the shows, the concerts, the movie shorts, the CBS special in New York . . .

Suddenly he switched to the publicity clippings, asked her to look at Liza's name, all the pictures and articles, the long and short interviews, the gossip columns, her wedding pictures outside Chelsea Registry Office, her Hollywood movie, and dozens of bits and pieces about her life there, and then Adam – and wedding pictures in the modern house on stilts in Stoneyvale. After that, the Broadway musical, smiling faces, big headlines, publicity shots galore, then the movie in Rome, many shots of her both in action on location with the fake earthquake and all the women and children following after her, and pictures of her with Sheldy Albright and great columns of print about their relationship – on to London, the biggest

TV show of all, pictures of Robbie before it was found that he wouldn't make it . . .

Finally, the Command Performance, shots of her arriving for rehearsal; Mim alongside, shots of her with other performers during rehearsal and many inches of speculation about the endlessly delayed marriage to Sheldon Albright, and Lizzie with Mim coming to the Palladium, on to the arrival of the Queen, her Lady-in-Waiting, her Secretary, the performance with shots of the Queen, and then the line-up for presentation afterwards, smiles all along – someone had even caught the mother in a dental display of glee, some kind of a high feather arrangement in her long brassy curls . . .

Dr. Bronson overrode his distaste. 'There,' he said – 'that's Liza as they found her, sitting with pigeons all round, weeping.'

Lizzie was very quiet, very still. 'I'm really sorry for her . . .' she murmured. 'I'm sorry I was so unkind . . .'

Dr. Bronson closed down his large blue-veined lids, gave an inaudible sigh, then sat up and looked at his watch. 'Well, Lizzie – Dorothy . . . That must be all for today . . .'

'That boy . . .' Lizzie said, her hand moving tentatively for the album.

'Yes?' Dr. Bronson tried not to reach too eagerly for the page.

'His face . . .' Lizzie's eyes narrowed with strain. 'I've seen it . . . It makes a funny feeling in my chest. He fits with something . . .'

'Yes?'

'Funny. Laughing . . . Made me laugh. Big boy . . .'

'Yes, dear . . .'

Lizzie seemed to shrink into herself, to take on a childish sauciness. 'Rob . . . That's Robbie, me friend.'

'Robbie – Rob Grover, perhaps?'

She nodded. 'Robbie.' Suddenly she frowned, sat up.

'But that's nonsense. How could I know him?'

Go with care, Dr. Bronson thought. Her accent had quickly up-marketed again.

Lizzie jumped to her feet. 'I remember nothing,' she said. 'I was just play-acting to please you.'

Dr. Bronson braced his shoulders, stood up. 'He was here,' he said quietly, 'to visit you. Wanted to know if there was anything he could do to help. You were under sedation. When I told you about it, you said you didn't know who he was. I'd get in touch with him now, except he's in America. He should be back soon, though . . .'

'I don't know what you're talking about, Dr. Bronson. I've never even heard of him.' Lizzie flicked back her hair, hitched her jeans. 'See you tomorrow . . .'

'He told me something he remembered, Dorothy. He said he gave you a little Woolworth engagement ring when you were in your teens – and that your mother had thrown it in the dustbin.'

Lizzie stood like a statue, every part of her frozen to immobility. After a few minutes she turned slowly to face the doctor. 'Oh, my God – oh, my God – I remember, I remember . . .'

Dr. Bronson did not dare to move even his eyes.

Suddenly Lizzie sagged to the floor, hid her face in her hair, beat a slow, steady rhythm on the oak boards with her balled fists. 'Oh, Christ, Christ, how I hate her, how I hate her, how I hate her!'

Dr. Bronson drew in a long deep breath. Going to the intercom on his desk, he spoke softly. 'No more appointments until you hear from me.'

It did not come out at once, in a great rush, but over the next few weeks Lizzie moved in and out of nightmare sequences of anger that sometimes closed her throat as if with finely-powdered glass, of rage that exploded with such violence that most objects in her room were gradu-

393

ally smashed to pieces against the walls and floors, and she had even scratched her own arms and face in lieu of her mother's.

Mim could not understand at all why she was not allowed to visit, or what could possibly be the matter with Lizzie. To her way of thinking, 'these shrinks didn't know nothin'; all Lizzie needed was to come 'ome and let me look after 'er proper. Soon as she'd 'ad a bit of rest and lovin', she'd be right as rain. All the world was waitin' for 'er to come back, she could name 'er own price. And I won't interfere no more, Doc – I'll let *'er* choose what she wants to be in. That's fair, ain't it?'

'Keep the woman out,' Dr. Bronson ordered the staff, 'and don't mention her name!'

Lizzie barely slept. Her days and nights had no separation except for the meals brought along into her room, the cleaners, the visits of the only person in her life she could bear near her, who came and went regularly, talked to her, understood everything she told him . . .

She told him about all the times she'd been made to go up on huge stages and sing and dance, with her hair all screwed up and horrible sticky make-up all over her face, her lashes beaded up with mascara, and never any time to play or be with other kids. Even working at night . . .

And suddenly she came to Freddie! She wept with misery over him. SHE had taken him away, thrown him out – her Freddie, her dear old bear she loved, her first and only friend . . .

Until the big boy . . .

Lizzie's fists curled with the bitter feelings. 'She called him *dirty* – when we were only playing family. We didn't do anything wrong. *She* made us go to Madame . . .'

Lizzie tugged her hair, gritted her teeth. 'She spoiled everything, took everything away, never ever let me alone from the time I was a baby . . .'

'Bertie couldn't help me.'

With her eyes on the doctor's, filled with tears, she told him how Bert had loved her, called her Miss Cuddles, but it was no use, he couldn't help – and then he died, and there was no-one to speak up for her . . .

The doctor told her to cry as much as she liked, to say anything at all – he was not there to judge her, and it was best she remembered all the things that had hurt . . .

But there were so *many*. Lizzie twisted and turned in her bed as she dreamed of trying to escape from Mum – trying to get away, from the time she was a little girl right on through her marriages . . .

Never, never, had she been able to – *SHE* was always there, waiting, finding ways even when she was married, even when she had Adam . . .

'She'd use *any* trick – and she knew my weak spots – that I appreciated her, was grateful, that she made me laugh – and (oh, how could I?) I loved her!'

That wasn't weakness, the doctor said.

But Lizzie wasn't yet ready for explanations. The hate still surged in her like waves of fire. There seemed no end to it.

The doctor gave her periods of respite with sedation, and then led her to tell him more.

It was summer by the time Lizzie had emptied out her anger. She was drained, quiet, no longer wanted to talk.

Dr. Bronson urged her to sit in the garden, to come to meals with the others, to watch TV, listen to radio, read in the well-stocked library, to be idle, relaxed.

Lizzie liked the feeling. She was protected completely from her mother – and, though she would one day want to see Sheldy to thank him, she did not have to come to any conclusions about anything or anyone. The outside world did not exist. She was in limbo.

She began to look in the mirror again, to wonder what to wear . . .

She had no idea what she wanted to look like, what to do with her hair – so she just chose clothes at random and let her hair hang long and plain to her shoulders where it had grown.

Her *name* had come back to her, but any previous image of herself had been dissolved with the revelation that it was made for Mim. Where the hate had been, there was emptiness, nothing to replace it.

'Something *will* come,' the doctor said. 'But remember – there is no *redress*. No-one is to blame. Everyone was doing the best they could at the stage they were. You will have to let it all go. You will, once you're strong enough, have to take responsibility for your own life. The hardest lesson of all, dear Liza – for all of us.'

Lizzie couldn't bear to leave him, or this place – yet . . .

At last, one day, she agreed to see Sheldy. It was strange, terrible, brought everything back – but as he walked with her through the park on her first journey away from the clinic, the fear moved off, and it was pleasant to be with him, to be with a person from her own life on the outside.

At the last minute, she kissed him goodbye.

'Liza – it's so good to see you back to your old self,' he said. 'Will you come out with me again soon?'

She looked into his bright, ruddy face for a few moments. How could she convey to him that she was not 'her old self' – never would be again? On the other hand, there was no new self either. 'Yes, of course,' she said. 'I'm so grateful to you. You've helped me so much, Sheldy. I owe you my life . . .'

He made a cheerful grimace. When he kissed her, he held her a moment as if with finality. 'I still love you,' he said.

Waving to him from the big front door, she liked the way he moved quickly, shoulders back, looked at his watch . . .

Thank goodness she had not put a blight on him; he would always be his own man.

Not long after that, Miss Lister came to her room with an anxious face. 'Mr. Rob Grover has turned up again. You don't *have* to see him . . .'

Lizzie looked down at her T-shirt and blue denims, pushed at the long straight curtain of uncombed hair. 'Lord! I look so awful . . .'

Then she broke into a laugh, and the neat, dark, bespectacled woman with whom she had become good friends, laughed with her. Such trivia illustrated better than any words how far she'd come.

'Shall I send him up here, or would you like to see him downstairs?'

'Up here, I think. People might stare.'

'He looks all right,' Miss Lister said. 'I mean . . .'

'Oh, good.'

Lizzie felt the first definite response of what might be the beginning of the new self. She did not attempt to tidy up. She stood in the middle of the big room, waited.

There was a knock on the door. 'Come in,' she called, her voice still rising easily in the habit of singing.

Robbie walked in.

'Hello, Lizzie,' he said.

If it hadn't been for that accent, so unchanged, she would hardly have known him. His long brown hair was tied behind his head with a bow, his face, a chalk-white colour with sunken cheeks, seemed all mouth and big black-circled eyes, he was dressed in dirty, scuffed black leather from jacket and trousers to knee-high boots. Worst of all, as he moved forward to greet her, was the unwashed smell of him, the blast of foul breath as he put his black-nailed hand on her arm.

'Good to see ya,' he said, 'it really is. Best thing what's happened in a long time. You look different, as if you've been through . . . well, what you been through. But good, great.'

She wanted to kiss him, but could not. 'It's wonderful, Robbie, to see you at last. I tried so many times – but . . . That was part of it – you know, don't you?'

'Her.' He nodded gloomily. 'Yeah – I guessed.'

'Sit down, Robbie – over here on the couch. Would you like anything to drink, or eat – I have room service, sort of . . .'

'Naa . . . No appetite these days. Maybe a glass of water – me mouth's dry. I'm off the stuff, but I feel like 'ell. They say it takes time – 'ow much, I wonder?' He made an effort to smile, but it only flared the nostrils of his long nose, and his eyes were dull.

Lizzie got a glass of water, put it on the table in front of him, sat down beside him, gazed at him in sudden loss of contact. The moment was both real and unreal, merged, divided, merged . . .

He put his hand over hers. 'Maybe I shouldn't 'ave come, shouldn't 'ave bothered ya. I'm a depressin' kind of bloke these days.'

'No, no,' said Lizzie, her blue eyes seeming to wake, 'I'm very glad you did. I would have tried to find you . . .'

'You would?' His bleak, red-veined blue eyes denied any hope. 'I'm washed up, you know, baby. Did meself in. No way back. Gawd knows what comes next.'

Lizzie nodded. 'Same with me.'

He stirred, shifted his big shoulders, emanating pungent sweat. 'Aa – not the same. You're IT. They're just waitin' for you to come back and take up where you left off.'

Although she was safe from them, Lizzie gave an involuntary shiver.

He frowned. 'How are ya feelin', any'ow? Can you talk about it? Does it bother you?'

Lizzie swallowed just the semblance of a lump in her throat. 'Not to you, it doesn't.'

'Only if you want to . . .'

For a moment, Lizzie could not speak, only stare at him as if he were still in those dreams – then, slowly, she nodded. 'I want to,' she said . . .

Two hours later, they were still talking. Lizzie had got almost used to his smell. She thought about how he would be after a lot of baths, with clean clothes, with her looking after him and growing stronger and surer of himself every day. Perhaps . . .

'Oh, Robbie,' she said, her eyes filling. 'You were the one, the only one. Why did we lose our way?'

'Gawd knows, Lizzie. I never loved no-one but you – never. The girls I 'ad weren't anythin' – even Louisa. She got me on the heavy stuff, and I never could get shot of 'er.'

'Like me and Mum.' She could even say it now!

There was a long protracted silence between them.

'Well – I suppose I'd better scarper. Got any plans, Lizzie?'

She shook her head. The hair fell around her face.

'You goin' to be 'ere a bit?'

'I think so . . .'

'Could I come and see ya again? I mean, tell me if it's a ruddy pain . . .'

'Of course you can. Better ring first – so's to be sure.'

He nodded, up and down, up and down, made no move to go.

'Oh, Robbie – do take care of yourself. Please!' Lizzie put her hand on the leather patch at his knee, felt its worn roughness. Surely he was part of her, she thought. Surely they would be together again!

Suddenly his head was against her breasts. 'Lizzie, Lizzie, oh, I need you. I *need* you, Lizzie-girl!'

She put her arms around him, cradled his head. She loved him, she thought. She did love him still. She lifted his head, kissed him . . .

After a few moments, Robbie drew back. 'You're sorry for me,' he said. 'Don't be, love, don't add *me* to your troubles.'

'Robbie – don't say that – why do you say that?' Lizzie's eyes searched his face as if in search of some final key to the truth.

'Isn't that what you feel? – be honest.' He gently disentangled himself, stood up.

Lizzie listened to the squeak of his boots as he crossed to the door. 'Robbie . . .' she called. 'Robbie . . .'

He stopped, turned, gave her a long, doleful look. 'Yeah?'

'Give me time, darling – just give me time!'

He nodded, 'You got it.' He raised a grimy hand. 'Bless ya, me love. I wish ya all the 'appiness in the world.'

'Oh, Robbie . . .'

He closed the door.

A week later, Dr. Bronson called Lizzie to his office, asked her to sit down and delivered a blow so cruel that Lizzie could hardly believe her ears.

'Liza,' he said, both his paternal and avuncular tone somewhat diminished, 'we've got to talk about your plans, we've got to talk about practicalities – where you want to go, what you want to do about your clothes, your finances, your . . . life.'

'But . . .' Lizzie had scooped her hair onto the top of her head and held it there as if to understand him more clearly. 'Why now, suddenly? You want to kick me out?'

He smiled wryly. 'You said it; I didn't. No, seriously, it's more than time, Liza. It's not that we want the room – your money's as good as anyone's – but it's not doing you any good to stay hidden here any longer. You've got to move on, try your wings.'

Lizzie's heart started a slow, hard thumping. 'Just like that.'

'Just like that. I've been trying to ease you out, but you've refused the hints. I don't want well people here, I've got too many in the state you were in, in urgent need of help.'

Dr. Bronson drew a fresh sheet of paper towards him, lifted his gold pen. 'Let's make a list. For instance, what will you do for money? You don't want to start off without funds. I gather your mother has control of your earnings and savings . . .'

'I don't want any of it,' Lizzie said, nervously pocketing her hands. 'She can have the lot.'

'Come now, dear, until you work again, you must . . .'

'All right. Let her give me a thousand pounds and call it quits.'

'*That* won't get you far. You don't want to create unnecessary problems – you'll have enough, adjusting to the world again.'

Lizzie jumped up and paced about. 'I don't know, I know nothing about these things. She's kept me like a child . . .'

'Now, now. You also kept yourself that way. This is where it all begins for you, Liza – the growing up.'

'Is it grown up to be cushioned by money?' Lizzie looked at him earnestly. 'I mean it, Dr. B. Wouldn't I be learning more from having none?'

'A fine idea – but you're not up to it yet. The next time you might not have a Sheldon Albright or a Bronson Clinic behind you.'

Lizzie sat down. 'Yes. I see. You're right. Well, perhaps a sort of stipend, sent to some address each month, until I know where I'm heading.'

'Good. I suggest you talk to your mother, and the bank. An arrangement could be made.'

'I don't *want* to talk to her, or *see* her!'

'Liza, you'll have to, my dear. If I didn't think you needed to, that it would be a good thing, I wouldn't suggest it.'

401

'Oh, Lord . . .' The heartbeat was joined by flutters in her jean-flattened stomach.

'In fact, I've taken the step for you. She's coming here this afternoon at three.'

Lizzie's jaw went stiff. 'Oh, no. Please . . .'

'If you handle it well, Liza, it could be the seal on your release from her. The hardest part will be over. You can walk out of here in charge of your own future.'

Lizzie lowered her head. 'Bugger . . .' she murmured.

'Sorry?' Dr. Bronson leaned forward, cocked an ear.

'Nothing.' Lizzie stood up. 'Right. Looks as if you've dispensed with the case of Liza Lee. See you – after.' She went out, flicked the door shut.

Dr. Bronson's smile was cautious, philosophical.

Lizzie waited in the main hall, where the door stood open to admit men delivering some new equipment for the kitchens. She had refused to see Mim in anything but a communal room where there would be other people. This was only partly because she felt in need of protection: it might also put a damper on her mother's protests.

The sun was pressing through a light drizzle, and the square was caught in a lull between afternoon and rush-hour traffic. Lizzie sniffed the air with a faint thrill. Now that Dr. B. had given her the 'bum's rush', she had come to unexpectedly sudden terms with her departure, with her approaching transition from patient to person. It would be an adventure simply to walk along the street, decide where to go, where to live, where to eat, what to do!

A familiar car was driving up, parking quickly in front of the clinic. A door was flung open, a small figure jumping out swathed in layers of Indian-style clothes, a kind of poor man's Mrs. Gandhi with only the tip of a nose showing. "Ere, 'Arry,' Lizzie heard her call to the man who got out the other side and came quickly round, 'don't *you* come in. You keep yourself scarce. No tellin' what could 'appen. You be waitin', see.'

Before she drew back, Lizzie saw Harry Org's obedient nod, saw him return to his place behind the wheel of the car, saw her mother start marching up the stairs.

Lizzie resisted smoothing her hair, adjusting her white jumper, the belt of her black jeans, was glad she had not given in to lipstick.

'Well!' Mim was taken aback by the immediate confrontation of Lizzie herself. 'Crikey, there you *are*.'

'Hello, Mother.' Lizzie moved forward, extended her hand.

Mim's eyebrows, fully re-grown, gathered in above her nose. She resisted the hand, moved in for a kiss – but Lizzie's hand held her off.

'In here, please,' she said, leading her to a big sitting room to one side of the garden where afternoon tea was generally served. 'I hope you will have a cup of tea.'

The whites of Mim's eyes rolled at her from under one side of the gold-threaded sari hood. 'What's this – I 'oped we'd have a private chat. After all, it's the first time they'd let me at you, like I was a leper or somethin'.'

'I've nothing very private to say, actually.' Lizzie dared a straight look into the familiar face and eyes, and was relieved that no sweat leaped to her underarms.

'Well, I 'ave, me darlin'. Plenty, an' all.'

'This way.' Lizzie didn't seem to have heard. 'This is a nice table – you can see the birds feeding. I'll miss feeding them, it was fun.'

Mim's eyebrow line remained. 'That a fact?'

They sat at a small table covered with a white cloth, and a young woman came over immediately to ask if they wanted tea. 'Please, Kirsty – for two. Have you got carrot cake today?'

Kirsty, who wore her own dress and no apron, winked. 'Special for *you*.'

'Humourin' the loonies, eh? 'Ow do you stand it?' Mim looked about, gave a sniff of disdain. 'Nothin' but a rip-off, if you arst me. Probably run by the Mafia.'

Lizzie did not respond. She no longer loved, or hated, this curious little person. She saw her now in the context of *her* upbringing, *her* particular fate. She *understood* her denial of poverty, hardship, drabness, the ghastliness of war. She *understood* her dream. She *admired* her tenacity, fortitude, resourcefulness, ingenuity, resilience – and, of course, her actual talent. For *she* had devised the routines, designed the costumes, written the songs – and *she* would have done all the performing too, if she had not made one big mistake . . .

'What you thinkin' about, then, Lizzie? You give me the willies lookin' at me like that. You all right? They goin' to let you come 'ome now?'

'I'm not coming home.' Lizzie paused while the tea was served, and waited till Kirsty was out of earshot. 'I want to talk to you about a financial arrangement – until I'm on my own feet.'

'That's stupid, me love. I ain't pushin' you this time – I learned me lesson, didn't I? *But*, now you performed for the Queen, *'Er Royal Majesty*, you *got* to go on!' Mim's nod shook the sari hood from her head to reveal the cap of kinked red hair, parted straight down the middle and winged to the sides, giving her long nose and gaunt face a witch-like sharpness.

Lizzie restrained a stare, a mesmeric shudder like an old reflex. 'Look here, Mother,' she said, tucking her own hair vigorously behind her ears, 'I'm only going to explain this once. I am not going back into show business – ever. I am never going to perform anywhere, for anyone, for any reason. I am absolutely, completely through. If I sing it will be because I want to, because I feel like it. I am now going to be a private person. Whatever I do will be my own choice, my own business. Is that clear?' To prove that her hand did not shake, Lizzie lifted her teacup to her mouth and drank. 'Have some cake,' she said, signalling the end of her pronouncement.

In reverse order, Mim put her cup down. 'They done this to you 'ere, 'aven't they – at this rich man's funny farm? Kept you 'ere all this time, turnin' you against your own mother, tellin' you you don't want to perform no more. How'd they do it, me love, eh? With them fancy drugs, wires in your 'ead, brain-washin' you so's you'd stay on and be in their power?'

'Mother – you're wasting your breath, and your time.' Lizzie was detached enough to feel vaguely amused by the so-familiar predictability of this tirade. At the same time, she felt a strong urge to cut it short – whatever patience she had ever had was as suddenly gone as that bird from the feeding dish into the blue beyond the windows . . .

'I'd like to be able to reach an understanding with you,' she went on before Mim could answer, 'but I know now it isn't possible and never will be. So – let's discuss "practicalities". Finances. I only want a reasonable amount to live on, and only for a reasonable period. The rest is yours. You deserve every bit of it, too, Mother.'

'What's this "Mother" lark, then?'

'Part of it.'

Mim's lips pinched into fine pleats. She pushed her cup away as if it offended her. 'I'm goin' to sue these con artists, I am. What they done to you is *criminal!*'

'I'm *not* off my rocker, and I've never been saner, Mother.' ('No one can deny, or be denied, their self-identity without *some* form of damage,' Dr. B. had said, 'and sometimes escape to madness is the only way back to the self.')

Mim gave her a long hard stare that shifted from outrage to disbelief, to stunned recognition. 'You *mean* it, me love – don't you? You're throwin' your Mum out like an old pair of shoes. Your 'eart's as cold as ice. They made you *'ate* me!'

Lizzie looked away, feeling a vague sorrow. 'Not true,' she murmured.

'And what're *you* goin' to do – marry Mr. Money-bags, arter all?'

'No . . . not necessarily . . .'

'Who, then?'

'I can't say. Maybe no-one.'

'Who will you live with?'

'Me . . . myself.'

Mim lapsed into scowling silence. Lizzie, conscious of Kirsty and others in the room, waited. It was incredible but true – she could not contain her longing for this moment to be over.

'Well,' said Mim, finally. 'I know what *I* got to do. See this 'ere shrink hisself. Get a few things straight. You ain't 'eard the last of this, or of me, young miss – take me word!' She got up, swung her sari into place, left as briskly as flat-heeled sandals on thick-pile carpet would allow, and without a backward look.

And that, as it transpired, was almost the last Lizzie saw of her mother. There was to be just one more glimpse . . .

Faced with the irrefutable facts of the case, after some name-calling, claiming a 'broken 'eart', that her 'darlin' Lizzie had done 'er in', Mim had agreed to give her 'the bleedin' payoff' and marched out of Dr. B.'s office, out the door and down to Harry, still muttering that she would 'sue'.

Lizzie, standing by the same window by which she had watched her arrive, had had a momentary pang . . . What a sad finale to their twenty-seven years. Suppose she had over-estimated her mother's will and ability to survive?

Her sudden, 'Oy, 'Arry' came ringing up to Lizzie, tinny, imperious. 'Lookit!'

Lizzie followed the direction of her mother's familiar lift of eyebrows and chin. A thin little teenage girl was striding along towards them, her orange and green hair rising in eight-inch spikes from her scalp, her pert milk-white face and 'bee-sting' mouth daubed with brilliant red, her enormous eyes surrounded with huge black lines, immense drop earrings dragging at the lobes of her small rouged ears. Wearing a mixture of scruffy, funereal black clothes that came to an end just under her bottom, large-webbed black-net stockings with big holes and sharply-pointed, button-sided boots run over at the heels, she gave Mim a long, wise look, almost a wink in passing.

Mim raised a thumb, winked back. 'Cute, eh, 'Arry?' she called in to him, 'Ought to get 'er name . . .'

'Come on, old gel,' Harry called out, 'there's 'undreds like 'er these days . . .' He started the motor.

Mim cast a wistful look after the girl, then nodded, got into the car.

Lizzie's pang subsided.

A few days later, Lizzie stood in the hall that had come to feel like part of her first real home, her luggage packed and ready beside her. She had decided to go to a small hotel in Kensington as a start. From there, where? Alone, without props, her name changed yet again, with only her physical shape the same, what would her assets be? Would she go to school, make up for the education she had never had? Would she be able to find some kind of work? What was she capable of, besides performing?

And what was she left feeling? Love for children, for animals, people of all kinds? Hints of peace, a possible inner strength – and, yes, a sense of some power bigger than she was, that didn't exclude *her* . . .

She shook hands with the staff, kissed some, kissed and hugged Dr. B. with tears in her eyes. 'Trust in life, dear Elizabeth,' he said.

She nodded at the significance of the name, stuck on her floppy felt hat, the big dark glasses of her disguise, followed the driver down the steps to the taxi.

When she was inside, she waved up to them all. 'Thank you, oh, thank you,' she signalled with her smile.

Then the taxi started up, and the clinic moved behind her and out of view. Perhaps she would be back there some day, a dismal failure at survival . . .

But perhaps she wouldn't.

For now, at least, at last, she was *free* – on her way – and the way, whatever it was, would be her own.